Funny Bones

An Anthology of
Humorous Ghost Stories

Selected by

Dorothy Scarborough

LEONAUR

Funny Bones: an Anthology of Humorous Ghost Stories
Selected by Dorothy Scarborough

Originally published under the title
Humorous Ghost Stories

Leonaur is an imprint of Oakpast Ltd

ISBN: 978-1-84677-692-2 (hardcover)
ISBN: 978-1-84677-691-5 (softcover)

http://www.leonaur.com

Publisher's Notes

The views expressed in this book are not necessarily
those of the publisher.

Contents

Introduction

The humorous ghost is distinctly a modern character. In early literature wraiths took themselves very seriously, and insisted on a proper show of respectful fear on the part of those whom they honoured by haunting. A mortal was expected to rise when a ghost entered the room, and in case he was slow about it, his spine gave notice of what etiquette demanded. In the event of outdoor apparition, if a man failed to bare his head in awe, the roots of his hair reminded him of his remissness. Woman has always had the advantage over man in such emergency, in that her locks, being long and pinned up, are less easily moved—which may explain the fact (if it be a fact!) that in fiction women have shown themselves more self-possessed in ghostly presence than men. Or possibly a woman knows that a masculine spook is, after all, only a man, and therefore may be charmed into helplessness, while the feminine can be seen through by another woman and thus disarmed. The majority of the comic apparitions, curiously enough, are masculine. You don't often find women wraithed in smiles—perhaps because they resent being made ridiculous, even after they're dead. Or maybe the reason lies in the fact that men have written most of the comic or satiric ghost stories, and have chivalrously spared the gentler shades. And there are very few funny child-ghosts—you might almost say none, in comparison with the number of grown-ups. The number of ghost children of any or all types is small proportionately—perhaps because it seems an unnatural thing for a child to die under any circumstances, while to make of him a butt for jokes would be unfeeling. There are a few instances, as in the case of the ghost baby mentioned later, but very few.

Ancient ghosts were a long-faced lot. They didn't know how to play at all. They had been brought up in stern repression of frivolities as haunters—no matter how sportive they may have been in life—and in turn they cowed mortals into a servile submission. No doubt they thought of men and women as mere youngsters that must be taught their place, since any living person, however senile, would be thought juvenile compared with a timeless spook.

But in these days of individualism and radical liberalism, spooks as well as mortals are expanding their personalities and indulging in greater freedom. A ghost can call his shade his own now, and exhibit any mood he pleases. Even young female wraiths, demanding latchkeys, refuse to obey the frowning face of the clock, and engage in light-hearted ebullience to make the ghost of Mrs. Grundy turn a shade paler in horror. Nowadays haunters have more fun and freedom than the haunted. In fact, it's money in one's pocket these days to be dead, for ghosts have no rent problems, and dead men pay no bills. What officer would willingly pursue a ghostly tenant to his last lodging in order to serve summons on him? And suppose a ghost brought into court demanded trial by a jury of his peers? No—manifestly death has compensations not connected with the consolations of religion.

The marvel is that apparitions were so long in realizing their possibilities, in improving their advantages. The spectres in classic and medieval literature were malarial, vapourous beings without energy to do anything but threaten, and mortals never would have trembled with fear at their frown if they had known how feeble they were. At best a revenant could only rattle a rusty skeleton, or shake a mouldy shroud, or clank a chain—but as mortals cowered before his demonstrations, he didn't worry. If he wished to evoke the extreme of anguish from his host, he raised a menacing arm and uttered a windy word or two. Now it takes more than that to produce a panic. The up-to-date ghost keeps his skeleton in a garage or some place where it is cleaned and oiled and kept in good working order. The modern wraith has sold his sheet to the old clo'es man, and dresses as in life. Now the ghost has learned to have a variety of good times, and he can make the living squirm far more satisfyingly than in the past. The spook of to-day enjoys making his haunted laugh even while he groans in terror. He knows that there's no weapon, no threat, in horror, to be compared with ridicule.

Think what a solemn creature the Gothic ghost was! How little originality and initiative he showed and how dependent he was on his own atmosphere for thrills! His sole appeal was to the spinal column. The ghost of to-day touches the funny bone as well. He adds new horrors to being haunted, but new pleasures also. The modern spectre can be a joyous creature on occasion, as he can be, when he wishes, fearsome beyond the dreams of classic or Gothic revenant. He has a keen sense of humour and loves a good joke on a mortal, while he can even enjoy one on himself. Though his fun is of comparatively recent origin—it's less than a century since he learned to crack a smile—the laughing ghost is very much alive and sportively active. Some of these new spooks are notoriously good company. Many Americans there are to-day who would court being haunted by the captain and crew of Richard Middleton's Ghost Ship that landed in a turnip field and dispensed drink till they demoralized the denizens of village and graveyard alike. After that show of spirits, the turnips in that field tasted of rum, long after the ghost ship had sailed away into the blue.

The modern spook is possessed not only of humour but of a caustic satire as well. His jest is likely to have more than one point to it, and he can haunt so insidiously, can make himself so at home in his host's study or bedroom that a man actually welcomes a chat with him— only to find out too late that his human foibles have been mercilessly flayed. Pity the poor chap in H. C. Bunner's story, *The Interfering Spook*, for instance, who was visited nightly by a spectre that repeated to him all the silly and trite things he had said during the day, a ghost, moreover, that towered and swelled at every hackneyed phrase, till finally he filled the room and burst after the young man proposed to his admired one, and made subsequent remarks. Ghosts not only have appallingly long memories, but they possess a mean advantage over the living in that they have once been mortal, while the men and women they haunt haven't yet been ghosts. Suppose each one of us were to be haunted by his own inane utterances? True, we're told that we'll have to give account *some day* for every idle word, but recording angels seem more sympathetic than a sneering ghost at one's elbow. Ghosts can satirize more fittingly than anyone else the absurdities of certain psychic claims, as witness the delightful seriousness of the story *Back from that Bourne*, which appeared as a front page news story in the New York *Sun* years ago. I should think that some of the futile, laggard messenger-boy ghosts that one reads about nowadays would blush with shame before the wholesome raillery of the porgy fisherman.

The modern humorous ghost satirizes everything from the old-fashioned spectre (he's very fond of taking pot-shots at him) to the latest psychic manifestations. He laughs at ghosts that aren't experts in efficiency haunting, and he has a lot of fun out of mortals for being scared of spectres. He loves to shake the lugubrious terrors of the past before you, exposing their hollow futility, and he contrives to create new fears for you magically while you are laughing at him.

The new ghost hates conventionality and uses the old thrills only to show what dead batteries they come from. His really electrical effects are his own inventions. He needs no dungeon keeps and monkish cells to play about in—not he! He demands no rag nor bone nor clank of chain of his old equipment to start on his career. He can start up a moving picture show of his own, as in Ruth McEnery Stuart's *The Haunted Photograph*, and demonstrate a new kind of apparition. The ghost story of to-day gives you spinal sensations with a difference, as in the immortal *Transferred Ghost*, by Frank R. Stockton, where the suitor on the moonlit porch, attempting to tell his fair one that he dotes on her, sees the ghost of her ferocious uncle (who isn't dead!) kicking his heels against the railing, and hears his admonition that he'd better hurry up, as the live uncle is coming in sight. The thrill with which you read of the ghost in Ellis Parker Butler's *The Late John Wiggins*, who deposits his wooden leg with the family he is haunting, on the plea that it is too materialistic to be worn with ease, and therefore they must take care of it for him, doesn't altogether leave you even when you discover that the late John is a fraud, has never been a ghost nor used a wooden leg. But a terrifying leg-acy while you do believe in it!

The new ghost has a more nimble and versatile tongue as well as wit. In the older fiction and drama apparitions spoke seldom, and then merely as *ghosts*, not as individuals. And ghosts, like kings in drama, were of a dignity and must preserve it in their speech. Or perhaps the authors were doubtful as to the dialogue of shades, and compromised on a few stately ejaculations as being safely phantasmal speaking parts. But compare that usage with the rude freedom of some modern spooks, as John Kendrick Bangs's spectral cook of Bangletop, who lets fall her h's and twists grammar in a rare and diverting manner. For myself, I'd hate to be an old-fashioned ghost with no chance to keep up with the styles in slang. Think of having always—and always—to speak a dead language!

The humorous ghost is not only modern, but he is distinctively American. There are ghosts of all nationalities, naturally, but the spook that provides a joke—on his host or on himself—is Yankee in origin and development. The dry humour, the comic sense of the incongruous, the willingness to laugh at himself as at others, carry over into immaterialization as characteristic American qualities and are preserved in their true flavour. I don't assert, of course, that Americans have been the only ones in this field. The French and English selections in this volume are sufficient to prove the contrary. Gautier's *The Mummy's Foot* has a humour of a lightness and grace as delicate as the princess's little foot itself. There are various English stories of whimsical haunting, some of actual spooks and some of the hoax type. Hoax ghosts are fairly numerous in British as in American literature, one of the early specimens of the kind being *The Spectre of Tappington* in the *Ingoldsby Legends*. The files of *Blackwood's Magazine* reveal several examples, though not of high literary value.

Of the early specimens of the really amusing ghost that is an actual revenant is *The Ghost Baby*, in *Blackwood's*, which shows originality and humour, yet is too diffuse for printing here. In that we have a conventional young bachelor, engaged to a charming girl, who is entangled in social complications and made to suffer mental torment because, without his consent, he has been chosen as the nurse and guardian of a ghost baby that cradles after him wherever he goes. This is a rich story almost spoiled by being poorly told. I sigh to think of the laughs that Frank R. Stockton or John Kendrick Bangs or Gelett Burgess could have got out of the situation. There are other comic British spooks, as in Baring-Gould's *A Happy Release*, where a widow and a widower in love are haunted by the jealous ghosts of their respective spouses, till the phantom couple take a liking to each other and decide to let the living bury their dead. This is suggestive of Brander Matthews's earlier and cleverer story of a spectral courtship, in *The Rival Ghosts*. Medieval and later literature gave us many instances of a love affair or marriage between one spirit and one mortal, but it remained for the modern American to celebrate the nuptials of two ghosts. Think of being married when you know that you and the other party are going to live ever after—whether happily or no! Truly, the present terrors are more fearsome than the old!

The stories by Eden Phillpotts and Richard Middleton in this collection show the diversity of the English humour as associated with apparitions, and are entertaining in themselves. The *Canterville Ghost*, by Oscar Wilde, is one of his best short stories and is in his happiest vein of laughing satire. This travesty on the conventional traditions of the wraith is preposterously delightful, one of the cleverest ghost stories in our language. Zangwill has written engagingly of spooks, with a laughable story about Samuel Johnson. And there are others. But the fact remains that in spite of conceded and admirable examples, the humorous ghost story is for the most part American in creation and spirit. Washington Irving might be said to have started that fashion in skeletons and shades, for he has given us various comic haunters, some real and some make-believe. Frank R. Stockton gave his to funny spooks with a riotous and laughing pen. The spirit in his *Transferred Ghost* is impudently deathless, and has called up a train of

subsequent haunters. John Kendrick Bangs has made the darker re-
gions seem comfortable and homelike for us, and has created ghosts
so human and so funny that we look forward to being one—or more.
We feel downright neighbourly toward such spectres as the futile "last
ghost" Nelson Lloyd evokes for us, as we appreciate the satire of Rose
O'Neill's sophisticated wraith. The daring concept of Gelett Burgess's
Ghost Extinguisher is altogether American. The field is still comparatively limited, but a number of Americans have done distinctive work
in it. The spectre now wears motley instead of a shroud, and shakes his
jester's bells the while he rattles his bones. I dare any, however grouchy,
reader to finish the stories in this volume without having a kindlier
feeling toward ghosts!

   D. S.
New York
March, 1921

The Canterville Ghost

Oscar Wilde

1

When Mr. Hiram B. Otis, the American Minister, bought Canterville Chase, everyone told him he was doing a very foolish thing, as there was no doubt at all that the place was haunted. Indeed, Lord Canterville himself, who was a man of the most punctilious honour, had felt it his duty to mention the fact to Mr. Otis when they came to discuss terms.

"We have not cared to live in the place ourselves," said Lord Canterville, "since my grand-aunt, the Dowager Duchess of Bolton, was frightened into a fit, from which she never really recovered, by two skeleton hands being placed on her shoulders as she was dressing for dinner, and I feel bound to tell you, Mr. Otis, that the ghost has been seen by several living members of my family, as well as by the rector of the parish, the Rev. Augustus Dampier, who is a Fellow of King's College, Cambridge. After the unfortunate accident to the duchess, none of our younger servants would stay with us, and Lady Canterville often got very little sleep at night, in consequence of the mysterious noises that came from the corridor and the library."

"My Lord," answered the Minister, "I will take the furniture and the ghost at a valuation. I have come from a modern country, where we have everything that money can buy; and with all our spry young fellows painting the Old World red, and carrying off your best actors and prima-donnas, I reckon that if there were such a thing as a ghost in Europe, we'd have it at home in a very short time in one of our public museums, or on the road as a show."

"I fear that the ghost exists," said Lord Canterville, smiling, "though it may have resisted the overtures of your enterprising impresarios. It has been well known for three centuries, since 1584 in fact, and always makes its appearance before the death of any member of our family."

"Well, so does the family doctor for that matter, Lord Canterville. But there is no such thing, sir, as a ghost, and I guess the laws of Nature are not going to be suspended for the British aristocracy."

"You are certainly very natural in America," answered Lord Canterville, who did not quite understand Mr. Otis's last observation, "and if you don't mind a ghost in the house, it is all right. Only you must remember I warned you."

A few weeks after this, the purchase was concluded, and at the close of the season the Minister and his family went down to Canterville Chase. Mrs. Otis, who, as Miss Lucretia R. Tappan, of West 53rd Street, had been a celebrated New York belle, was now a very handsome, middle-aged woman, with fine eyes, and a superb profile. Many American ladies on leaving their native land adopt an appearance of chronic ill-health, under the impression that it is a form of European refinement, but Mrs. Otis had never fallen into this error. She had a magnificent constitution, and a really wonderful amount of animal spirits. Indeed, in many respects, she was quite English, and was an excellent example of the fact that we have really everything in common with America nowadays, except, of course, language. Her eldest son, christened Washington by his parents in a moment of patriotism, which he never ceased to regret, was a fair-haired, rather good-looking young man, who had qualified himself for American diplomacy by leading the German at the Newport Casino for three successive seasons, and even in London was well known as an excellent dancer. Gardenias and the peerage were his only weaknesses. Otherwise he was extremely sensible. Miss Virginia E. Otis was a little girl of fifteen, lithe and lovely as a fawn, and with a fine freedom in her large blue eyes. She was a wonderful Amazon, and had once raced old Lord Bilton on her pony twice round the park, winning by a length and a half, just in front of the Achilles statue, to the huge delight of the young Duke of Cheshire, who proposed for her on the spot, and was sent back to Eton that very night by his guardians, in floods of tears. After Virginia came the twins, who were usually called "The Stars and Stripes," as they were always getting swished. They were delightful boys, and, with the exception of the worthy Minister, the only true republicans of the family.

As Canterville Chase is seven miles from Ascot, the nearest railway station, Mr. Otis had telegraphed for a wagonette to meet them, and they started on their drive in high spirits. It was a lovely July evening, and the air was delicate with the scent of the pinewoods. Now and then they heard a wood-pigeon brooding over its own sweet voice, or saw, deep in the rustling fern, the burnished breast of the pheasant. Little squirrels peered at them from the beech-trees as they went by, and the rabbits scudded away through the brushwood and over the mossy knolls, with their white tails in the air. As they entered the avenue of Canterville Chase, however, the sky became suddenly overcast with clouds, a curious stillness seemed to hold the atmosphere, a great flight of rooks passed silently over their heads, and, before they reached the house, some big drops of rain had fallen.

Standing on the steps to receive them was an old woman, neatly dressed in black silk, with a white cap and apron. This was Mrs. Umney, the housekeeper, whom Mrs. Otis, at Lady Canterville's earnest request, had consented to keep in her former position. She made them each a low curtsy as they alighted, and said in a quaint, old-fashioned manner, "I bid you welcome to Canterville Chase." Following her, they passed through the fine Tudor hall into the library, a long, low room, paneled in black oak, at the end of which was a large stained glass window. Here they found tea laid out for them, and, after taking off their wraps, they sat down and began to look round, while Mrs. Umney waited on them.

Suddenly Mrs. Otis caught sight of a dull red stain on the floor just by the fireplace, and, quite unconscious of what it really signified, said to Mrs. Umney, "I am afraid something has been spilled there."

"Yes, madam," replied the old housekeeper in a low voice, "blood has been spilled on that spot."

"How horrid!" cried Mrs. Otis; "I don't at all care for blood-stains in a sitting-room. It must be removed at once."

The old woman smiled, and answered in the same low, mysterious voice, "It is the blood of Lady Eleanore de Canterville, who was murdered on that very spot by her own husband, Sir Simon de Canterville, in 1575. Sir Simon survived her nine years, and disappeared suddenly under very mysterious circumstances. His body has never been discovered, but his guilty spirit still haunts the Chase. The blood-stain has been much admired by tourists and others, and cannot be removed."

"That is all nonsense," cried Washington Otis; "Pinkerton's Champion Stain Remover and Paragon Detergent will clean it up in no time," and before the terrified housekeeper could interfere, he had fallen upon his knees, and was rapidly scouring the floor with a small stick of what looked like a black cosmetic. In a few moments no trace of the blood-stain could be seen.

"I knew Pinkerton would do it," he exclaimed, triumphantly, as he looked round at his admiring family; but no sooner had he said these words than a terrible flash of lightning lit up the sombre room, a fearful peal of thunder made them all start to their feet, and Mrs. Umney fainted.

"What a monstrous climate!" said the American Minister, calmly, as he lit a long cheroot. "I guess the old country is so overpopulated that they have not enough decent weather for everybody. I have always been of opinion that emigration is the only thing for England."

"My dear Hiram," cried Mrs. Otis, "what can we do with a woman who faints?"

"Charge it to her like breakages," answered the Minister; "she won't faint after that"; and in a few moments Mrs. Umney certainly came to. There was no doubt, however, that she was extremely upset, and she sternly warned Mr. Otis to beware of some trouble coming to the house.

"I have seen things with my own eyes, sir," she said, "that would make any Christian's hair stand on end, and many and many a night I have not closed my eyes in sleep for the awful things that are done here." Mr. Otis, however, and his wife warmly assured the honest soul that they were not afraid of ghosts, and, after invoking the blessings of Providence on her new master and mistress, and making arrangements for an increase of salary, the old housekeeper tottered off to her own room.

2

The storm raged fiercely all that night, but nothing of particular note occurred. The next morning, however, when they came down to breakfast, they found the terrible stain of blood once again on the floor. "I don't think it can be the fault of the Paragon Detergent," said Washington, "for I have tried it with everything. It must be the ghost." He accordingly rubbed out the stain a second time, but the second morning it appeared again. The third morning also it was there, though the library had been locked up at night by Mr. Otis himself, and the key carried upstairs. The whole family were now quite interested; Mr. Otis began to suspect that he had been too dogmatic in his denial of the existence of ghosts, Mrs. Otis expressed her intention of joining the Psychical Society, and Washington prepared a long letter to Messrs. Myers and Podmore on the subject of the permanence of sanguineous stains when connected with crime. That night all doubts about the objective existence of phantasmata were removed forever.

16

The day had been warm and sunny; and, in the cool of the evening, the whole family went out to drive. They did not return home till nine o'clock, when they had a light supper. The conversation in no way turned upon ghosts, so there were not even those primary conditions of receptive expectations which so often precede the presentation of psychical phenomena. The subjects discussed, as I have since learned from Mr. Otis, were merely such as form the ordinary conversation of cultured Americans of the better class, such as the immense superiority of Miss Fanny Devonport over Sarah Bernhardt as an actress; the difficulty of obtaining green corn, buckwheat cakes, and hominy, even in the best English houses; the importance of Boston in the development of the world-soul; the advantages of the baggage-check system in railway travelling; and the sweetness of the New York accent as compared to the London drawl. No mention at all was made of the supernatural, nor was Sir Simon de Canterville alluded to in any way. At eleven o'clock the family retired, and by half-past all the lights were out. Some time after, Mr. Otis was awakened by a curious noise in the corridor, outside his room. It sounded like the clank of metal, and seemed to be coming nearer every moment. He got up at once, struck a match, and looked at the time. It was exactly one o'clock. He was quite calm, and felt his pulse, which was not at all feverish. The strange noise still continued, and with it he heard distinctly the sound of footsteps. He put on his slippers, took a small oblong phial out of his dressing-case, and opened the door. Right in front of him he saw, in the wan moonlight, an old man of terrible aspect. His eyes were as red burning coals; long gray hair fell over his shoulders in matted coils; his garments, which were of antique cut, were soiled and ragged, and from his wrists and ankles hung heavy manacles and rusty gyves.

"My dear sir," said Mr. Otis, "I really must insist on your oiling those chains, and have brought you for that purpose a small bottle of the Tammany Rising Sun Lubricator. It is said to be completely efficacious upon one application, and there are several testimonials to that effect on the wrapper from some of our most eminent native divines. I shall leave it here for you by the bedroom candles, and will be happy to supply you with more, should you require it." With these words the United States Minister laid the bottle down on a marble table, and, closing his door, retired to rest.

For a moment the Canterville ghost stood quite motionless in natural indignation; then, dashing the bottle violently upon the polished floor, he fled down the corridor, uttering hollow groans, and emitting a ghastly green light. Just, however, as he reached the top of the great oak staircase, a door was flung open, two little white-robed figures appeared, and a large pillow whizzed past his head! There was evidently no time to be lost, so, hastily adopting the Fourth dimension of Space as a means of escape, he vanished through the wainscoting, and the house became quite quiet.

On reaching a small secret chamber in the left wing, he leaned up against a moonbeam to recover his breath, and began to try and realize his position. Never, in a brilliant and uninterrupted career of three hundred years, had he been so grossly insulted. He thought of the Dowager Duchess, whom he had frightened into a fit as she stood before the glass in her lace and diamonds; of the four housemaids, who had gone into hysterics when he merely grinned at them through the curtains on one of the spare bedrooms; of the rector of the parish, whose candle he had blown out as he was coming late one night from the library, and who had been under the care of Sir William Gull ever since, a perfect martyr to nervous disorders; and of old Madame de Tremouillac, who, having wakened up one morning early and seen a skeleton seated in an arm-chair by the fire reading her diary, had been confined to her bed for six weeks with an attack of brain fever, and, on her recovery, had become reconciled to the Church, and broken off her connection with that notorious sceptic, Monsieur de Voltaire. He remembered the terrible night when the wicked Lord Canterville was found choking in his dressing-room, with the knave of diamonds half-way down his throat, and confessed, just before he died, that he had cheated Charles James Fox out of £50,000 at Crockford's by means of that very card, and swore that the ghost had made him swallow it. All his great achievements came back to him again, from the butler who had shot himself in the pantry because he had seen a green hand tapping at the windowpane, to the beautiful Lady Stutfield, who was always obliged to wear a black velvet band round her throat to hide the mark of five fingers burnt upon her white skin, and who drowned herself at last in the carp-pond at the end of the King's Walk. With the enthusiastic egotism of the true artist, he went over his most celebrated performances, and smiled bitterly to himself as he recalled to mind his last appearance as "Red Reuben, or the Strangled Babe," his début as "Gaunt Gibeon, the Blood-sucker of Bexley Moor," and the furore he had excited one lovely June evening by merely playing nine-pins with his own bones upon the lawn-tennis ground. And after all this some wretched modern Americans were to come and offer him the Rising Sun Lubricator, and throw pillows at his head! It was quite unbearable. Besides, no ghost in history had ever been treated in this manner. Accordingly, he determined to have vengeance, and remained till daylight in an attitude of deep thought.

3

The next morning, when the Otis family met at breakfast, they discussed the ghost at some length. The United States Minister was naturally a little annoyed to find that his present had not been accepted. "I have no wish," he said, "to do the ghost any personal injury, and I must say that, considering the length of time he has been in the house, I don't think it is at all polite to throw pillows at him,"—a very just remark, at which, I am sorry to say, the twins burst into shouts of laughter. "Upon the other hand," he continued, "if he really declines to use the Rising Sun Lubricator, we shall have to take his chains from him. It would be quite impossible to sleep, with such a noise going on outside the bedrooms."

For the rest of the week, however, they were undisturbed, the only thing that excited any attention being the continual renewal of the blood-stain on the library floor. This certainly was very strange, as the door was always locked at night by Mr. Otis, and the windows kept closely barred. The chameleon-like colour, also, of the stain excited a good deal of comment. Some mornings it was a dull (almost Indian) red, then it would be vermilion, then a rich purple, and once when they came down for family prayers, according to the simple rites of the Free American Reformed Episcopalian Church, they found it a bright emerald-green. These kaleidoscopic changes naturally amused the party very much, and bets on the subject were freely made every evening. The only person who did not enter into the joke was little Virginia, who, for some unexplained reason, was always a good deal distressed at the sight of the blood-stain, and very nearly cried the morning it was emerald-green.

The second appearance of the ghost was on Sunday night. Shortly after they had gone to bed they were suddenly alarmed by a fearful crash in the hall. Rushing downstairs, they found that a large suit of old armour had become detached from its stand, and had fallen on the stone floor, while seated in a high-backed chair was the Canterville ghost, rubbing his knees with an expression of acute agony on his face. The twins, having brought their pea-shooters with them, at once discharged two pellets on him, with that accuracy of aim which can only be attained by long and careful practice on a writing-master, while the

United States Minister covered him with his revolver, and called upon him, in accordance with Californian etiquette, to hold up his hands! The ghost started up with a wild shriek of rage, and swept through them like a mist, extinguishing Washington Otis's candle as he passed, and so leaving them all in total darkness. On reaching the top of the staircase he recovered himself, and determined to give his celebrated peal of demoniac laughter. This he had on more than one occasion found extremely useful. It was said to have turned Lord Raker's wig gray in a single night, and had certainly made three of Lady Canterville's French governesses give warning before their month was up. He accordingly laughed his most horrible laugh, till the old vaulted roof rang and rang again, but hardly had the fearful echo died away when a door opened, and Mrs. Otis came out in a light blue dressing-gown. "I am afraid you are far from well," she said, "and have brought you a bottle of Doctor Dobell's tincture. If it is indigestion, you will find it a most excellent remedy." The ghost glared at her in fury, and began at once to make preparations for turning himself into a large black dog, an accomplishment for which he was justly renowned, and to which the family doctor always attributed the permanent idiocy of Lord Canterville's uncle, the Hon. Thomas Horton. The sound of approaching footsteps, however, made him hesitate in his fell purpose, so he contented himself with becoming faintly phosphorescent, and vanished with a deep churchyard groan, just as the twins had come up to him.

On reaching his room he entirely broke down, and became a prey to the most violent agitation. The vulgarity of the twins, and the gross materialism of Mrs. Otis, were naturally extremely annoying, but what really distressed him most was that he had been unable to wear the suit of mail. He had hoped that even modern Americans would be thrilled by the sight of a spectre in armour, if for no more sensible reason, at least out of respect for their national poet Longfellow, over whose graceful and attractive poetry he himself had whiled away many a weary hour when the Cantervilles were up in town. Besides it was his own suit. He had worn it with great success at the Kenilworth tournament, and had been highly complimented on it by no less a person than the Virgin Queen herself. Yet when he had put it on, he had been completely overpowered by the weight of the huge breastplate and steel casque, and had fallen heavily on the stone pavement, barking both his knees severely, and bruising the knuckles of his right hand.

For some days after this he was extremely ill, and hardly stirred out of his room at all, except to keep the blood-stain in proper repair. However, by taking great care of himself, he recovered, and resolved to make a third attempt to frighten the United States Minister and his family. He selected Friday, August 17th, for his appearance, and spent most of that day in looking over his wardrobe, ultimately deciding in favour of a large slouched hat with a red feather, a winding-sheet frilled at the wrists and neck, and a rusty dagger. Towards evening a violent storm of rain came on, and the wind was so high that all the windows and doors in the old house shook and rattled. In fact, it was just such weather as he loved. His plan of action was this. He was to make his way quietly to Washington Otis's room, gibber at him from the foot of the bed, and stab himself three times in the throat to the sound of low music. He bore Washington a special grudge, being quite aware that it was he who was in the habit of removing the famous Canterville blood-stain by means of Pinkerton's Paragon Detergent. Having reduced the reckless and foolhardy youth to a condition of abject terror, he was then to proceed to the room occupied by the United States Minister and his wife, and there to place a clammy hand on Mrs. Otis's forehead, while he hissed into her trembling husband's ear the awful secrets of the charnel-house. With regard to little Virginia, he had not quite made up his mind. She had never insulted him in any way, and was pretty and gentle. A few hollow groans from the wardrobe, he thought, would be more than sufficient, or, if that failed to wake her, he might grabble at the counterpane with palsy-twitching fingers. As for the twins, he was quite determined to teach them a lesson. The first thing to be done was, of course, to sit upon their chests, so as to produce the stifling sensation of nightmare. Then, as their beds were quite close to each other, to stand between them in the form of a green, icy-cold corpse, till they became paralyzed with fear, and finally, to throw off the winding-sheet, and crawl round the room, with white, bleached bones and one rolling eyeball in the character of "Dumb Daniel, or the Suicide's Skeleton," a role in which he had on more than one occasion produced a great effect, and which he considered quite equal to his famous part of "Martin the Maniac, or the Masked Mystery."

At half-past ten he heard the family going to bed. For some time he was disturbed by wild shrieks of laughter from the twins, who, with the light-hearted gayety of schoolboys, were evidently amusing themselves before they retired to rest, but at a quarter-past eleven all was still, and, as midnight sounded, he sallied forth. The owl beat against the window-panes, the raven croaked from the old yew-tree, and the wind wandered moaning round the house like a lost soul; but the Otis family slept unconscious of their doom, and high above the rain and storm he could hear the steady snoring of the Minister for the United States. He stepped stealthily out of the wainscoting, with an evil smile on his cruel, wrinkled mouth, and the moon hid her face in a cloud as he stole past the great oriel window, where his own arms and those of his murdered wife were blazoned in azure and gold. On and on he glided, like an evil shadow, the very darkness seeming to loathe him as he passed. Once he thought he heard something call, and stopped; but it was only the baying of a dog from the Red Farm, and he went on, muttering strange sixteenth century curses, and ever and anon brandishing the rusty dagger in the midnight air. Finally he reached the corner of the passage that led to luckless Washington's room. For a moment he paused there, the wind blowing his long gray locks about his head, and twisting into grotesque and fantastic folds the nameless horror of the dead man's shroud. Then the clock struck the quarter, and he felt the time was come. He chuckled to himself, and turned the corner; but no sooner had he done so than, with a piteous wail of terror, he fell back, and hid his blanched face in his long, bony hands. Right in front of him was standing a horrible spectre, motionless as a carven image, and monstrous as a madman's dream! Its head was bald and burnished; its face round, and fat, and white; and hideous laughter seemed to have writhed its features into an eternal grin. From the eyes streamed rays of scarlet light, the mouth was a wide well of fire, and a hideous garment, like to his own, swathed with its silent snows the Titan form. On its breast was a placard with strange writing in antique characters, some scroll of shame it seemed, some record of wild sins, some awful calendar of crime, and, with its right hand, it bore aloft a falchion of gleaming steel.

Never having seen a ghost before, he naturally was terribly frightened, and, after a second hasty glance at the awful phantom, he fled back to his room, tripping up in his long winding-sheet as he sped down the corridor, and finally dropping the rusty dagger into the Minister's jack-boots, where it was found in the morning by the butler. Once in the privacy of his own apartment, he flung himself down on a small pallet-bed, and hid his face under the clothes. After a time, however, the brave old Canterville spirit asserted itself, and he determined to go and speak to the other ghost as soon as it was daylight. Accordingly, just as the dawn was touching the hills with silver, he returned towards the spot where he had first laid eyes on the grisly phantom, feeling that, after all, two ghosts were better than one, and that, by the aid of his new friend, he might safely grapple with the twins. On reaching the spot, however, a terrible sight met his gaze. Something had evidently happened to the spectre, for the light had entirely faded from its hollow eyes, the gleaming falchion had fallen from its hand, and it was leaning up against the wall in a strained and uncomfortable attitude. He rushed forward and seized it in his arms, when, to his horror, the head slipped off and rolled on the floor, the body assumed a recumbent posture, and he found himself clasping a white dimity bed-curtain, with a sweeping-brush, a kitchen cleaver, and a hollow turnip lying at his feet! Unable to understand this curious transformation, he clutched the placard with feverish haste, and there, in the gray morning light, he read these fearful words:

YE OTIS GHOSTE
Ye Onlie True and Originale Spook
Beware of Ye Imitationes
All others are counterfeite

The whole thing flashed across him. He had been tricked, foiled, and outwitted! The old Canterville look came into his eyes; he ground his toothless gums together; and, raising his withered hands high above his head, swore according to the picturesque phraseology of the antique school, that, when Chanticleer had sounded twice his merry horn, deeds of blood would be wrought, and murder walk abroad with silent feet.

Hardly had he finished this awful oath when, from the red-tiled roof of a distant homestead, a cock crew. He laughed a long, low, bitter laugh, and waited. Hour after hour he waited, but the cock, for some strange reason, did not crow again. Finally, at half-past seven, the arrival of the housemaids made him give up his fearful vigil, and he stalked back to his room, thinking of his vain oath and baffled purpose. There he consulted several books of ancient chivalry, of which he was exceedingly fond, and found that, on every occasion on which this oath had been used, Chanticleer had always crowed a second time. "Perdition seize the naughty fowl," he muttered, "I have seen the day when, with my stout spear, I would have run him through the gorge, and made him crow for me an 'twere in death!" He then retired to a comfortable lead coffin, and stayed there till evening.

4

The next day the ghost was very weak and tired. The terrible excitement of the last four weeks was beginning to have its effect. His nerves were completely shattered, and he started at the slightest noise. For five days he kept his room, and at last made up his mind to give up the point of the blood-stain on the library floor. If the Otis family did not want it, they clearly did not deserve it. They were evidently people on a low, material plane of existence, and quite incapable of appreciating the symbolic value of sensuous phenomena. The question of phantasmic apparitions, and the development of astral bodies, was of course quite a different matter, and really not under his control. It was his solemn duty to appear in the corridor once a week, and to gibber from the large oriel window on the first and third Wednesdays in every month, and he did not see how he could honourably escape from his obligations. It is quite true that his life had been very evil, but, upon the other hand, he was most conscientious in all things connected with the supernatural. For the next three Saturdays, accordingly, he traversed the corridor as usual between midnight and three o'clock, taking every possible precaution against being either heard or seen. He removed his boots, trod as lightly as possible on the old worm-eaten boards, wore a large black velvet cloak, and was careful to use the Rising Sun Lubricator for oiling his chains. I am bound to acknowledge that it was with a good deal of difficulty that he brought himself to adopt this last mode of protection. However, one night, while the family were at dinner, he slipped into Mr. Otis's bedroom and carried off the bottle. He felt a little humiliated at first, but afterwards was sensible enough to see that there was a great deal to be said for the invention, and, to a certain degree, it served his purpose. Still, in spite of everything he was not left unmolested. Strings were continually being stretched across the corridor, over which he tripped in the dark, and on one occasion, while dressed for the part of "Black Isaac, or the Huntsman of Hogley Woods," he met with a severe fall, through treading on a butter-slide, which the twins had constructed from the entrance of the Tapestry Chamber to the top of the oak staircase. This last insult so enraged him that he resolved to make one final effort to assert his dignity and social position, and determined to visit the insolent young Etonians the next night in his celebrated character of "Reckless Rupert, or the Headless Earl."

He had not appeared in this disguise for more than seventy years; in fact, not since he had so frightened pretty Lady Barbara Modish by means of it, that she suddenly broke off her engagement with the present Lord Canterville's grandfather, and ran away to Gretna Green with handsome Jack Castletown, declaring that nothing in the world would induce her to marry into a family that allowed such a horrible phantom to walk up and down the terrace at twilight. Poor Jack was afterwards shot in a duel by Lord Canterville on Wandsworth Common, and Lady Barbara died of a broken heart at Tunbridge Wells before the year was out, so, in every way, it had been a great success. It was, however, an extremely difficult "make-up," if I may use such a theatrical expression in connection with one of the greatest mysteries of the supernatural, or, to employ a more scientific term, the higher-natural world, and it took him fully three hours to make his preparations. At last everything was ready, and he was very pleased with his appearance. The big leather riding-boots that went with the dress were just a little too large for him, and he could only find one of the two horse-pistols, but, on the whole, he was quite satisfied, and at a quarter-past one he glided out of the wainscoting and crept down the corridor. On reaching the room occupied by the twins, which I should mention was called the Blue Bed Chamber on account of the colour of its hangings, he found the door just ajar. Wishing to make an effective entrance, he flung it wide open, when a heavy jug of water fell right down on him, wetting him to the skin, and just missing his left shoulder by a couple of inches. At the same moment he heard stifled shrieks of laughter proceeding from the four-post bed. The shock to his nervous system was so great that he fled back to his room as hard as he could go, and the next day he was laid up with a severe cold. The only thing that at all consoled him in the whole affair was the fact that he had not brought his head with him, for, had he done so, the consequences might have been very serious.

He now gave up all hope of ever frightening this rude American family, and contented himself, as a rule, with creeping about the passages in list slippers, with a thick red muffler round his throat for fear of draughts, and a small arquebus, in case he should be attacked by the twins. The final blow he received occurred on the 19th of September. He had gone downstairs to the great entrance-hall feeling sure that there, at any rate, he would be quite unmolested, and was amusing himself by making satirical remarks on the large Saroni photographs of the United States Minister and his wife, which had now taken the place of the Canterville family pictures. He was simply but neatly clad in a long shroud, spotted with churchyard mould, had tied up his jaw with a strip of yellow linen, and carried a small lantern and a sexton's spade. In fact, he was dressed for the character of "Jonas the Graveless, or the Corpse-Snatcher of Chertsey Barn," one of his most remarkable impersonations, and one which the Cantervilles had every reason to remember, as it was the real origin of their quarrel with their neighbour, Lord Rufford. It was about a quarter-past two o'clock in the morning, and, as far as he could ascertain, no one was stirring. As he was strolling towards the library, however, to see if there were any traces left of the bloodstain, suddenly there leaped out on him from a dark corner two figures, who waved their arms wildly above their heads, and shrieked out *"Boo!"* in his ear.

Seized with a panic, which, under the circumstances, was only natural, he rushed for the staircase, but found Washington Otis waiting for him there with the big garden-syringe, and being thus hemmed in by his enemies on every side, and driven almost to bay, he vanished into the great iron stove, which, fortunately for him, was not lit, and had to make his way home through the flues and chimneys, arriving at his own room in a terrible state of dirt, disorder, and despair.

After this he was not seen again on any nocturnal expedition. The twins lay in wait for him on several occasions, and strewed the passages with nutshells every night to the great annoyance of their parents and the servants, but it was of no avail. It was quite evident that his feelings were so wounded that he would not appear. Mr. Otis consequently resumed his great work on the history of the Democratic party, on which he had been engaged for some years; Mrs. Otis organized a wonderful clam-bake, which amazed the whole county; the boys took to lacrosse, euchre, poker, and other American national games, and Virginia rode about the lanes on her pony, accompanied by the young Duke of Cheshire, who had come to spend the last week of his holidays at Canterville Chase. It was generally assumed that the ghost had gone away, and, in fact, Mr. Otis wrote a letter to that effect to Lord Canterville, who, in reply, expressed his great pleasure at the news, and sent his best congratulations to the Minister's worthy wife.

The Otises, however, were deceived, for the ghost was still in the house, and though now almost an invalid, was by no means ready to let matters rest, particularly as he heard that among the guests was the young Duke of Cheshire, whose grand-uncle, Lord Francis Stilton, had once bet a hundred guineas with Colonel Carbury that he would play dice with the Canterville ghost, and was found the next morning lying on the floor of the card-room in such a helpless paralytic state that, though he lived on to a great age, he was never able to say anything again but "Double Sixes." The story was well known at the time, though, of course, out of respect to the feelings of the two noble families, every attempt was made to hush it up, and a full account of all the circumstances connected with it will be found in the third volume of Lord Tattle's *Recollections of the Prince Regent and his Friends*. The ghost, then, was naturally very anxious to show that he had not lost his influence over the Stiltons, with whom, indeed, he was distantly connected, his own first cousin having been married *en secondes noces* to the Sieur de Bulkeley, from whom, as everyone knows, the Dukes of Cheshire are lineally descended. Accordingly, he made arrangements for appearing to Virginia's little lover in his celebrated impersonation of "The Vampire Monk, or the Bloodless Benedictine," a performance so horrible that when old Lady Startup saw it, which she did on one fatal New Year's Eve, in the year 1764, she went off into the most piercing shrieks, which culminated in violent apoplexy, and died in three days, after disinheriting the Cantervilles, who were her nearest relations, and leaving all her money to her London apothecary. At the last moment, however, his terror of the twins prevented his leaving his room, and the little duke slept in peace under the great feathered canopy in the Royal Bedchamber, and dreamed of Virginia.

5

A few days after this, Virginia and her curly-haired cavalier went out riding on Brockley meadows, where she tore her habit so badly in getting through a hedge that, on their return home, she made up her mind to go up by the back staircase so as not to be seen. As she was running past the Tapestry Chamber, the door of which happened to be open, she fancied she saw someone inside, and thinking it was her mother's maid, who sometimes used to bring her work there, looked in to ask her to mend her habit. To her immense surprise, however, it was the Canterville ghost himself! He was sitting by the window, watching the ruined gold of the yellowing trees fly through the air, and the red leaves dancing madly down the long avenue. His head was leaning on his hand, and his whole attitude was one of extreme depression. Indeed, so forlorn, and so much out of repair did he look, that little Virginia, whose first idea had been to run away and lock herself in her room, was filled with pity, and determined to try and comfort him. So light was her footfall, and so deep his melancholy, that he was not aware of her presence till she spoke to him.

"I am so sorry for you," she said, "but my brothers are going back to Eton to-morrow, and then, if you behave yourself, no one will annoy you."

"It is absurd asking me to behave myself," he answered, looking round in astonishment at the pretty little girl who had ventured to address him, "quite absurd. I must rattle my chains, and groan through keyholes, and walk about at night, if that is what you mean. It is my only reason for existing."

"It is no reason at all for existing, and you know you have been very wicked. Mrs. Umney told us, the first day we arrived here, that you had killed your wife."

"Well, I quite admit it," said the ghost, petulantly, "but it was a purely family matter and concerned no one else."

"It is very wrong to kill anyone," said Virginia, who at times had a sweet puritan gravity, caught from some old New England ancestor.

"Oh, I hate the cheap severity of abstract ethics! My wife was very plain, never had my ruffs properly starched, and knew nothing about cookery. Why, there was a buck I had shot in Hogley Woods, a magnificent pricket, and do you know how she had it sent to table? However, it is no matter now, for it is all over, and I don't think it was very nice of her brothers to starve me to death, though I did kill her."

"Starve you to death? Oh, Mr. Ghost—I mean Sir Simon, are you hungry? I have a sandwich in my case. Would you like it?"

"No, thank you, I never eat anything now; but it is very kind of you, all the same, and you are much nicer than the rest of your horrid, rude, vulgar, dishonest family."

"Stop!" cried Virginia, stamping her foot, "it is you who are rude, and horrid, and vulgar, and as for dishonesty, you know you stole the paints out of my box to try and furbish up that ridiculous blood-stain in the library. First you took all my reds, including the vermilion, and I couldn't do any more sunsets, then you took the emerald-green and the chrome-yellow, and finally I had nothing left but indigo and Chinese white, and could only do moonlight scenes, which are always depressing to look at, and not at all easy to paint. I never told on you, though I was very much annoyed, and it was most ridiculous, the whole thing; for who ever heard of emerald-green blood?"

"Well, really," said the Ghost, rather meekly, "what was I to do? It is a very difficult thing to get real blood nowadays, and, as your brother began it all with his Paragon Detergent, I certainly saw no reason why I should not have your paints. As for colour, that is always a matter of taste: the Cantervilles have blue blood, for instance, the very bluest in England; but I know you Americans don't care for things of this kind."

"You know nothing about it, and the best thing you can do is to emigrate and improve your mind. My father will be only too happy to give you a free passage, and though there is a heavy duty on spirits of every kind, there will be no difficulty about the Custom House, as the officers are all Democrats. Once in New York, you are sure to be a great success. I know lots of people there who would give a hundred thousand dollars to have a grandfather, and much more than that to have a family ghost."

"I don't think I should like America."

"I suppose because we have no ruins and no curiosities," said Virginia, satirically.

"No ruins! no curiosities!" answered the Ghost; "you have your navy and your manners."

"Good evening; I will go and ask papa to get the twins an extra week's holiday."

"Please don't go, Miss Virginia," he cried; "I am so lonely and so unhappy, and I really don't know what to do. I want to go to sleep and I cannot."

"That's quite absurd! You have merely to go to bed and blow out the candle. It is very difficult sometimes to keep awake, especially at church, but there is no difficulty at all about sleeping. Why, even babies know how to do that, and they are not very clever."

"I have not slept for three hundred years," he said sadly, and Virginia's beautiful blue eyes opened in wonder; "for three hundred years I have not slept, and I am so tired."

Virginia grew quite grave, and her little lips trembled like rose-leaves. She came towards him, and kneeling down at his side, looked up into his old withered face.

"Poor, poor ghost," she murmured; "have you no place where you can sleep?"

"Far away beyond the pinewoods," he answered, in a low, dreamy voice, "there is a little garden. There the grass grows long and deep, there are the great white stars of the hemlock flower, there the nightingale sings all night long. All night long he sings, and the cold crystal moon looks down, and the yew-tree spreads out its giant arms over the sleepers."

Virginia's eyes grew dim with tears, and she hid her face in her hands.

"You mean the Garden of Death," she whispered.

"Yes, death. Death must be so beautiful. To lie in the soft brown earth, with the grasses waving above one's head, and listen to silence. To have no yesterday, and no to-morrow. To forget time, to forget life, to be at peace. You can help me. You can open for me the portals of death's house, for love is always with you, and love is stronger than death is."

Virginia trembled, a cold shudder ran through her, and for a few moments there was silence. She felt as if she was in a terrible dream.

Then the ghost spoke again, and his voice sounded like the sighing of the wind.

"Have you ever read the old prophecy on the library window?"

"Oh, often," cried the little girl, looking up; "I know it quite well. It is painted in curious black letters, and is difficult to read. There are only six lines:

"'When a golden girl can win
"Prayer from out the lips of sin,
"When the barren almond bears,
"And a little child gives away its tears,
"Then shall all the house be still
"And peace come to Canterville.'

"But I don't know what they mean."

"They mean," he said, sadly, "that you must weep with me for my sins, because I have no tears, and pray with me for my soul, because I have no faith, and then, if you have always been sweet, and good, and gentle, the angel of death will have mercy on me. You will see fearful shapes in darkness, and wicked voices will whisper in your ear, but they will not harm you, for against the purity of a little child the powers of Hell cannot prevail."

Virginia made no answer, and the ghost wrung his hands in wild despair as he looked down at her bowed golden head. Suddenly she stood up, very pale, and with a strange light in her eyes. "I am not afraid," she said firmly, "and I will ask the angel to have mercy on you."

He rose from his seat with a faint cry of joy, and taking her hand bent over it with old-fashioned grace and kissed it. His fingers were as cold as ice, and his lips burned like fire, but Virginia did not falter, as he led her across the dusky room. On the faded green tapestry were broidered little huntsmen. They blew their tasselled horns and with their tiny hands waved to her to go back. "Go back! little Virginia," they cried, "go back!" but the ghost clutched her hand more tightly, and she shut her eyes against them. Horrible animals with lizard tails and goggle eyes blinked at her from the carven chimney-piece, and murmured, "Beware! little Virginia, beware! we may never see you again," but the ghost glided on more swiftly, and Virginia did not listen. When they reached the end of the room he stopped, and muttered some words she could not understand. She opened her eyes, and saw the wall slowly fading away like a mist, and a great black cavern in front of her. A bitter cold wind swept round them, and she felt something pulling at her dress. "Quick, quick," cried the ghost, "or it will be too late," and in a moment the wainscoting had closed behind them, and the Tapestry Chamber was empty.

6

About ten minutes later, the bell rang for tea, and, as Virginia did not come down, Mrs. Otis sent up one of the footmen to tell her. After a little time he returned and said that he could not find Miss Virginia anywhere. As she was in the habit of going out to the garden every evening to get flowers for the dinner-table, Mrs. Otis was not at all alarmed at first, but when six o'clock struck, and Virginia did not appear, she became really agitated, and sent the boys out to look for her, while she herself and Mr. Otis searched every room in the house. At half-past six the boys came back and said that they could find no trace of their sister anywhere. They were all now in the greatest state of excitement, and did not know what to do, when Mr. Otis suddenly remembered that, some few days before, he had given a band of gipsies permission to camp in the park. He accordingly at once set off for Blackfell Hollow, where he knew they were, accompanied by his eldest son and two of the farm-servants. The little Duke of Cheshire, who was perfectly frantic with anxiety, begged hard to be allowed to go too, but Mr. Otis would not allow him, as he was afraid there might be a scuffle. On arriving at the spot, however, he found that the gipsies had gone, and it was evident that their departure had been rather sudden, as the fire was still burning, and some plates were lying on the grass. Having sent off Washington and the two men to scour the district, he ran home, and dispatched telegrams to all the police inspectors in the county, telling them to look out for a little girl who had been kidnapped by tramps or gipsies. He then ordered his horse to be brought round, and after insisting on his wife and the three boys sitting down to dinner, rode off down the Ascot road with a groom. He had hardly, however, gone a couple of miles, when he heard somebody galloping after him, and, looking round, saw the little duke coming up on his pony, with his face very flushed, and no hat. "I'm awfully sorry, Mr. Otis," gasped out the boy, "but I can't eat any dinner as long as Virginia is lost. Please don't be angry with me; if you had let us be engaged last year, there would never have been all this trouble. You won't send me back, will you? I can't go! I won't go!"

The Minister could not help smiling at the handsome young scapegrace, and was a good deal touched at his devotion to Virginia, so leaning down from his horse, he patted him kindly on the shoulders, and said, "Well, Cecil, if you won't go back, I suppose you must come with me, but I must get you a hat at Ascot."

"Oh, bother my hat! I want Virginia!" cried the little duke, laughing, and they galloped on to the railway station. There Mr. Otis inquired of the station-master if anyone answering to the description of Virginia had been seen on the platform, but could get no news of her. The station-master, however, wired up and down the line, and assured him that a strict watch would be kept for her, and, after having bought a hat for the little duke from a linen-draper, who was just putting up his shutters, Mr. Otis rode off to Bexley, a village about four miles away, which he was told was a well-known haunt of the gipsies, as there was a large common next to it. Here they roused up the rural policeman, but could get no information from him, and, after riding all over the common, they turned their horses' heads homewards, and reached the Chase about eleven o'clock, dead tired and almost heartbroken. They found Washington and the twins waiting for them at the gatehouse with lanterns, as the avenue was very dark. Not the slightest trace of Virginia had been discovered. The gipsies had been caught on Brockley meadows, but she was not with them, and they had explained their sudden departure by saying that they had mistaken the date of Chorton Fair, and had gone off in a hurry for fear they should be late. Indeed, they had been quite distressed at hearing of Virginia's disappearance, as they were very grateful to Mr. Otis for having allowed them to camp in his park, and four of their number had stayed behind to help in the search. The carp-pond had been dragged, and the whole Chase thoroughly gone over, but without any result. It was evident that, for that night at any rate, Virginia was lost to them; and it was in a state of the deepest depression that Mr. Otis and the boys walked up to the house, the groom following behind with the two horses and the pony. In the hall they found a group of frightened servants, and lying on a sofa in the library was poor Mrs. Otis, almost out of her mind with terror and anxiety, and having her forehead bathed with eau de cologne by the old housekeeper. Mr. Otis at once insisted on her having something to eat, and ordered up supper for the whole party. It was a melancholy meal, as hardly anyone spoke, and even the twins were awestruck and subdued, as they were very fond of their sister. When they had finished, Mr. Otis, in spite of the entreaties of the little duke, ordered them all to bed, saying that nothing more could be done that night, and that he would telegraph in the morning to Scotland Yard for some detectives to be sent down immediately. Just as they were passing out of the dining-room, midnight began to boom from the clock tower, and when the last stroke sounded they heard a crash and a sudden shrill cry; a dreadful peal of thunder shook the house, a strain of unearthly music floated through the air, a panel at the top of the staircase flew back with a loud noise, and out on the landing, looking very pale and white, with a little casket in her hand, stepped Virginia. In a moment they had all rushed up to her. Mrs. Otis clasped her passionately in her arms, the Duke smothered her with violent kisses, and the twins executed a wild war-dance round the group.

"Good heavens! child, where have you been?" said Mr. Otis, rather angrily, thinking that she had been playing some foolish trick on them. "Cecil and I have been riding all over the country looking for you, and your mother has been frightened to death. You must never play these practical jokes any more."

"Except on the ghost! except on the ghost!" shrieked the twins, as they capered about.

"My own darling, thank God you are found; you must never leave my side again," murmured Mrs. Otis, as she kissed the trembling child, and smoothed the tangled gold of her hair.

"Papa," said Virginia, quietly, "I have been with the ghost. He is dead, and you must come and see him. He had been very wicked, but he was really sorry for all that he had done, and he gave me this box of beautiful jewels before he died."

The whole family gazed at her in mute amazement, but she was quite grave and serious; and, turning round, she led them through the opening in the wainscoting down a narrow secret corridor, Washington following with a lighted candle, which he had caught up from the table. Finally, they came to a great oak door, studded with rusty nails. When Virginia touched it, it swung back on its heavy hinges, and they found themselves in a little low room, with a vaulted ceiling, and one tiny grated window. Embedded in the wall was a huge iron ring, and chained to it was a gaunt skeleton, that was stretched out at full length on the stone floor, and seemed to be trying to grasp with its long fleshless fingers an old-fashioned trencher and ewer, that were placed just out of its reach. The jug had evidently been once filled with water, as it was covered inside with green mould. There was nothing on the trencher but a pile of dust. Virginia knelt down beside the skeleton, and, folding her little hands together, began to pray silently, while the rest of the party looked on in wonder at the terrible tragedy whose secret was now disclosed to them.

"Hallo!" suddenly exclaimed one of the twins, who had been looking out of the window to try and discover in what wing of the house the room was situated. "Hallo! the old withered almond-tree has blossomed. I can see the flowers quite plainly in the moonlight."

"God has forgiven him," said Virginia, gravely, as she rose to her feet, and a beautiful light seemed to illumine her face.

"What an angel you are!" cried the young duke, and he put his arm round her neck, and kissed her.

7

Four days after these curious incidents, a funeral started from Canterville Chase at about eleven o'clock at night. The hearse was drawn by eight black horses, each of which carried on its head a great tuft of nodding ostrich-plumes, and the leaden coffin was covered by a rich purple pall, on which was embroidered in gold the Canterville coat-of-arms. By the side of the hearse and the coaches walked the servants with lighted torches, and the whole procession was wonderfully impressive. Lord Canterville was the chief mourner, having come up specially from Wales to attend the funeral, and sat in the first carriage along with little Virginia. Then came the United States Minister and his wife, then Washington and the three boys, and in the last carriage was Mrs. Umney. It was generally felt that, as she had been frightened by the ghost for more than fifty years of her life, she had a right to see the last of him. A deep grave had been dug in the corner of the churchyard, just under the old yew-tree, and the service was read in the most impressive manner by the Rev. Augustus Dampier. When the ceremony was over, the servants, according to an old custom observed in the Canterville family, extinguished their torches, and, as the coffin was being lowered into the grave, Virginia stepped forward, and laid on it a large cross made of white and pink almond-blossoms. As she did so, the moon came out from behind a cloud, and flooded with its silent silver the little churchyard, and from a distant copse a nightingale began to sing. She thought of the ghost's description of the Garden of Death, her eyes became dim with tears, and she hardly spoke a word during the drive home.

The next morning, before Lord Canterville went up to town, Mr. Otis had an interview with him on the subject of the jewels the ghost had given to Virginia. They were perfectly magnificent, especially a certain ruby necklace with old Venetian setting, which was really a superb specimen of sixteenth-century work, and their value was so great that Mr. Otis felt considerable scruples about allowing his daughter to accept them.

"My lord," he said, "I know that in this country mortmain is held to apply to trinkets as well as to land, and it is quite clear to me that these jewels are, or should be, heirlooms in your family. I must beg you, accordingly, to take them to London with you, and to regard them simply as a portion of your property which has been restored to you under certain strange conditions. As for my daughter, she is merely a child, and has as yet, I am glad to say, but little interest in such appurtenances of idle luxury. I am also informed by Mrs. Otis, who, I may say, is no mean authority upon art,—having had the privilege of spending several winters in Boston when she was a girl,—that these gems are of great monetary worth, and if offered for sale would fetch a tall price. Under these circumstances, Lord Canterville, I feel sure that you will recognize how impossible it would be for me to allow them to remain in the possession of any member of my family; and, indeed, all such vain gauds and toys, however suitable or necessary to the dignity of the British aristocracy, would be completely out of place among those who have been brought up on the severe, and I believe immortal, principles of Republican simplicity. Perhaps I should mention that Virginia is very anxious that you should allow her to retain the box, as a memento of your unfortunate but misguided ancestor. As it is extremely old, and consequently a good deal out of repair, you may perhaps think fit to comply with her request. For my own part, I confess I am a good deal surprised to find a child of mine expressing sympathy with medievalism in any form, and can only account for it by the fact that Virginia was born in one of your London suburbs shortly after Mrs. Otis had returned from a trip to Athens."

Lord Canterville listened very gravely to the worthy Minister's speech, pulling his gray moustache now and then to hide an involuntary smile, and when Mr. Otis had ended, he shook him cordially by the hand, and said: "My dear sir, your charming little daughter rendered my unlucky ancestor, Sir Simon, a very important service, and I and my family are much indebted to her for her marvellous courage and pluck. The jewels are clearly hers, and, egad, I believe that if I were heartless enough to take them from her, the wicked old fellow would be out of his grave in a fortnight, leading me the devil of a life. As for their being heirlooms, nothing is an heirloom that is not so mentioned in a will or legal document, and the existence of these jewels has been quite unknown. I assure you I have no more claim on them than your butler, and when Miss Virginia grows up, I dare say she will be pleased to have pretty things to wear. Besides, you forget, Mr. Otis, that you took the furniture and the ghost at a valuation, and anything that belonged to the ghost passed at once into your possession, as, whatever activity Sir Simon may have shown in the corridor at night, in point of law he was really dead, and you acquired his property by purchase."

Mr. Otis was a good deal distressed at Lord Canterville's refusal, and begged him to reconsider his decision, but the good-natured peer was quite firm, and finally induced the Minister to allow his daughter to retain the present the ghost had given her, and when, in the spring of 1890, the young Duchess of Cheshire was presented at the Queen's first drawing-room on the occasion of her marriage her jewels were the universal theme of admiration. For Virginia received the coronet, which is the reward of all good little American girls, and was married to her boy-lover as soon as he came of age. They were both so charming, and they loved each other so much, that everyone was delighted at the match, except the old Marchioness of Dumbleton, who had tried to catch the Duke for one of her seven unmarried daughters, and had given no less than three expensive dinner-parties for that purpose, and, strange to say, Mr. Otis himself. Mr. Otis was extremely fond of the young Duke personally, but, theoretically, he objected to titles, and, to use his own words, "was not without apprehension lest, amid the enervating influences of a pleasure-loving aristocracy, the true principles of Republican simplicity should be forgotten." His objections, however, were completely over-ruled, and I believe that when he walked up the aisle of St. George's, Hanover Square, with his daughter leaning on his arm, there was not a prouder man in the whole length and breadth of England.

The duke and duchess, after the honeymoon was over, went down to Canterville Chase, and on the day after their arrival they walked over in the afternoon to the lonely churchyard by the pinewoods. There had been a great deal of difficulty at first about the inscription on Sir Simon's tombstone, but finally it had been decided to engrave on it simply the initials of the old gentleman's name, and the verse from the library window. The duchess had brought with her some lovely roses, which she strewed upon the grave, and after they had stood by it for some time they strolled into the ruined chancel of the old abbey. There the duchess sat down on a fallen pillar, while her husband lay at her feet smoking a cigarette and looking up at her beautiful eyes. Suddenly he threw his cigarette away, took hold of her hand, and said to her, "Virginia, a wife should have no secrets from her husband."

"Dear Cecil! I have no secrets from you."

"Yes, you have," he answered, smiling, "you have never told me what happened to you when you were locked up with the ghost."

"I have never told anyone, Cecil," said Virginia, gravely.

"I know that, but you might tell me."

"Please don't ask me, Cecil, I cannot tell you. Poor Sir Simon! I owe him a great deal. Yes, don't laugh, Cecil, I really do. He made me see what Life is, and what Death signifies, and why Love is stronger than both."

The duke rose and kissed his wife lovingly.

"You can have your secret as long as I have your heart," he murmured.

"You have always had that, Cecil."

"And you will tell our children some day, won't you?"

Virginia blushed.

The Ghost-Extinguisher

Gelett Burgess

My attention was first called to the possibility of manufacturing a practicable ghost-extinguisher by a real-estate agent in San Francisco.

"There's one thing," he said, "that affects city property here in a curious way. You know we have a good many murders, and, as a consequence, certain houses attain a very sensational and undesirable reputation. These houses it is almost impossible to let; you can scarcely get a decent family to occupy them rent-free. Then we have a great many places said to be haunted. These were dead timber on my hands until I happened to notice that the Japanese have no objections to spooks. Now, whenever I have such a building to rent, I let it to Japs at a nominal figure, and after they've taken the curse off, I raise the rent, the Japs move out, the place is renovated, and in the market again."

The subject interested me, for I am not only a scientist, but a speculative philosopher as well. The investigation of those phenomena that lie upon the threshold of the great unknown has always been my favourite field of research. I believed, even then, that the Oriental mind, working along different lines than those which we pursue, has attained knowledge that we know little of. Thinking, therefore, that these Japs might have some secret inherited from their misty past, I examined into the matter.

I shall not trouble you with a narration of the incidents which led up to my acquaintance with Hoku Yamanochi. Suffice it to say that I found in him a friend who was willing to share with me his whole lore of quasi-science. I call it this advisedly, for science, as we Occidentals use the term, has to do only with the laws of matter and sensation; our scientific men, in fact, recognize the existence of nothing else. The Buddhistic philosophy, however, goes further.

According to its theories, the soul is sevenfold, consisting of different shells or envelopes—something like an onion—which are shed as life passes from the material to the spiritual state. The first, or lowest, of these is the corporeal body, which, after death, decays and perishes. Next comes the vital principle, which, departing from the body, dissipates itself like an odour, and is lost. Less gross than this is the astral body, which, although immaterial, yet lies near to the consistency of matter. This astral shape, released from the body at death, remains for a while in its earthly environment, still preserving more or less definitely the imprint of the form which it inhabited.

It is this relic of a past material personality, this outworn shell, that appears, when galvanized into an appearance of life, partly materialized, as a ghost. It is not the soul that returns, for the soul, which is immortal, is composed of the four higher spiritual essences that surround the ego, and are carried on into the next life. These astral bodies, therefore, fail to terrify the Buddhists, who know them only as shadows, with no real volition. The Japs, in point of fact, have learned how to exterminate them.

There is a certain powder, Hoku informed me, which, when burnt in their presence, transforms them from the rarefied, or semi-spiritual, condition to the state of matter. The ghost, so to speak, is precipitated into and becomes a material shape which can easily be disposed of. In this state it is confined and allowed to disintegrate slowly where it can cause no further annoyance.

This long-winded explanation piqued my curiosity, which was not to be satisfied until I had seen the Japanese method applied. It was not long before I had an opportunity. A particularly revolting murder having been committed in San Francisco, my friend Hoku Yamanochi applied for the house, and, after the police had finished their examination, he was permitted to occupy it for a half-year at the ridiculous price of three dollars a month. He invited me to share his quarters, which were large and luxuriously furnished.

For a week, nothing abnormal occurred. Then, one night, I was awakened by terrifying groans followed by a blood-curdling shriek which seemed to emerge from a large closet in my room, the scene of the late atrocity. I confess that I had all the covers pulled over my head and was shivering with horror when my Japanese friend entered, wearing a pair of flowered-silk pyjamas. Hearing his voice, I peeped forth, to see him smiling reassuringly.

"You some kind of very foolish fellow," he said. "I show you how to fix him!"

He took from his pocket three conical red pastilles, placed them upon a saucer and lighted them. Then, holding the fuming dish in one outstretched hand, he walked to the closed door and opened it. The shrieks burst out afresh, and, as I recalled the appalling details of the scene which had occurred in this very room only five weeks ago, I shuddered at his temerity. But he was quite calm.

Soon, I saw the wraith-like form of the recent victim dart from the closet. She crawled under my bed and ran about the room, endeavouring to escape, but was pursued by Hoku, who waved his smoking plate with indefatigable patience and dexterity.

At last he had her cornered, and the spectre was caught behind a curtain of odorous fumes. Slowly the figure grew more distinct, assuming the consistency of a heavy vapour, shrinking somewhat in the operation. Hoku now hurriedly turned to me.

"You hully up, bling me one pair bellows pletty quick!" he commanded.

I ran into his room and brought the bellows from his fireplace. These he pressed flat, and then carefully inserting one toe of the ghost into the nozzle and opening the handles steadily, he sucked in a portion of the unfortunate woman's anatomy, and dexterously squirted the vapour into a large jar, which had been placed in the room for the purpose. Two more operations were necessary to withdraw the phantom completely from the corner and empty it into the jar. At last the transfer was effected and the receptacle securely stoppered and sealed.

"In formeryore-time," Hoku explained to me, "old pliests sucked ghost with mouth and spit him to inside of vase with acculacy. Modern-time method more better for stomach and epiglottis."

"How long will this ghost keep?" I inquired.

"Oh, about four, five hundled years, maybe," was his reply. "Ghost now change from spilit to matter, and comes under legality of matter as usual science."

"What are you going to do with her?" I asked.

"Send him to Buddhist temple in Japan. Old pliest use him for high celemony," was the answer.

My next desire was to obtain some of Hoku Yamanochi's ghostpowder and analyze it. For a while it defied my attempts, but, after many months of patient research, I discovered that it could be produced, in all its essential qualities, by means of a fusion of formaldehyde and *hypophenyltrybrompropionic* acid in an electrified vacuum. With this product I began a series of interesting experiments.

As it became necessary for me to discover the habitat of ghosts in considerable numbers, I joined the American Society for Psychical Research, thus securing desirable information in regard to haunted houses. These I visited persistently, until my powder was perfected and had been proved efficacious for the capture of any ordinary house-broken phantom. For a while I contented myself with the mere sterilization of these spectres, but, as I became surer of success, I began to attempt the transfer of ghosts to receptacles wherein they could be transported and studied at my leisure, classified and preserved for future reference.

Hoku's bellows I soon discarded in favour of a large-sized bicycle-pump, and eventually I had constructed one of my own, of a pattern which enabled me to inhale an entire ghost at a single stroke. With this powerful instrument I was able to compress even an adult life-sized ghost into a two-quart bottle, in the neck of which a sensitive valve (patented) prevented the spectre from emerging during process.

My invention was not yet, however, quite satisfactory. While I had no trouble in securing ghosts of recent creation—spirits, that is, who were yet of almost the consistency of matter—on several of my trips abroad in search of material I found in old manor houses or ruined castles many spectres so ancient that they had become highly rarefied and tenuous, being at times scarcely visible to the naked eye. Such elusive spirits are able to pass through walls and elude pursuit with ease. It became necessary for me to obtain some instrument by which their capture could be conveniently effected.

The ordinary fire-extinguisher of commerce gave me the hint as to how the problem could be solved. One of these portable hand-instruments I filled with the proper chemicals. When inverted, the ingredients were commingled in *vacuo* and a vast volume of gas was liberated. This was collected in the reservoir provided with a rubber tube having a nozzle at the end. The whole apparatus being strapped upon my back, I was enabled to direct a stream of powerful precipitating gas in any desired direction, the flow being under control through the agency of a small stopcock. By means of this ghost-extinguisher I was enabled to pursue my experiments as far as I desired.

So far my investigations had been purely scientific, but before long the commercial value of my discovery began to interest me. The ruinous effects of spectral visitations upon real estate induced me to realize some pecuniary reward from my ghost-extinguisher, and I began to advertise my business. By degrees, I became known as an expert in my original line, and my professional services were sought with as much confidence as those of a veterinary surgeon. I manufactured the Gerrish Ghost-Extinguisher in several sizes, and put it on the market, following this venture with the introduction of my justly celebrated Gerrish Ghost-Grenades. These hand-implements were made to be kept in racks conveniently distributed in country houses for cases of sudden emergency. A single grenade, hurled at any spectral form, would, in breaking, liberate enough *formaldybrom* to coagulate the most perverse spirit, and the resulting vapour could easily be removed from the room by a housemaid with a common broom.

This branch of my business, however, never proved profitable, for the appearance of ghosts, especially in the United States, is seldom anticipated. Had it been possible for me to invent a preventive as well as a remedy, I might now be a millionaire; but there are limits even to modern science.

Having exhausted the field at home, I visited England in the hope of securing customers among the country families there. To my surprise, I discovered that the possession of a family spectre was considered as a permanent improvement to the property, and my offers of service in ridding houses of ghostly tenants awakened the liveliest resentment. As a layer of ghosts I was much lower in the social scale than a layer of carpets.

Disappointed and discouraged, I returned home to make a further study of the opportunities of my invention. I had, it seemed, exhausted the possibilities of the use of unwelcome phantoms. Could I not, I thought, derive a revenue from the traffic in desirable spectres? I decided to renew my investigations.

The nebulous spirits preserved in my laboratory, which I had graded and classified, were, you will remember, in a state of suspended animation. They were, virtually, embalmed apparitions, their inevitable decay delayed, rather than prevented. The assorted ghosts that I had now preserved in hermetically sealed tins were thus in a state of unstable equilibrium. The tins once opened and the vapour allowed to dissipate, the original astral body would in time be reconstructed and the warmed-over spectre would continue its previous career. But this process, when naturally performed, took years. The interval was quite too long for the phantom to be handled in any commercial way. My problem was, therefore, to produce from my tinned Essence of Ghost a spectre that was capable of immediately going into business and that could haunt a house while you wait.

It was not until radium was discovered that I approached the solution of my great problem, and even then months of indefatigable labour were necessary before the process was perfected. It has now been well demonstrated that the emanations of radiant energy sent forth by this surprising element defy our former scientific conceptions of the constitution of matter. It was for me to prove that the vibratory activity of radium (whose amplitudes and intensity are undoubtedly four-dimensional) effects a sort of allotropic modification in the particles of that imponderable ether which seems to lie halfway between matter and pure spirit. This is as far as I need to go in my explanation, for a full discussion involves the use of *quaternions* and the method of least squares. It will be sufficient for the layman to know that my preserved phantoms, rendered radio-active, would, upon contact with the air, resume their spectral shape.

The possible extension of my business now was enormous, limited only by the difficulty in collecting the necessary stock. It was by this time almost as difficult to get ghosts as it was to get radium. Finding that a part of my stock had spoiled, I was now possessed of only a few dozen cans of apparitions, many of these being of inferior quality. I immediately set about replenishing my raw material. It was not enough for me to pick up a ghost here and there, as one might get old mahogany; I determined to procure my phantoms in wholesale lots.

Accident favoured my design. In an old volume of *Blackwood's Magazine* I happened, one day, to come across an interesting article upon the battle of Waterloo. It mentioned, incidentally, a legend to the effect that every year, upon the anniversary of the celebrated victory, spectral squadrons had been seen by the peasants charging battalions of ghostly grenadiers. Here was my opportunity.

I made elaborate preparations for the capture of this job lot of phantoms upon the next anniversary of the fight. Hard by the fatal ditch which engulfed Napoleon's cavalry I stationed a corps of able assistants provided with rapid-fire extinguishers ready to enfilade the famous sunken road. I stationed myself with a No. 4 model magazine-hose, with a four-inch nozzle, directly in the path which I knew would be taken by the advancing squadron.

It was a fine, clear night, lighted, at first, by a slice of new moon; but later, dark, except for the pale illumination of the stars. I have seen many ghosts in my time—ghosts in garden and garret, at noon, at dusk, at dawn, phantoms fanciful, and spectres sad and spectacular—but never have I seen such an impressive sight as this nocturnal charge of cuirassiers, galloping in goblin glory to their time-honoured doom. From afar the French reserves presented the appearance of a nebulous mass, like a low-lying cloud or fog-bank, faintly luminous, shot with fluorescent gleams. As the squadron drew nearer in its desperate charge, the separate forms of the troopers shaped themselves, and the galloping guardsmen grew ghastly with supernatural splendour.

Although I knew them to be immaterial and without mass or weight, I was terrified at their approach, fearing to be swept under the hoofs of the nightmares they rode. Like one in a dream, I started to run, but in another instant they were upon me, and I turned on my stream of *formaldybrom*. Then I was overwhelmed in a cloud-burst of wild warlike wraiths.

The column swept past me, over the bank, plunging to its historic fate. The cut was piled full of frenzied, scrambling spectres, as rank after rank swept down into the horrid gut. At last the ditch swarmed full of writhing forms and the carnage was dire.

My assistants with the extinguishers stood firm, and although almost unnerved by the sight, they summoned their courage, and directed simultaneous streams of *formaldybrom* into the struggling mass of phantoms. As soon as my mind returned, I busied myself with the huge tanks I had prepared for use as receivers. These were fitted with a mechanism similar to that employed in portable forges, by which the heavy vapour was sucked off. Luckily the night was calm, and I was enabled to fill a dozen cylinders with the precipitated ghosts. The segregation of individual forms was, of course, impossible, so that men and horses were mingled in a horrible mixture of fricasseed spirits. I intended subsequently to empty the soup into a large reservoir and allow the separate spectres to reform according to the laws of spiritual cohesion.

Circumstances, however, prevented my ever accomplishing this result. I returned home, to find awaiting me an order so large and important that I had no time in which to operate upon my cylinders of cavalry.

My patron was the proprietor of a new sanatorium for nervous invalids, located near some medicinal springs in the Catskills. His building was unfortunately located, having been built upon the site of a once-famous summer hotel, which, while filled with guests, had burnt to the ground, scores of lives having been lost. Just before the patients were to be installed in the new structure, it was found that the place was haunted by the victims of the conflagration to a degree that rendered it inconvenient as a health resort. My professional services were requested, therefore, to render the building a fitting abode for convalescents. I wrote to the proprietor, fixing my charge at five thousand dollars. As my usual rate was one hundred dollars per ghost, and over a hundred lives were lost at the fire, I considered this price reasonable, and my offer was accepted.

The sanatorium job was finished in a week. I secured one hundred and two superior spectral specimens, and upon my return to the laboratory, put them up in heavily embossed tins with attractive labels in colours .

My delight at the outcome of this business was, however, soon transformed to anger and indignation. The proprietor of the health resort, having found that the spectres from his place had been sold, claimed a rebate upon the contract price equal to the value of the modified ghosts transferred to my possession. This, of course, I could not allow. I wrote, demanding immediate payment according to our agreement, and this was peremptorily refused. The manager's letter was insulting in the extreme. The Pied Piper of Hamelin was not worse treated than I felt myself to be; so, like the piper, I determined to have my revenge.

I got out the twelve tanks of Waterloo ghost-hash from the store-rooms, and treated them with radium for two days. These I shipped to the Catskills billed as hydrogen gas. Then, accompanied by two trustworthy assistants, I went to the sanatorium and preferred my demand for payment in person. I was ejected with contumely. Before my hasty exit, however, I had the satisfaction of noticing that the building was filled with patients. Languid ladies were seated in wicker chairs upon the piazzas, and frail anaemic girls filled the corridors. It was a hospital of nervous wrecks whom the slightest disturbance would throw into a panic. I suppressed all my finer feelings of mercy and kindness and smiled grimly as I walked back to the village.

That night was black and lowering, fitting weather for the pandemonium I was about to turn loose. At ten o'clock, I loaded a wagon with the tanks of compressed cohorts, and, muffled in heavy overcoats, we drove to the sanatorium. All was silent as we approached; all was dark. The wagon concealed in a grove of pines, we took out the tanks one by one, and placed them beneath the ground-floor windows. The sashes were easily forced open, and raised enough to enable us to insert the rubber tubes connected with the iron reservoirs. At midnight everything was ready.

I gave the word, and my assistants ran from tank to tank, opening the stopcocks. With a hiss as of escaping steam the huge vessels emptied themselves, vomiting forth clouds of vapour, which, upon contact with the air, coagulated into strange shapes as the white of an egg does when dropped into boiling water. The rooms became instantly filled with dismembered shades of men and horses seeking wildly to unite themselves with their proper parts.

Legs ran down the corridors, seeking their respective trunks, arms writhed wildly reaching for missing bodies, heads rolled hither and yon in search of native necks. Horses' tails and hoofs whisked and hurried in quest of equine ownership until, reorganized, the spectral steeds galloped about to find their riders.

Had it been possible, I would have stopped this riot of wraiths long ere this, for it was more awful than I had anticipated, but it was already too late. Cowering in the garden, I began to hear the screams of awakened and distracted patients. In another moment, the front door of the hotel was burst open, and a mob of hysterical women in expensive nightgowns rushed out upon the lawn, and huddled in shrieking groups.

I fled into the night.

I fled, but Napoleon's men fled with me. Compelled by I know not what fatal astral attraction, perhaps the subtle affinity of the creature for the creator, the spectral shells, moved by some mysterious mechanics of spiritual being, pursued me with fatuous fury. I sought refuge, first, in my laboratory, but, even as I approached, a lurid glare foretold me of its destruction. As I drew nearer, the whole ghost-factory was seen to be in flames; every moment crackling reports were heard, as the over-heated tins of phantasmagoria exploded and threw their supernatural contents upon the night. These liberated ghosts joined the army of Napoleon's outraged warriors, and turned upon me. There was not enough *formaldybrom* in all the world to quench their fierce energy. There was no place in all the world safe for me from their visitation. No ghost-extinguisher was powerful enough to lay the host of spirits that haunted me henceforth, and I had neither time nor money left with which to construct new Gatling quick-firing tanks.

It is little comfort to me to know that one hundred nervous invalids were completely restored to health by means of the terrific shock which I administered.

"Dey Ain't No Ghosts"

Ellis Parker Butler

Once 'pon a time dey was a li'l' black boy whut he name was Mose. An' whin he come erlong to be 'bout knee-high to a mewel, he 'gin to git powerful 'fraid ob ghosts, 'ca'se dat am sure a mighty ghostly location whut he lib' in, 'ca'se dey 's a grabeyard in de hollow, an' a buryin'-ground on de hill, an' a cemuntary in betwixt an' between, an' dey ain't nuffin' but trees nowhar excipt in de clearin' by de shanty an' down de hollow whar de pumpkin-patch am.

An' whin de night come erlong, dey ain't no sounds *at* all whut kin be heard in dat locality but de rain-doves, whut mourn out, "Oo-*oo*-o-o-o!" jes dat trembulous *an'* scary, an' de owls, whut mourn out, "Whut-*whoo*-o-o-o!" more trembulous an' scary dan dat, an' de wind, whut mourn out, "You-*you*-o-o-o!" mos' scandalous' trembulous an' scary ob all. Dat a powerful onpleasant locality for a li'l' black boy whut he name was Mose.

'Ca'se dat li'l' black boy he so specially black he can't be seen in de dark *at* all 'cept by de whites ob he eyes. So whin he go' outen de house *at* night, he ain't dast shut he eyes, 'ca'se den ain't nobody can see him in de least. He jes as invidsible as nuffin'. An' who know' but whut a great, big ghost bump right into him 'ca'se it can't see him? An' dat shore w'u'd scare dat li'l' black boy powerful' bad, 'ca'se yever'body knows whut a cold, damp pussonality a ghost is.

So whin dat li'l' black Mose go' outen de shanty at night, he keep' he eyes wide open, you may be shore. By day he eyes 'bout de size ob butter-pats, an' come sundown he eyes 'bout de size ob saucers; but whin he go' outen de shanty at night, he eyes am de size ob de white chiny plate whut set on de mantel; an' it powerful' hard to keep eyes whut am de size ob dat from a-winkin' an' a-blinkin'.

So whin Hallowe'en come' erlong, dat li'l' black Mose he jes mek' up he mind he ain't gwine outen he shack *at* all. He cogitate he gwine stay right snug in de shack wid he pa an' he ma, 'ca'se de rain-doves tek notice dat de ghosts are philanderin' roun' de country, 'ca'se dey mourn out, "Oo-*oo*-o-o-o!" an' de owls dey mourn out, "Whut-*whoo*-o-o-o!" an' de wind mourn out, "You-*you*-o-o-o!" De eyes ob dat li'l' black Mose dey as big as de white chiny plate whut set on de mantel by side de clock, an' de sun jes a-settin'.

So dat all right. Li'l' black Mose he scrooge' back in de corner by de fireplace, an' he 'low' he gwine stay dere till he gwine *to* bed. But byme-by Sally Ann, whut live' up de road, draps in, an' Mistah Sally Ann, whut is her husban', he draps in, an' Zack Badget an' de school-teacher whut board' at Unc' Silas Diggs's house drap in, an' a powerful lot ob folks drap in. An' li'l' black Mose he seen dat gwine be one s'prise-party, an' he right down cheerful 'bout dat.

So all dem folks shake dere hands an' 'low "Howdy," an' some ob dem say: "Why, dere's li'l' Mose! Howdy, li'l' Mose?" An' he so please' he jes grin' an' grin', 'ca'se he ain't reckon whut gwine happen. So byme-by Sally Ann, whut live up de road, she say', "Ain't no sort o' Hallowe'en lest we got a jack-o'-lantern." An' de school-teacher, whut board at Unc' Silas Diggs's house, she 'low', "Hallowe'en jes no Hallowe'en *at* all 'thout we got a jack-o'-lantern." An' li'l' black Mose he stop' a-grinnin', an' he scrooge' so far back in de corner he 'mos' scrooge frough de wall. But dat ain't no use, 'ca'se he ma say', "Mose, go on down to de pumpkin-patch an' fotch a pumpkin."

"I ain't want to go," say' li'l' black Mose.

"Go on erlong wid yo'," say' he ma, right commandin'.

"I ain't want to go," say' Mose ag'in.

"Why ain't yo' want to go?" he ma ask'.

"'Ca'se I's afraid ob de ghosts," say' li'l' black Mose, an' dat de particular truth an' no mistake.

"Dey ain't no ghosts," say' de school-teacher, whut board at Unc' Silas Diggs's house, right peart.

"'Co'se dey ain't no ghosts," say' Zack Badget, whut dat 'fear'd ob ghosts he ain't dar' come to li'l' black Mose's house ef de school-teacher ain't ercompany him.

"Go 'long wid your ghosts!" say li'l' black Mose's ma.

"Wha' yo' pick up dat nomsense?" say' he pa. "Dey ain't no ghosts."

An' dat whut all dat s'prise-party 'low: dey ain't no ghosts. An' dey 'low dey mus' hab a jack-o'-lantern or de fun all sp'iled. So dat li'l' black boy whut he name is Mose he done got to fotch a pumpkin from de pumpkin-patch down de hollow. So he step' outen de shanty an' he stan' on de doorstep twell he get' he eyes pried open as big as de bottom ob he ma's wash-tub, mostly, an' he say', "Dey ain't no ghosts." An' he put' one foot on de ground, an' dat was de fust step.

An' de rain-dove say', "OO-*oo*-o-o-o!"

An' li'l' black Mose he tuck anudder step.

An' de owl mourn' out, "Whut-*whoo*-o-o-o!"

An' li'l' black Mose he tuck anudder step.

An' de wind sob' out, "You-*you*-o-o-o!"

An' li'l' black Mose he tuck one look ober he shoulder, an' he shut he eyes so tight dey hurt round de aidges, an' he pick' up he foots an' run. Yas, sah, he run' right peart fast. An' he say': "Dey ain't no ghosts. Dey ain't no ghosts." An' he run' erlong de paff whut lead' by de buryin'-ground on de hill, 'ca'se dey ain't no fince eround dat buryin'-ground *at* all.

No fince; jes' de big trees whut de owls an' de rain-doves sot in an' mourn an' sob, an' whut de wind sigh an' cry frough. An byme-by somefin' jes' *brush*' li'l' Mose on de arm, which mek' him run jes a bit more faster. An' byme-by somefin' jes brush' li'l' Mose on de cheek, which mek' him run erbout as fast as he can. An' byme-by somefin' grab' li'l' Mose by de aidge of he coat, an' he fight' an' struggle' an' cry out: "Dey ain't no ghosts. Dey ain't no ghosts." An' dat ain't nuffin' but de wild brier whut grab' him, an' dat ain't nuffin' but de leaf ob a tree whut brush' he cheek, an' dat ain't nuffin' but de branch ob a hazel-bush whut brush' he arm. But he downright scared jes de same, an' he ain't lose no time, 'ca'se de wind an' de owls an' de rain-doves dey signerfy whut ain't no good. So he scoot' past dat buryin'-ground whut on de hill, an' dat cemuntary whut betwixt an' between, an' dat grabeyard in de hollow, twell he come' to de pumpkin-patch, an' he rotch' down an' tek' erhold ob de bestest pumpkin whut in de patch. An' he right smart scared. He jes' de mostest scared li'l' black boy whut yever was. He ain't gwine open he eyes fo' nuffin', 'ca'se de wind go, "You-*you*-o-o-o!" an' de owls go, "Whut-*whoo*-o-o-o!" an' de rain-doves go, "Oo-*oo*-o-o-o!"

He jes speculate', "Dey ain't no ghosts," an' wish' he hair don't stand on ind dat way. An' he jes cogitate', "Dey ain't no ghosts," an' wish' he goose-pimples don't rise up dat way. An' he jes 'low', "Dey ain't no ghosts," an' wish' he backbone ain't all trembulous wid chills dat way. So he rotch' down, an' he rotch' down, twell he git' a good hold on dat pricklesome stem of dat bestest pumpkin whut in de patch, an' he jes yank' dat stem wid all he might.

49

"*Let loosen my head!*" say' a big voice all on a suddent.

Dat li'l' black boy whut he name is Mose he jump' 'most outen he skin. He open' he eyes, an' he 'gin to shake like de aspen-tree, 'ca'se whut dat a-standin' right dar behint him but a 'mendjous big ghost! Yas, sah, dat de bigges', whites' ghost whut yever was. An' it ain't got no head. Ain't got no head *at* all! Li'l' black Mose he jes drap' on he knees an' he beg' an' pray':

"Oh, 'scuse me! 'Scuse me, Mistah Ghost!" he beg'. "Ah ain't mean no harm *at* all."

"Whut for you try to take my head?" ask' de ghost in dat fearsome voice whut like de damp wind outen de cellar.

"'Scuse me! 'Scuse me!" beg' li'l' Mose. "Ah ain't know dat was yo' head, an' I ain't know you was dar *at* all. 'Scuse me!"

"Ah 'scuse you ef you do me dis favour,' say de ghost. "Ah got somefin' powerful *im*portant to say unto you, an' Ah can't say hit 'ca'se Ah ain't got no head; an' whin Ah ain't got no head, Ah ain't got no mouf, an' whin Ah ain't got no mouf, Ah can't talk *at* all."

An' dat right logical fo' shore. Can't nobody talk whin he ain't got no mouf, an' can't nobody have no mouf whin he ain't got no head, an' whin li'l' black Mose he look', he see' dat ghost ain't got no head *at* all. Nary head.

So de ghost say':

"Ah come on down yere fo' to git a pumpkin fo' a head, an' Ah pick' dat *ixact* pumpkin whut yo' gwine tek, an' Ah don't like dat one bit. No, sah. Ah feel like Ah pick yo' up an' carry yo' away, an' nobody see you no more for yever. But Ah got somefin' powerful *im*portant to say unto yo', an' if yo' pick up dat pumpkin an' sot it on de place whar my head ought to be, Ah let you off dis time, 'ca'se Ah ain't been able to talk fo' so long Ah right hongry to say somefin'."

So li'l' black Mose he heft up dat pumpkin, an' de ghost he bend' down, an' li'l' black Mose he sot dat pumpkin on dat ghostses neck. An' right off dat pumpkin head 'gin' to wink an' blink like a jack-o'-lantern, an' right off dat pumpkin head 'gin' to glimmer an' glow frough de mouf like a jack-o'-lantern, an' right off dat ghost start' to speak. Yas, sah, dass so.

"Whut yo' want to say unto me?" *in*quire' li'l' black Mose.

"Ah want to tell yo'," say' de ghost, "dat yo' ain't need yever be skeered of ghosts, 'ca'se dey ain't no ghosts."

An' whin he say dat, de ghost jes vanish' away like de smoke in July. He ain't even linger round dat locality like de smoke in Yoctober. He jes dissipate' outen de air, an' he gone *in*tirely.

So li'l' Mose he grab' up de nex' bestest pumpkin an' he scoot'. An' whin he come' to de grabeyard in de hollow, he goin' erlong same as yever, on'y faster, whin he reckon' he'll pick up a club *in* case he gwine have trouble. An' he rotch' down an' rotch' down an' tek' hold of a likely appearin' hunk o' wood whut right dar. An' whin he grab' dat hunk of wood—

"*Let loosen my leg!*" say' a big voice all on a suddent.

Dat li'l' black boy 'most jump' outen he skin, 'ca'se right dar in de paff is six 'mendjus big ghostes an' de bigges' ain't got but one leg. So li'l' black Mose jes natchully handed dat hunk of wood to dat bigges' ghost, an' he say':

"'Scuse me, Mistah Ghost; Ah ain't know dis your leg."

An' whut dem six ghostes do but stand round an' confabulate? Yas, sah, dass so. An' whin dey do so, one say':

"'Pears like dis a mighty likely li'l' black boy. Whut we gwine do fo' to *re*ward him fo' politeness?"

An' annuder say':

"Tell him whut de truth is 'bout ghostes."

So de bigges' ghost he say':

"Ah gwine tell yo' somefin' *im*portant whut yever'body don't know: Dey *ain't* no ghosts."

An' whin he say' dat, de ghostes jes natchully vanish away, an' li'l' black Mose he proceed' up de paff. He so scared he hair jes yank' at de roots, an' whin de wind go', "Oo-*oo*-o-o-o!" an' de owl go', "Whut-*whoo*-o-o-o!" an' de rain-doves go, "You-*you*-o-o-o-!" he jes tremble' an' shake'. An' byme-by he come' to de cemuntary whut betwixt an' between, an' he shore is mighty skeered, 'ca'se dey is a whole comp'ny of ghostes lined up along de road, an' he 'low' he ain't gwine spind no more time palaverin' wid ghostes. So he step' offen de road fo' to go round erbout, an' he step' on a pine-stump whut lay right dar.

"*Git offen my chest!*" say' a big voice all on a suddent, 'ca'se dat stump am been selected by de captain ob de ghostes for to be he chest, 'ca'se he ain't got no chest betwixt he shoulders an' he legs. An' li'l' black Mose he hop' offen dat stump right peart. Yes, *sah*; right peart.

"'Scuse me! 'Scuse me!" dat li'l' black Mose beg' an' plead', an' de ghostes ain't know whuther to eat him all up or not, 'ca'se he step on de boss ghostes's chest dat a-way. But byme-by they 'low they let him go 'ca'se dat was an accident, an' de captain ghost he say', "Mose, you Mose, Ah gwine let you off dis time, 'ca'se you ain't nuffin' but a misabul li'l' tremblin' nigger; but Ah want you should *re*mimber one thing mos' particular'."

"Ya-yas, sah," say' dat li'l' black boy; "Ah'll remember. Whut is dat Ah got to remember?"

De captain ghost he swell' up, an' he swell' up, twell he as big as a house, an' he say' in a voice whut shake' de ground:

"Dey ain't no ghosts."

So li'l' black Mose he bound to remimber dat, an' he rise' up an' mek' a bow, an' he proceed' toward home right libely. He do, indeed.

An' he gwine along jes as fast as he kin, whin he come' to de aidge ob de buryin'-ground whut on de hill, an' right dar he bound to stop, 'ca'se de kentry round about am so populate' he ain't able to go frough. Yas, sah, seem' like all de ghostes in de world habin' a conference right dar. Seem' like all de ghosteses whut yever was am havin' a convintion on dat spot. An' dat li'l' black Mose so skeered he jes fall' down on a' old log whut dar an' screech' an' moan'. An' all on a suddent de log up and spoke:

"*Get offen me! Get offen me!*" yell' dat log.

So li'l' black Mose he git' offen dat log, an' no mistake.

An' soon as he git' offen de log, de log uprise, an' li'l' black Mose he see' dat dat log am de king ob all de ghostes. An' whin de king uprise, all de congergation crowd round li'l' black Mose, an' dey am about leben millium an' a few lift ober. Yas, sah; dat de reg'lar annyul Hallowe'en convintion whut li'l' black Mose interrup'. Right dar am all de sperits in de world, an' all de ha'nts in de world, an' all de hobgoblins in de world, an' all de ghouls in de world, an' all de spicters in de world, an' all de ghostes in de world. An' whin dey see' li'l' black Mose, dey all gnash dey teef an' grin' 'ca'se it gettin' erlong toward dey-all's lunch-time. So de king, whut he name old Skull-an'-Bones, he step' on top ob li'l' Mose's head, an' he say':

"Gin'l'min, de convintion will come to order. De sicretary please note who is prisint. De firs' business whut come' before de convintion am: whut we gwine do to a li'l' black boy whut stip' on de king an' maul' all ober de king an' treat' de king dat disrespictful'."

An li'l' black Mose jes moan' an' sob':

"'Scuse me! 'Scuse me, Mistah King! Ah ain't mean no harm *at* all."

But nobody ain't pay no *at*tintion to him *at* all, 'ca'se yevery one lookin' at a monstrous big ha'nt whut name Bloody Bones, whut rose up an' spoke.

"Your Honor, Mistah King, an' gin'l'min *an*' ladies," he say', "dis am a right bad case ob *lasy majesty*, 'ca'se de king been step on. Whin yivery li'l' black boy whut choose' gwine wander round *at* night an' stip on de king ob ghostes, it ain't no time for to palaver, it ain't no time for to prevaricate, it ain't no time for to cogitate, it ain't no time do nuffin' but tell de truth, an' de whole truth, an' nuffin' but de truth."

An' all dem ghostes sicond de motion, an' dey confabulate out loud erbout dat, an' de noise soun' like de rain-doves goin', "Oo-*oo*-o-o-o!" an' de owls goin', "Whut-*whoo*-o-o-o!" an' de wind goin', "You-*you*-o-o-o!" So dat risolution am passed unanermous, an' no mistake.

So de king ob de ghostes, whut name old Skull-an'-Bones, he place' he hand on de head ob li'l' black Mose, an' he hand feel like a wet rag, an' he say':

"Dey ain't no ghosts."

An' one ob de hairs whut on de head of li'l' black Mose turn' white.

An' de monstrous big ha'nt whut he name Bloody Bones he lay he hand on de head ob li'l' black Mose, an' he hand feel like a toadstool in de cool ob de day, an' he say':

"Dey ain't no ghosts."

An' anudder ob de hairs whut on de head ob li'l' black Mose turn' white.

An' a heejus sperit whut he name Moldy Pa'm place' he hand on de head ob li'l' black Mose, an' he hand feel like de yunner side ob a lizard, an' he say':

"Dey ain't no ghosts."

An' anudder ob de hairs whut on de head ob li'l' black Mose turn white *as* snow.

An' a perticklar bend-up hobgoblin he put' he hand on de head ob li'l' black Mose, an' he mek' dat same *re*mark, an' dat whole convintion ob ghostes an' spicters an' ha'nts an' yiver'thing, which am more 'n a millium, pass by so quick dey-all's hands feel lak de wind whut blow outen de cellar whin de day am hot, an' dey-all say, "Dey ain't no ghosts." Yas, sah, dey-all say dem wo'ds so fas' it soun' like de wind whin it moan frough de turkentine-trees whut behind de cider-priss. An' yivery hair whut on li'l' black Mose's head turn' white. Dat whut happen' whin a li'l' black boy gwine meet a ghost convintion dat-a-way. Dat's so he ain' gwine forgit to remember dey ain't no ghostes. 'Ca'se ef a li'l' black boy gwine imaginate dey *is* ghostes, he gwine be skeered in de dark. An' dat a foolish thing for to imaginate.

So prisintly all de ghostes am whiff away, like de fog outen de holler whin de wind blow' on it, an' li'l' black Mose he ain' see no ca'se for to remain in dat locality no longer. He rotch' down, an' he raise' up de pumpkin, an' he perambulate' right quick to he ma's shack, an' he lift' up de latch, an' he open' de do', an' he yenter' in. An' he say':

"Yere's de pumpkin."

An' he ma an' he pa, an' Sally Ann, whut live up de road, an' Mistah Sally Ann, whut her husban', an' Zack Badget, an' de school-teacher whut board at Unc' Silas Diggs's house, an' all de powerful lot of folks whut come to de doin's, dey all scrooged back in de cornder ob de shack, 'ca'se Zack Badget he been done tell a ghost-tale, an' de rain-doves gwine, "Oo-*oo*-o-o-o!" an' de owls am gwine, "Whut-*whoo*-o-o-o!" and de wind it gwine, "You-*you*-o-o-o!" an' yiver'body power-ful skeered. 'Ca'se li'l' black Mose he come' a-fumblin' an' a-rattlin' at de do' jes whin dat ghost-tale mos' skeery, an' yiver'body gwine imaginate dat he a ghost a-fumblin' an' a-rattlin' at de do'. Yas, sah. So li'l' black Mose he turn' he white head, an' he look' roun' an' peer' roun', an' he say':

"Whut you all skeered fo'?"

'Ca'se ef anybody skeered, he want' to be skeered too. Dat's natural. But de school-teacher, whut live at Unc' Silas Diggs's house, she say':

"Fo' de lan's sake, we fought you was a ghost!"

So li'l' black Mose he sort ob sniff an' he sort ob sneer, an' he 'low':

"Huh! dey ain't no ghosts."

Den he ma she powerful took back dat li'l' black Mose he gwine be so uppetish an' contrydict folks whut know 'rifmeticks an' alge-bricks an' gin'ral countin' widout fingers, like de school-teacher whut board at Unc' Silas Diggs's house knows, an' she say':

"Huh! whut you know 'bout ghosts, anner ways?"

An' li'l' black Mose he jes kinder stan' on one foot, an' he jes kinder suck' he thumb, an' he jes kinder 'low':

"I don't know nuffin' erbout ghosts, 'ca'se dey ain't no ghosts."

So he pa gwine whop him fo' tellin' a fib 'bout dey ain' no ghosts whin yiver'body know' dey is ghosts; but de school-teacher, whut board at Unc' Silas Diggs's house, she tek' note de hair ob li'l' black Mose's head am plumb white, an' she tek' note li'l' black Mose's face am de colour ob wood-ash, so she jes retch' one arm round dat li'l' black boy, an' she jes snuggle' him up, an' she say':

"Honey lamb, don't you be skeered; ain' nobody gwine hurt you. How you know dey ain't no ghosts?"

An' li'l' black Mose he kinder lean' up 'g'inst de school-teacher whut board at Unc' Silas Diggs's house, an' he 'low':

"'Ca'se—'ca'se—'ca'se I met de cap'n ghost, an' I met de gin'ral ghost, an' I met de king ghost, an' I met all de ghostes whut yiver was in de whole worl', an' yivery ghost say' de same thing: 'Dey ain't no ghosts.' An' if de cap'n ghost an' de gin'ral ghost an' de king ghost an' all de ghostes in de whole worl' don't know ef dar am ghostes, who does?"

"Das right; das right, honey lamb," say' de school-teacher. And she say': "I been s'picious dey ain' no ghostes dis long whiles, an' now I know. Ef all de ghostes say dey ain' no ghosts, dey *ain'* no ghosts."

So yiver'body 'low' dat so 'cep' Zack Badget, whut been tellin' de ghost-tale, an' he ain' gwine say "Yis" an' he ain' gwine say "No," 'ca'se he right sweet on de school-teacher; but he know right well he done seen plinty ghostes in he day. So he boun' to be sure fust. So he say' to li'l' black Mose:

"'T ain't likely you met up wid a monstrous big ha'nt whut live' down de lane whut he name Bloody Bones?"

"Yas," say' li'l' black Mose; "I done met up wid him."

"An' did old Bloody Bones done tol' you dey ain' no ghosts?" say Zack Badget.

"Yas," say' li'l' black Mose, "he done tell me perzackly dat."

"Well, if *he* tol' you dey ain't no ghosts," say' Zack Badget, "I got to 'low dey ain't no ghosts, 'ca'se he ain' gwine tell no lie erbout it. I know dat Bloody Bones ghost sence I was a piccaninny, an' I done met up wif him a powerful lot o' times, an' he ain't gwine tell no lie erbout it. Ef dat perticklar ghost say' dey ain't no ghosts, dey *ain't* no ghosts."

So yiver'body say':

"Das right; dey ain' no ghosts."

An' dat mek' li'l' black Mose feel mighty good, 'ca'se he ain' lak ghostes. He reckon' he gwine be a heap mo' comfortable in he mind sence he know' dey ain' no ghosts, an' he reckon' he ain' gwine be skeered of nuffin' never no more. He ain' gwine min' de dark, an' he ain' gwine min' de rain-doves whut go', "Oo-*oo*-o-o-o!" an' he ain' gwine min' de owls whut go', "Who-*whoo*-o-o-o!" an' he ain' gwine min' de wind whut go', "You-*you*-o-o-o!" nor nuffin', nohow. He gwine be brave as a lion, sence he know' fo' sure dey ain' no ghosts. So prisintly he ma say':

"Well, time fo' a li'l' black boy whut he name is Mose to be gwine up de ladder to de loft to bed."

An' li'l' black Mose he 'low' he gwine wait a bit. He 'low' he gwine jes wait a li'l' bit. He 'low' he gwine be no trouble *at* all ef he jes been let wait twell he ma she gwine up de ladder to de loft to bed, too. So he ma she say':

"Git erlong wid yo'! Whut yo' skeered ob whin dey ain't no ghosts?"

An' li'l' black Mose he scrooge', and he twist', an' he pucker' up de mouf, an' he rub' he eyes, an' prisintly he say' right low:

"I ain' skeered ob ghosts whut am, 'ca'se dey ain' no ghosts."

"Den whut *am* yo' skeered ob?" ask he ma.

"Nuffin," say' de li'l' black boy whut he name is Mose; "but I jes feel kinder oneasy 'bout de ghosts whut ain't."

Jes lak white folks! Jes lak white folks!

The Transferred Ghost

Frank R. Stockton

The country residence of Mr. John Hinckman was a delightful place to me, for many reasons. It was the abode of a genial, though somewhat impulsive, hospitality. It had broad, smooth-shaven lawns and towering oaks and elms; there were bosky shades at several points, and not far from the house there was a little rill spanned by a rustic bridge with the bark on; there were fruits and flowers, pleasant people, chess, billiards, rides, walks, and fishing. These were great attractions; but none of them, nor all of them together, would have been sufficient to hold me to the place very long. I had been invited for the trout season, but should, probably, have finished my visit early in the summer had it not been that upon fair days, when the grass was dry, and the sun was not too hot, and there was but little wind, there strolled beneath the lofty elms, or passed lightly through the bosky shades, the form of my Madeline.

This lady was not, in very truth, my Madeline. She had never given herself to me, nor had I, in any way, acquired possession of her. But as I considered her possession the only sufficient reason for the continuance of my existence, I called her, in my reveries, mine. It may have been that I would not have been obliged to confine the use of this possessive pronoun to my reveries had I confessed the state of my feelings to the lady.

But this was an unusually difficult thing to do. Not only did I dread, as almost all lovers dread, taking the step which would in an instant put an end to that delightful season which may be termed the ante-interrogatory period of love, and which might at the same time terminate all intercourse or connection with the object of my passion; but I was, also, dreadfully afraid of John Hinckman. This gentleman was a good friend of mine, but it would have required a bolder man than I was at that time to ask him for the gift of his niece, who was the head of his household, and, according to his own frequent statement, the main prop of his declining years. Had Madeline acquiesced in my general views on the subject, I might have felt encouraged to open the matter to Mr. Hinckman; but, as I said before, I had never asked her whether or not she would be mine. I thought of these things at all hours of the day and night, particularly the latter.

I was lying awake one night, in the great bed in my spacious chamber, when, by the dim light of the new moon, which partially filled the room, I saw John Hinckman standing by a large chair near the door. I was very much surprised at this for two reasons. In the first place, my host had never before come into my room; and, in the second place, he had gone from home that morning, and had not expected to return for several days. It was for this reason that I had been able that evening to sit much later than usual with Madeline on the moonlit porch. The figure was certainly that of John Hinckman in his ordinary dress, but there was a vagueness and indistinctness about it which presently assured me that it was a ghost. Had the good old man been murdered? and had his spirit come to tell me of the deed, and to confide to me the protection of his dear——? My heart fluttered at what I was about to think, but at this instant the figure spoke.

"Do you know," he said, with a countenance that indicated anxiety, "if Mr. Hinckman will return to-night?"

I thought it well to maintain a calm exterior, and I answered:

"We do not expect him."

"I am glad of that," said he, sinking into the chair by which he stood. "During the two years and a half that I have inhabited this house, that man has never before been away for a single night. You can't imagine the relief it gives me."

And as he spoke he stretched out his legs, and leaned back in the chair. His form became less vague, and the colours of his garments more distinct and evident, while an expression of gratified relief succeeded to the anxiety of his countenance.

"Two years and a half!" I exclaimed. "I don't understand you."

"It is fully that length of time," said the ghost, "since I first came here. Mine is not an ordinary case. But before I say anything more about it, let me ask you again if you are sure Mr. Hinckman will not return to-night."

"I am as sure of it as I can be of anything," I answered. "He left to-day for Bristol, two hundred miles away."

"Then I will go on," said the ghost, "for I am glad to have the op-

58

portunity of talking to someone who will listen to me; but if John Hinckman should come in and catch me here, I should be frightened out of my wits."

"This is all very strange," I said, greatly puzzled by what I had heard. "Are you the ghost of Mr. Hinckman?"

This was a bold question, but my mind was so full of other emotions that there seemed to be no room for that of fear.

"Yes, I am his ghost," my companion replied, "and yet I have no right to be. And this is what makes me so uneasy, and so much afraid of him. It is a strange story, and, I truly believe, without precedent. Two years and a half ago, John Hinckman was dangerously ill in this very room. At one time he was so far gone that he was really believed to be dead. It was in consequence of too precipitate a report in regard to this matter that I was, at that time, appointed to be his ghost. Imagine my surprise and horror, sir, when, after I had accepted the position and assumed its responsibilities, that old man revived, became convalescent, and eventually regained his usual health. My situation was now one of extreme delicacy and embarrassment. I had no power to return to my original unembodiment, and I had no right to be the ghost of a man who was not dead. I was advised by my friends to quietly maintain my position, and was assured that, as John Hinckman was an elderly man, it could not be long before I could rightfully assume the position for which I had been selected. But I tell you, sir," he continued, with animation, "the old fellow seems as vigorous as ever, and I have no idea how much longer this annoying state of things will continue. I spend my time trying to get out of that old man's way. I must not leave this house, and he seems to follow me everywhere. I tell you, sir, he haunts me."

"That is truly a queer state of things," I remarked. "But why are you afraid of him? He couldn't hurt you."

"Of course he couldn't," said the ghost. "But his very presence is a shock and terror to me. Imagine, sir, how you would feel if my case were yours."

I could not imagine such a thing at all. I simply shuddered.

"And if one must be a wrongful ghost at all," the apparition continued, "it would be much pleasanter to be the ghost of some man other than John Hinckman. There is in him an irascibility of temper, accompanied by a facility of invective, which is seldom met with. And what would happen if he were to see me, and find out, as I am sure he would, how long and why I had inhabited his house, I can scarcely conceive. I have seen him in his bursts of passion; and, although he did not hurt the people he stormed at any more than he would hurt me, they seemed to shrink before him."

All this I knew to be very true. Had it not been for this peculiarity of Mr. Hinckman, I might have been more willing to talk to him about his niece.

"I feel sorry for you," I said, for I really began to have a sympathetic feeling toward this unfortunate apparition. "Your case is indeed a hard one. It reminds me of those persons who have had doubles, and I suppose a man would often be very angry indeed when he found that there was another being who was personating himself."

"Oh! the cases are not similar at all," said the ghost. "A double or *doppelgänger* lives on the earth with a man; and, being exactly like him, he makes all sorts of trouble, of course. It is very different with me. I am not here to live with Mr. Hinckman. I am here to take his place. Now, it would make John Hinckman very angry if he knew that. Don't you know it would?"

I assented promptly.

"Now that he is away I can be easy for a little while," continued the ghost; "and I am so glad to have an opportunity of talking to you. I have frequently come into your room, and watched you while you slept, but did not dare to speak to you for fear that if you talked with me Mr. Hinckman would hear you, and come into the room to know why you were talking to yourself."

"But would he not hear you?" I asked.

"Oh, no!" said the other: "there are times when anyone may see me, but no one hears me except the person to whom I address myself."

"But why did you wish to speak to me?" I asked.

"Because," replied the ghost, "I like occasionally to talk to people, and especially to someone like yourself, whose mind is so troubled and perturbed that you are not likely to be frightened by a visit from one of us. But I particularly wanted to ask you to do me a favour. There is every probability, so far as I can see, that John Hinckman will live a long time, and my situation is becoming insupportable. My great object at present is to get myself transferred, and I think that you may, perhaps, be of use to me."

"Transferred!" I exclaimed. "What do you mean by that?"

"What I mean," said the other, "is this: Now that I have started on my career I have got to be the ghost of somebody, and I want to be the ghost of a man who is really dead."

"I should think that would be easy enough," I said. "Opportunities must continually occur."

"Not at all! not at all!" said my companion quickly. "You have no idea what a rush and pressure there is for situations of this kind. Whenever a vacancy occurs, if I may express myself in that way, there are crowds of applications for the ghost-ship."

"I had no idea that such a state of things existed," I said, becoming quite interested in the matter. "There ought to be some regular system, or order of precedence, by which you could all take your turns like customers in a barber's shop."

"Oh dear, that would never do at all!" said the other. "Some of us would have to wait forever. There is always a great rush whenever a good ghost-ship offers itself—while, as you know, there are some positions that no one would care for. And it was in consequence of my being in too great a hurry on an occasion of the kind that I got myself into my present disagreeable predicament, and I have thought that it might be possible that you would help me out of it. You might know of a case where an opportunity for a ghost-ship was not generally expected, but which might present itself at any moment. If you would give me a short notice, I know I could arrange for a transfer."

"What do you mean?" I exclaimed. "Do you want me to commit suicide? Or to undertake a murder for your benefit?"

"Oh, no, no, no!" said the other, with a vapoury smile. "I mean nothing of that kind. To be sure, there are lovers who are watched with considerable interest, such persons having been known, in moments of depression, to offer very desirable ghost-ships; but I did not think of anything of that kind in connection with you. You were the only person I cared to speak to, and I hoped that you might give me some information that would be of use; and, in return, I shall be very glad to help you in your love affair."

"You seem to know that I have such an affair," I said.

"Oh, yes!" replied the other, with a little yawn. "I could not be here so much as I have been without knowing all about that."

There was something horrible in the idea of Madeline and myself having been watched by a ghost, even, perhaps, when we wandered together in the most delightful and bosky places. But, then, this was quite an exceptional ghost, and I could not have the objections to him which would ordinarily arise in regard to beings of his class.

"I must go now," said the ghost, rising: "but I will see you somewhere to-morrow night. And remember—you help me, and I'll help you."

I had doubts the next morning as to the propriety of telling Madeline anything about this interview, and soon convinced myself that I must keep silent on the subject. If she knew there was a ghost about the house, she would probably leave the place instantly. I did not mention the matter, and so regulated my demeanour that I am quite sure Madeline never suspected what had taken place. For some time I had wished that Mr. Hinckman would absent himself, for a day at least, from the premises. In such case I thought I might more easily nerve myself up to the point of speaking to Madeline on the subject of our future collateral existence; and, now that the opportunity for such speech had really occurred, I did not feel ready to avail myself of it. What would become of me if she refused me?

I had an idea, however, that the lady thought that, if I were going to speak at all, this was the time. She must have known that certain sentiments were afloat within me, and she was not unreasonable in her wish to see the matter settled one way or the other. But I did not feel like taking a bold step in the dark. If she wished me to ask her to give herself to me, she ought to offer me some reason to suppose that she would make the gift. If I saw no probability of such generosity, I would prefer that things should remain as they were.

* * * * * * * *

That evening I was sitting with Madeline in the moonlit porch. It was nearly ten o'clock, and ever since supper-time I had been working myself up to the point of making an avowal of my sentiments. I had not positively determined to do this, but wished gradually to reach the proper point, when, if the prospect looked bright, I might speak. My companion appeared to understand the situation—at least, I imagined that the nearer I came to a proposal the more she seemed to expect it. It was certainly a very critical and important epoch in my life. If I spoke, I should make myself happy or miserable forever, and if I did not speak I had every reason to believe that the lady would not give me another chance to do so.

Sitting thus with Madeline, talking a little, and thinking very hard over these momentous matters, I looked up and saw the ghost, not a dozen feet away from us. He was sitting on the railing of the porch, one leg thrown up before him, the other dangling down as he leaned against a post. He was behind Madeline, but almost in front of me, as I sat facing the lady. It was fortunate that Madeline was looking out over the landscape, for I must have appeared very much startled. The ghost had told me that he would see me some time this night, but I did not think he would make his appearance when I was in the company of Madeline. If she should see the spirit of her uncle, I could not answer for the consequences. I made no exclamation, but the ghost evidently saw that I was troubled.

"Don't be afraid," he said—"I shall not let her see me; and she cannot hear me speak unless I address myself to her, which I do not intend to do."

I suppose I looked grateful.

"So you need not trouble yourself about that," the ghost continued; "but it seems to me that you are not getting along very well with your affair. If I were you, I should speak out without waiting any longer. You will never have a better chance. You are not likely to be interrupted; and, so far as I can judge, the lady seems disposed to listen to you favourably; that is, if she ever intends to do so. There is no knowing when John Hinckman will go away again; certainly not this summer. If I were in your place, I should never dare to make love to Hinckman's niece if he were anywhere about the place. If he should catch anyone offering himself to Miss Madeline, he would then be a terrible man to encounter."

I agreed perfectly to all this.

"I cannot bear to think of him!" I ejaculated aloud.

"Think of whom?" asked Madeline, turning quickly toward me.

Here was an awkward situation. The long speech of the ghost, to which Madeline paid no attention, but which I heard with perfect distinctness, had made me forget myself.

It was necessary to explain quickly. Of course, it would not do to admit that it was of her dear uncle that I was speaking; and so I mentioned hastily the first name I thought of.

"Mr. Vilars," I said.

This statement was entirely correct; for I never could bear to think of Mr. Vilars, who was a gentleman who had, at various times, paid much attention to Madeline.

"It is wrong for you to speak in that way of Mr. Vilars," she said. "He is a remarkably well educated and sensible young man, and has very pleasant manners. He expects to be elected to the legislature this fall, and I should not be surprised if he made his mark. He will do well in a legislative body, for whenever Mr. Vilars has anything to say he knows just how and when to say it."

This was spoken very quietly, and without any show of resentment, which was all very natural, for if Madeline thought at all favourably of me she could not feel displeased that I should have disagreeable emotions in regard to a possible rival. The concluding words contained a hint which I was not slow to understand. I felt very sure that if Mr. Vilars were in my present position he would speak quickly enough.

"I know it is wrong to have such ideas about a person," I said, "but I cannot help it."

The lady did not chide me, and after this she seemed even in a softer mood. As for me, I felt considerably annoyed, for I had not wished to admit that any thought of Mr. Vilars had ever occupied my mind.

"You should not speak aloud that way," said the ghost, "or you may get yourself into trouble. I want to see everything go well with you, because then you may be disposed to help me, especially if I should chance to be of any assistance to you, which I hope I shall be."

I longed to tell him that there was no way in which he could help me so much as by taking his instant departure. To make love to a young lady with a ghost sitting on the railing nearby, and that ghost the apparition of a much-dreaded uncle, the very idea of whom in such a position and at such a time made me tremble, was a difficult, if not an impossible, thing to do; but I forbore to speak, although I may have looked my mind.

"I suppose," continued the ghost, "that you have not heard anything that might be of advantage to me. Of course, I am very anxious to hear; but if you have anything to tell me, I can wait until you are alone. I will come to you to-night in your room, or I will stay here until the lady goes away."

"You need not wait here," I said; "I have nothing at all to say to you."

Madeline sprang to her feet, her face flushed and her eyes ablaze.

"Wait here!" she cried. "What do you suppose I am waiting for? Nothing to say to me indeed!—I should think so! What should you have to say to me?"

"Madeline!" I exclaimed, stepping toward her, "let me explain."

But she had gone.

Here was the end of the world for me! I turned fiercely to the ghost.

"Wretched existence!" I cried. "You have ruined everything. You have blackened my whole life. Had it not been for you—"

But here my voice faltered. I could say no more.

"You wrong me," said the ghost. "I have not injured you. I have tried only to encourage and assist you, and it is your own folly that has done this mischief. But do not despair. Such mistakes as these can be explained. Keep up a brave heart. Good-by."

And he vanished from the railing like a bursting soap-bubble.

I went gloomily to bed, but I saw no apparitions that night except those of despair and misery which my wretched thoughts called up. The words I had uttered had sounded to Madeline like the basest insult. Of course, there was only one interpretation she could put upon them.

As to explaining my ejaculations, that was impossible. I thought the matter over and over again as I lay awake that night, and I determined that I would never tell Madeline the facts of the case. It would be better for me to suffer all my life than for her to know that the ghost of her uncle haunted the house. Mr. Hinckman was away, and if she knew of his ghost she could not be made to believe that he was not dead. She might not survive the shock! No, my heart could bleed, but I would never tell her.

The next day was fine, neither too cool nor too warm; the breezes were gentle, and nature smiled. But there were no walks or rides with Madeline. She seemed to be much engaged during the day, and I saw but little of her. When we met at meals she was polite, but very quiet and reserved. She had evidently determined on a course of conduct and had resolved to assume that, although I had been very rude to her, she did not understand the import of my words. It would be quite proper, of course, for her not to know what I meant by my expressions of the night before.

I was downcast and wretched, and said but little, and the only bright streak across the black horizon of my woe was the fact that she did not appear to be happy, although she affected an air of unconcern. The moonlit porch was deserted that evening, but wandering about the house I found Madeline in the library alone. She was reading, but I went in and sat down near her. I felt that, although I could not do so fully, I must in a measure explain my conduct of the night before. She listened quietly to a somewhat laboured apology I made for the words I had used.

"I have not the slightest idea what you meant," she said, "but you were very rude."

I earnestly disclaimed any intention of rudeness, and assured her, with a warmth of speech that must have made some impression upon her, that rudeness to her would be an action impossible to me. I said a great deal upon the subject, and implored her to believe that if it were not for a certain obstacle I could speak to her so plainly that she would understand everything.

She was silent for a time, and then she said, rather more kindly, I thought, than she had spoken before:

"Is that obstacle in any way connected with my uncle?"

"Yes," I answered, after a little hesitation, "it is, in a measure, connected with him."

She made no answer to this, and sat looking at her book, but not reading. From the expression of her face, I thought she was somewhat softened toward me. She knew her uncle as well as I did, and she may have been thinking that, if he were the obstacle that prevented my speaking (and there were many ways in which he might be that obstacle), my position would be such a hard one that it would excuse some wildness of speech and eccentricity of manner. I saw, too, that the warmth of my partial explanations had had some effect on her, and I began to believe that it might be a good thing for me to speak my mind without delay. No matter how she should receive my proposition, my relations with her could not be worse than they had been the previous night and day, and there was something in her face which encouraged me to hope that she might forget my foolish exclamations of the evening before if I began to tell her my tale of love.

I drew my chair a little nearer to her, and as I did so the ghost burst into the room from the doorway behind her. I say burst, although no door flew open and he made no noise. He was wildly excited, and waved his arms above his head. The moment I saw him, my heart fell within me. With the entrance of that impertinent apparition, every hope fled from me. I could not speak while he was in the room.

I must have turned pale; and I gazed steadfastly at the ghost, almost without seeing Madeline, who sat between us.

"Do you know," he cried, "that John Hinckman is coming up the hill? He will be here in fifteen minutes; and if you are doing anything in the way of love-making, you had better hurry it up. But this is not what I came to tell you. I have glorious news! At last I am transferred! Not forty minutes ago a Russian nobleman was murdered by the Nihilists. Nobody ever thought of him in connection with an immediate ghost-ship. My friends instantly applied for the situation for me, and obtained my transfer. I am off before that horrid Hinckman comes up the hill. The moment I reach my new position, I shall put off this hated semblance. Good-by. You can't imagine how glad I am to be, at last, the real ghost of somebody."

"Oh!" I cried, rising to my feet, and stretching out my arms in utter wretchedness, "I would to Heaven you were mine!"

"I *am* yours," said Madeline, raising to me her tearful eyes.

The Mummy's Foot

Théophile Gautier

I had sauntered idly into the shop of one of those dealers in old curiosities—*bric-à-brac* as they say in that Parisian argot, so absolutely unintelligible elsewhere in France.

You have no doubt often glanced through the windows of some of these shops, which have become numerous since it is so fashionable to buy antique furniture, that the humblest stockbroker feels obliged to have a room furnished in medieval style.

Something is there which belongs alike to the shop of the dealer in old iron, the warehouse of the merchant, the laboratory of the chemist, and the studio of the painter: in all these mysterious recesses, where but a discreet half-light filters through the shutters, the most obviously antique thing is the dust: the cobwebs are more genuine than the laces, and the old pear-tree furniture is more modern than the mahogany which arrived but yesterday from America.

The warehouse of my dealer in *bric-à-brac* was a veritable Capharnaüm; all ages and all countries seemed to have arranged a rendezvous there; an Etruscan terra cotta lamp stood upon a Boule cabinet, with ebony panels decorated with simple filaments of inlaid copper: a duchess of the reign of Louis XV stretched nonchalantly her graceful feet under a massive Louis XIII table with heavy, spiral oaken legs, and carvings of intermingled flowers and grotesque figures.

In a corner glittered the ornamented breastplate of a suit of damascened armour of Milan. The shelves and floor were littered with porcelain cupids and nymphs, Chinese monkeys, vases of pale green enamel, cups of Dresden and old Sèvres.

Upon the denticulated shelves of sideboards, gleamed huge Japanese plaques, with red and blue designs outlined in gold, side by side with the enamels of Bernard Palissy, with serpents, frogs, and lizards in relief.

From ransacked cabinets tumbled cascades of silvery-gleaming China silk, the shimmering brocade pricked into luminous beads by a slanting sunbeam; while portraits of every epoch smiled through their yellowed varnish from frames more or less tarnished.

The dealer followed me watchfully through the tortuous passages winding between the piles of furniture, warding off with his hands the perilous swing of my coat tail, observing my elbows with the disquieting concern of an antiquarian and a usurer.

He was an odd figure—this dealer; an enormous skull, smooth as a knee, was surrounded by a scant aureole of white hair, which, by contrast, emphasized the salmon-coloured tint of his complexion, and gave a wrong impression of patriarchal benevolence, corrected, however, by the glittering of two small, yellow eyes which shifted in their orbits like two *louis d'or* floating on quicksilver. The curve of his nose gave him an aquiline silhouette, which suggested the Oriental or Jewish type. His hands, long, slender, with prominent veins and sinews protruding like the strings on a violin, with nails like the claws on the membranous wings of the bat moved with a senile trembling painful to behold, but those nervously quivering hands became firmer than pincers of steel, or the claws of a lobster, when they picked up any precious object, an onyx cup, a Venetian glass, or a platter of Bohemian crystal. This curious old fellow had an air so thoroughly rabbinical and cabalistic, that, from mere appearance, he would have been burned at the stake three centuries ago.

"Will you not buy something from me to-day, sir? Here is a *kris* from Malay, with a blade which undulates like a flame; look at these grooves for the blood to drip from, these teeth reversed so as to tear out the entrails in withdrawing the weapon; it is a fine specimen of a ferocious weapon, and will be an interesting addition to your trophies; this two-handed sword is very beautiful—it is the work of Joseph de la Herz; and this *cauchelimarde* with its carved guard—what superb workmanship!"

"No, I have enough weapons and instruments of carnage; I should like to have a small figure, any sort of object which can be used for a paper weight; for I cannot endure those commonplace bronzes for sale at the stationers which one sees invariably on everybody's desk."

The old gnome, rummaging among his ancient wares, displayed before me some antique bronzes—pseudo-antique, at least, fragments of malachite, little Hindu and Chinese idols, jade monkeys, incarnations of Brahma and Vishnu, marvellously suitable for the purpose— scarcely divine—of holding papers and letters in place.

I was hesitating between a porcelain dragon covered with constellations of warts, its jaws embellished with teeth and tusks, and a hideous little Mexican fetish, representing realistically the god Vitziliputzili, when I noticed a charming foot, which at first I supposed was a fragment of some antique Venus.

It had that beautiful tawny reddish tint, which gives the Florentine bronzes their warm, life-like appearance, so preferable to the verdigris tones of ordinary bronzes, which might be taken readily for statues in a state of putrefaction; a satiny lustre gleamed over its curves, polished by the amorous kisses of twenty centuries; for it must have been a Corinthian bronze, a work of the finest period, moulded perhaps by Lysippus himself.

"That foot will do," I said to the dealer, who looked at me with an ironical, crafty expression, as he handed me the object I asked for, so that I might examine it more carefully.

I was surprised at its lightness. It was not a metal foot but in reality a foot of flesh, an embalmed foot, a mummy's foot; on examining it more closely, one could distinguish the grain of the skin, and the almost imperceptible imprint of the weave of the wrappings. The toes were slender, delicate, with perfect nails, pure and transparent as agate; the great toe, slightly separated from the others, in the antique manner was in pleasing contrast to the position of the other toes, and gave a suggestion of the freedom and lightness of a bird's foot. The sole, faintly streaked with almost invisible lines, showed that it had never touched the ground, or come in contact with anything but the finest mats woven from the rushes of the Nile, and the softest rugs of panther skin.

"Ha, ha! You want the foot of the Princess Hermonthis," said the dealer with a strange, mocking laugh, staring at me with his owlish eyes. "Ha, ha, ha, for a paper weight! An original idea! an artist's idea! If anyone had told old Pharaoh that the foot of his adored daughter would be used for a paper weight, particularly whilst he was having a mountain of granite hollowed out in which to place her triple coffin, painted and gilded, covered with hieroglyphics, and beautiful pictures of the judgment of souls, it would truly have surprised him," continued the queer little dealer, in low tones, as though talking to himself.

"How much will you charge me for this fragment of a mummy?"

"Ah, as much as I can get; for it is a superb piece; if I had the mate to it, you could not have it for less than five hundred *francs*—the daughter of a Pharaoh! there could be nothing more choice."

"Assuredly it is not common; but, still, how much do you want for it? First, however, I want to acquaint you with one fact, which is, that my fortune consists of only five *louis*. I will buy anything that costs five *louis*, but nothing more expensive. You may search my vest pockets, and my most secret bureau drawers, but you will not find one miserable five *franc* piece besides."

"Five *louis* for the foot of the Princess Hermonthis! It is very little, too little, in fact, for an authentic foot," said the dealer, shaking his head and rolling his eyes with a peculiar rotary motion. "Very well, take it, and I will throw in the outer covering," he said, rolling it in a shred of old damask—"very beautiful, genuine damask, which has never been redyed; it is strong, yet it is soft," he muttered, caressing the frayed tissue, in accordance with his dealer's habit of praising an article of so little value, that he himself thought it good for nothing but to give away.

He dropped the gold pieces into a kind of medieval pouch which was fastened at his belt, while he repeated:

"The foot of the Princess Hermonthis to be used for a paper weight!"

Then, fastening upon me his phosphorescent pupils he said, in a voice strident as the wails of a cat which has just swallowed a fish bone:

"Old Pharaoh will not be pleased; he loved his daughter—that dear man."

"You speak of him as though you were his contemporary; no matter how old you may be, you do not date back to the pyramids of Egypt," I answered laughingly from the threshold of the shop.

I returned home, delighted with my purchase.

To make use of it at once, I placed the foot of the exalted Princess Hermonthis on a stack of papers—sketches of verses, undecipherable mosaics of crossed out words, unfinished articles, forgotten letters, posted in the desk drawer, a mistake often made by absent-minded people; the effect was pleasing, bizarre, and romantic.

Highly delighted with this decoration, I went down into the street, and took a walk with all the importance and pride proper to a man who has the inexpressible advantage over the passersby he elbows, of possessing a fragment of the Princess Hermonthis, daughter of Pharaoh.

I thought people who did not possess, like myself, a paper weight so genuinely Egyptian, were objects of ridicule, and it seemed to me the proper business of the sensible man to have a mummy's foot upon his desk.

Happily, an encounter with several friends distracted me from my raptures over my recent acquisition, I went to dinner with them, for it would have been hard for me to dine alone.

When I returned at night, with my brain somewhat muddled by the effects of a few glasses of wine, a vague whiff of oriental perfume tickled delicately my olfactory nerves. The heat of the room had warmed the natron, the bitumen, and the myrrh in which the *paraschites* who embalmed the dead had bathed the body of the Princess; it was a delicate, yet penetrating perfume, which four thousand years had not been able to dissipate.

The Dream of Egypt was for the Eternal; its odours have the solidity of granite, and last as long.

In a short time I drank full draughts from the black cup of sleep; for an hour or two all remained in obscurity; Oblivion and Nothingness submerged me in their sombre waves.

Nevertheless the haziness of my perceptions gradually cleared away, dreams began to brush me lightly in their silent flight.

The eyes of my soul opened, and I saw my room as it was in reality. I might have believed myself awake, if I had not had a vague consciousness that I was asleep, and that something very unusual was about to take place.

The odour of myrrh had increased in intensity, and I had a slight headache, which I very naturally attributed to several glasses of champagne that we had drunk to unknown gods, and to our future success.

I scrutinized my room with a feeling of expectation, which there was nothing to justify. Each piece of furniture was in its usual place; the lamp, softly shaded by the milky whiteness of its ground crystal globe, burned upon the console, the water colours glowed from under the Bohemian glass; the curtains hung in heavy drooping folds; everything suggested tranquillity and slumber.

Nevertheless, after a few moments the quiet of the room was disturbed, the woodwork creaked furtively, the ash-covered log suddenly spurted out a blue flame, and the surfaces of the plaques seemed like metallic eyes, watching, like myself, for what was about to happen.

By chance my eyes fell on the table on which I had placed the foot of the Princess Hermonthis.

Instead of remaining in the state of immobility proper to a foot which has been embalmed for four thousand years, it moved about in an agitated manner, twitching, leaping about over the papers like a frightened frog; one might have thought it in contact with a galvanic battery; I could hear distinctly the quick tap of the little heel, hard as the hoof of a gazelle.

I became rather dissatisfied with my purchase, for I like paper weights of sedentary habits—besides I found it very unnatural for feet to move about without legs, and I began to feel something closely resembling fear.

Suddenly I noticed a movement of one of the folds of my curtains, and I heard a stamping like that made by a person hopping about on one foot. I must admit that I grew hot and cold by turns, that I felt a mysterious breeze blowing down my back, and that my hair stood on end so suddenly that it forced my night-cap to a leap of several degrees.

The curtains partly opened, and I saw the strangest figure possible advancing.

It was a young girl, as coffee-coloured as Amani the dancer, and of a perfect beauty of the purest Egyptian type. She had slanting almond-shaped eyes, with eyebrows so black that they appeared blue; her nose was finely chiselled, almost Grecian in its delicacy; she might have been taken for a Corinthian statue of bronze, had not her prominent cheekbones and rather African fullness of lips indicated without a doubt the hieroglyphic race which dwelt on the banks of the Nile.

Her arms, thin, spindle shaped, like those of very young girls, were encircled with a kind of metal ornament, and bracelets of glass beads; her hair was twisted into little cords; on her breast hung a green paste idol, identified by her whip of seven lashes as Isis, guide of souls—a golden ornament shone on her forehead, and slight traces of rouge were visible on the coppery tints of her cheeks.

As for her costume, it was very odd.

Imagine a *pagne* made of narrow strips bedizened with red and black hieroglyphics, weighted with bitumen, and apparently belonging to a mummy newly unswathed.

In one of those flights of fancy usual in dreams, I could hear the hoarse, rough voice of the dealer of *bric-à-brac* reciting in a monotonous refrain, the phrase he had kept repeating in his shop in so enigmatic a manner.

"Old Pharaoh will not be pleased—he loved his daughter very much—that dear man."

One peculiar detail, which was hardly reassuring, was that the apparition had but one foot, the other was broken off at the ankle.

She approached the table, where the mummy's foot was fidgeting and tossing about with redoubled energy. She leaned against the edge, and I saw her eyes fill with pearly tears.

Although she did not speak, I fully understood her feelings. She looked at the foot, for it was in truth her own, with an expression of coquettish sadness, which was extremely charming; but the foot kept jumping and running about as though it were moved by springs of steel.

Two or three times she stretched out her hand to grasp it, but did not succeed.

Then began between the Princess Hermonthis and her foot, which seemed to be endowed with an individuality of its own, a very bizarre dialogue, in an ancient Coptic tongue, such as might have been spoken thirty centuries before, among the sphinxes of the Land of Ser; fortunately, that night I understood Coptic perfectly.

The Princess Hermonthis said in a tone of voice sweet and tremulous as the tones of a crystal bell:

"Well, my dear little foot, you always flee from me, yet I took the best of care of you; I bathed you with perfumed water, in a basin of alabaster; I rubbed your heel with pumice stone, mixed with oil of palm; your nails were cut with golden scissors, and polished with a hippopotamus' tooth; I was careful to select for you painted and embroidered *tatbebs*, with turned up toes, which were the envy of all the young girls of Egypt; on your great toe, you wore rings representing the sacred Scarab, and you supported one of the lightest bodies that could be desired by a lazy foot."

The foot answered in a pouting, regretful voice:

"You know well that I no longer belong to myself. I have been bought and paid for; the old dealer knew what he was about. He bears you a grudge for having refused to marry him. This is a trick he has played on you. The Arab who forced open your royal tomb, in the subterranean pits of the Necropolis of Thebes, was sent there by him. He wanted to prevent you from attending the reunion of the shades, in the cities of the lower world. Have you five pieces of gold with which to ransom me?"

"Alas, no! My jewels, my rings, my purses of gold and of silver have all been stolen from me," answered the Princess Hermonthis with a sigh.

"Princess," I then cried out, "I have never kept possession of anyone's foot unjustly; even though you have not the five *louis* which it cost me, I will return it to you gladly; I should be wretched, were I the cause of the lameness of so charming a person as the Princess Hermonthis."

I delivered this discourse in a courtly, troubadour-like manner, which must have astonished the beautiful Egyptian.

She looked at me with an expression of deepest gratitude, and her eyes brightened with bluish lights.

She took her foot, which this time submitted, and, like a woman about to put on her brodekin, she adjusted it to her leg with great dexterity.

This operation finished, she took a few steps about the room, as though to assure herself that she was in reality no longer lame.

"Ah, how happy my father will be, he who was so wretched because of my mutilation—he who, from the day of my birth, set a whole nation to work to hollow out a tomb so deep that he might preserve me intact until that supreme last day, when souls must be weighed in the scales of Amenti! Come with me to my father; he will be happy to receive you, for you have given me back my foot."

I found this proposition quite natural. I decked myself out in a dressing-gown of huge sprawling design, which gave me an extremely Pharaohesque appearance; I hurriedly put on a pair of Turkish slippers, and told the Princess Hermonthis that I was ready to follow her.

Before setting out, Hermonthis detached from her necklace the little green paste image and placed it on the scattered papers which strewed the table.

"It is no more than right," she said smilingly, "that I should replace your paper weight."

She gave me her hand, which was soft and cool as the skin of a serpent, and we departed. For a time we sped with the rapidity of an arrow, through a misty expanse of space, in which almost indistinguishable silhouettes flashed by us, on the right and left.

For an instant we saw nothing but sea and sky.

A few minutes later, towering obelisks, pillars, the sloping outlines of the sphinx, were designed against the horizon.

We had arrived.

The princess conducted me to the side of a mountain of red granite in which there was an aperture so low and narrow that, had it not been marked by two monoliths covered with bizarre carvings, it would have been difficult to distinguish from the fissures in the rock.

Hermonthis lighted a torch and led the way.

The corridors were hewn through the living rock. The walls, with panels covered with hieroglyphics, and representations of allegorical processions, must have been the work of thousands of hands for thousands of years; the corridors, of an interminable length, ended in square rooms, in the middle of which pits had been constructed, to which we descended by means of *crampons* or spiral staircases. These pits led us into other rooms, from which opened out other corridors embellished in the same bizarre manner with sparrow-hawks, serpents coiled in circles, the symbolic *tau*, *pedum*, and *baris*, prodigious works which no living eye should ever see, interminable legends in granite which only the dead throughout eternity have time to read.

At last we reached a hall so vast, so boundless, so immeasurable, that its limits could not be discerned. As far as the eye could see, extended files of gigantic columns, between which sparkled livid stars of yellow light. These glittering points of light revealed incalculable depths beyond.

The Princess Hermonthis, still holding my hand, greeted graciously the mummies of her acquaintance.

My eyes gradually became accustomed to the shadowy twilight, and I began to distinguish the objects around me.

I saw, seated upon their thrones, the kings of the subterranean races. They were dignified old personages, or dried up, shrivelled, wrinkled-like parchment, and blackened with naphtha and bitumen. On their heads they wore *pschents* of gold, and their breastplates and *gorgets* scintillated with precious stones; their eyes had the fixedness of the sphinx, and their long beards were whitened by the snows of centuries. Behind them stood their embalmed subjects, in the rigid and constrained postures of Egyptian art, preserving eternally the attitudes prescribed by the hieratic code. Behind the subjects, the cats, ibexes, and crocodiles contemporary with them, rendered still more monstrous by their wrappings, mewed, beat their wings, and opened and closed their huge jaws in foolish grimaces.

All the Pharaohs were there—Cheops, Chephrenes, Psammetichus, Sesostri, Amenoteph, all the dark-skinned rulers of the country of the pyramids, and the royal sepulchres; on a still higher platform sat enthroned the kings Chronos, and Xixouthros, who were contemporary with the deluge, and Tubal-Cain, who preceded it.

The beard of King Xixouthros had grown to such lengths that it had already wound itself seven times around the granite table against which he leaned, lost in reverie, as though in slumber.

Further in the distance, through a dim exhalation, across the mists of eternities, I beheld vaguely the seventy-two pre-Adamite kings, with their seventy-two peoples, vanished forever.

The Princess Hermonthis, after allowing me a few moments to enjoy this dizzying spectacle, presented me to Pharaoh, her father, who nodded to me in a most majestic manner.

"I have found my foot—I have found my foot!" cried the Princess, clapping her little hands, with every indication of uncontrollable joy. "It was this gentleman who returned it to me."

The races of Kheme, the races of Nahasi, all the races, black, bronze, and copper-coloured, repeated in a chorus:

"The Princess Hermonthis has found her foot."

Xixouthros himself was deeply affected.

He raised his heavy eyelids, stroked his moustache, and regarded me with his glance charged with the centuries.

"By Oms, the dog of Hell, and by Tmei, daughter of the Sun and of Truth, here is a brave and worthy young man," said Pharaoh, extending toward me his sceptre which terminated in a lotus flower. "What recompense do you desire?"

Eagerly, with that audacity which one has in dreams, where nothing seems impossible, I asked him for the hand of the Princess Hermonthis. Her hand in exchange for her foot, seemed to me an antithetical recompense, in sufficiently good taste.

Pharaoh opened wide his eyes of glass, surprised at my pleasantry, as well as my request.

"From what country are you, and what is your age?"

"I am a Frenchman, and I am twenty-seven years old, venerable Pharaoh."

"Twenty-seven years old! And he wishes to espouse the Princess Hermonthis, who is thirty centuries old!" exclaimed in a chorus all the thrones, and all the circles of nations.

Hermonthis alone did not seem to think my request improper.

"If you were even two thousand years old," continued the old king, "I would gladly bestow upon you the Princess; but the disproportion is too great; besides, our daughters must have husbands who will last, and you no longer know how to preserve yourselves. Of the last persons who were brought here, scarcely fifteen centuries ago, nothing now remains but a pinch of ashes. Look! my flesh is as hard as basalt, my bones are bars of steel. I shall be present on the last day, with the body and features I had in life. My daughter Hermonthis will last longer than a statue of bronze. But at that time the winds will have dissipated the last grains of your dust, and Isis herself, who knew how to recover the fragments of Osiris, would hardly be able to recompose your being. See how vigorous I still am, and how powerful is the strength of my arm," said he, shaking my hand in the English fashion, in a way that cut my fingers with my rings.

His grasp was so strong that I awoke, and discovered my friend Alfred, who was pulling me by the arm, and shaking me, to make me get up.

"Oh, see here, you maddening sleeper! Must I have you dragged into the middle of the street, and have fireworks put off close to your ear, in order to waken you? It is afternoon. Don't you remember that you promised to call for me and take me to see the Spanish pictures of M. Aguada?"

"Good heavens! I forgot all about it," I answered, dressing hurriedly. "We can go there at once—I have the permit here on my table." I crossed over to get it; imagine my astonishment when I saw, not the mummy's foot I had bought the evening before, but the little green paste image left in its place by the Princess Hermonthis!

The Rival Ghosts

Brander Matthews

The good ship sped on her way across the calm Atlantic. It was an outward passage, according to the little charts which the company had charily distributed, but most of the passengers were homeward bound, after a summer of rest and recreation, and they were counting the days before they might hope to see Fire Island Light. On the lee side of the boat, comfortably sheltered from the wind, and just by the door of the captain's room (which was theirs during the day), sat a little group of returning Americans. The duchess (she was down on the purser's list as Mrs. Martin, but her friends and familiars called her the Duchess of Washington Square) and Baby Van Rensselaer (she was quite old enough to vote, had her sex been entitled to that duty, but as the younger of two sisters she was still the baby of the family)—the Duchess and Baby Van Rensselaer were discussing the pleasant English voice and the not unpleasant English accent of a manly young lordling who was going to America for sport. Uncle Larry and Dear Jones were enticing each other into a bet on the ship's run of the morrow.

"I'll give you two to one she don't make 420," said Dear Jones.

"I'll take it," answered Uncle Larry. "We made 427 the fifth day last year." It was Uncle Larry's seventeenth visit to Europe, and this was therefore his thirty-fourth voyage.

"And when did you get in?" asked Baby Van Rensselaer. "I don't care a bit about the run, so long as we get in soon."

"We crossed the bar Sunday night, just seven days after we left Queenstown, and we dropped anchor off Quarantine at three o'clock on Monday morning."

"I hope we sha'n't do that this time. I can't seem to sleep any when the boat stops."

"I can, but I didn't," continued Uncle Larry, "because my stateroom was the most for'ard in the boat, and the donkey-engine that let down the anchor was right over my head."

"So you got up and saw the sun rise over the bay," said Dear Jones, "with the electric lights of the city twinkling in the distance, and the first faint flush of the dawn in the east just over Fort Lafayette, and the rosy tinge which spread softly upward, and—"

"Did you both come back together?" asked the duchess.

"Because he has crossed thirty-four times you must not suppose he has a monopoly in sunrises," retorted Dear Jones. "No; this was my own sunrise; and a mighty pretty one it was too."

"I'm not matching sunrises with you," remarked Uncle Larry calmly; "but I'm willing to back a merry jest called forth by my sunrise against any two merry jests called forth by yours."

"I confess reluctantly that my sunrise evoked no merry jest at all." Dear Jones was an honest man, and would scorn to invent a merry jest on the spur of the moment.

"That's where my sunrise has the call," said Uncle Larry, complacently.

"What was the merry jest?" was Baby Van Rensselaer's inquiry, the natural result of a feminine curiosity thus artistically excited.

"Well, here it is. I was standing aft, near a patriotic American and a wandering Irishman, and the patriotic American rashly declared that you couldn't see a sunrise like that anywhere in Europe, and this gave the Irishman his chance, and he said, 'Sure ye don't have'm here till we're through with 'em over there.'"

"It is true," said Dear Jones, thoughtfully, "that they do have some things over there better than we do; for instance, umbrellas."

"And gowns," added the duchess.

"And antiquities."—this was Uncle Larry's contribution.

"And we do have some things so much better in America!" protested Baby Van Rensselaer, as yet uncorrupted by any worship of the effete monarchies of despotic Europe. "We make lots of things a great deal nicer than you can get them in Europe—especially ice-cream."

"And pretty girls," added Dear Jones; but he did not look at her.

"And spooks," remarked Uncle Larry, casually.

"Spooks?" queried the duchess.

"Spooks. I maintain the word. Ghost, if you like that better, or spectres. We turn out the best quality of spook—"

"You forget the lovely ghost stories about the Rhine and the Black Forest," interrupted Miss Van Rensselaer, with feminine inconsistency.

"I remember the Rhine and the Black Forest and all the other haunts of elves and fairies and hobgoblins; but for good honest spooks there is no place like home. And what differentiates our spook—*spiritus Americanus*—from the ordinary ghost of literature is that it responds to the American sense of humour. Take Irving's stories, for example. The 'Headless Horseman'—that's a comic ghost story. And Rip Van Winkle—consider what humour, and what good humour, there is in the telling of his meeting with the goblin crew of Hendrik Hudson's men! A still better example of this American way of dealing with legend and mystery is the marvellous tale of the rival ghosts."

"The rival ghosts!" queried the duchess and Baby Van Rensselaer together. "Who were they?"

"Didn't I ever tell you about them?" answered Uncle Larry, a gleam of approaching joy flashing from his eye.

"Since he is bound to tell us sooner or later, we'd better be resigned and hear it now," said Dear Jones.

"If you are not more eager, I won't tell it at all."

"Oh, do, Uncle Larry! you know I just dote on ghost stories," pleaded Baby Van Rensselaer.

"Once upon a time," began Uncle Larry—"in fact, a very few years ago—there lived in the thriving town of New York a young American called Duncan—Eliphalet Duncan. Like his name, he was half Yankee and half Scotch, and naturally he was a lawyer, and had come to New York to make his way. His father was a Scotchman who had come over and settled in Boston and married a Salem girl. When Eliphalet Duncan was about twenty he lost both of his parents. His father left him enough money to give him a start, and a strong feeling of pride in his Scotch birth; you see there was a title in the family in Scotland, and although Eliphalet's father was the younger son of a younger son, yet he always remembered, and always bade his only son to remember, that this ancestry was noble. His mother left him her full share of Yankee grit and a little old house in Salem which had belonged to her family for more than two hundred years. She was a Hitchcock, and the Hitchcocks had been settled in Salem since the year 1. It was a great-great-grandfather of Mr. Eliphalet Hitchcock who was foremost in the time of the Salem witchcraft craze. And this little old house which she left to my friend, Eliphalet Duncan, was haunted."

"By the ghost of one of the witches, of course?" interrupted Dear Jones.

"Now how could it be the ghost of a witch, since the witches were all burned at the stake? You never heard of anybody who was burned having a ghost, did you?" asked Uncle Larry.

"That's an argument in favour of cremation, at any rate," replied Dear Jones, evading the direct question.

"It is, if you don't like ghosts. I do," said Baby Van Rensselaer.

"And so do I," added Uncle Larry. "I love a ghost as dearly as an Englishman loves a lord."

"Go on with your story," said the duchess, majestically overruling all extraneous discussion.

"This little old house at Salem was haunted," resumed Uncle Larry. "And by a very distinguished ghost—or at least by a ghost with very remarkable attributes."

"What was he like?" asked Baby Van Rensselaer, with a premonitory shiver of anticipatory delight.

"It had a lot of peculiarities. In the first place, it never appeared to the master of the house. Mostly it confined its visitations to unwelcome guests. In the course of the last hundred years it had frightened away four successive mothers-in-law, while never intruding on the head of the household."

"I guess that ghost had been one of the boys when he was alive and in the flesh." This was Dear Jones's contribution to the telling of the tale.

"In the second place," continued Uncle Larry, "it never frightened anybody the first time it appeared. Only on the second visit were the ghost-seers scared; but then they were scared enough for twice, and they rarely mustered up courage enough to risk a third interview. One of the most curious characteristics of this well-meaning spook was that it had no face—or at least that nobody ever saw its face."

"Perhaps he kept his countenance veiled?" queried the duchess, who was beginning to remember that she never did like ghost stories.

"That was what I was never able to find out. I have asked several people who saw the ghost, and none of them could tell me anything about its face, and yet while in its presence they never noticed its features, and never remarked on their absence or concealment. It was only afterwards when they tried to recall calmly all the circumstances of meeting with the mysterious stranger that they became aware that they had not seen its face. And they could not say whether the features were covered, or whether they were wanting, or what the trouble was. They knew only that the face was never seen. And no matter how often they might see it, they never fathomed this mystery. To this day nobody knows whether the ghost which used to haunt the little old house in Salem had a face, or what manner of face it had."

"How awfully weird!" said Baby Van Rensselaer. "And why did the ghost go away?"

"I haven't said it went away," answered Uncle Larry, with much dignity.

"But you said it *used* to haunt the little old house at Salem, so I supposed it had moved. Didn't it?" the young lady asked.

"You shall be told in due time. Eliphalet Duncan used to spend most of his summer vacations at Salem, and the ghost never bothered him at all, for he was the master of the house—much to his disgust, too, because he wanted to see for himself the mysterious tenant at will of his property. But he never saw it, never. He arranged with friends to call him whenever it might appear, and he slept in the next room with the door open; and yet when their frightened cries waked him the ghost was gone, and his only reward was to hear reproachful sighs as soon as he went back to bed. You see, the ghost thought it was not fair of Eliphalet to seek an introduction which was plainly unwelcome."

Dear Jones interrupted the story-teller by getting up and tucking a heavy rug more snugly around Baby Van Rensselaer's feet, for the sky was now overcast and gray, and the air was damp and penetrating.

"One fine spring morning," pursued Uncle Larry, "Eliphalet Duncan received great news. I told you that there was a title in the family in Scotland, and that Eliphalet's father was the younger son of a younger son. Well, it happened that all Eliphalet's father's brothers and uncles had died off without male issue except the eldest son of the eldest son, and he, of course, bore the title, and was Baron Duncan of Duncan. Now the great news that Eliphalet Duncan received in New York one fine spring morning was that Baron Duncan and his only son had been yachting in the Hebrides, and they had been caught in a black squall, and they were both dead. So my friend Eliphalet Duncan inherited the title and the estates."

"How romantic!" said the duchess. "So he was a baron!"

"Well," answered Uncle Larry, "he was a baron if he chose. But he didn't choose."

"More fool he!" said Dear Jones, sententiously.

"Well," answered Uncle Larry, "I'm not so sure of that. You see, Eliphalet Duncan was half Scotch and half Yankee, and he had two eyes to the main chance. He held his tongue about his windfall of luck until he could find out whether the Scotch estates were enough to keep up the Scotch title. He soon discovered that they were not, and that the late Lord Duncan, having married money, kept up such state as he could out of the revenues of the dowry of Lady Duncan. And Eliphalet, he decided that he would rather be a well-fed lawyer in New York, living comfortably on his practice, than a starving lord in Scotland, living scantily on his title."

"But he kept his title?" asked the Duchess.

"Well," answered Uncle Larry, "he kept it quiet. I knew it, and a friend or two more. But Eliphalet was a sight too smart to put 'Baron Duncan of Duncan, Attorney and Counsellor at Law,' on his shingle."

"What has all this got to do with your ghost?" asked Dear Jones, pertinently.

"Nothing with that ghost, but a good deal with another ghost. Eliphalet was very learned in spirit lore—perhaps because he owned the haunted house at Salem, perhaps because he was a Scotchman by descent. At all events, he had made a special study of the wraiths and white ladies and banshees and bogies of all kinds whose sayings and doings and warnings are recorded in the annals of the Scottish nobility. In fact, he was acquainted with the habits of every reputable spook in the Scotch peerage. And he knew that there was a Duncan ghost attached to the person of the holder of the title of Baron Duncan of Duncan."

"So, besides being the owner of a haunted house in Salem, he was also a haunted man in Scotland?" asked Baby Van Rensselaer.

"Just so. But the Scotch ghost was not unpleasant, like the Salem ghost, although it had one peculiarity in common with its transatlantic fellow-spook. It never appeared to the holder of the title, just as the other never was visible to the owner of the house. In fact, the Duncan ghost was never seen at all. It was a guardian angel only. Its sole duty was to be in personal attendance on Baron Duncan of Duncan, and to warn him of impending evil. The traditions of the house told that the Barons of Duncan had again and again felt a premonition of ill fortune. Some of them had yielded and withdrawn from the venture they had undertaken, and it had failed dismally. Some had been obstinate, and had hardened their hearts, and had gone on reckless to defeat and to death. In no case had a Lord Duncan been exposed to peril without fair warning."

"Then how came it that the father and son were lost in the yacht off the Hebrides?" asked Dear Jones.

"Because they were too enlightened to yield to superstition. There is extant now a letter of Lord Duncan, written to his wife a few minutes before he and his son set sail, in which he tells her how hard he has had to struggle with an almost overmastering desire to give up the trip. Had he obeyed the friendly warning of the family ghost, the letter would have been spared a journey across the Atlantic."

"Did the ghost leave Scotland for America as soon as the old baron died?" asked Baby Van Rensselaer, with much interest.

"How did he come over," queried Dear Jones—"in the steerage, or as a cabin passenger?"

"I don't know," answered Uncle Larry, calmly, "and Eliphalet didn't know. For as he was in no danger, and stood in no need of warning, he couldn't tell whether the ghost was on duty or not. Of course he was on the watch for it all the time. But he never got any proof of its presence until he went down to the little old house of Salem, just before the Fourth of July. He took a friend down with him—a young fellow who had been in the regular army since the day Fort Sumter was fired on, and who thought that after four years of the little unpleasantness down South, including six months in Libby, and after ten years of fighting the bad Indians on the plains, he wasn't likely to be much frightened by a ghost. Well, Eliphalet and the officer sat out on the porch all the evening smoking and talking over points in military law. A little after twelve o'clock, just as they began to think it was about time to turn in, they heard the most ghastly noise in the house. It wasn't a shriek, or a howl, or a yell, or anything they could put a name to. It was an indeterminate, inexplicable shiver and shudder of sound, which went wailing out of the window. The officer had been at Cold Harbor, but he felt himself getting colder this time. Eliphalet knew it was the ghost who haunted the house. As this weird sound died away, it was followed by another, sharp, short, blood-curdling in its intensity. Something in this cry seemed familiar to Eliphalet, and he felt sure that it proceeded from the family ghost, the warning wraith of the Duncans."

"Do I understand you to intimate that both ghosts were there together?" inquired the duchess, anxiously.

"Both of them were there," answered Uncle Larry. "You see, one of them belonged to the house, and had to be there all the time, and the other was attached to the person of Baron Duncan, and had to follow him there; wherever he was, there was that ghost also. But Eliphalet, he had scarcely time to think this out when he heard both sounds again, not one after another, but both together, and something told him—some sort of an instinct he had—that those two ghosts didn't agree, didn't get on together, didn't exactly hit it off; in fact, that they were quarrelling."

"Quarrelling ghosts! Well, I never!" was Baby Van Rensselaer's remark.

"It is a blessed thing to see ghosts dwell together in unity," said Dear Jones.

84

And the duchess added, "It would certainly be setting a better example."

"You know," resumed Uncle Larry, "that two waves of light or of sound may interfere and produce darkness or silence. So it was with these rival spooks. They interfered, but they did not produce silence or darkness. On the contrary, as soon as Eliphalet and the officer went into the house, there began at once a series of spiritualistic manifestations—a regular dark séance. A tambourine was played upon, a bell was rung, and a flaming banjo went singing around the room."

"Where did they get the banjo?" asked Dear Jones, sceptically.

"I don't know. Materialized it, maybe, just as they did the tambourine. You don't suppose a quiet New York lawyer kept a stock of musical instruments large enough to fit out a strolling minstrel troupe just on the chance of a pair of ghosts coming to give him a surprise party, do you? Every spook has its own instrument of torture. Angels play on harps, I'm informed, and spirits delight in banjos and tambourines. These spooks of Eliphalet Duncan's were ghosts with all modern improvements, and I guess they were capable of providing their own musical weapons. At all events, they had them there in the little old house at Salem the night Eliphalet and his friend came down. And they played on them, and they rang the bell, and they rapped here, there, and everywhere. And they kept it up all night."

"All night?" asked the awe-stricken duchess.

"All night long," said Uncle Larry, solemnly; "and the next night too. Eliphalet did not get a wink of sleep, neither did his friend. On the second night the house ghost was seen by the officer; on the third night it showed itself again; and the next morning the officer packed his gripsack and took the first train to Boston. He was a New Yorker, but he said he'd sooner go to Boston than see that ghost again. Eliphalet wasn't scared at all, partly because he never saw either the domiciliary or the titular spook, and partly because he felt himself on friendly terms with the spirit world, and didn't scare easily. But after losing three nights' sleep and the society of his friend, he began to be a little impatient, and to think that the thing had gone far enough. You see, while in a way he was fond of ghosts, yet he liked them best one at a time. Two ghosts were one too many. He wasn't bent on making a collection of spooks. He and one ghost were company, but he and two ghosts were a crowd."

"What did he do?" asked Baby Van Rensselaer.

"Well he couldn't do anything. He waited awhile, hoping they would get tired; but he got tired out first. You see, it comes natural to a spook to sleep in the daytime, but a man wants to sleep nights, and they wouldn't let him sleep nights. They kept on wrangling and quarrelling incessantly; they manifested and they dark-séanced as regularly as the old clock on the stairs struck twelve; they rapped and they rang bells and they banged the tambourine and they threw the flaming banjo about the house, and, worse than all, they swore."

"I did not know that spirits were addicted to bad language," said the duchess.

"How did he know they were swearing? Could he hear them?" asked Dear Jones.

"That was just it," responded Uncle Larry; "he could not hear them—at least, not distinctly. There were inarticulate murmurs and stifled rumblings. But the impression produced on him was that they were swearing. If they had only sworn right out, he would not have minded it so much, because he would have known the worst. But the feeling that the air was full of suppressed profanity was very wearing, and after standing it for a week he gave up in disgust and went to the White Mountains."

"Leaving them to fight it out, I suppose," interjected Baby Van Rensselaer.

"Not at all," explained Uncle Larry. "They could not quarrel unless he was present. You see, he could not leave the titular ghost behind him, and the domiciliary ghost could not leave the house. When he went away he took the family ghost with him, leaving the house ghost behind. Now spooks can't quarrel when they are a hundred miles apart any more than men can."

"And what happened afterwards?" asked Baby Van Rensselaer, with a pretty impatience.

"A most marvellous thing happened. Eliphalet Duncan went to the White Mountains, and in the car of the railroad that runs to the top of Mount Washington he met a classmate whom he had not seen for years, and this classmate introduced Duncan to his sister, and this sister was a remarkably pretty girl, and Duncan fell in love with her at first sight, and by the time he got to the top of Mount Washington he was so deep in love that he began to consider his own unworthiness, and to wonder whether she might ever be induced to care for him a little—ever so little."

"I don't think that is so marvellous a thing," said Dear Jones, glancing at Baby Van Rensselaer.

"Who was she?" asked the duchess, who had once lived in Philadelphia.

"She was Miss Kitty Sutton, of San Francisco, and she was a daughter of old Judge Sutton, of the firm of Pixley & Sutton."

"A very respectable family," assented the duchess.

"I hope she wasn't a daughter of that loud and vulgar old Mrs. Sutton whom I met at Saratoga one summer four or five years ago?" said Dear Jones.

"Probably she was," Uncle Larry responded.

"She was a horrid old woman. The boys used to call her Mother Gorgon."

"The pretty Kitty Sutton with whom Eliphalet Duncan had fallen in love was the daughter of Mother Gorgon. But he never saw the mother, who was in Frisco, or Los Angeles, or Santa Fé, or somewhere out West, and he saw a great deal of the daughter, who was up in the White Mountains. She was travelling with her brother and his wife, and as they journeyed from hotel to hotel Duncan went with them, and filled out the quartet. Before the end of the summer he began to think about proposing. Of course he had lots of chances, going on excursions as they were every day. He made up his mind to seize the first opportunity, and that very evening he took her out for a moonlight row on Lake Winipiseogee. As he handed her into the boat he resolved to do it, and he had a glimmer of suspicion that she knew he was going to do it, too."

"Girls," said Dear Jones, "never go out in a rowboat at night with a young man unless you mean to accept him."

"Sometimes it's best to refuse him, and get it over once for all," said Baby Van Rensselaer, impersonally.

"As Eliphalet took the oars he felt a sudden chill. He tried to shake it off, but in vain. He began to have a growing consciousness of impending evil. Before he had taken ten strokes—and he was a swift oarsman—he was aware of a mysterious presence between him and Miss Sutton."

"Was it the guardian-angel ghost warning him off the match?" interrupted Dear Jones.

"That's just what it was," said Uncle Larry. "And he yielded to it, and kept his peace, and rowed Miss Sutton back to the hotel with his proposal unspoken."

"More fool he," said Dear Jones. "It will take more than one ghost to keep me from proposing when my mind is made up." And he looked at Baby Van Rensselaer.

"The next morning," continued Uncle Larry, "Eliphalet overslept himself, and when he went down to a late breakfast he found that the

Suttons had gone to New York by the morning train. He wanted to follow them at once, and again he felt the mysterious presence overpowering his will. He struggled two days, and at last he roused himself to do what he wanted in spite of the spook. When he arrived in New York it was late in the evening. He dressed himself hastily, and went to the hotel where the Suttons were, in the hope of seeing at least her brother. The guardian angel fought every inch of the walk with him, until he began to wonder whether, if Miss Sutton were to take him, the spook would forbid the banns. At the hotel he saw no one that night, and he went home determined to call as early as he could the next afternoon, and make an end of it. When he left his office about two o'clock the next day to learn his fate, he had not walked five blocks before he discovered that the wraith of the Duncans had withdrawn his opposition to the suit. There was no feeling of impending evil, no resistance, no struggle, no consciousness of an opposing presence. Eliphalet was greatly encouraged. He walked briskly to the hotel; he found Miss Sutton alone. He asked her the question, and got his answer."

"She accepted him, of course?" said Baby Van Rensselaer.

"Of course," said Uncle Larry. "And while they were in the first flush of joy, swapping confidences and confessions, her brother came into the parlour with an expression of pain on his face and a telegram in his hand. The former was caused by the latter, which was from Frisco, and which announced the sudden death of Mrs. Sutton, their mother."

"And that was why the ghost no longer opposed the match?" questioned Dear Jones.

"Exactly. You see, the family ghost knew that Mother Gorgon was an awful obstacle to Duncan's happiness, so it warned him. But the moment the obstacle was removed, it gave its consent at once."

The fog was lowering its thick, damp curtain, and it was beginning to be difficult to see from one end of the boat to the other. Dear Jones tightened the rug which enwrapped Baby Van Rensselaer, and then withdrew again into his own substantial coverings.

Uncle Larry paused in his story long enough to light another of the tiny cigars he always smoked.

"I infer that Lord Duncan"—the duchess was scrupulous in the bestowal of titles—"saw no more of the ghosts after he was married."

"He never saw them at all, at any time, either before or since. But they came very near breaking off the match, and thus breaking two young hearts."

"You don't mean to say that they knew any just cause or impediment why they should not forever after hold their peace?" asked Dear Jones.

"How could a ghost, or even two ghosts, keep a girl from marrying the man she loved?" This was Baby Van Rensselaer's question.

"It seems curious, doesn't it?" and Uncle Larry tried to warm himself by two or three sharp pulls at his fiery little cigar. "And the circumstances are quite as curious as the fact itself. You see, Miss Sutton wouldn't be married for a year after her mother's death, so she and Duncan had lots of time to tell each other all they knew. Eliphalet got to know a good deal about the girls she went to school with; and Kitty soon learned all about his family. He didn't tell her about the title for a long time, as he wasn't one to brag. But he described to her the little old house at Salem. And one evening towards the end of the summer, the wedding-day having been appointed for early in September, she told him that she didn't want a bridal tour at all; she just wanted to go down to the little old house at Salem to spend her honeymoon in peace and quiet, with nothing to do and nobody to bother them. Well, Eliphalet jumped at the suggestion: it suited him down to the ground. All of a sudden he remembered the spooks, and it knocked him all of a heap. He had told her about the Duncan banshee, and the idea of having an ancestral ghost in personal attendance on her husband tickled her immensely. But he had never said anything about the ghost which haunted the little old house at Salem. He knew she would be frightened out of her wits if the house ghost revealed itself to her, and he saw at once that it would be impossible to go to Salem on their wedding trip. So he told her all about it, and how whenever he went to Salem the two ghosts interfered, and gave dark séances and manifested and materialized and made the place absolutely impossible. Kitty listened in silence, and Eliphalet thought she had changed her mind. But she hadn't done anything of the kind."

"Just like a man—to think she was going to," remarked Baby Van Rensselaer.

"She just told him she could not bear ghosts herself, but she would not marry a man who was afraid of them."

"Just like a girl—to be so inconsistent," remarked Dear Jones.

Uncle Larry's tiny cigar had long been extinct. He lighted a new one, and continued: "Eliphalet protested in vain. Kitty said her mind was made up. She was determined to pass her honeymoon in the little old house at Salem, and she was equally determined not to go there as long as there were any ghosts there. Until he could assure her that the spectral tenant had received notice to quit, and that there was no danger of manifestations and materializing, she refused to be married at all. She did not intend to have her honeymoon interrupted by two wrangling ghosts, and the wedding could be postponed until he had made ready the house for her."

"She was an unreasonable young woman," said the duchess.

"Well, that's what Eliphalet thought, much as he was in love with her. And he believed he could talk her out of her determination. But he couldn't. She was set. And when a girl is set, there's nothing to do but to yield to the inevitable. And that's just what Eliphalet did. He saw he would either have to give her up or to get the ghosts out; and as he loved her and did not care for the ghosts, he resolved to tackle the ghosts. He had clear grit, Eliphalet had—he was half Scotch and half Yankee and neither breed turns tail in a hurry. So he made his plans and he went down to Salem. As he said good-by to Kitty he had an impression that she was sorry she had made him go; but she kept up bravely, and put a bold face on it, and saw him off, and went home and cried for an hour, and was perfectly miserable until he came back the next day."

"Did he succeed in driving the ghosts away?" asked Baby Van Rensselaer, with great interest.

"That's just what I'm coming to," said Uncle Larry, pausing at the critical moment, in the manner of the trained story-teller. "You see, Eliphalet had got a rather tough job, and he would gladly have had an extension of time on the contract, but he had to choose between the girl and the ghosts, and he wanted the girl. He tried to invent or remember some short and easy way with ghosts, but he couldn't. He wished that somebody had invented a specific for spooks—something that would make the ghosts come out of the house and die in the yard. He wondered if he could not tempt the ghosts to run in debt, so that he might get the sheriff to help him. He wondered also whether the ghosts could not be overcome with strong drink—a dissipated spook, a spook with delirium tremens, might be committed to the inebriate asylum. But none of these things seemed feasible."

"What did he do?" interrupted Dear Jones. "The learned counsel will please speak to the point."

"You will regret this unseemly haste," said Uncle Larry, gravely, "when you know what really happened."

"What was it, Uncle Larry?" asked Baby Van Rensselaer. "I'm all impatience."

And Uncle Larry proceeded:

"Eliphalet went down to the little old house at Salem, and as soon as the clock struck twelve the rival ghosts began wrangling as before. Raps here, there, and everywhere, ringing bells, banging tambourines, strumming banjos sailing about the room, and all the other manifestations and materializations followed one another just as they had the summer before. The only difference Eliphalet could detect was a stronger flavour in the spectral profanity; and this, of course, was only a vague impression, for he did not actually hear a single word. He waited awhile in patience, listening and watching. Of course he never saw either of the ghosts, because neither of them could appear to him. At last he got his dander up, and he thought it was about time to interfere, so he rapped on the table, and asked for silence. As soon as he felt that the spooks were listening to him he explained the situation to them. He told them he was in love, and that he could not marry unless they vacated the house. He appealed to them as old friends, and he laid claim to their gratitude. The titular ghost had been sheltered by the Duncan family for hundreds of years, and the domiciliary ghost had had free lodging in the little old house at Salem for nearly two centuries. He implored them to settle their differences, and to get him out of his difficulty at once. He suggested that they had better fight it out then and there, and see who was master. He had brought down with him all needful weapons. And he pulled out his valise, and spread on the table a pair of navy revolvers, a pair of shotguns, a pair of duelling swords, and a couple of Bowie knives. He offered to serve as second for both parties, and to give the word when to begin. He also took out of his valise a pack of cards and a bottle of poison, telling them that if they wished to avoid carnage they might cut the cards to see which one should take the poison. Then he waited anxiously for their reply. For a little space there was silence. Then he became conscious of a tremulous shivering in one corner of the room, and he remembered that he had heard from that direction what sounded like a frightened sigh when he made the first suggestion of the duel. Something told him that this was the domiciliary ghost, and that it was badly scared. Then he was impressed by a certain movement in the opposite corner of the room, as though the titular ghost were drawing himself up with offended dignity. Eliphalet couldn't exactly see those things, because he never saw the ghosts, but he felt them. After a silence of nearly a minute a voice came from the corner where the family ghost stood—a voice strong and full, but trembling slightly with suppressed passion. And this voice told Eliphalet it was plain enough that he had not long been the head of the Duncans, and that he had never properly considered the characteristics of his race if now he supposed that one of his blood could draw his sword against a woman. Eliphalet said he had never suggested that the Duncan ghost should raise his hand against a woman, and all he wanted was that the Duncan ghost should fight the other ghost. And then the voice told Eliphalet that the other ghost was a woman."

"What?" said Dear Jones, sitting up suddenly. "You don't mean to tell me that the ghost which haunted the house was a woman?"

"Those were the very words Eliphalet Duncan used," said Uncle Larry; "but he did not need to wait for the answer. All at once he recalled the traditions about the domiciliary ghost, and he knew that what the titular ghost said was the fact. He had never thought of the sex of a spook, but there was no doubt whatever that the house ghost was a woman. No sooner was this firmly fixed in Eliphalet's mind than he saw his way out of the difficulty. The ghosts must be married!—for then there would be no more interference, no more quarrelling, no more manifestations and materializations, no more dark séances, with their raps and bells and tambourines and banjos. At first the ghosts would not hear of it. The voice in the corner declared that the Duncan wraith had never thought of matrimony. But Eliphalet argued with them, and pleaded and persuaded and coaxed, and dwelt on the advantages of matrimony. He had to confess, of course, that he did not know how to get a clergyman to marry them; but the voice from the corner gravely told him that there need be no difficulty in regard to that, as there was no lack of spiritual chaplains. Then, for the first time, the house ghost spoke, a low, clear, gentle voice, and with a quaint, old-fashioned New England accent, which contrasted sharply with the broad Scotch speech of the family ghost. She said that Eliphalet Duncan seemed to have forgotten that she was married. But this did not upset Eliphalet at all; he remembered the whole case clearly, and he told her she was not a married ghost, but a widow, since her husband had been hanged for murdering her. Then the Duncan ghost drew attention to the great disparity in their ages, saying that he was nearly four hundred and fifty years old, while she was barely two hundred. But Eliphalet had not talked to juries for nothing; he just buckled to, and coaxed those ghosts into matrimony. Afterwards he came to the conclusion that they were willing to be coaxed, but at the time he thought he had pretty hard work to convince them of the advantages of the plan."

"Did he succeed?" asked Baby Van Rensselaer, with a woman's interest in matrimony.

"He did," said Uncle Larry. "He talked the wraith of the Duncans and the spectre of the little old house at Salem into a matrimonial engagement. And from the time they were engaged he had no more trouble with them. They were rival ghosts no longer. They were married by their spiritual chaplain the very same day that Eliphalet Duncan met Kitty Sutton in front of the railing of Grace Church. The ghostly bride and bridegroom went away at once on their bridal tour, and Lord and Lady Duncan went down to the little old house at Salem to pass their honeymoon."

Uncle Larry stopped. His tiny cigar was out again. The tale of the rival ghosts was told. A solemn silence fell on the little party on the deck of the ocean steamer, broken harshly by the hoarse roar of the fog-horn.

The Water Ghost of Harrowby Hall

John Kendrick Bangs

The trouble with Harrowby Hall was that it was haunted, and, what was worse, the ghost did not content itself with merely appearing at the bedside of the afflicted person who saw it, but persisted in remaining there for one mortal hour before it would disappear.

It never appeared except on Christmas Eve, and then as the clock was striking twelve, in which respect alone was it lacking in that originality which in these days is a *sine qua non* of success in spectral life. The owners of Harrowby Hall had done their utmost to rid themselves of the damp and dewy lady who rose up out of the best bedroom floor at midnight, but without avail. They had tried stopping the clock, so that the ghost would not know when it was midnight; but she made her appearance just the same, with that fearful miasmatic personality of hers, and there she would stand until everything about her was thoroughly saturated.

Then the owners of Harrowby Hall caulked up every crack in the floor with the very best quality of hemp, and over this were placed layers of tar and canvas; the walls were made waterproof, and the doors and windows likewise, the proprietors having conceived the notion that the unexorcised lady would find it difficult to leak into the room after these precautions had been taken; but even this did not suffice. The following Christmas Eve she appeared as promptly as before, and frightened the occupant of the room quite out of his senses by sitting down alongside of him and gazing with her cavernous blue eyes into his; and he noticed, too, that in her long, aqueously bony fingers bits of dripping seaweed were entwined, the ends hanging down, and these ends she drew across his forehead until he became like one insane. And then he swooned away, and was found unconscious in his bed the next morning by his host, simply saturated with sea-water and fright, from

94

the combined effects of which he never recovered, dying four years later of pneumonia and nervous prostration at the age of seventy-eight.

The next year the master of Harrowby Hall decided not to have the best spare bedroom opened at all, thinking that perhaps the ghost's thirst for making herself disagreeable would be satisfied by haunting the furniture, but the plan was as unavailing as the many that had preceded it.

The ghost appeared as usual in the room—that is, it was supposed she did, for the hangings were dripping wet the next morning, and in the parlour below the haunted room a great damp spot appeared on the ceiling. Finding no one there, she immediately set out to learn the reason why, and she chose none other to haunt than the owner of the Harrowby himself. She found him in his own cosy room drinking whiskey—whiskey undiluted—and felicitating himself upon having foiled her ghost-ship, when all of a sudden the curl went out of his hair, his whiskey bottle filled and overflowed, and he was himself in a condition similar to that of a man who has fallen into a water-butt. When he recovered from the shock, which was a painful one, he saw before him the lady of the cavernous eyes and seaweed fingers. The sight was so unexpected and so terrifying that he fainted, but immediately came to, because of the vast amount of water in his hair, which, trickling down over his face, restored his consciousness.

Now it so happened that the master of Harrowby was a brave man, and while he was not particularly fond of interviewing ghosts, especially such quenching ghosts as the one before him, he was not to be daunted by an apparition. He had paid the lady the compliment of fainting from the effects of his first surprise, and now that he had come to he intended to find out a few things he felt he had a right to know. He would have liked to put on a dry suit of clothes first, but the apparition declined to leave him for an instant until her hour was up, and he was forced to deny himself that pleasure. Every time he would move she would follow him, with the result that everything she came in contact with got a ducking. In an effort to warm himself up he approached the fire, an unfortunate move as it turned out, because it brought the ghost directly over the fire, which immediately was extinguished. The whiskey became utterly valueless as a comforter to his chilled system, because it was by this time diluted to a proportion of ninety per cent of water. The only thing he could do to ward off the evil effects of his encounter he did, and that was to swallow ten two-grain quinine pills, which he managed to put into his mouth before the ghost had time to interfere. Having done this, he turned with some asperity to the ghost, and said:

"Far be it from me to be impolite to a woman, madam, but I'm hanged if it wouldn't please me better if you'd stop these infernal visits of yours to this house. Go sit out on the lake, if you like that sort of thing; soak the water-butt, if you wish; but do not, I implore you, come into a gentleman's house and saturate him and his possessions in this way. It is damned disagreeable."

"Henry Hartwick Oglethorpe," said the ghost, in a gurgling voice, "you don't know what you are talking about."

"Madam," returned the unhappy householder, "I wish that remark were strictly truthful. I was talking about you. It would be shillings and pence—nay, pounds, in my pocket, madam, if I did not know you."

"That is a bit of specious nonsense," returned the ghost, throwing a quart of indignation into the face of the master of Harrowby. "It may rank high as repartee, but as a comment upon my statement that you do not know what you are talking about, it savours of irrelevant impertinence. You do not know that I am compelled to haunt this place year after year by inexorable fate. It is no pleasure to me to enter this house, and ruin and mildew everything I touch. I never aspired to be a shower-bath, but it is my doom. Do you know who I am?"

"No, I don't," returned the master of Harrowby. "I should say you were the Lady of the Lake, or Little Sallie Waters."

"You are a witty man for your years," said the ghost.

"Well, my humour is drier than yours ever will be," returned the master.

"No doubt. I'm never dry. I am the Water Ghost of Harrowby Hall, and dryness is a quality entirely beyond my wildest hope. I have been the incumbent of this highly unpleasant office for two hundred years to-night."

"How the deuce did you ever come to get elected?" asked the master.

"Through a suicide," replied the spectre. "I am the ghost of that fair maiden whose picture hangs over the mantelpiece in the drawing-room. I should have been your great-great-great-great-great-aunt if I had lived, Henry Hartwick Oglethorpe, for I was the own sister of your great-great-great-great-grandfather."

"But what induced you to get this house into such a predicament?"

"I was not to blame, sir," returned the lady. "It was my father's fault. He it was who built Harrowby Hall, and the haunted chamber was to have been mine. My father had it furnished in pink and yellow, knowing well that blue and gray formed the only combination of colour I could tolerate. He did it merely to spite me, and, with what I deem a proper spirit, I declined to live in the room; whereupon my father said I could live there or on the lawn, he didn't care which. That night I ran from the house and jumped over the cliff into the sea."

"That was rash," said the master of Harrowby.

"So I've heard," returned the ghost. "If I had known what the consequences were to be I should not have jumped; but I really never realized what I was doing until after I was drowned. I had been drowned a week when a sea-nymph came to me and informed me that I was to be one of her followers forever afterwards, adding that it should be my doom to haunt Harrowby Hall for one hour every Christmas Eve throughout the rest of eternity. I was to haunt that room on such Christmas Eves as I found it inhabited; and if it should turn out not to be inhabited, I was and am to spend the allotted hour with the head of the house."

"I'll sell the place."

"That you cannot do, for it is also required of me that I shall appear as the deeds are to be delivered to any purchaser, and divulge to him the awful secret of the house."

"Do you mean to tell me that on every Christmas Eve that I don't happen to have somebody in that guest-chamber, you are going to haunt me wherever I may be, ruining my whiskey, taking all the curl out of my hair, extinguishing my fire, and soaking me through to the skin?" demanded the master.

"You have stated the case, Oglethorpe. And what is more," said the water ghost, "it doesn't make the slightest difference where you are, if I find that room empty, wherever you may be I shall douse you with my spectral pres—"

Here the clock struck one, and immediately the apparition faded away. It was perhaps more of a trickle than a fade, but as a disappearance it was complete.

"By St. George and his Dragon!" ejaculated the master of Harrowby, wringing his hands. "It is guineas to hot-cross buns that next Christmas there's an occupant of the spare room, or I spend the night in a bathtub."

But the master of Harrowby would have lost his wager had there been anyone there to take him up, for when Christmas Eve came again he was in his grave, never having recovered from the cold contracted that awful night. Harrowby Hall was closed, and the heir to the estate was in London, where to him in his chambers came the same experience that his father had gone through, saving only that, being younger and stronger, he survived the shock. Everything in his rooms was ruined—his clocks were rusted in the works; a fine collection of water-colour drawings was entirely obliterated by the onslaught of the water ghost; and what was worse, the apartments below his were drenched with the water soaking through the floors, a damage for which he was compelled to pay, and which resulted in his being requested by his landlady to vacate the premises immediately.

The story of the visitation inflicted upon his family had gone abroad, and no one could be got to invite him out to any function save afternoon teas and receptions. Fathers of daughters declined to permit him to remain in their houses later than eight o'clock at night, not knowing but that some emergency might arise in the supernatural world which would require the unexpected appearance of the water ghost in this on nights other than Christmas Eve, and before the mystic hour when weary churchyards, ignoring the rules which are supposed to govern polite society, begin to yawn. Nor would the maids themselves have aught to do with him, fearing the destruction by the sudden incursion of aqueous femininity of the costumes which they held most dear.

So the heir of Harrowby Hall resolved, as his ancestors for several generations before him had resolved, that something must be done. His first thought was to make one of his servants occupy the haunted room at the crucial moment; but in this he failed, because the servants themselves knew the history of that room and rebelled. None of his friends would consent to sacrifice their personal comfort to his, nor was there to be found in all England a man so poor as to be willing to occupy the doomed chamber on Christmas Eve for pay.

Then the thought came to the heir to have the fireplace in the room enlarged, so that he might evaporate the ghost at its first appearance, and he was felicitating himself upon the ingenuity of his plan, when he remembered what his father had told him—how that no fire could withstand the lady's extremely contagious dampness. And then he bethought him of steam-pipes. These, he remembered, could lie hundreds of feet deep in water, and still retain sufficient heat to drive the water away in vapour; and as a result of this thought the haunted room was heated by steam to a withering degree, and the heir for six months attended daily the Turkish baths, so that when Christmas Eve came he could himself withstand the awful temperature of the room.

The scheme was only partially successful. The water ghost appeared at the specified time, and found the heir of Harrowby prepared; but hot as the room was, it shortened her visit by no more than five minutes in the hour, during which time the nervous system of the young master was well-nigh shattered, and the room itself was cracked and warped to an extent which required the outlay of a large sum of money to remedy. And worse than this, as the last drop of the water ghost was slowly sizzling itself out on the floor, she whispered to her would-be conqueror that his scheme would avail him nothing, because there was still water in great plenty where she came from, and that next year would find her rehabilitated and as exasperatingly saturating as ever.

It was then that the natural action of the mind, in going from one extreme to the other, suggested to the ingenious heir of Harrowby the means by which the water ghost was ultimately conquered, and happiness once more came within the grasp of the house of Oglethorpe.

The heir provided himself with a warm suit of fur under-clothing. Donning this with the furry side in, he placed over it a rubber garment, tight-fitting, which he wore just as a woman wears a jersey. On top of this he placed another set of under-clothing, this suit made of wool, and over this was a second rubber garment like the first. Upon his head he placed a light and comfortable diving helmet, and so clad, on the following Christmas Eve he awaited the coming of his tormentor.

It was a bitterly cold night that brought to a close this twenty-fourth day of December. The air outside was still, but the temperature was below zero. Within all was quiet, the servants of Harrowby Hall awaiting with beating hearts the outcome of their master's campaign against his supernatural visitor.

The master himself was lying on the bed in the haunted room, clad as has already been indicated, and then—

The clock clanged out the hour of twelve.

There was a sudden banging of doors, a blast of cold air swept through the halls, the door leading into the haunted chamber flew open, a splash was heard, and the water ghost was seen standing at the side of the heir of Harrowby, from whose outer dress there streamed rivulets of water, but whose own person deep down under the various garments he wore was as dry and as warm as he could have wished.

"Ha!" said the young master of Harrowby. "I'm glad to see you."

"You are the most original man I've met, if that is true," returned the ghost. "May I ask where did you get that hat?"

"Certainly, madam," returned the master, courteously. "It is a little portable observatory I had made for just such emergencies as this. But, tell me, is it true that you are doomed to follow me about for one mortal hour—to stand where I stand, to sit where I sit?"

"That is my delectable fate," returned the lady.

"We'll go out on the lake," said the master, starting up.

"You can't get rid of me that way," returned the ghost. "The water won't swallow me up; in fact, it will just add to my present bulk."

"Nevertheless," said the master, firmly, "we will go out on the lake."

"But, my dear sir," returned the ghost, with a pale reluctance, "it is fearfully cold out there. You will be frozen hard before you've been out ten minutes."

"Oh no, I'll not," replied the master. "I am very warmly dressed. Come!" This last in a tone of command that made the ghost ripple.

And they started.

They had not gone far before the water ghost showed signs of distress.

"You walk too slowly," she said. "I am nearly frozen. My knees are so stiff now I can hardly move. I beseech you to accelerate your step."

"I should like to oblige a lady," returned the master, courteously, "but my clothes are rather heavy, and a hundred yards an hour is about my speed. Indeed, I think we would better sit down here on this snowdrift, and talk matters over."

"Do not! Do not do so, I beg!" cried the ghost. "Let me move on. I feel myself growing rigid as it is. If we stop here, I shall be frozen stiff."

"That, madam," said the master slowly, and seating himself on an ice-cake—"that is why I have brought you here. We have been on this spot just ten minutes; we have fifty more. Take your time about it, madam, but freeze, that is all I ask of you."

"I cannot move my right leg now," cried the ghost, in despair, "and my overskirt is a solid sheet of ice. Oh, good, kind Mr. Oglethorpe, light a fire, and let me go free from these icy fetters."

"Never, madam. It cannot be. I have you at last."

"Alas!" cried the ghost, a tear trickling down her frozen cheek. "Help me, I beg. I congeal!"

"Congeal, madam, congeal!" returned Oglethorpe, coldly. "You have drenched me and mine for two hundred and three years, madam. To-night you have had your last drench."

"Ah, but I shall thaw out again, and then you'll see. Instead of the comfortably tepid, genial ghost I have been in my past, sir, I shall be iced-water," cried the lady, threateningly.

"No, you won't, either," returned Oglethorpe; "for when you are frozen quite stiff, I shall send you to a cold-storage warehouse, and there shall you remain an icy work of art forever more."

"But warehouses burn."

"So they do, but this warehouse cannot burn. It is made of asbestos and surrounding it are fireproof walls, and within those walls the temperature is now and shall forever be 416 degrees below the zero point; low enough to make an icicle of any flame in this world—or the next," the master added, with an ill-suppressed chuckle.

"For the last time let me beseech you. I would go on my knees to you, Oglethorpe, were they not already frozen. I beg of you do not doo—"

Here even the words froze on the water-ghost's lips and the clock struck one. There was a momentary tremor throughout the ice-bound form, and the moon, coming out from behind a cloud, shone down on the rigid figure of a beautiful woman sculptured in clear, transparent ice. There stood the ghost of Harrowby Hall, conquered by the cold, a prisoner for all time.

The heir of Harrowby had won at last, and to-day in a large storage house in London stands the frigid form of one who will never again flood the house of Oglethorpe with woe and sea-water.

As for the heir of Harrowby, his success in coping with a ghost has made him famous, a fame that still lingers about him, although his victory took place some twenty years ago; and so far from being unpopular with the fair sex, as he was when we first knew him, he has not only been married twice, but is to lead a third bride to the altar before the year is out.

Back from That Bourne

Anonymous

Practical Working of Materialization in Maine
A Strange Story from Pocock Island—
A Materialized Spirit that Will not Go back
The First Glimpse of What May yet Cause Very Extensive
Trouble in this World.

The Sun, Saturday, December 19, 1874

We are permitted to make extracts from a private letter which bears the signature of a gentleman well known in business circles, and whose veracity we have never heard called in question. His statements are startling and well-nigh incredible, but if true, they are susceptible of easy verification. Yet the thoughtful mind will hesitate about accepting them without the fullest proof, for they spring upon the world a social problem of stupendous importance. The dangers apprehended by Mr. Malthus and his followers become remote and commonplace by the side of this new and terrible issue.

The letter is dated at Pocock Island, a small township in Washington County, Maine, about seventeen miles from the mainland and nearly midway between Mt. Desert and the Grand Menan. The last state census accords to Pocock Island a population of 311, mostly engaged in the porgy fisheries. At the Presidential election of 1872 the island gave Grant a majority of three. These two facts are all that we are able to learn of the locality from sources outside of the letter already referred to.

The letter, omitting certain passages which refer solely to private matters, reads as follows:

But enough of the disagreeable business that brought me here to this bleak island in the month of November. I have a singular story to tell you. After our experience together at Chittenden I know you will not reject statements because they are startling.

My friend, there is upon Pocock Island a materialized spirit which (or who) refuses to be dematerialized. At this moment and within a quarter of a mile from me as I write, a man who died and was buried four years ago, and who has exploited the mysteries beyond the grave, walks, talks, and holds interviews with the inhabitants of the island, and is, to all appearances, determined to remain permanently upon this side of the river. I will relate the circumstances as briefly as I can.

JOHN NEWBEGIN

In April, 1870, John Newbegin died and was buried in the little cemetery on the landward side of the island. Newbegin was a man of about forty-eight, without family or near connections, and eccentric to a degree that sometimes inspired questions as to his sanity. What money he had earned by many seasons' fishing upon the banks was invested in quarters of two small mackerel schooners, the remainder of which belonged to John Hodgeson, the richest man on Pocock, who was estimated by good authorities to be worth thirteen or fourteen thousand dollars.

Newbegin was not without a certain kind of culture. He had read a good deal of the odds and ends of literature and, as a simple-minded islander expressed it in my hearing, knew more bookfuls than anybody on the island. He was naturally an intelligent man; and he might have attained influence in the community had it not been for his utter aimlessness of character, his indifference to fortune, and his consuming thirst for rum.

Many yachtsmen who have had occasion to stop at Pocock for water or for harbour shelter during eastern cruises, will remember a long, listless figure, astonishingly attired in blue army pants, rubber boots, loose toga made of some bright chintz material, and very bad hat, staggering through the little settlement, followed by a rabble of jeering brats, and pausing to strike uncertain blows at those within reach of the dead sculpin which he usually carried round by the tail. This was John Newbegin.

HIS SUDDEN DEATH

As I have already remarked, he died four years ago last April. The *Mary Emmeline*, one of the little schooners in which he owned, had returned from the eastward, and had smuggled, or 'run in' a quantity of St. John brandy. Newbegin had a solitary and protracted debauch. He was missed from his accustomed walks for several days, and when the islanders broke into the hovel where he lived, close down to the seaweed and almost within reach of the incoming tide, they found him dead on the floor, with an emptied demijohn hard by his head.

After the primitive custom of the island, they interred John Newbegin's remains without coroner's inquest, burial certificate, or funeral services, and in the excitement of a large catch of porgies that summer, soon forgot him and his friendless life. His interest in the *Mary Emmeline* and the *Prettyboat* recurred to John Hodgeson; and as nobody came forward to demand an administration of the estate, it was never administered. The forms of law are but loosely followed in some of these marginal localities.

HIS REAPPEARANCE AT POCOCK

Well, my dear —, four years and four months had brought their quota of varying seasons to Pocock Island when John Newbegin reappeared under the following circumstances:

In the latter part of last August, as you may remember, there was a heavy gale all along our Atlantic coast. During this storm the squadron of the Naugatuck Yacht Club, which was returning from a summer cruise as far as Campobello, was forced to take shelter in the harbour to the leeward of Pocock Island. The gentlemen of the club spent three days at the little settlement ashore. Among the party was Mr. R— E—, by which name you will recognize a medium of celebrity, and one who has been particularly successful in materializations. At the desire of his companions, and to relieve the tedium of their detention, Mr. E— improvised a cabinet in the little schoolhouse at Pocock, and gave a séance, to the delight of his fellow yachtsmen and the utter bewilderment of such natives as were permitted to witness the manifestations.

The conditions appeared unusually favourable to spirit appearances and the séance was upon the whole perhaps the most remarkable that Mr. E— ever held. It was all the more remarkable because the surroundings were such that the most prejudiced sceptic could discover no possibility of trickery.

The first form to issue from the wood closet which constituted the cabinet, when Mr. E— had been tied therein by a committee of old sailors from the yachts, was that of an Indian chief who announced himself as Hock-a-mock, and who retired after dancing a 'Harvest Moon' *pas seul*, and declaring himself in very emphatic terms, as opposed to the present Indian policy of the Administration. Hock-a-mock was succeeded by the aunt of one of the yachtsmen, who identified herself beyond question by allusion to family matters and by displaying the scar of a burn upon her left arm, received while making tomato catsup upon earth. Then came successively a child whom none present recognized, a French Canadian who could not talk English, and a portly gentleman who introduced himself as William King, first Governor of Maine. These in turn re-entered the cabinet and were seen no more.

It was some time before another spirit manifested itself, and Mr. E— gave directions that the lights be turned down still further. Then the door of the wood closet was slowly opened and a singular figure in rubber boots and a species of Dolly Varden garment emerged, bringing a dead fish in his right hand.

His Determination to Remain

The city men who were present, I am told, thought that the medium was masquerading in grotesque habiliments for the more complete astonishment of the islanders, but these latter rose from their seats and exclaimed with one consent: 'It is John Newbegin!' And then, in not unnatural terror of the apparition they turned and fled from the schoolroom, uttering dismal cries.

John Newbegin came calmly forward and turned up the solitary kerosene lamp that shed uncertain light over the proceedings. He then sat down in the teacher's chair, folded his arms, and looked complacently about him.

'You might as well untie the medium,' he finally remarked. 'I propose to remain in the materialized condition.'

And he did remain. When the party left the schoolhouse among them walked John Newbegin, as truly a being of flesh and blood as any man of them. From that day to this, he has been a living inhabitant of Pocock Island, eating, drinking, (water only) and sleeping after the manner of men. The yachtsmen who made sail for Bar Harbor the very next morning, probably believe that he was a fraud hired for the occasion by Mr. E—. But the people of Pocock, who laid him out, dug his grave, and put him into it four years ago, know that John Newbegin has come back to them from a land they know not of.

A Singular Member of Society

The idea, of having a ghost—somewhat more condensed it is true than the traditional ghost—as a member was not at first over pleasing to the 311 inhabitants of Pocock Island. To this day, they are a little sensitive upon the subject, feeling evidently that if the matter got abroad, it might injure the sale of the really excellent porgy oil which is the product of their sole manufacturing interest. This reluctance to advertise the skeleton in their closet, superadded to the slowness of these obtuse, fishy, matter-of-fact people to recognize the transcendent importance of the case, must be accepted as explanation of the fact that John Newbegin's spirit has been on earth between three and four months, and yet the singular circumstance is not known to the whole country.

But the Pocockians have at last come to see that a spirit is not necessarily a malevolent spirit, and accepting his presence as a fact in their stolid, unreasoning way, they are quite neighbourly and sociable with Mr. Newbegin.

I know that your first question will be: 'Is there sufficient proof of his ever having been dead?' To this I answer unhesitatingly, 'Yes.' He was too well-known a character and too many people saw the corpse to admit of any mistake on this point. I may add here that it was at one time proposed to disinter the original remains, but that project was abandoned in deference to the wishes of Mr. Newbegin, who feels a natural delicacy about having his first set of bones disturbed from motives of mere curiosity.

An Interview With A Dead Man

You will readily believe that I took occasion to see and converse with John Newbegin. I found him affable and even communicative. He is perfectly aware of his doubtful status as a being, but is in hopes that at some future time there may be legislation that shall correctly define his position and the position of any spirit who may follow him into the material world. The only point upon which he is reticent is his experience during the four years that elapsed between his death and his reappearance at Pocock. It is to be presumed that the memory is not a pleasant one: at least he never speaks of this period. He candidly admits, however, that he is glad to get back to earth and that he embraced the very first opportunity to be materialized.

Mr. Newbegin says that he is consumed with remorse for the wasted years of his previous existence. Indeed, his conduct during the past three months would show that this regret is genuine. He has discarded his eccentric costume, and dresses like a reasonable spirit. He has not touched liquor since his reappearance. He has embarked in the porgy oil business, and his operations already rival that of Hodgeson, his old partner in the *Mary Emmeline* and the *Prettyboat*. By the way, Newbegin threatens to sue Hodgeson for his quarter in each of these vessels, and this interesting case therefore bids fair to be thoroughly investigated in the courts.

As a business man, he is generally esteemed on the Island, although there is a noticeable reluctance to discount his paper at long dates. In short, Mr. John Newbegin is a most respectable citizen (if a dead man can be a citizen) and has announced his intention of running for the next Legislature!

In Conclusion

And now, my dear ——, I have told you the substance of all I know respecting this strange, strange case. Yet, after all, why so strange? We accepted materialization at Chittenden. Is this any more than the logical issue of that admission? If the spirit may return to earth, clothed in flesh and blood and all the physical attributes of humanity, why may it not remain on earth as long as it sees fit?

Thinking of it from whatever standpoint, I cannot but regard John Newbegin as the pioneer of a possibly large immigration from the spirit world. The bars once down, a whole flock will come trooping back to earth. Death will lose its significance altogether. And when I think of the disturbance which will result in our social relations, of the overthrow of all accepted institutions, and of the nullification of all principles of political economy, law, and religion, I am lost in perplexity and apprehension.

The Ghost-Ship

Richard Middleton

Fairfield is a little village lying near the Portsmouth Road, about halfway between London and the sea. Strangers, who now and then find it by accident, call it a pretty, old-fashioned place; we who live in it and call it home don't find anything very pretty about it, but we should be sorry to live anywhere else. Our minds have taken the shape of the inn and the church and the green, I suppose. At all events, we never feel comfortable out of Fairfield.

Of course the cockneys, with their vasty houses and noise-ridden streets, can call us rustics if they choose; but for all that, Fairfield is a better place to live in than London. Doctor says that when he goes to London his mind is bruised with the weight of the houses, and he was a cockney born. He had to live there himself when he was a little chap, but he knows better now. You gentlemen may laugh—perhaps some of you come from London-way, but it seems to me that a witness like that is worth a gallon of arguments.

Dull? Well, you might find it dull, but I assure you that I've listened to all the London yarns you have spun to-night, and they're absolutely nothing to the things that happen at Fairfield. It's because of our way of thinking, and minding our own business. If one of your Londoners was set down on the green of a Saturday night when the ghosts of the lads who died in the war keep tryst with the lasses who lie in the churchyard, he couldn't help being curious and interfering, and then the ghosts would go somewhere where it was quieter. But we just let them come and go and don't make any fuss, and in consequence Fairfield is the ghostiest place in all England. Why, I've seen a headless man sitting on the edge of the well in broad daylight, and the children playing about his feet as if he were their father. Take my word for it, spirits know when they are well off as much as human beings.

Still, I must admit that the thing I'm going to tell you about was queer even for our part of the world, where three packs of ghost-hounds hunt regularly during the season, and blacksmith's great-grandfather is busy all night shoeing the dead gentlemen's horses. Now that's a thing that wouldn't happen in London, because of their interfering ways; but blacksmith he lies up aloft and sleeps as quiet as a lamb. Once when he had a bad head he shouted down to them not to make so much noise, and in the morning he found an old guinea left on the anvil as an apology. He wears it on his watch-chain now. But I must get on with my story; if I start telling you about the queer happenings at Fairfield, I'll never stop.

It all came of the great storm in the spring of '97, the year that we had two great storms. This was the first one, and I remember it well, because I found in the morning that it had lifted the thatch of my pigsty into the widow's garden as clean as a boy's kite. When I looked over the hedge, widow—Tom Lamport's widow that was—was prodding for her nasturtiums with a daisy grubber. After I had watched her for a little I went down to the Fox and Grapes to tell landlord what she had said to me. Landlord he laughed, being a married man and at ease with the sex. "Come to that," he said, "the tempest has blowed something into my field. A kind of a ship I think it would be."

I was surprised at that until he explained that it was only a ghost-ship, and would do no hurt to the turnips. We argued that it had been blown up from the sea at Portsmouth, and then we talked of something else. There were two slates down at the parsonage and a big tree in Lumley's meadow. It was a rare storm.

I reckon the wind had blown our ghosts all over England. They were coming back for days afterward with foundered horses, and as footsore as possible, and they were so glad to get back to Fairfield that some of them walked up the street crying like little children. Squire said that his great-grandfather's great-grandfather hadn't looked so dead-beat since the battle of Naseby, and he's an educated man.

What with one thing and another, I should think it was a week before we got straight again, and then one afternoon I met the land-lord on the green, and he had a worried face. "I wish you'd come and have a look at that ship in my field," he said to me. "It seems to me it's leaning real hard on the turnips. I can't bear thinking what the missus will say when she sees it."

I walked down the lane with him, and, sure enough, there was a ship in the middle of his field, but such a ship as no man had seen on the water for three hundred years, let alone in the middle of a turnip field. It was all painted black, and covered with carvings, and there was a great bay-window in the stern, for all the world like the squire's drawing-room. There was a crowd of little black cannon on deck and looking out of her port-holes, and she was anchored at each end to the hard ground. I have seen the wonders of the world on picture-postcards, but I have never seen anything to equal that.

"She seems very solid for a ghost-ship," I said, seeing that landlord was bothered.

"I should say it's a betwixt and between," he answered, puzzling it over; "but it's going to spoil a matter of fifty turnips, and missus she'll want it moved." We went up to her and touched the side, and it was as hard as a real ship. "Now, there's folks in England would call that very curious," he said.

Now, I don't know much about ships, but I should think that that ghost-ship weighed a solid two hundred tons, and it seemed to me that she had come to stay; so that I felt sorry for landlord, who was a married man. "All the horses in Fairfield won't move her out of my turnips," he said, frowning at her.

Just then we heard a noise on her deck, and we looked up and saw that a man had come out of her front cabin and was looking down at us very peaceably. He was dressed in a black uniform set off with rusty gold lace, and he had a great cutlass by his side in a brass sheath. "I'm Captain Bartholomew Roberts," he said in a gentleman's voice, "put in for recruits. I seem to have brought her rather far up the harbour."

"Harbour!" cried landlord. "Why, you're fifty miles from the sea!"

Captain Roberts didn't turn a hair. "So much as that, is it?" he said coolly. "Well, it's of no consequence."

Landlord was a bit upset at this. "I don't want to be unneighbour-ly," he said, "but I wish you hadn't brought your ship into my field. You see, my wife sets great store on these turnips."

The captain took a pinch of snuff out of a fine gold box that he pulled out of his pocket, and dusted his fingers with a silk handker-chief in a very genteel fashion. "I'm only here for a few months," he said, "but if a testimony of my esteem would pacify your good lady, I should be content," and with the words he loosed a great gold brooch from the neck of his coat and tossed it down to landlord.

Landlord blushed as red as a strawberry. "I'm not denying she's fond of jewellery," he said; "but it's too much for half a sackful of tur-nips." Indeed it was a handsome brooch.

The captain laughed. "Tut, man!" he said, "it's a forced sale, and you deserve a good price. Say no more about it," and nodding good day to us, he turned on his heel and went into the cabin. Landlord walked back up the lane like a man with a weight off his mind. "That tempest has blowed me a bit of luck," he said; "the missus will be main pleased with that brooch. It's better than blacksmith's guinea any day."

'97 was Jubilee year—the year of the second Jubilee, you remember, and we had great doings at Fairfield, so that we hadn't much time to bother about the ghost-ship, though, anyhow, it isn't our way to meddle in things that don't concern us. Landlord he saw his tenant once or twice when he was hoeing his turnips, and passed the time of day and landlord's wife wore her new brooch to church every Sunday. But we didn't mix much with the ghosts at any time, all except an idiot lad there was in the village, and he didn't know the difference between a man and a ghost, poor innocent! On Jubilee day, however, somebody told Captain Roberts why the church bells were ringing, and he hoisted a flag and fired off his guns like a loyal Englishman. 'T is true the guns were shotted, and one of the round shot knocked a hole in Farmer Johnstone's barn, but nobody thought much of that in such a season of rejoicing.

It wasn't till our celebrations were over that we noticed that anything was wrong in Fairfield. 'T was shoemaker who told me first about it one morning at the Fox and Grapes. "You know my great-great-uncle?" he said to me.

"You mean Joshua, the quiet lad?" I answered, knowing him well.

"Quiet!" said shoemaker, indignantly. "Quiet you call him, coming home at three o'clock every morning as drunk as a magistrate and waking up the whole house with his noise!"

"Why, it can't be Joshua," I said, for I knew him for one of the most respectable young ghosts in the village.

"Joshua it is," said shoemaker; "and one of these nights he'll find himself out in the street if he isn't careful."

This kind of talk shocked me, I can tell you, for I don't like to hear a man abusing his own family, and I could hardly believe that a steady youngster like Joshua had taken to drink. But just then in came butcher Aylwin in such a temper that he could hardly drink his beer. "The young puppy! The young puppy!" he kept on saying, and it was some time before shoemaker and I found out that he was talking about his ancestor that fell at Senlac.

"Drink?" said shoemaker, hopefully, for we all like company in our misfortunes, and butcher nodded grimly. "The young noodle!" he said, emptying his tankard.

Well, after that I kept my ears open, and it was the same story all

111

over the village. There was hardly a young man among all the ghosts of Fairfield who didn't roll home in the small hours of the morning the worse for liquor. I used to wake up in the night and hear them stumble past my house, singing outrageous songs. The worst of it was that we couldn't keep the scandal to ourselves, and the folk at Greenhill began to talk of "sodden Fairfield" and taught their children to sing a song about us:

Sodden Fairfield, sodden Fairfield, Has no use for bread and butter, Rum for breakfast, rum for dinner, Rum for tea, and rum for supper!

We are easy-going in our village, but we didn't like that.

Of course we soon found out where the young fellows went to get the drink, and landlord was terribly cut up that his tenant should have turned out so badly; but his wife wouldn't hear of parting with the brooch, so he couldn't give the captain notice to quit. But as time went on, things grew from bad to worse, and at all hours of the day you would see those young reprobates sleeping it off on the village green. Nearly every afternoon a ghost-wagon used to jolt down to the ship with a lading of rum, and though the older ghosts seemed inclined to give the captain's hospitality the go-by, the youngsters were neither to hold nor to bind.

So one afternoon when I was taking my nap, I heard a knock at the door, and there was parson, looking very serious, like a man with a job before him that he didn't altogether relish.

"I'm going down to talk to the captain about all this drunkenness in the village, and I want you to come with me," he said straight out.

I can't say that I fancied the visit much myself, and I tried to hint to parson that as, after all, they were only a lot of ghosts, it didn't much matter.

"Dead or alive, I'm responsible for their good conduct," he said, "and I'm going to do my duty and put a stop to this continued disorder. And you are coming with me, John Simmons."

So I went, parson being a persuasive kind of man.

We went down to the ship, and as we approached her, I could see the captain tasting the air on deck. When he saw parson, he took off his hat very politely, and I can tell you that I was relieved to find that he had a proper respect for the cloth. Parson acknowledged his salute, and spoke out stoutly enough.

"Sir, I should be glad to have a word with you."

"Come on board, sir; come on board," said the captain, and I could tell by his voice that he knew why we were there.

Parson and I climbed up an uneasy kind of ladder, and the captain took us into the great cabin at the back of the ship, where the bay-window was. It was the most wonderful place you ever saw in your life, all full of gold and silver plate, swords with jewelled scabbards, carved oak chairs, and great chests that looked as though they were bursting with guineas. Even parson was surprised, and he did not shake his head very hard when the captain took down some silver cups and poured us out a drink of rum. I tasted mine, and I don't mind saying that it changed my view of things entirely. There was nothing betwixt and between about that rum, and I felt that it was ridiculous to blame the lads for drinking too much of stuff like that. It seemed to fill my veins with honey and fire.

Parson put the case squarely to the captain, but I didn't listen much to what he said. I was busy sipping my drink and looking through the window at the fishes swimming to and fro over landlord's turnips. Just then it seemed the most natural thing in the world that they should be there, though afterward, of course, I could see that that proved it was a ghost-ship.

But even then I thought it was queer when I saw a drowned sailor float by in the thin air, with his hair and beard all full of bubbles. It was the first time I had seen anything quite like that at Fairfield.

All the time I was regarding the wonders of the deep, parson was telling Captain Roberts how there was no peace or rest in the village owing to the curse of drunkenness, and what a bad example the youngsters were setting to the older ghosts. The captain listened very attentively, and put in a word only now and then about boys being boys and young men sowing their wild oats. But when parson had finished his speech, he filled up our silver cups and said to parson with a flourish:

"I should be sorry to cause trouble anywhere where I have been made welcome, and you will be glad to hear that I put to sea to-morrow night. And now you must drink me a prosperous voyage."

So we all stood up and drank the toast with honour, and that noble rum was like hot oil in my veins.

After that, captain showed us some of the curiosities he had brought back from foreign parts, and we were greatly amazed, though afterward I couldn't clearly remember what they were. And then I found myself walking across the turnips with parson, and I was telling him of the glories of the deep that I had seen through the window of the ship. He turned on me severely.

"If I were you, John Simmons," he said, "I should go straight home to bed." He has a way of putting things that wouldn't occur to an ordinary man, has parson, and I did as he told me.

Well, next day it came on to blow, and it blew harder and harder, till about eight o'clock at night I heard a noise and looked out into the garden. I dare say you won't believe me,—it seems a bit tall even to me,—but the wind had lifted the thatch of my pigsty into the widow's garden a second time. I thought I wouldn't wait to hear what widow had to say about it, so I went across the green to the Fox and Grapes, and the wind was so strong that I danced along on tiptoe like a girl at the fair. When I got to the inn, landlord had to help me shut the door. It seemed as though a dozen goats were pushing against it to come in out of the storm.

"It's a powerful tempest," he said, drawing the beer. "I hear there's a chimney down at Dickory End."

"It's a funny thing how these sailors know about the weather," I answered. "When captain said he was going to-night, I was thinking it would take a capful of wind to carry the ship back to sea; and now here's more than a capful."

"Ah, yes," said landlord; "it's to-night he goes true enough, and mind you, though he treated me handsome over the rent, I'm not sure it's a loss to the village. I don't hold with gentrice, who fetch their drink from London instead of helping local traders to get their living."

"But you haven't got any rum like his," I said, to draw him out.

His neck grew red above his collar, and I was afraid I'd gone too far; but after a while he got his breath with a grunt.

"John Simmons," he said, "if you've come down here this windy night to talk a lot of fool's talk, you've wasted a journey."

Well, of course then I had to smooth him down with praising his rum, and Heaven forgive me for swearing it was better than captain's. For the like of that rum no living lips have tasted save mine and parson's. But somehow or other I brought landlord round, and presently we must have a glass of his best to prove its quality.

"Beat that if you can," he cried, and we both raised our glasses to our mouths, only to stop halfway and look at each other in amaze. For the wind that had been howling outside like an outrageous dog had all of a sudden turned as melodious as the carol-boys of a Christmas eve.

"Surely that's not my Martha," whispered landlord, Martha being his great-aunt who lived in the loft overhead.

We went to the door, and the wind burst it open so that the handle was driven clean into the plaster of the wall, but we didn't think about that at the time; for over our heads, sailing very comfortably through the windy stars, was the ship that had passed the summer in landlord's field. Her port-holes and her bay-window were blazing with lights, and there was a noise of singing and fiddling on her decks. "He's gone!" shouted landlord above the storm, "and he's taken half the village with him." I could only nod in answer, not having lungs like bellows of leather.

In the morning we were able to measure the strength of the storm, and over and above my pigsty, there was damage enough wrought in the village to keep us busy. True it is that the children had to break down no branches for the firing that autumn, since the wind had strewn the woods with more than they could carry away. Many of our ghosts were scattered abroad, but this time very few came back, all the young men having sailed with captain; and not only ghosts, for a poor half-witted lad was missing, and we reckoned that he had stowed himself away or perhaps shipped as cabin-boy, not knowing any better.

What with the lamentations of the ghost girls and the grumblings of families who had lost ancestors, the village was upset for a while, and the funny thing was that it was the folk who had complained most of the carryings-on of the youngsters who made most noise now that they were gone. I hadn't any sympathy with shoemaker or butcher, who ran about saying how much they missed their lads, but it made me grieve to hear the poor bereaved girls calling their lovers by name on the village green at nightfall. It didn't seem fair to me that they should have lost their men a second time, after giving up life in order to join them, as like as not. Still, not even a spirit can be sorry forever, and after a few months we made up our mind that the folk who had sailed in the ship were never coming back; and we didn't talk about it any more.

And then one day, I dare say it would be a couple of years after, when the whole business was quite forgotten, who should come traipsing along the road from Portsmouth but the daft lad who had gone away with the ship without waiting till he was dead to become a ghost. You never saw such a boy as that in all your life. He had a great rusty cutlass hanging to a string at his waist, and he was tattooed all over in fine colours, so that even his face looked like a girl's sampler. He had a handkerchief in his hand full of foreign shells and old-fashioned pieces of small money, very curious, and he walked up to the well outside his mother's house and drew himself a drink as if he had been nowhere in particular.

The worst of it was that he had come back as soft-headed as he went, and try as we might, we couldn't get anything reasonable out of him. He talked a lot of gibberish about keelhauling and walking the plank and crimson murders—things which a decent sailor should know nothing about, so that it seemed to me that for all his manners captain had been more of a pirate than a gentleman mariner. But to draw sense out of that boy was as hard as picking cherries off a crabtree. One silly tale he had that he kept on drifting back to, and to hear him you would have thought that it was the only thing that happened to him in his life.

"We was at anchor," he would say, "off an island called the Basket of Flowers, and the sailors had caught a lot of parrots and we were teaching them to swear. Up and down the decks, up and down the decks, and the language they used was dreadful. Then we looked up and saw the masts of the Spanish ship outside the harbour. Outside the harbour they were, so we threw the parrots into the sea, and sailed out to fight. And all the parrots were drowned in the sea, and the language they used was dreadful."

That's the sort of boy he was—nothing but silly talk of parrots when we asked him about the fighting. And we never had a chance of teaching him better, for two days after he ran away again, and hasn't been seen since.

That's my story, and I assure you that things like that are happening at Fairfield all the time. The ship has never come back, but somehow, as people grow older, they seem to think that one of these windy nights she'll come sailing in over the hedges with all the lost ghosts on board. Well, when she comes, she'll be welcome. There's one ghost lass that has never grown tired of waiting for her lad to return. Every night you'll see her out on the green, straining her poor eyes with looking for the mast-lights among the stars. A faithful lass you'd call her, and I'm thinking you'd be right.

Landlord's field wasn't a penny the worse for the visit; but they do say that since then the turnips that have been grown in it have tasted of rum.

The Transplanted Ghost

Wallace Irwin

When Aunt Elizabeth asked me to spend Christmas with her at Seven Oaks she appended a peculiar request to her letter. "Like a good fellow," she wrote, "won't you drop off at Perkinsville, Ohio, on your way, and take a look at Gauntmoor Castle? They say it's a wonderful old pile; and its history is in many ways connected with that of our own family. As long as you're the last of the Geoffray Pierreponts, such things ought to interest you." Like her auburn namesake who bossed the Thames of yore, sweet, red-haired, romantic autocrat, Aunt Elizabeth! Her wishes were commands.

"What the deuce is Aunt Elizabeth up to now?" I asked Tim Cole, my law partner, whom I found in my rooms smoking my tobacco. "Why should I be inspecting Gauntmoor Castle—and what is a castle named Gauntmoor doing in Perkinsville, Ohio, anyway? Perkinsville sounds like the Middle West, and Gauntmoor sounds like the Middle Ages."

"Right in both analyses," said the pipe-poaching Tim. "Castle Gauntmoor *is* from the Middle Ages, and we all know about where in Ohio Perkinsville is. But is it possible that you, twenty-seven years old and a college graduate, haven't heard of Thaddeus Hobson, the Marvellous Millionaire?" I shook my head. "The papers have been full of Hobson in the past two or three years," said Tim. "It was in 1898, I think, that Fate jumped Thaddeus Hobson to the golden Olympus. He was first head salesman in the village hardware store, then he formulated so successful a scheme to clean up the Tin Plate Combine that he put away a fabulous number of millions in a year, and subsequently went to England. Finally he set his heart on Norman architecture. After a search he found the ancient Castle Gauntmoor still habitable and for sale. He thrilled the British comic papers by his offer to buy the castle and move it to America. Hobson saw the property, telegraphed to London, and closed the deal in two hours. And an army of labourers at once began taking the Gauntmoor to pieces, stone by stone.

"Transporting that relic to America involved a cost in labour and ingenuity comparable with nothing that has yet happened. Moving the Great Pyramid would be a lighter job, perhaps. Thousands of tons of scarred and medieval granite were carried to the railroads, freighted to the sea, and dragged across the Atlantic in whopping big lighters chartered for the job. And the next the newspapers knew, the monster was set up in Perkinsville, Ohio."

"But why did he do it?" I asked.

"Who knows?" said Tim. "Ingrowing sentiment—unlimited capital—wanted to do something for the Home Town, probably; wanted to beautify the village that gave him his start—and didn't know how to go at it. Well, so long!" he called out, as I seized my hat and streaked for the train.

****

It was dinner time when the train pulled in at Perkinsville. The town was as undistinguished as I expected. I was too hungry to care about castles at the moment, so I took the 'bus for the Commercial Hotel, an establishment that seemed to live up to its name, both in sentiment and in accommodation. The landlord, Mr. Spike, referred bitterly to the castle, which, he explained, was, by its dominating presence, "spoilin' the prosperous appearance of Perkinsville." Dinner over, he led me to a side porch.

"How does Perkinsville look with that—with that curio squattin' on top of it?" asked Mr. Spike sternly, as he pointed over the local livery stable, over Smith Brothers' Plough Works, over Odd Fellows' Hall, and up, up to the bleak hills beyond, where, poised like a stony coronet on a giant's brow, rose the great Norman towers and frowning buttresses of Gauntmoor Castle. I rubbed my eyes. No, it *couldn't* be real—it must be a wizard's work!

"What's old Hobson got out of it?" said Mr. Spike in my ear. "Nothin' but an old stone barn, where he can set all day nursin' a grouch and keepin' his daughter Anita—they do say he does—under lock and key for fear somebody's goin' to marry her for her money."

Mr. Spike looked up at the ramparts defiantly, even as the Saxon churl must have gazed in an earlier, far sadder land.

"It's romantic," I suggested.

"Yes, *darn* rheumatic," agreed Mr. Spike.

118

"Is it open for visitors?" I asked innocently.

"Hobson?" cackled Spike. "He'd no more welcome a stranger to that place than he'd welcome—a ghost. He's a hol-ee terror, Hobson!"

Mr. Spike turned away to referee a pool game down in the barroom.

The fires of a December sunset flared behind Gauntmoor and cast the grim shadows of Medievalism over Mediocrity, which lay below. Presently the light faded, and I grew tired of gazing. Since Hobson would permit no tourists to inspect his castle, why was I here on this foolish trip? Already I was planning to wire Aunt Elizabeth a sarcastic reference to being marooned at Christmas with a castle on my hands, when a voice at my shoulder said suddenly:

"Mr. Hobson sends his compliments, sir, and wants to know would Mr. Pierrepont come up to Gauntmoor for the night?"

A groom in a plum-coloured livery stood at my elbow. A light station wagon was waiting just outside. How the deuce did Hobson know my name? What did he want of me at Gauntmoor this time of night? Yet prospects of bed and breakfast away from the Commercial lured me strangely.

"Sure, Mr. Pierrepont will be delighted," I announced, leaping into the vehicle, and soon we were mounting upward, battling with the winds around the time-scarred walls. The wagon stopped at the great gate. A horn sounded from within, the gate swung open, a drawbridge fell with a hideous creaking of machinery, and we passed in, twenty or thirty feet above the snow-drifted moat. Beyond the portcullis a dim door swung open. Some sort of seneschal met us with a light and led us below the twilight arches, where beyond, I could catch glimpses of the baileys and courts and the donjon tower against the heavy ramparts.

The wind hooted through the high galleries as we passed; but the west wing, from its many windows and loopholes, blazed with cheerful yellow light. It looked nearly cosy. Into a tall, gaunt tower we plunged, down a winding staircase, and suddenly we came into a vast hall, stately with tapestries and innumerable monkish carvings—and all brightly lighted with electricity!

A little fat man sat smoking in a chair near the fire. When I entered he was in his shirt sleeves, reading a newspaper, but when a footman announced my name the little man, in a state of great nervousness, jumped to his feet and threw on a coat, fidgeting painfully with the armholes. As he came toward me, I noticed that he was perfectly bald. He looked dyspeptic and discontented, like a practical man trying vainly to adjust his busy habits to a lazy life. Obviously he didn't go with the rest of the furniture.

"Pleased to see you, Mr. Pierrepont," he said, looking me over carefully as if he thought of buying me. "Geoffray Pierrepont—tut, tut!—ain't it queer!"

"Queer!" I said rather peevishly. "What's queer about it?"

"Excuse me, did I say queer? I didn't mean to be impolite, sir—I was just thinking, that's all."

You could hear the demon Army of the Winds scaling the walls outside.

"Maybe you thought it kind of abrupt, Mr. Pierrepont, me asking you up here so unceremonious," he said. "My daughter Annie, she tells me I ought to live up to the looks of the place; but I've got my notions. To tell you the truth, I'm in an awful quandary about this Antique Castle business and when I heard you was at the hotel, I thought you might help me out some way. You see you—"

He led me to a chair and offered me a fat cigar.

"Young man," he said, "when you get your head above water and make good in the world—if you ever do—don't fool with curios, don't monkey with antiques. Keep away from castles. They're like everything else sold by curio dealers—all humbug. Look nice, yes. But get 'em over to America and they either fall to pieces or the paint comes off. Whether it's a chair or a castle—same old story. The sly scallywags that sell you the goods won't live up to their contracts."

"Hasn't Gauntmoor all the ancient inconveniences a Robber Baron could wish?" I asked.

"It ain't," announced Mr. Hobson. "Though it looks all right to a stranger, perhaps. There may be castles in the Old World got it on Gauntmoor for size—thank God I didn't buy 'em!—but for looks you can't beat Gauntmoor."

"Comfortable?" I asked.

"Can't complain. Modern plumbed throughout. Hard to heat, but I put an electric-light plant in the cellar. Daughter Annie's got a Colonial suite in the North Tower."

"Well," I suggested, "if there's anything the castle lacks, you can buy it."

"There's one thing money *can't* buy," said Mr. Hobson, leaning very close and speaking in a sibilant whisper. "And that's ghosts!"

"But who wants ghosts?" I inquired.

"Now look here," said Mr. Hobson. "I'm a business man. When I bought Gauntmoor, the London scallywags that sold it to me gave me distinctly to understand that this was a Haunted Castle. They showed me a haunted chamber, showed me the haunted wall where the ghost walks, guaranteed the place to be the Spook Headquarters of the British Isles—and see what I got!" He snapped his fingers in disgust.

"No results?"

"Results? Stung! I've slept in that haunted room upstairs for a solid year. I've gazed night after night over the haunted rampart. I've even hired spiritualists to come and cut their didoes in the towers and donjon keep. No use. You can't get ghosts where they ain't."

I expressed my sympathy.

"I'm a plain man," said Hobson. "I ain't got any ancestors back of father, who was a blacksmith, and a good one, when sober. Somebody else's ancestors is what I looked for in this place—and I've got 'em, too, carved in wood and stone in the chapel out back of the tower. But statues and carvings ain't like ghosts to add tone to an ancient lineage."

"Is there any legend?" I asked.

"Haven't you heard it?" he exclaimed, looking at me sharply out of his small gray eyes. "It seems, 'way back in the sixteenth century, there was a harum-scarum young feller living in a neighbouring castle, and he took an awful shine to Lady Katherine, daughter of the Earl of Cummyngs, who was boss of this place at that time. Now the young man who loved Miss—I mean Lady—Katherine was a sort of wild proposition. Old man wouldn't have him around the place; but young man kept hanging on till Earl ordered him off. Finally the old gent locked Lady Kitty in the donjon tower," said Mr. Hobson.

"Too much shilly-shallying in *this* generation," he went on. "Every house that's got a pretty girl ought to have a donjon keep. I've got both." He paused and wiped his brow.

"This fresh young kid I'm telling you about, he thought he knew more than the old folks, so he got a rope ladder and climbed up the masonry one night, intending to bust into the tower where the girl was. But just as he got half across the wall—out yonder—his foot slipped and he broke his neck in the moat below. Consequence, Lady Kitty goes crazy and old Earl found dead a week later in his room. It was Christmas Eve when the boy was killed. That's the night his ghost's supposed to walk along the ramparts, give a shriek, and drop off—but the irritating thing about it all is, it don't ever happen."

"And now, Mr. Hobson," I said, throwing away the butt of my cigar, "why am *I* here? What have I got to do with all this ghost business?"

"I want you to stay," said Hobson, beseechingly. "To-morrow night's Christmas Eve. I've figured it out that your influence, somehow, you being of the same blood, as it were, might encourage the ghost to come out and save the reputation of the castle."

A servant brought candles, and Hobson turned to retire.

"The same blood!" I shouted after him. "What on earth is the name of the ghost?"

"When he was alive his name was—Sir Geoffray de Pierrepont," said Thaddeus Hobson, his figure fading into the dimness beyond.

I followed the servant with the candle aloft through chill and carven corridors, through galleries lined with faded portraits of forgotten lords. "Wheels!" I kept saying to myself. "The old man evidently thinks it takes a live Pierrepont to coax a dead one," and I laughed nervously as I entered the vast brown bedroom. I had to get on a chair in order to climb into the four-poster, a cheerful affair that looked like a royal funeral barge. At my head I noticed a carved device, seven mailed hands snatching at a sword with the motto: *cave adsum!*

"Beware, I am here!" I translated. Who was here? Ghosts? Fudge! What hideous scenes had this chamber beheld of yore? What might not happen here now? Where, by the way, was old Hobson's daughter, Anita? Might not anything be possible? I covered my head with the bedclothes.

****

Next morning being mild and bright for December, and Thaddeus Hobson and his mysterious daughter not having showed up for breakfast, I amused myself by inspecting the exterior of the castle. In daylight I could see that Gauntmoor, as now restored, consisted of only a portion of the original structure. On the west side, near a sheer fall of forty or fifty feet, stood the donjon tower, a fine piece of medieval barbarism with a peaked roof. And, sure enough! I saw it all now. Running along the entire west side of the castle was a wonderful wall, stretching above the moat to a dizzy height. It was no difficult matter to mount this wall from the courtyard, above which it rose no more than eight or ten feet. I ascended by a rude sentry's staircase, and once on top I gazed upward at the tall medieval prison-place, which reared above me like a clumsy stone chimney. Just as I stood, at the top of the wall, I was ten or twelve feet below the lowest window of the donjon tower. This, then, was the wall that the ancient Pierrepont had scaled, and yonder was the donjon window that he had planned to plunder on that fatal night so long ago. And this was where Pierrepont the Ghost was supposed to appear!

How the lover of spectral memory had managed to scale that wall from the outside, I could not quite make out. But once *on* the wall, it was no trick to snatch the damsel from her durance vile. Just drop a long rope ladder from the wall to the moat, then crawl along the narrow ledge—got to be careful with a job like that—then up to the window of the donjon keep, and away with the Lady Fair. Why, that window above the ramparts would be an easy climb for a fellow with strong arms and a little nerve, as the face of the tower from the wall to the window was studded with ancient spikes and the projecting ends of beams.

I counted the feet, one, two, three—and as I looked up at the window, a small, white hand reached out and a pink slip of paper dropped at my feet. It read:

Dear Sir. I'm Miss Hobson. I'm locked in the donjon tower. Father always locks me here when there's a young man about. It's a horrid, uncomfortable place. Won't you hurry and go?
Yours respectfully,
A. Hobson

I knew it was easy. I swung myself aloft on the spikes and stones leading to the donjon window. When I was high enough I gazed in, my chin about even with the sill. And there I saw the prettiest girl I ever beheld, gazing down at a book tranquilly, as though gentlemanly rescuers were common as toads around that tower. She wore something soft and golden; her hair was night-black, and her eyes were that peculiar shade of gray that—but what's the use?

"Pardon," I said, holding on with my right hand, lifting my hat with my left. "Pardon, am I addressing Miss Annie Hobson?"

"You are not," she replied, only half looking up. "You are addressing Miss Anita Hobson. Calling me Annie is another little habit father ought to break himself of." She went on reading.

"Is that a very interesting book?" I asked, because I didn't like to go without saying something more.

"It isn't!" She arose suddenly and hurled the book into a corner. "It's Anthony Hope—and if there's anything I hate it's him. Father always gives me *Prisoner of Zenda* and *Ivanhoe* to read when he locks me into this donjon. Says I ought to read up on the situation. Do you think so?"

"There are some other books in the library," I suggested. "Bernard Shaw and Kipling, you know. I'll run over and get you one."

"That's fine—but no!" she besought, reaching out her hand to detain me. "No, don't go! If you went away you'd never come back. They never do."

"Who never do?"

"The young men. The very instant father sees one coming he pops me in the tower and turns the key. You see," she explained, "when I was in Italy I was engaged to a duke—he was a silly little thing and I was glad when he turned out bogus. But father took the deception awfully to heart and swore I should never be married for my money. Yet I don't see what else a young girl can expect," she added quite simply.

I could have mentioned several hundred things.

"He has no right!" I said sternly. "It's barbarous for him to treat a girl that way—especially his daughter."

"Hush!" she said. "Dad's a good sort. But you can't measure him by other people's standards. And yet—oh, it's maddening, this life! Day after day—loneliness. Nothing but stone walls and rusty armour and books. We're rich, but what do we get out of it? I have nobody of my own age to talk to. How the years are passing! After a while—I'll be—an old maid. I'm twenty-one now!" I heard a sob. Her pretty head was bowed in her hands.

Desperately I seized the bars of the window and miraculously they parted. I leaned across the sill and drew her hands gently down.

"Listen to me," I said. "If I break in and steal you away from this, will you go?"

"Go?" she said. "Where?"

"My aunt lives at Seven Oaks, less than an hour from here by train. You can stay there till your father comes to his reason."

"It's quite like father *never* to come to his reason," she reflected. "Then I should have to be self-supporting. Of course, I should appreciate employment in a candy shop—I think I know all the principal kinds."

"Will you go?" I asked.

"Yes," she replied simply, "I'll go. But how can I get away from here?"

"To-night," I said, "is Christmas Eve, when Pierrepont the Ghost is supposed to walk along the wall—right under this window. You don't believe that fairy story, do you?"

"No."

"Neither do I. But can't you see? The haunted wall begins at my window on one end of the castle and ends at your window on the other. The bars of your cell, I see, are nearly all loose."

"Yes," she laughed, "I pried them out with a pair of scissors."

I could hear Hobson's voice across the court giving orders to servants.

"Your father's coming. Remember to-night," I whispered.

"Midnight," she said softly, smiling out at me. I could have faced flocks and flocks of dragons for her at that moment. The old man was coming nearer. I swung to the ground and escaped into a ruined court.

Well, the hours that followed were anxious and busy for me. I worked in the glamour of romance like a soldier about to do some particularly brave and foolish thing. From the window of my room I looked down on the narrow, giddy wall below. It *was* a brave and foolish thing. Among the rubbish in an old armoury I found a coil of stout rope, forty or fifty feet of it. This I smuggled away. From a remote hall I borrowed a Crusader's helmet and spent the balance of the afternoon in my room practicing with a sheet across my shoulders, shroud-fashion.

We dined grandly at eight, the old man and I. He drank thirstily and chatted about the ghost, as you might discuss the chances in a coming athletic event. After what seemed an age he looked at his watch and cried: "Whillikens! Eleven o'clock already! Well, I'll be going up to watch from the haunted room. I think, Jeff, that you'll bring me luck to-night."

"I am sure I shall!" I answered sardonically, as he departed.

Three quarters of an hour later, wearing the Crusader's helmet and swathed in a bed sheet, I let myself down from the window to the haunted wall below. It was moonlight, bitter cold as I crouched on the wall, waiting for the stroke of twelve, when I should act the spook and walk along that precarious ledge to rescue Anita.

The "haunted wall," I observed from where I stood, was shaped like an irregular crescent, being in plain view of Hobson's "haunted room" at the middle, but not so at its north and south ends, where my chamber and Anita's tower were respectively situated. I pulled out my watch from under my winding-sheet. Three minutes of twelve. I drew down the visor of my helmet and gathered up my cerements preparatory to walking the hundred feet of wall which would bring me in sight of the haunted room where old Hobson kept his vigil. Two minutes, one minute I waited, when—I suddenly realized I was not alone.

A man wearing a long cloak and a feather in his cap was coming toward me along the moonlit masonry. Aha! So I was not the only masquerading swain calling on the captive princess in the prison tower. A jealous pang shot through me as I realized this.

The man was within twenty feet of me, when I noticed something. He was not walking on the wall. *He was walking on air, three or four feet above the wall.* Nearer and nearer came the man—the Thing—now into the light of the moon, whose beams seemed to strike through his misty tissue like the thrust of a sword. I was horribly scared. My knees loosened under me, and I clutched the vines at my back to save me from falling into the moat below. Now I could see his face, and somehow fear seemed to leave me. His expression was so young and human.

"Ghost of the Pierrepont," I thought, "whether you walk in shadow or in light, you lived among a race of Men!"

His noble, pallid face seemed to burn with its own pale light, but his eyes were in darkness. He was now within two yards of me. I could see the dagger at his belt. I could see the gory cut on his forehead. I attempted to speak, but my voice creaked like a rusty hinge. He neither heeded nor saw me; and when he came to the spot where I stood, he did not turn out for me. He walked *through* me! And when next I saw him he was a few feet beyond me, standing in mid-air over the moat and gazing up at the high towers like one revisiting old scenes. Again he floated toward me and poised on the wall four feet from where I stood.

"What do you here to-night?" suddenly spoke, or seemed to speak, a voice that was like the echo of a silence.

No answer came from my frozen tongue. Yet I would gladly have spoken, because somehow I felt a great sympathy for this boyish spirit.

"It has been many earth-years," he said, "since I have walked these towers. And ah, cousin, it has been many miles that I have been called to-night to answer the summons of my race. And this fortress—what power has moved it overseas to this mad kingdom? Magic!"

His eyes seemed suddenly to blaze through the shadows.

"Cousin," he again spoke, "it is to you that I come from my far-off English tomb. It was your need called me. It is no pious deed brings you to this wall to-night. You are planning to pillage these towers unworthily, even as I did yesterday. Death was my portion, and broken hearts to the father I wronged and the girl I sought."

"But it is the father wrongs the girl here," I heard myself saying.

"He who rules these towers to-day is of stern mind but loving heart," said the ghost. "Patience. By the Star that redeems the world, love should not be won *to-night* by stealth, but by—love."

He raised his hands toward the tower, his countenance radiant with an undying passion.

"*She* called to me and died," he said, "and her little ghost comes not to earth again for any winter moon or any summer wind."

"But you—you come often?" my voice was saying.

"No," said the ghost, "only on Christmas Eve. Yule is the tide of spectres; for then the thoughts of the world are so beautiful that they enter our dreams and call us back."

He turned to go, and a boyish, friendly smile rested a moment on his pale face.

"Farewell, Sir Geoffray de Pierrepont," he called to me.

Into the misty moonlight the ghost floated to that portion of the wall directly opposite the haunted room. From where I stood I could not see this chamber. After a moment I shook my numb senses to life. My first instinct was one of strong human curiosity, which impelled me to follow far enough to see the effect of the apparition on old Hobson, who must be watching at the window.

I tiptoed a hundred feet along the wall and peered around a turret up to a room above, where Hobson's head could easily be seen in a patch of light. The ghost, at that moment, was walking just below, and the effect on the old man, appalling though it was, was ludicrous as well. He was leaning far out of the window, his mouth wide open; and the entire disk of his fat, hairless head was as pallid as the moon itself. The spectre, who was now rounding the curve of the wall near the tower, swerved suddenly, and as suddenly seemed to totter headlong into the abyss below. As he dropped, a wild laugh broke through the frosty air. It wasn't from the ghost. It came from above—yes, it emanated from Thaddeus Hobson, who had, apparently, fallen back, leaving the window empty. Lights began breaking out all over the castle. In another moment I should be caught in my foolish disguise. With the courage of a coward, I turned and ran full tilt along the dizzy ledge and back to my window, where I lost no seconds scrambling up the rope that led to my room.

With all possible haste I threw aside my sheet and helmet and started downstairs. I had just wrestled with a ghost; I would now have it out with the old man. The castle seemed ablaze below. I saw the flash of a light skirt in the picture gallery, and Anita, pale as the vision I had so lately beheld, came running toward me.

"Father—saw it!" she panted. "He had some sort of sinking spell—he's better now—isn't it awful!" She clung to me, sobbing hysterically.

Before I realized what I had done, I was holding her close in my arms.

"Don't!" I cried. "It was a good ghost—he had a finer spirit than mine. He came to-night for you, dear, and for me. It was a foolish thing we planned."

"Yes, but I wanted, I wanted to go!" she sobbed now crying frankly on my shoulder.

"You *are* going with me," I said fiercely, raising her head. "But not over any ghost-ridden breakneck wall. We're going this time through the big front door of this old castle, American fashion, and there'll be an automobile waiting outside and a parson at the other end of the line."

We found Thaddeus Hobson alone, in the vast hall looking blankly at the fire.

"Jeff," he said solemnly, "you sure brought me luck to-night if you can call it such being scared into a human icicle. Br-r-r! Shall I ever get the cold out of my backbone? But somehow, somehow that foggy feller outside sort of changed my look on things. It made me feel *kinder* toward living folks. Ain't it strange!"

"Mr. Hobson," I said, "I think the ghost has made us *all* see things differently. In a word, sir, I have a confession to make—if you don't mind."

And I told him briefly of my accidental meeting with Anita in the donjon, of the practical joke we planned, of our sudden meeting with the *real* ghost on the ramparts. Mr. Hobson listened, his face growing redder and redder. At the finish of my story he suddenly leaped to his feet and brought his fist down on the table with a bang.

"Well, you little devils!" he said admiringly, and burst into loud laughter. "You're a spunky lad, Jeff. And there ain't any doubt that the de Pierreponts are as good stuff as you can get in the ancestry business. The Christmas supper is spread in the banquet hall. Come, de Pierrepont, will you sup with the old Earl?"

****

The huge oaken banquet hall, lined with rich hangings, shrunk us to dwarfs by its vastness. Golden goblets were at each place. A butler, dressed in antique livery, threw a red cloak over Hobson's fat shoulders. It was a whim of the old man's.

As we took our places, I noticed the table was set for four.

"Whose is the extra place?" I asked.

The old man at first made no reply. At last he turned to me earnestly and said: "Do you believe in ghosts?"

"No," I replied. "Yet how else can I explain that vision I saw on the ramparts?"

"Is the fourth place for him?" Anita almost whispered.

The old man nodded mutely and raised a golden goblet.

"To the Transplanted Ghost!" I said. It was an empty goblet that I touched to my lips.

128

The Last Ghost in Harmony

Nelson Lloyd

From his perch on the blacksmith's anvil he spoke between the puffs of his post-prandial pipe. The fire in the forge was out and the day was going slowly, through the open door of the shop and the narrow windows, westward to the mountains. In the advancing shadow, on the pile of broken wheels on the work-bench, on keg and barrel, they sat puffing their post-prandial pipes and listening.

****

For a partner in business I want a truthful man, but for a companion give me one with imagination. To my mind imagination is the spice of life. There is nothing so uninteresting as a fact, for when you know it that is the end of it. When life becomes nothing but facts it won't be worth living; yet in a few years the race will have no imagination left. It is being educated out. Look at the children. When I was young the bogey man was as real to me as pa and nearly as much to be feared of, but just yesterday I was lectured for merely mentioning him to my neffy. So with ghosts. We was taught to believe in ghosts the same as we was in Adam or Noar. Nowadays nobody believes in them. It is unscientific, and if you are superstitious you are considered ignorant and laughed at. Ghosts are the product of the imagination, but if I imagine I see one he is as real to me as if he actually exists, isn't he? Therefore he does exist. That's logic. You fellows have become scientific and admits only what you see and feel, and don't depend on your imagination for anything. Such being the case, I myself admit that the sperrits no longer ha'nt the burying-ground or play around your houses. I admit it because the same condition exact existed in Harmony when I was there, and because of what was told me by Robert J. Dinkle about two years after he died, and because of what occurred between me and him and the Rev. Mr. Spiegelnail.

Harmony was a highly intellectual town. About the last man there with any imagination or interesting ideas, excepting me, of course, was Robert J. Dinkle. Yet he had an awful reputation, and when he died it was generally stated privately that the last landmark of ignorance and superstition had been providentially removed. You know he had always been seeing things, but we set it down to his fondness for hard cider or his natural propensity for joshing. With him gone there was no one left to report the doings of the sperrit-world. In fact, so widespread was the light of reason, as the Rev. Mr. Spiegelnail called it, that the burying-ground became a popular place for moonlight strolls. Even I walked through it frequent on my way home from Miss Wheedle's, with whom I was keeping company, and it never occurred to me to go any faster there, or to look back over my shoulder, for I didn't believe in such foolishness. But to the most intellectual there comes times of doubt about things they know nothing of nor understand. Such a time come to me, when the wind was more mournfuller than usual in the trees, and the clouds scudded along overhead, casting peculiar shadders. My imagination got the best of my intellect. I hurried. I looked back over my shoulder. I shivered, kind of. Natural I see nothing in the burying-ground, yet at the end of town I was still uneasy-like, though half laughing at myself. It was so quiet; not a light burned anywhere, and the square seemed lonelier than the cemetery, and the store was so deserted, so ghostly in the moonlight, that I just couldn't keep from peering around at it.

Then, from the empty porch, from the empty bench—empty, I swear, for I could see plain, so clear was the night—from absolute nothing come as pleasant a voice as ever I hear.

"Hello!" it says.

My blood turned icy-like and the chills waved up and down all through me. I couldn't move.

The voice came again, so natural, so familiar, that I warmed some, and rubbed my eyes and stared.

There, sitting on the bench, in his favourite place, was the late Robert J. Dinkle, gleaming in the moonlight, the front door showing right through him.

"I must appear pretty distinct," he says in a proud-like way. "Can't you see me very plain?"

See him plain! I should think so. Even the patches on his coat was visible, and only for the building behind him, he never looked more natural, and hearing him so pleasant, set me thinking. This, says I, is the sperrit of the late Robert J. Dinkle. In life he never did me any harm and in his present misty condition is likely to do less; if he is looking for trouble I'm not afraid of a bit of fog. Such being the case, I says, I shall address him as soon as I am able.

But Robert got tired waiting, and spoke again in an anxious tone, a little louder, and ruther complaining, "Don't I show up good?" says he.

"I never see you looking better," I answered, for my voice had came back, and the chills were quieter, and I was fairly ca'm and dared even to move a little nearer.

A bright smile showed on his pale face. "It is a relief to be seen at last," he cried, most cheerful. "For years I've been trying to do a little ha'nting around here, and no one would notice me. I used to think mebbe my material was too delicate and gauzy, but I've conceded that, after all, the stuff is not to blame."

He heaved a sigh so natural that I forgot all about his being a ghost. Indeed, taken all in all, I see that he had improved, was solemner, had a sweeter expression and wasn't likely to give in to his old propensity for joshing.

"Set down and we will talk it over," he went on most winning. "Really, I can't do any harm, but please be a little afraid and then I will show up distincter. I must be getting dim now."

"You are," says I, for though I was on the porch edging nearer him most bold, I could hardly see him.

Without any warning he gave an awful groan that brought the chills waving back most violent. I jumped and stared, and as I stared he stood out plainer and solider in the moonlight.

"That's better," he said with a jolly chuckle; "now you do believe in me, don't you? Well, set there nervous-like, on the edge of the bench and don't be too ca'm-like, or I'll disappear."

The ghost's orders were followed explicit. But with him setting there so natural and pleasant it was hard to be frightened and more than once I forgot. He, seeing me peering like my eyesight was bad, would give a groan that made my blood curdle. Up he would flare again, gleaming in the moonlight full and strong.

"Harmony's getting too scientific, too intellectual," he said, speaking very melancholic. "What can't be explained by arithmetic or geography is put down as impossible. Even the preachers encourage such idees and talk about Adam and Eve being allegories. As a result, the graveyard has become the slowest place in town. You simply can't ha'nt anything around here. A man hears a groan in his room and

131

he gets up and closes the shutters tighter, or throws a shoe at a rat, or swears at the wind in the chimney. A few sperrits were hanging around when I was first dead, but they were complaining very bad about the hard times. There used to be plenty of good society in the burying-ground, they said, but one by one they had to quit. All the old Berrys had left. Mr. Whoople retired when he was taken for a white mule. Mrs. Morris A. Klump, who once oppyrated 'round the deserted house beyond the mill had gave up in disgust just a week before my arrival. I tried to encourage the few remaining, explained how the sperritualists were working down the valley and would strike town any time, but they had lost all hope—kept fading away till only me was left. If things don't turn for the better soon I must go, too. It's awful discouraging. And lonely! Why folks ramble around the graves like even I wasn't there. Just last night my boy Ossy came strolling along with the lady he is keeping company with, and where do you s'pose they set down to rest, and look at the moon and talk about the silliest subjecks? Right on my headstone! I stood in front of them and did the ghostliest things till I was clean tired out and discouraged. They just would not pay the least attention."

The poor old ghost almost broke down and cried. Never in life had I known him so much affected, and it went right to my heart to see him wiping his eyes with his handkercher and snuffling.

"Mebbe you don't make enough noise when you ha'nt," says I most sympathetic.

"I do all the regular acts," says he, a bit het up by my remark. "We always were kind of limited. I float around and groan, and talk foolish, and sometimes I pull off bedclothes or reveal the hiding-place of buried treasure. But what good does it do in a town so intellectual as Harmony?"

I have seen many folks who were down on their luck, but never one who so appealed to me as the late Robert J. Dinkle. It was the way he spoke, the way he looked, his general patheticness, his very helplessness, and deservingness. In life I had known him well, and as he was now I liked him better. So I did want to do something for him. We sat studying for a long time, him smoking very violent, blowing clouds of fog outen his pipe, me thinking up some way to help him. And idees allus comes to them who sets and waits.

"The trouble is partly as you say, Robert," I allowed after a bit, "and again partly because you can't make enough noise to awaken the slumbering imagination of intellectual Harmony. With a little natural help from me though, you might stir things up in this town."

You never saw a gladder smile or a more gratefuller look than that poor sperrit gave me.

"Ah," he says, "with your help I could do wonders. Now who'll we begin on?"

"The Rev. Mr. Spiegelnail," says I, "has about all the imagination left in Harmony—of course excepting me."

Robert's face fell visible. "I have tried him repeated and often," he says, kind of argumentative-like. "All the sign he made was to complain that his wife talked in her sleep."

I wasn't going to argue—not me. I was all for action, and lost no time in starting. Robert J., he followed me like a dog, up through town to our house, where I went in, leaving him outside so as not to disturb mother. There I got me a hammer and nails with the heavy lead sinker offen my fishnet, and it wasn't long before the finest tick-tack you ever saw was working against the Spiegelnails' parlour window, with me in a lilac-bush operating the string that kept the weight a-swinging. Before the house was an open spot where the moon shone full and clear, where Robert J. walked up and down, about two feet off the ground, waving his arms slow-like and making the melancholiest groans. Now I have been to *Uncle Tom's Cabin* frequent, but in all my life I never see such acting. Yet what was the consequences? Up went the window above, and the Rev. Mr. Spiegelnail showed out plain in the moonlight.

"Who is there?" he called very stern. You had otter see Robert then. It was like tonic to him. He rose up higher and began to beat his arms most violent and to gurgle tremendous. But the preacher never budged.

"You boys otter be ashamed of yourselves," he says in a severe voice.

"Louder, louder," I calls to Robert J., in answering which he began the most awful contortions.

"You can hear me perfectly plain," says the dominie, now kind of sad-like. "It fills my old heart with sorrow to see that yous all have gone so far astray."

Hearing that, so calm, so distinct, so defiant, made Robert J. stop short and stare. To remind him I gave the weight an extra thump, and it was so loud as to bring forth Mrs. Spiegelnail, her head showing plain as she peered out over the preacher's shoulder. The poor discouraged ghost took heart, striking his tragicest attitude, one which he told me afterwards was his pride and had been got out of a book. But what was the result?

"Does you hear anyone in the bushes, dear?" inquires Mr. Spiegelnail, cocking his ears and listening.

"It must be Ossy Dinkle and them bad friends of his," says she, in her sour tone.

Poor Robert! Hearing that, he about gave up hope.

"Don't I show up good?" he asks in an anxious voice.

"I can see you distinct," says I, very sharp. "You never looked better."

Down went the window—so sudden, so unexpected that I did not know what to make of it. Robert J. thought he did, and over me he came floating, most delighted.

"I must have worked," he said, laughing like he'd die, a-doubling up and holding his sides to keep from splitting. "At last I have showed up distinct; at last I am of some use in the world. You don't realize what a pleasure it is to know that you are fulfilling your mission and living up to your reputation."

Poor old ghost! He was for talking it all over then and there and settled down on a soft bunch of lilacs, and fell to smoking fog and chattering. It did me good to see him so happy and I was inclined to puff up a bit at my own success in the ha'nting line. But it was not for long. The rattle of keys warned us. The front door flew open and out bounded the Rev. Mr. Spiegelnail, clearing the steps with a jump, and flying over the lawn. All thought of the late Robert J. Dinkle left me then, for I had only a few feet start of my pastor. You see I shouldn't a-hurried so only I sung bass in the choir and I doubt if I could have convinced him that I was working in the interests of Science and Truth. Fleeing was instinct. Gates didn't matter. They were took on the wing, and down the street I went with the preacher's hot breath on my neck. But I beat him. He tired after the first spurt and was soon left behind, so I could double back home to bed.

Robert, he was for giving up entirely.

"I simply won't work," says he to me, when I met him on the store porch that next night. "A hundred years ago such a bit of ha'nting would have caused the town to be abandoned; to-day it is attributed to natural causes."

"Because," says I, "we left behind such evidences of material manifestations as strings and weights on the parlour window."

"S'pose we work right in the house?" says he, brightening up. "You can hide in the closet and groan while I act."

Now did you ever hear anything innocenter than that? Yet he meant it so well I did not even laugh.

"I'm too fond of my pastor," I says, "to let him catch me in his closet. A far better spot for our work is the short cut he takes home from church after Wednesday evening meeting. We won't be so loud, but more dignified, melancholier, and tragic. You overacted last night, Robert," I says. "Next time pace up and down like you were deep in thought and sigh gentle. Then if he should see you it would be nice to take his arm and walk home with him."

I think I had the right idea of ha'nting, and had I been able to keep up Robert J. Dinkle's sperrits and to train him regular I could have aroused the slumbering imagination of Harmony, and brought life to the burying-ground. But he was too easy discouraged. He lacked perseverance. For if ever Mr. Spiegelnail was on the point of seeing things it was that night as he stepped out of the woods. He had walked slow and meditating till he come opposite where I was. Now I didn't howl or groan or say anything particular. What I did was to make a noise that wasn't animal, neither was it human, nor was it regulation ghostly. As I had stated to the late Robert J. Dinkle, what was needed for ha'nting was something new and original. And it certainly ketched Mr. Spiegelnail's attention. I see him stop. I see his lantern shake. It appeared like he was going to dive into the bushes for me, but he changed his mind. On he went, quicker, kind as if he wasn't afraid, yet was, on to the open, where the moon brought out Robert beautiful as he paced slowly up and down, his head bowed like he was studying. Still the preacher never saw him, stepped right through him, in fact. I give the dreadful sound again. That stopped him. He turned, raised the lantern before him, put his hand to his ear, and seemed to be looking intense and listening. Hardly ten feet away stood Robert, all a-trembling with excitement, but the light that showed through him was as steady as a rock, as the dominie watched and listened, so quiet and ca'm. He lowered the lantern, rubbed his hands across his eyes, stepped forward and looked again. The ghost was perfect. As I have stated, he was excited and his sigh shook a little, but he was full of dignity and sadity. He shouldn't have lost heart so soon. I was sure then that he almost showed up plain to the preacher and he would have grown on Mr. Spiegelnail had he kept on ha'nting him instead of giving in because that one night the pastor walked on to the house fairly cool. He did walk quicker, I know, and he did peer over his shoulder twicet and I did hear the kitchen door bang in a relieved way. But when we consider the stuff that ghosts are made of we hadn't otter expect them to be heroes. They are too foggy and gauzy to have much perseverance—judging at least from Robert J.

"I simply can't work any more," says he, when I came up to him, as he sat there in the path, his elbows on his knees, his head on his hands, his eyes studying the ground most mournful.

"But Robert—" I began, thinking to cheer him up.

He didn't hear; he wouldn't listen—just faded away.

Had he only held out there is no telling what he might have done in his line. Often, since then, have I thought of him and figgered on his tremendous possibilities. That he had possibilities I am sure. Had I only realized it that last night we went out ha'nting, he never would have got away from me. But the realization came too late. It came in church the very next Sunday, with the usual announcements after the long prayer, as Mr. Spiegelnail was leaning over the pulpit eying the congregation through big smoked glasses.

Says he in a voice that was full of sadness: "I regret to announce that for the first time in twenty years union services will be held in this town next Sabbath." Setting in the choir, reading my music marks, I heard the preacher's words and started, for I saw at once that something unusual was happening, or had happened, or was about to happen. "Unfortunately," said Mr. Spiegelnail, continuing, "I shall have to turn my pulpit over to Brother Spiker of the Baptist Church, for my failing eyesight renders it necessary that I go at once to Philadelphia, to consult an oculist. Some of my dear brethren may think this an unusual step, but I should not desert them without cause. They may think, perhaps, that I am making much ado about nothing and could be treated just as well in Harrisburg. To such let me explain that I am suffering from astigmatism. It is not so much that I cannot see, but that I sees things which I know are not there—a defect in sight which I feel needs the most expert attention. Sunday-school at half-past nine; divine service at eleven. I take for my text 'And the old men shall see visions.'"

How I did wish the late Robert J. Dinkle could have been in church that morning. It would have so gladdened his heart to hear that he had partly worked, for if he worked partly, then surely, in time, he would have worked complete. For me, I was just wild with excitement, and was so busy thinking of him and how glad he would be, that I didn't hear the sermon at all, and in planning new ways of ha'nting I forgot to sing in the last anthem. You see, I figgered lively times ahead for Harmony—a general return to the good old times when folks had imagination and had something more in their heads than facts. I had only to get Robert again, and with him working it would not be long till all the old Berrys and Mrs. Klump showed up distinct and plain. But I wasn't well posted in the weak characters of shades, for I thought, of course, I could find my sperrit friend easy when night came. Yet I didn't. I set on the store porch shivering till the moon was high up over the ridge. He just wouldn't come. I called for him soft-like and got no answer. Down to the burying-ground I went and set on his headstone. It was the quietest place you ever see. The clouds was scudding overhead; the wind was sighing among the leaves; and through the trees the moon was gleaming so clear and distinct you could almost read the monnyments. It was just a night when things should have been lively there—a perfect night for ha'nting. I called for Robert. I listened. He never answered. I heard only a bull-frog a-bellering in the pond, a whippoorwill whistling in the grove, and a dog howling at the moon.

The Ghost of Miser Brimpson

Eden Phillpotts

1

Penniless and proud he was; and that pair don't draw a man to pleasant places when they be in double harness. There's only one thing can stop 'em if they take the bit between their teeth, and that's a woman. So there, you might say, lies the text of the tale of Jonathan Drake, of Dunnabridge Farm, a tenement in the Forest of Dartymoor. 'Twas Naboth's vineyard to Duchy, and the greedy thing would have given a very fair price for it, without a doubt; but the Drake folk held their land, and wouldn't part with it, and boasted a freehold of fifty acres in the very midst of the Forest. They did well, too, and moved with the times, and kept their heads high for more generations than I can call home; and then they comed to what all families, whether gentle or simple, always come to soon or late. And that's a black sheep for bellwether. Bad uns there'll be in every generation of a race; but the trouble begins when a bad un chances to be up top; and if the head of the family is a drunkard, or a spendthrift, or built on too free and flowing a pattern for this work-a-day shop, then the next generation may look out for squalls, as the sailor-men say.

'Twas Jonathan's grandfather that did the harm at Dunnabridge. He had sport in his blood, on his mother's side, and 'twas horses ran him into trouble. He backed 'em, and was ruined; and then his son bred 'em, and didn't do very much better. So, when the pair of 'em dropped out of the hunt, and died with their backs to the wall, one after t'other, it looked as if the game was up for them to follow. By good chance, however, Tom Drake had but one child—a boy—the Jonathan as I be telling about; and when his father and grandfather passed away, within a year of each other, Dunnabridge was left to

138

Tom's widow and her son, him then being twenty-two. She was for selling Dunnabridge and getting away from Dartymoor, because the place had used her bad, and she hated the sight of it; but Jonathan, a proud chap even then, got the lawyers to look into the matter, and they told him that 'twasn't vital for Dunnabridge to be sold, though it might ease his pocket, and smooth his future to do so, 'specially as Duchy wanted the place rather bad, and had offered the value of it. And Jonathan's mother was on the side of Duchy, too, and went on her knees to the man to sell; but he wouldn't. He had a bee in his bonnet sometimes, and he said that all the Drakes would rise out of their graves to Widecombe churchyard, and haunt his rising up and going down if he were to do such a thing, just to suit his own convenience, and be rid of the place. So he made a plan with the creditors. It figured out that his father and grandfather had owed near a thousand pound between them; and Jonathan actually set himself to pay it off to the last penny. 'Twas the labour of years; but by the time he was thirty-three he done it—at what cost of scrimping and screwing, only his mother might have told. She never did tell, however, for she died two year before the last item was paid. Some went as far as to declare that 'twas her son's miserly ways hurried her into her grave; and, for all I know, they may have done so, for 'tis certain, in her husband's life, she had a better time. Tom was the large-hearted, juicy, easy sort, as liked meat on the table, and plenty to wash it down; and he loved Mercy Jane Drake very well; and, when he died, the only thought that troubled him was leaving her; and the last thing he advised his son was to sell Dunnabridge, and take his mother off the Moor down to the "in country" where she'd come from.

But Jonathan was made of different stuff, and 'twas rumoured by old people that had known the family for several generations that he favoured an ancient forefather by name of Brimpson Drake. This bygone man was a miser and the richest of the race. He'd lived in the days when we were at war with France and America, and when Princetown sprang up, and a gert war-prison was built there to cage all the chaps we got on our hands through winning such a lot o' sea battles. And Miser Brimpson was said to have made thousands by helping rich fellows to escape from the prison. Truth and falsehood mixed made up his story as 'twas handed down. But one thing appeared to be fairly true about it; which was, that when the miser died, and Dunnabridge went to his cousin, the horse racer, not a penny of his fortune ever came into the sight of living men. So some said 'twas all nonsense, and he never had no money at all, but only pretended to it; and others again, declared that he knew too well who'd follow in his shoes at Dunnabridge, and hid his money accordingly, so that no Drake should have it. For he hated his heirs as only a miser can hate 'em.

So things stood when Mercy Jane died and Jonathan was left alone. He paid all his relations' debts, and he had his trouble and the honour of being honourable for his pains. Everybody respected him something wonderful; but, all the same, a few of his mother's friends always did say that 'twas a pity he put his dead father's good name afore his living mother's life. However, we'm not built in the pattern of our fellow-creatures, and 'tis only fools that waste time blaming a man for being himself.

Jonathan went his stern way; and then, in the lonely days after his parent was taken, when he lived at Dunnabridge, with nought but two hinds and a brace of sheep-dogs, 'twas suddenly borne in upon his narrow sight that there might be other women still in the world, though his mother had gone out of it. And he also discovered, doubtless, that a home without a woman therein be merely the cruel mockery of what a home should be.

A good few folk watched Jonathan to see what he'd do about it, and no doubt a maiden here and there was interested too; because, though a terrible poor man, he wasn't bad to look at, though rather hard about the edge of the jaw, and rather short and stern in his manners to human creatures and beasts alike.

And then beginned his funny courting—if you can call it courting, where a poor man allows hisself the luxury of pride at the wrong time, and makes a show of hisself in consequence. At least that's my view; but you must know that a good few, quite as wise as me, took t'other side, and held that Jonathan covered his name with glory when he changed his mind about Hyssop Burges. That was her bitter name, but a pleasanter girl never walked on shoe-leather. She was Farmer Stonewer's niece to White Works, and he took her in for a charity, and always said that 'twas the best day's work as ever he had done. A straight, hardworking, cheerful sort of a girl, with nothing to name about her very special save a fine shape and a proud way of holding her head in the air and looking her fellow creatures in the eyes. Proud she was for certain, and terrible partickler as to her friends; but there happened to be that about Jonathan that made flint to her steel. He knowed she was penniless, or he'd not have looked at her twice; and when, after a short, fierce sort of courting, she took him, everybody felt pleased about it but Farmer Stonewer, who couldn't abide the thought of losing Hyssop, though his wife had warned him any time this four year that 'twas bound to happen.

Farmer and the girl were sitting waiting for Jonathan one night; and she was a bit nervous, and he was trying for to calm her.

"Jonathan must be told," she says. "It can't go on no longer."

"Then tell him," says her uncle. "Good powers!" he says; "to see you, one would think the news was the worst as could ever fall between a pair o' poor lovers, instead of the best."

"I know him a lot better than you," she tells Farmer; "and I know how plaguey difficult he can be where money's the matter. He very near throwed me over when, in a weak moment, I axed him to let me buy my own tokening-ring. Red as a turkey's wattles did he flame, and said I'd insulted him; and now, when he hears the secret, I can't for the life of me guess how he'll take it."

"'Twas a pity you didn't tell him when he offered for you," declared Hyssop's aunt. "Proud he is as a silly peacock, and terrible frightened of seeming to look after money, or even casting his eye where it bides; but he came to you without any notion of the windfall, and he loved you for yourself, like an honest man; and you loved him the same way; and right well you know that if your old cousin had left you five thousand pound instead of five hundred, Jonathan Drake was the right chap for you. He can't blame himself, for not a soul on Dartymoor but us three has ever heard tell about the money."

"But he'll blame me for having money at all," answered the girl. "He said a dozen times afore he offered for me, that he'd never look at a woman if she'd got more cash than what he had himself. That's why I couldn't bring myself to confess to it—and lose him. And, after we was tokened, it got to be harder still."

"Why not bide till you'm married, then?" asked Mrs. Stonewer. "Since it have gone so long, let it go longer, and surprise him with the news on the wedding-night—eh, James?"

"No," answered Farmer. "'Enough is as good as a feast.' 'Tis squandering blessings to do that at such a time. Keep the news till some rainy day, when he's wondering how to get round a tight corner. That's the moment to tell him; and that's the moment he's least likely to make a face at the news."

But Hyssop wouldn't put it off no more; she said as she'd not have any further peace till the murder was out. And that very night, sure enough when Jonathan comed over from Dunnabridge for his bit of love-making, and the young couple had got the farm parlour to themselves, she plumped it out, finding him in a very kindly mood. They

141

never cuddled much, for he wasn't built that way; but he'd not disdain to sit beside her and put his arm around her now and again, when she picked up his hand and drew it round. Then, off and on, she'd rub her cheek against his mutton-chop whiskers, till he had to kiss her in common politeness.

Well, Hyssop got it out—Lord alone knows how, as she said afterwards. She got it out, and told him that an old, aged cousin had died, and left her a nice little skuat[1] of money; and how she'd never touched a penny but let it goody in the bank; and how she prayed and hoped 'twould help 'em to Dunnabridge; and how, of course, he must have the handling of it, being a man, and so cruel clever in such things. She went on and on, pretty well frightened to stop and hear him. But, after she'd said it over about a dozen times, her breath failed her, and she shut her mouth, and tried to smile, and looked up terrible anxious and pleading at Jonathan.

His hard gray eyes bored into her like a brace of gimlets, and in return for all her talk he axed but one question.

"How long have you had this here money?" he said.

She told the truth, faltering and shaking under his glare.

"Four years and upwards, Jonathan."

"That's years and years afore I axed you to marry me?"

"Yes, Jonathan."

"And you remember what I said about never marrying anybody as had more than what I have?"

"Yes, Jonathan."

"And you full know how many a time I told you that, after I paid off all my father's debts, I had nought left, and 'twould be years afore I could build up anything to call money?"

"Yes, Jonathan."

"Very well, then!" he cried out, and his brow crooked down and his fists clenched. "Very well, you've deceived me deliberate, and if you'd do that in one thing, you would in another. I'm going out of this house this instant moment, and you can tell your relations why 'tis. I'm terrible sorry, Hyssop Burges, for no man will ever love you better than what I did; and so you'd have lived to find out when all this here courting tomfoolery was over, and you'd come to be my wife. But now I'll have none of you, for you've played with me. And so—so I'll bid you good-bye!"

He went straight out without more speech; and she tottered, weeping, to her uncle and aunt. They couldn't believe their senses; and Jimmy

---

1. Skuat, windfall.

Stonewer declared thereon that any man who could make himself such a masterpiece of a fool as Jonathan had done that night, was better out of the marriage state than in it. He told Hyssop as she'd had a marvellous escape from a prize zany; and his wife said the same. But the girl couldn't see it like that. She knowed Jonathan weren't a prize zany, and his raging pride didn't anger her, for she admired it something wonderful, and it only made her feel her loss all the crueller to see what a terrible rare, haughty sort of a chap he was. There were a lot of other men would have had her, and twice as many again, if they'd known about the money; but they all seemed as tame as robins beside her hawk of a Jonathan. She had plenty of devil in her, too, when it came to the fighting pitch; and now, while he merely said that the match was broken off through a difference of opinion, and gave no reason for it, she set to work with all her might to get him back again, and used her love-sharpened wits so well as she knew how, to best him into matrimony.

2

In truth she made poor speed. Jonathan was always civil afterwards; but you might as soon have tried to thaw an iceberg with a box of matches as to get him round again by gentleness and affection. He was the sort that can't be won with kindness. He felt he'd treated the world better than the world had treated him, and the thought shrivelled his heart a bit. Always shy and suspicious, you might say; and yet, underneath it, the most honourable and upright and high-minded man you could wish to meet. Hyssop loved him like her life, and she got a bit poorly in health after their sad quarrel. Then chance willed it that, going down from Princetown to Plymouth by train—to see a chemist, and get something to make her eat—who should be in the selfsame carriage but Mr. Drake and his hind, Thomas Parsons.

There was others there, too; and it fell out that an old fellow as knowed Jonathan's grandfather before him, brought up the yarn about Miser Brimpson, and asked young Drake if he took any stock in it.

Of course the man pooh-poohed such foolery, and told the old chap not to talk nonsense like that in the ear of the nineteenth century; but when Jonathan and Parsons had got out of the train—which they did do at Yelverton station—Hyssop, as knowed the old man, axed him to tell more about the miser; and he explained, so well as he knew how, that Brimpson Drake had made untold thousands out of the French and American prisoners, and that, without doubt, 'twas all hidden even to this day at Dunnabridge.

"Of course Jonathan's too clever to believe such a tale—like his father before him; but his grandfather believed it, and the old blid spent half his time poking about the farm. Only, unfortunately, he didn't have no luck. But 'tis there for sure; and if Jonathan had enough faith he'd come by it—not by digging and wasting time and labour, but by doing what is right and proper when you'm dealing with such matters."

"And what might that be?" axed Miss Burges.

Just then, however, the train for Plymouth ran up, and the old man told her that he'd explain some other time.

"This generation laughs at such things," he said; "but they laugh best who laugh last, and, for all we can say to the contrary, 'tis nought but his conceit and pride be standing between that stiff-necked youth and the wealth of a bank."

Hyssop, she thought a lot upon this; but she hadn't no need to go to the old chap again, as she meant to do, for when she got home, her uncle—Farmer Stonewer—knowed all about the matter, and told her how 'twas a very rooted opinion among the last generation that a miser's spirit never could leave its hidden hoard till the stuff was brought to light, and in human hands once more.

"Millions of good money has been found in that manner, if all we hear is true," declared Farmer Jimmy; "and if one miser has been known to walk, which nobody can deny, then why shouldn't another? Them as believe in such dark things—and I don't say I do, and I don't say I don't—them as know of such mysteries happening in their own recollection, or in the memory of their friends, would doubtless say that Miser Brimpson still creeps around his gold now and again; and if that money be within the four corners of Dunnabridge Farm, and if Jonathan happed to be on the lookout on the rightful night and at the rightful moment, 'tis almost any odds but he might see his forbear sitting over his money-bags like a hen on a clutch of eggs, and so recover the hoard."

"But faith's needed for such a deed," Mrs. Stonewer told her niece; "and that pig-headed creature haven't no faith. Too proud, he is, to believe in anything he don't understand. 'Twas even so with Lucifer afore him. If you told him—Jonathan—this news, he'd rather let the money go than set off ghost-hunting in cold blood. Yet there it is: and a humbler-minded fashion of chap, with the Lord on his side, and a trustful heart in his bosom, might very like recover all them tubs of cash the miser come by."

"And then he'd have thousands to my poor tens," said Hyssop. "Not that he'd ever come back to me now, I reckon."

But, all the same, she knowed by the look in Jonathan's eye when

144

they met, that he loved her still, and that his silly, proud heart was hungering after her yet, though he'd rather have been drawn under a harrow than show a spark of what was burning there.

And so, upon this nonsense about a buried treasure she set to work again to use her brains, and see if there might be any road out of the trouble by way of Miser Brimpson's ghost.

What she did, none but them as helped her ever knew, until the story comed round to me; but 'twas the cleverest thing that ever I heard of a maiden doing, and it worked a wonder. In fact, I can't see but a single objection to the plot, though that was a serious thing for the girl. It lay in the fact that there had to be a secret between Hyssop and her husband; and she kept it close as the grave until the grave itself closed over him. Yet 'twas an innocent secret, too; and, when all's said, 'tisn't a wedded pair in five hundred as haven't each their one little cupboard fast locked, with the key throwed away.

Six months passed by, and Jonathan worked as only he knowed how to work, and tried to forget his sad disappointment by dint of toil. Early and late he laboured, and got permission to reclaim a bit of moor for a "newtake," and so added a very fair three acres to his farm. He noticed about this time that his hind, Parsons, did oft drag up the subject of Miser Brimpson Drake; and first Jonathan laughed, and then he was angered, and bade Thomas hold his peace. But, though a very obedient and humble sort of man, Parsons would hark back to the subject, and tell how his father had known a man who was own brother to a miser; and how, when the miser died, his own brother had seen him clear as truth in the chimley-corner of his room three nights after they'd buried him; and how they made search, and found, not three feet from where the ghost had stood, a place in the wall with seventeen golden sovereigns hid in it, and a white witch's cure for glanders. Thomas Parsons swore on the Book to this; and he said, as a certain fact, that New Year's Night was the time most misers walked; and he advised Jonathan not to be dead to his own interests.

"At least, as a thinking man, that believes in religion and the powers of the air, in Bible word, you might give it a chance," said Thomas; and then Jonathan told him to shut his mouth, and not shame Dunnabridge by talking such childish nonsense.

The next autumn Jonathan went up beyond Exeter to buy some of they black-faced, horned Scotch sheep, and he wanted for Parsons to go with him; but his man falled ill the night afore, and so young Hacker went instead.

Drake reckoned then that Thomas Parsons would have to leave, for

Dunnabridge weren't a place for sick folk; and he'd made up his mind after he came back to turn the old chap off; but Thomas was better when the master got home, so the question of sacking him was let be, and Jonathan contented himself by telling Tom that, if he falled ill again, 'twould be the last time. And Parsons said that was as it should be; but he hoped that at his age—merely sixty-five or thereabout—he wouldn't be troubled with his breathing parts again for half a score o' years at least. He added that he'd done his work as usual while the master was away; but he didn't mention that Hyssop Burges had made so bold as to call at Dunnabridge with a pony and cart, and that she'd spent a tidy long time there, and gone all over the house and farmyard, among other places, afore she drove off again.

And the next chapter of the story was told by Jonathan himself to his two men on the first day of the following year.

There was but little light of morning just then, and the three of 'em were putting down some bread and bacon and a quart of tea by candlelight in the Dunnabridge kitchen, when Thomas saw that his master weren't eating nothing to name. Instead, he went out to the barrel and drawed himself a pint of ale, and got along by the peat fire with it, and stuck his boots so nigh the scads as he dared without burning 'em.

"What's amiss?" said Thomas. "Don't say you'm sick, master. And if you be, I lay no liquor smaller than brandy will fetch you round."

"I bain't sick," answered Jonathan shortly.

He seemed in doubt whether to go on. Then he resolved to do so.

"There was a man in the yard last night," he said; "and, if I thought as either of you chaps knowed anything about it, I'd turn you off this instant, afore you'd got the bacon out of your throats."

"A man? Never!" cried Parsons.

"How was it the dog didn't bark?" asked Hacker.

"How the devil do I know why he didn't bark?" answered Jonathan, dark as night, and staring in the fire. One side of his face was red with the flames, and t'other side blue as steel along of the daylight just beginning to filter in at the window.

"All I can say is this," he added. "I turned in at half-after ten, just after that brace of old fools to Brownberry went off to see the New Year in. I slept till midnight; then something woke me with a start. What 'twas, I can't tell, but some loud sound near at hand, no doubt. I was going off again when I heard more row—a steady sound repeated over and over. And first I thought 'twas owls; and then I heard 'twas not. You might have said 'twas somebody thumping on a barrel; but, at any rate, I woke up, and sat up, and found the noise was in the yard.

"I looked out of my chamber window then, and the moon was bright as day, and the stars sparkling likewise; and there, down by 'the Judge's Table' where the thorn-tree grows, I see a man standing by the old barrel as plain as I see you chaps now."

"The Judge's Table" be a wonnerful curiosity at Dunnabridge, and if you go there you'll do well to axe to see it. 'Tis a gert slab of moor-stone said to have come from Crokern Torr, where the tinners held theer parliament in the ancient times. Now it bides over a water-trough with a white-thorn tree rising up above.

Jonathan took his breath when he'd got that far, and fetched his pipe out of his pocket and lighted it. Then he drank off half the beer, and spat in the fire, and went on.

"A man so tall as me, if not taller. He'd got one of them old white beaver hats on his head, and he wore a flowing white beard, so long as my plough-horse's tail, and he walked up and down, up and down over the stones, like a sailor walks up and down on the deck of a ship. I shouted to the chap, but he didn't take no more notice than the moon. Up and down he went; and then I told him, if he wasn't off inside two minutes, I'd get my fowling-piece and let fly. Still he paid no heed; and I don't mind saying to you men that, for half a second, I felt creepy-crawly and goose-flesh down the back. But 'twas only the cold, I reckon, for my window was wide open, and I'd been leaning out of it for a good while into ten degrees of frost.

"After that, I got angry, and went down house and hitched the gun off the hooks over the mantelpiece, and ran out, just as I was, in nought but my boots and my nightshirt. The hour was so still as the grave at first, and the moon shone on the river far below and lit up the eaves and windows; and then, through the silence, I heard Widecombe bells ringing in the New Year. But the old night-bird in his top hat was gone. Not a hair of his beard did he leave behind. I looked about, and then up came the dog, barking like fury, not knowing who I was, dressed that way, till he heard my voice. And that's the tale; and who be that curious old rascal I'd much like to know."

They didn't answer at first, and the daylight gained on 'em. Then old Parsons spoke up, and wagged his head and swore that 'twas no man his master had seen, but a creature from the other world.

"I'll lay my life," he said, "'twas the spectrum of Miser Brimpson as you saw walking; and I'll take oath by the New Year that 'twas his way to show where his stuff be buried. For God's sake," he says, "if you don't want to get into trouble with unknown creatures, go out and pull up the cobblestones, and see if there's anything underneath 'em."

But Jonathan made as though the whole thing was nonsense, and wouldn't let neither Thomas nor Hacker move a pebble. Only, the next day, he went off to a very old chap called Samuel Windeatt, whose father had been a boy at the time of the War Prison, and was said to have seen and known Miser Brimpson in the flesh. And the old man declared that, in his childish days, he'd heard of the miser, and that he certainly wore a beaver hat and had a white beard a yard long. So Jonathan came home again more thoughtful than afore, and finally—though he declared that he was ashamed to do it—he let Tom over persuade him; and two days after the three men set to work where Drake had seen the spectrum.

They dug and they dug, this way and that; and Jonathan found nought, and Parsons found nought; but Hacker came upon a box, and they dragged it out of the earth, and underneath of it was another box like the first. They was a pair of old rotten wood chests, by the look of them, made of boards nailed together with rusty nails. No locks or keys they had; but that was no matter, for they fell abroad at a touch, and inside of them was a lot of plate—candlesticks, snuffers, tea-kettles, table silver, and the like.

"Thunder!" cried out Jonathan. "'Tis all pewter trash, not worth a five-pound note! Us'll dig again."

And dig they did for a week, till the farmyard in that place was turned over like a trenched kitchen-garden. But not another teaspoon did they find.

Meantime, however, somebody as understood such things explained to young Drake that the stuff unearthed was not pewter, nor yet Britannia metal neither, but old Sheffield plate, and worth plenty of good money at that.

Jonathan felt too mazed with the event to do anything about it for a month; then he went to Plymouth, and took a few pieces of the find in his bag. And the man what he showed 'em to was so terrible interested that nothing would do but he must come up to Dunnabridge and see the lot. He offered two hundred and fifty pound for the things on the nail; so Jonathan saw very clear that they must be worth a good bit more. They haggled for a week, and finally the owner went up to Exeter and got another chap to name a price. In the long run, the dealers halved the things, and Jonathan comed out with a clear three hundred and fifty-four pound.

3

He wasn't very pleased to talk about his luck, and inquisitive people got but little out of him on the subject; but, of course, Parsons and Hacker spoke free and often on the subject, for 'twas the greatest adventure as had ever come to them in their lives; and, from telling the tale over and over old Parsons got to talk about it as if he'd seen the ghost himself.

Then, after he'd chewed over the matter for a space of three or four months, and spring was come again, Jonathan Drake went off one night to White Works, just the same as he used to do when he was courting Hyssop Burges; and there was the little party as usual, with Mrs. Stonewer knitting, and Farmer reading yesterday's newspaper, and Hyssop sewing in her place by her aunt.

"Well!" says Farmer Jimmy, "wonders never cease! And to see you again here be almost so big a wonder as that they tell about of the old miser's tea-things. I'm sure we all give you joy, Jonathan; and I needn't tell you as we was cruel pleased to hear about it."

The young man thanked them very civilly, and said how 'twas a coorious come-along-of-it, and he didn't hardly know what to think of the matter even to that day.

"I should reckon 'twas a bit of nonsense what I'd dreamed," he said; "but money's money, as who should know better than me? And, by the same token, I want a few words with Hyssop if she'm willing to give me ten minutes of her time."

"You'm welcome, Mr. Drake," she said.

He started at the surname; but she got up, and they went off just in the usual way to the parlour; and when they was there, she sat down in her old corner of the horsehair sofa and looked at him. But he didn't sit down—not at first. He walked about fierce and talked fierce.

"I'll axe one question afore I go on, and, if the answer's what I fear, I'll trouble you no more," he said. "In a word, be you tokened again? I suppose you be, for you're not the sort to go begging. Say it quick if 'tis so, and I'll be off and trouble you no further."

"No, Mr. Drake. I'm free as the day you—you throwed me over," she answered, in a very quiet little voice.

He snorted at that, but was too mighty thankful to quarrel with the words. She could see he began to grow terrible excited now; and he walked up and down, taking shorter and shorter strides this way and that, like a hungry caged tiger as knows his bit of horse-flesh be on the way.

At last he bursts out again.

"There was a lot of lies told about that old plate us found at Dunnabridge. But the truth of the matter is, that I sold it for three hundred and fifty-four pounds."

"So Tom Parsons told uncle. A wonderful thing; and we sat up all night talking about it, Mr. Drake."

"For God's sake call me 'Jonathan'!" he cried out; "and tell me—tell me what the figure of your legacy was. You must tell me—you can't withhold it. 'Tis life or death—to me."

She'd never seen him so excited, but very well knowed what was in his mind.

"If you must know, you must," she answered. "I thought I told you when—when—"

"No, you didn't. I wouldn't bide to hear. Whatever 'twas, you'd got more than me, and that was all I cared about; but now, if by good fortune 'tis less than mine, you understand—"

"Of course 'tis less. A hundred and eighty pound and the interest—a little over two hundred in all—is what I've gotten."

"Thank God!" he said.

Then he axed her if she could marry him still, or if she knew too much about his ways and his ideas to care about doing so.

And she took him again.

* * * * * * * *

You see, Hyssop Burges was my mother, and when father died I had the rights of the story from her. By that time the old people at White Works and Tom Parsons was all gone home, and the secret remained safe enough with Hyssop herself.

The great difficulty was to put half her money and more, slap into Jonathan's hands without his knowing how it got there; and, even when the game with the ghost was hit upon, 'twas hard to know how to do it clever. Hyssop wanted to hide golden sovereigns at Dunnabridge; but her uncle, with wonnerful wit, pointed out that they'd all be dated; and to get three hundred sovereigns and more a hundred years old could never have been managed. Then old Thomas, who was in the secret, of course, and played the part of Miser Brimpson, and got five pounds for doing it so clever, and another five after from his master, when the stuff was found—he thought upon trinkums and jewels; and finally Mrs. Stonewer, as had a friend in the business, said that Sheffield plate would do the trick. And she was right. The plate was bought for three hundred and eighty pound, and kept close at White Works till 'twas known that Jonathan meant to go away and bide away some days. Then my mother drove across with it; and Thomas made the cases wi' old rotten boards, and they drove a slant hole under the cobbles, and got all vitty again long afore young Drake came back home.

"Me and Jonathan was wedded in the fall of that year," said my mother to me when she told the tale. "And, come the next New Year's Night, he was at our chamber window as the clock struck twelve, and bided there looking out into the yard for an hour, keen as the hawk that he was. He thought I must be asleep; but well I knowed he was seeking for an old man in a beaver hat wi' a long white beard, and well I knowed he'd never see him again. Of course your father took good care not to tell me the next morning that he'd been on the lookout for the ghost."

And my mother, in her own last days, oft dwelt on that trick; and sometimes she'd say, as the time for meeting father got nearer and nearer, "I wonder if 'twill make any difference in heaven, where no secrets be hid?" And, knowing father so well as I had, I felt very sure as it might make a mighty lot of difference. So, in my crafty way, I hedged, and told mother that, for my part, I felt sartain there were some secrets that wouldn't even be allowed to come out at Judgment Day, for fear of turning heaven into t'other place; and that this was one of 'em. She always used to fret at that, however.

"I want for it to come out," she'd say. "And, if Jonathan don't know, I shall certainly tell him. I've kept it in long enough, and I can't trust myself to do it no more. He've got to know, and, with all eternity to get over it and forgive me in, I have a right to be hopeful that he will."

Hyssop Drake died in that fixed resolve; and I'm sure I trust that, when 'tis my turn to join my parents again, I shall find no shadow between 'em. But there's a lot of doubt about it—knowing father.

The Haunted Photograph

Ruth McEnery Stuart

To the ordinary observer it was just a common photograph of a cheap summer hotel. It hung sumptuously framed in plush, over the Widow Morris's mantel, the one resplendent note in an otherwise modest home, in a characteristic Queen Anne village.

One had only to see the rapt face of its owner as she sat in her weeds before the picture, which she tearfully pronounced "a strikin' likeness," to sympathize with the townsfolk who looked askance at the bereaved woman, even while they bore with her delusion, feeling sure that her sudden sorrow had set her mind agog.

When she had received the picture through the mail, some months before the fire which consumed the hotel—a fire through which she had not passed, but out of which she had come a widow—she proudly passed it around among the friends waiting with her at the post-office, replying to their questions as they admired it:

"Oh, yes! That's where he works—if you can call it work. He's the head steward in it. All that row o' winders where you see the awnin's down, they're his—an' them that ain't down, they're his, too—that is to say, it's his jurisdiction.

"You see, he's got the whip hand over the cook an' the sto'eroom, an' that key don't go out o' his belt unless he knows who's gettin' what—an' he's firm. Morris always was. He's like the iron law of the Ephesians."

"What key?"

It was an old lady who held the picture at arm's length, the more closely to scan it, who asked the question. She asked it partly to know, as neither man nor key appeared in the photograph, and partly to parry the "historic allusion"—a disturbing sort of fire for which Mrs. Morris was rather noted and which made some of her most loyal townsfolk a bit shy of her.

"Oh, I ain't referrin' to the picture," she hastened to explain. "I mean the keys thet he always carries in his belt. The reg'lar joke there is to call him 'St. Peter,' an' he takes it in good part, for, he declares, if there *is* such a thing *as* a similitude to the kingdom o' Heaven *in* a hotel, why, it's in the providential supply department which, in a manner, hangs to his belt. He always humours a joke—'specially on himself.'"

No one will ever know through what painful periods of unrequited longing the Widow Morris had sought solace in this, her only cherished "relic," after the "half hour of sky-works" which had made her, in her own vernacular, "a lonely, conflagrated widow, with a heart full of ashes," before the glad moment when it was given her to discern in it an unsuspected and novel value. First had come, as a faint gleam of comfort, the reflection that although her dear lost one was not in evidence in the picture, he had really been inside the building when the photograph was taken, and so, of course, *he must be in there yet!*

At first she experienced a slight disappointment that her man was not visible, at door or window. But it was only a passing regret. It was really better to feel him surely and broadly within—at large in the great house, free to pass at will from one room to another. To have had him fixed, no matter how effectively, would have been a limitation. As it was, she pressed the picture to her bosom as she wondered if, perchance, he would not some day come out of his hiding to meet her.

It was a muffled pleasure and tremulously entertained at first, but the very whimsicality of it was an appeal to her sensitized imagination, and so, when finally the thing did really happen, it is small wonder that it came somewhat as a shock.

It appears that one day, feeling particularly lonely and forlorn, and having no other comfort, she was pressing her tear-stained face against the row of window-shutters in the room without awnings, this being her nearest approach to the alleged occupant's bosom, when she was suddenly startled by a peculiar swishing sound, as of wind-blown rain, whereupon she lifted her face to perceive that it was indeed raining, and then, glancing back at the photograph, she distinctly saw her husband rushing from one window to another, drawing down the sashes on the side of the house that would have been exposed to the real shower whose music was in her ears.

This was a great discovery, and, naturally enough, it set her weeping, for, she sobbed, it made her feel, for a minute, that she had lost her widowhood and that, after the shower, he'd be coming home.

It might well make any one cry to suddenly lose the pivot upon which his emotions are swung. At any rate, Mrs. Morris cried. She said that she cried all night, first because it seemed so spooky to see him whose remains she had so recently buried on faith, waiving recognition in the debris, dashing about now in so matter-of-fact a way.

And then she wept because, after all, he did not come.

This was the formal beginning of her sense of personal companionship in the picture—companionship, yes, of delight in it, for there is even delight in tears—in some situations in life. Especially is this true of one whose emotions are her only guides, as seems to have been the case with the Widow Morris.

After seeing him draw the window-sashes—and he had drawn them *down*, ignoring her presence—she sat for hours, waiting for the rain to stop. It seemed to have set in for a long spell, for when she finally fell asleep, "from sheer disappointment, 'long towards morning,'" it was still raining, but when she awoke the sun shone and all the windows in the picture were up again.

This was a misleading experience, however, for she soon discovered that she could not count upon any line of conduct by the man in the hotel, as the fact that it had one time rained in the photograph at the same time that it rained outside was but a coincidence and she was soon surprised to perceive all quiet along the hotel piazza, not even an awning flapping, while the earth, on her plane, was torn by storms.

On one memorable occasion when her husband had appeared, flapping the window-panes from within with a towel, she had thought for one brief moment that he was beckoning to her, and that she might have to go to him, and she was beginning to experience terror, with shortness of breath and other premonitions of sudden passing, when she discovered that he was merely killing flies, and she flurriedly fanned herself with the asbestos mat which she had seized from the stove beside her, and staggered out to a seat under the mulberries, as she stammered:

"I do declare, Morris'll be the death of me yet. He's 'most as much care to me dead as he was alive—I made sure—made sure he'd come after me!"

Then, feeling her own fidelity challenged, she hastened to add:

"Not that I hadn't rather go to him than to take any trip in the world, but—but I never did fancy that hotel, and since I've got used to seein' him there so constant, I feel sure that's where we'd put up. My belief is, anyway, that if there's hereafters for some things, there's hereafters for all. From what I can gather, I reckon I'm a kind of a cross between a Swedenborgian and a Gates-ajar—that, of course, engrafted on to a Methodist. Now, that hotel, when it was consumed by fire, which to it was the same as mortal death, why, it either ascended into Heaven, in smoke, or it fell, in ashes—to the other place. If it died worthy, like as not it's undergoin' repairs now for a 'mansion,' jasper cupolas, an'—but, of course, such as that could be run up in a twinklin'.

"Still, from what I've heard, it's more likely gone *down* to its deserts. It would seem hard for a hotel with so many awned-off corridors an' palmed embrasures with *tete-a-tete* sofas, to live along without sin."

She stood on her step-ladder, wiping the face of the picture as she spoke, and as she began to back down she discovered the cat under her elbow, glaring at the picture.

"Yes, Kitty! Spit away!" she exclaimed. "Like as not you see even more than I do!"

And as she slipped the ladder back into the closet, she remarked—this to herself, strictly:

"If it hadn't 'a' been for poor puss, I'd 'a' had a heap more pleasure out o' this picture than what I have had—or will be likely to have again. The way she's taken on, I've almost come to hate it!"

A serpent had entered her poor little Eden—even the green-eyed monster constrictor, who, if given full swing, would not spare a bone of her meagre comfort.

A neighbour who chanced to come in at the time, unobserved overheard the last remark, and Mrs. Morris, seeing that she was there, continued in an unchanged tone, while she gave her a chair:

"Of course, Mis' Withers, you can easy guess who I refer to. I mean that combly-featured wench that kep' the books an' answered the telephone at the hotel—when she found the time from her meddlin'. Somehow, I never thought about her bein' *burned in* with Morris till puss give her away. Puss never did like the girl when she was alive, an' the first time I see her scratch an' spit at the picture, just the way she used to do whenever *she* come in sight, why, it just struck me like a clap o' thunder out of a clear sky that puss knew who she was a-spittin' at—an' I switched around sudden—an' glanced up sudden—an'—

"Well, what I seen, I seen! There was that beautied-up typewriter settin' in the window-sill o' Morris's butler's pantry—an' if she didn't wink at me malicious, then I don't know malice when I see it. An' she used her fingers against her nose, too, most defiant and impolite. So I says to puss I says, 'Puss,' I says, 'there's *goin's on* in that hotel, sure as fate. Annabel Bender has got the better o' me, for once!' An', tell the truth, it did spoil the photograph for me for a while, for, of course, after that, if I didn't see him somewheres on the watch for his faithful spouse, I'd say to myself, 'He's inside there with that pink-featured hussy!'

"You know, a man's a man, Mis' Withers—'specially Morris, an' with his lawful wife cut off an' indefinitely divorced by a longevitied family—an' another burned in with him—well, his faithfulness is put to a trial by fire, as you might say. So, as I say, it spoiled the picture for me, for a while.

"An', to make matters worse, it wasn't any time before I recollected that Campbellite preacher thet was burned in with them, an' with that my imagination run riot, an' I'd think to myself, '*If* they're inclined, they cert'n'y have things handy!' Then I'd ketch myself an' say, 'Where's your faith in Scripture, Mary Marthy Matthews, named after two Bible women an' born daughter to an apostle? What's the use?' I'd say, an' so, first an' last, I'd get a sort o' alpha an' omega comfort out o' the passage about no givin' in marriage. Still, there'd be times, pray as I would, when them three would loom up, him an' her—*an'* the Campbellite preacher. I know his license to marry would run out *in time*, but for eternity, of course we don't know. Seem like everything would last forever—an' then again, if I've got a widow's freedom, Morris must be classed as a widower, if he's anything.

"Then I'd get some relief in thinkin' about his disposition. Good as he was, Morris was fickle-tasted, not in the long run, but day in an' day out, an' even if he'd be taken up with her he'd get a distaste the minute he reelized she'd be there interminable. That's Morris. Why, didn't he used to get nervous just seein' *me* around, an' me his own selected? An' didn't I use to make some excuse to send him over to Mame Maddern's ma's ma's—so's he'd be harmlessly diverted? She was full o' talk, and she was ninety-odd an' asthmatic, but he'd come home from them visits an' call me his child wife. I've had my happy moments!

"You know a man'll get tired of himself, even, if he's condemned to it too continual, and think of that blondinetted typewriter for a steady diet—to a man like Morris! Imagine her when her hair dye started to give out—green streaks in that pompadour! So, knowin' my man, I'd take courage an' I'd think, 'Seein' me cut off, he'll soon be wantin' me more than ever'—an' so he does. It's got so now that, glance up at that hotel any time I will, I can generally find him on the lookout, an' many's the time I've stole in an' put on a favouryte apron o' his with blue bows on it, when we'd be alone an' nobody to remark about me breakin' my mournin'. Dear me, how full o' b'oyancy he was—a regular boy at thirty-five, when he passed away!"

Was it any wonder that her friends exchanged glances while Mrs. Morris entertained them in so droll a way? Still, as time passed and she not only brightened in the light of her delusion, but proceeded to meet the conditions of her own life by opening a small shop in her home, and when she exhibited a wholesome sense of profit and loss, her neighbours were quite ready to accept her on terms of mental responsibility.

With occupation and a modest success, emotional disturbance was surely giving place to an even calm, when, one day, something happened.

Mrs. Morris sat behind her counter, sorting notions, puss asleep beside her, when she heard the swish of thin silk, with a breath of familiar perfume, and, looking up, whom did she see but the blond lady of her troubled dreams striding bodily up to the counter, smiling as she swished.

At the sight the good woman first rose to her feet, and then as suddenly dropped—flopped—breathless and white—backward—and had to be revived, so that for the space of some minutes things happened very fast—that is, if we may believe the flurried testimony of the blonde, who, in going over it, two hours later, had more than once to stop for breath.

"Well, say!" she panted. "Did you ever! *Such* a turn as took her! I hadn't no more 'n stepped in the door when she succumbed, green as the Ganges, into her own egg-basket—an' it full! An' she was on the eve o' floppin' back into the prunin' scizzor points up, when I scrambled over the counter, breakin' my straight-front in two, which she's welcome to, poor thing! Then I loaned her my smellin'-salts, which she held her breath against until it got to be a case of smell or die, an' she smelt! Then it was a case of temporary spasms for a minute, the salts spillin' out over her face, but when the accident evapourated, an' she opened her eyes, rational, I thought to myself, 'Maybe she don't know she's keeled an' would be humiliated if she did,' so I acted callous, an' I says, offhand like, I says, pushin' her apron around behind her over its *vice versa*, so's to cover up the eggs, which I thought had better be broke to her gently, I says, 'I just called in, Mis' Morris, to borry your recipe for angel-cake—or maybe get you to bake one for us' (I knew she baked on orders). An' with that, what does she do but go over again, limp as wet starch, down an' through every egg in that basket, solid *an'* fluid!

"Well, by this time, a man who had seen her at her first worst an' run for a doctor, he come in with three, an' whilst they were bowin' to each other an' backin', I giv' 'er stimulus an' d'rectly she turned upon me one remembrable gaze, an' she says, 'Doctors,' says she, 'would you think they'd have the gall to try to get me to cook for 'em? They've ordered angel-ca—' An' with that, over she toppled again, no pulse nor nothin', same as the dead!"

While the blonde talked she busied herself with her loosely falling locks, which she tried vainly to entrap.

"An' yet you say she ain't classed as crazy? I'd say it of her, sure! An' so old Morris is dead—burned in that old hotel! Well, well! Poor old fellow! Dear old place! What times I've had!"

She spoke through a mouthful of gilt hairpins and her voice was as an Aeolian harp.

"An' he burned in it—an' she's a widow yet! Yes, I did hear there'd been a fire, but you never can tell. I thought the chimney might 'a' burned out—an' I was in the thick of bein' engaged to the night clerk at the Singin' Needles Hotel at Pineville at the time—an' there's no regular mail there. I thought the story might be exaggerated. Oh no, I didn't marry the night clerk. I'm a bride now, married to the head steward, same rank as poor old Morris—an' we're just *as* happy! I used to pleg Morris about *her* hair, but I'd have to let up on that now. Mine's as red again as hers. No, not my hair—*mine's* hair. It's as red as a flannen drawer, every bit an' grain!

"But, say," she added, presently, "when she gets better, just tell her never mind about that recipe. I copied it out of her recipe book whilst she was under the weather, an' dropped a dime in her cash-drawer. I recollect how old Morris used to look forward to her angel-cakes week-ends he'd be goin' home, an' you know there's nothin' like havin' ammunition, in marriage, even if you never need it. Mine's in that frame of mind now that transforms my gingerbread into angel-cake, but the time may come when I'll have to beat my eggs to a fluff even for angel-cake, so's not to have it taste like gingerbread to him.

"Oh no, he's not with me this trip. I just run down for a lark to show my folks my ring an' things, an' let 'em see it's really so. He give me considerable jewellery. His First's taste run that way, an' they ain't no children.

"Yes, this amethyst is the weddin'-ring. I selected that on account of him bein' a widower. It's the nearest I'd come to wearin' second mournin' for a woman I can't exactly grieve after. The year not bein' up is why he stayed home this trip. He didn't like to be seen traversin' the same old haunts with Another till it *was* up. I wouldn't wait because, tell the truth, I was afraid. He ain't like a married man with me about money yet, an' it's liable to seize him any day. He might say that he couldn't afford the trip, or that we couldn't, which would amount to the same thing. I rather liked him bein' a little ticklish about goin' around with me for a while. It's one thing to do a thing an' another to be brazen about it—it—

"But if she don't get better"—the reversion was to the Widow Morris—"if she don't get her mind poor thing! there's a fine insane asylum just out of Pineville, an' I'd like the best in the world to look out for her. It would make an excuse for me to go in. They say they have high old times there. Some days they let the inmates do 'most any old thing that's harmless. They even give 'em unpoisonous paints an' let 'em paint each other up. One man insisted he was a barber-pole an' ringed himself accordingly, an' then another chased him around for a stick of peppermint candy. Think of all that inside a close fence, an' a town so dull an' news-hungry—

"Yes, they say Thursdays is paint days, an', of course, Fridays, they are scrub days. They pass around turpentine an' hide the matches. But, of course, Mis' Morris may get the better of it. 'Tain' every woman that can stand widowin', an' sometimes them that has got the least out of marriage will seem the most deprived to lose it—so they say."

The blonde was a person of words.

* * * * * * * *

When Mrs. Morris had fully revived and, after a restoring "night's sleep" had got her bearings, and when she realized clearly that her supposed rival had actually shown up in the flesh, she visibly braced up. Her neighbours understood that it must have been a shock "to be suddenly confronted with any souvenir of the hotel fire"—so one had expressed it—and the incident soon passed out of the village mind.

It was not long after this incident that the widow confided to a friend that she was coming to depend upon Morris for advice in her business.

"Standing as he does, in that hotel door—between two worlds, as you might say—why, he sees both ways, and oftentimes he'll detect an event *on the way to happening,* an' if it don't move too fast, why, I can hustle an' get the better of things." It was as if she had a private wire for advance information—and she declared herself happy.

Indeed, a certain ineffable light such as we sometimes see in the eyes of those newly in love came to shine from the face of the widow, who did not hesitate to affirm, looking into space as she said it:

"Takin' all things into consideration, I can truly say that I have never been so truly and ideely married as since my widowhood." And she smiled as she added:

"Marriage, the earthly way, is vicissitudinous, for everybody knows that anything is liable to happen to a man at large."

There had been a time when she lamented that her picture was not "life-sized" as it would seem so much more natural, but she immediately reflected that that hotel would never have gotten into her little house, and that, after all, the main thing was having "him" under her own roof.

As the months passed Mrs. Morris, albeit she seemed serene and of peaceful mind, grew very white and still. Fire is white in its ultimate intensity. The top, spinning its fastest, is said to "sleep"—and the dancing dervish is "still." So, misleading signs sometimes mark the danger-line.

"Under-eating and over-thinking" was what the doctor said while he felt her translucent wrist and prescribed nails in her drinking-water. If he secretly knew that kind nature was gently letting down the bars so that a waiting spirit might easily pass—well, he was a doctor, not a minister. His business was with the body, and he ordered repairs.

She was only thirty-seven and "well" when she passed painlessly out of life. It seemed to be simply a case of going.

There were several friends at her bedside the night she went, and to them she turned, feeling the time come:

"I just wanted to give out that the first thing I intend to do when I'm relieved is to call by there for Morris"—she lifted her weary eyes to the picture as she spoke—"for Morris—and I want it understood that it'll be a vacant house from the minute I depart. So, if there's any other woman that's calculatin' to have any carryin's-on from them windows—why, she'll be disappointed—she or they. The one obnoxious person I thought was in it *wasn't*. My imagination was tempted of Satan an' I was misled. So it must be sold for just what it is—just a photographer's photograph. If it's a picture with a past, why, everybody knows what that past is, and will respect it. I have tried to conquer myself enough to bequeath it to the young lady I suspicioned, but human nature is frail, an' I can't quite do it, although doubtless she would like it as a souvenir. Maybe she'd find it a little too souvenirish to suit my wifely taste, and yet—if a person is going to die—

"I suppose I might legate it to her, partly to recompense her for her discretion in leaving that hotel when she did—an' partly for undue suspicion—

"There's a few debts to be paid, but there's eggs an' things that'll pay them, an' there's no need to have the hen settin' in the window showcase any longer. It was a good advertisement, but I've often thought it might be embarrassin' to her." She was growing weaker, but she roused herself to amend:

"Better raffle the picture for a dollar a chance an' let the proceeds go to my funeral—an' I want to be buried in the hotel-fire general grave, commingled with him—an' what's left over after the debts are paid, I bequeath to *her*—to make amends—an' if she don't care to come for it, let every widow in town draw for it. But she'll come. 'Most any woman'll take any trip, if it's paid for—But look!" she raised her eyes excitedly toward the mantel, "Look! What's that he's wavin'? It looks—oh yes, it is—it's our wings—two pairs—mine a little smaller. I s'pose it'll be the same old story—I'll never be able to keep up—to keep up with him—an' I've been so hap—

"Yes, Morris—I'm comin'—"

And she was gone—into a peaceful sleep from which she easily passed just before dawn.

When all was well over, the sitting women rose with one accord and went to the mantel, where one even lighted an extra candle more clearly to scan the mysterious picture.

Finally one said:

"You may think I'm queer, but it does look different to me already!"

"So it does," said another, taking the candle. "Like a house for rent. I declare, it gives me the cold shivers."

"I'll pay my dollar gladly, and take a chance for it," whispered a third, "but I wouldn't let such a thing as that enter my happy home—"

"Neither would I!"

"Nor me, neither. I've had trouble enough. My husband's first wife's portrait has brought me discord enough—an' it was a straight likeness. I don't want any more pictures to put in the hen-house loft."

So the feeling ran among the wives.

"Well," said she who was blowing out the candle, "I'll draw for it—an' take it if I win it, an' consider it a sort of inheritance. I never inherited anything but indigestion."

The last speaker was a maiden lady, and so was she who answered, chuckling:

"That's what I say! Anything for a change. There'd be some excitement in a picture where a man was liable to show up. It's more than I've got now. I do declare it's just scandalous the way we're gigglin', an' the poor soul hardly out o' hearin'. She had a kind heart, Mis' Morris had, an' she made herself happy with a mighty slim chance—"

"Yes, she did—and I only wish there'd been a better man waitin' for her in that hotel."

The Ghost that Got the Button

Will Adams

One autumn evening, when the days were shortening and the darkness fell early on Hotchkiss and the frost was beginning to adorn with its fine glistening lace the carbine barrels of the night sentries as they walked post, Sergeants Hansen and Whitney and Corporal Whitehall had come to Stone's room after supper, feeling the need common to all men in the first cold nights of the year for a cosy room, a good smoke, and congenial companionship.

The steam heat, newly turned on, wheezed and whined through the radiator: the air was blue and dense with tobacco smoke; the three sergeants reposed in restful, if inelegant attitudes, and Whitehall, his feet on the window sill and his wooden chair tilted back, was holding forth between puffs at a very battered pipe about an old coloured woman who kept a little saloon in town.

"So she got mad at those K troop men," he said. "An' nex' day when Turner stopped there for a drink she says: 'You git outer yere! You men fum de Arsenic wid de crossbones on you caps, I ain't lettin' you in; but de Medical Corpses an' de Non-efficient Officers, dey may come.'"

The laugh that followed was interrupted by the approach of a raucous, shrieking noise that rose and fell in lugubrious cadence. "What the deuce!" exclaimed Whitehall, starting up.

"That's Bill," explained Stone. "Bill Sullivan. He thinks he's singin'. Funny you never heard him before, Kid, but then he's not often taken that way, thank the Lord."

"Come in, Bill," he called, "an' tell us what's the matter. Feel sick? Where's the pain?" he asked as big Bill appeared in the doorway.

"Come in, hombre, an' rest yo'self," invited Whitney, and hospitably handed over his tobacco-pouch. "What was that tune yo'all were singin' out yonder?"

"Thanks," responded Bill, settling down. "That there tune was *I Wonder Where You Are To-night, My Love*."

"Sounded like *Sister's Teeth Are Plugged with Zinc*," commented Whitney.

"Or *Lookin' Through the Knot Hole in Papa's Wooden Leg*," said Whitehall.

"Or *He Won't Buy the Ashman a Manicure Set*," added Stone.

"No," reiterated Bill solemnly. "It was like I told yer; *I Wonder Where You Are To-night, My Love*, and it's a corker, too! I seen a feller an' a goil sing it in Kelly's Voddyville Palace out ter Cheyenne onct. Foist he'd sing one voise an' then she'd sing the nex'. He was dressed like a soldier, an' while he sang they was showin' tabloids o' what the goil was a-doin' behind him; an' then when she sang her voise he'd be in the tabloid, an' when it got ter the last voise, an' he was dyin' on a stretcher in a ambulance, everybody in the house was a-cryin' so yer could hardly hear her. It was great! My!" continued Bill, spreading out his great paws over the radiator, "ain't this the snappy evenin'? Real cold. Somehow it 'minds me of the cold we had in China that time of the Boxers, after we'd got ter the Legations; the nights was cold just like this is."

"Why, Bill," said Whitney, "I never knew yo'all were there then. Why did yo' never tell us befo'? What were yo' with?"

"Fourteenth Infantry," responded Bill proudly. "It's a great ol' regiment—don't care if they *are* doughboys."

"What company was you in?" inquired Hansen, ponderously taking his pipe from his mouth and breaking silence for the first time.

"J Company, same as this."

At this reply Stone opened his mouth abruptly to say something, but thought better of it and shut up again.

"It was blame cold them nights a week or so after we was camped in the Temple of Agriculture (that's what they called it—I dunno why), but say! the heat comin' up from Tientsin was fryin'! It was jus' boilin', bakin', an' bubblin'—worse a heap than anythin' we'd had in the islands. We chucked away mos' every last thing on that hike but canteens an' rifles. It was a darn fool thing ter do—the chuckin' was, o' course—but it come out all right, 'cause extree supplies follered us up on the Pie-ho in junks. Ain't that a funny name fer a river? Pie-ho? Every time I got homesick I'd say that river, an' then I'd see Hogan's Dairy Lunch fer Ladies an' Gents on the ol' Bowery an' hear the kid Mick Hogan yellin': 'Draw one in the dark! White wings—let her flop! Pie-ho!' an' it helped me a heap." Bill settled himself and stretched.

"But what I really wanted to tell youse about," said he, "was somepin' that happened one o' these here cold nights. It gits almighty cold there in September, an' it was sure the spookiest show I ever seen. Even Marm Haggerty's table rappin's in Hester Street never come up to it.

"There was three of us fellers who ran in a bunch them days: me an' Buck Dugan, my bunkie, from the Bowery like me (he was a corporal), an' Ranch Fields—we called him that 'cause he always woiked on a ranch before he come into the Fourteenth. They was great fellers, Buck an' Ranch was. Buck, now—yer couldn't phase him, yer couldn't never phase him, no matter what sort o' job yer put him up against he'd slide through slick as a greased rat. The Cap'n, he knew it, too. Onct when we was fightin' an' hadn't no men to spare, he lef' Buck on guard over about twenty-five Boxer prisoners in a courtyard an' tells him he dassent let one escape. But Buck wants ter git into the fight with the rest of the boys, an' when he finds that if he leaves them Chinos loose in the yard alone they'll git out plenty quick, what does he do but tie 'em tight up by their pigtails to some posts. He knows they can't undo them tight knots backwards, an' no Chink would cut his pigtail if he *did* have a knife—he'd die foist—an' so Buck skidoos off to the fight, an', sure enough, when the Cap'n wants them Boxers, they're ready, tied up an' waitin'. That was his sort, an', gee, but he was smart!

"We was all right int'rested in them Allies, o' course, an' watched 'em clost; but, 'Bill,' says Buck ter me one night, 'its been woikin in me nut that these here fellers ain't so different from what we know a'ready. Excep' fer their uniform an' outfits, we've met 'em all before but the Japs. Why, look a-here,' says he, 'foist, there's the white men— the English—ain't they jus' like us excep' that they're thicker an' we're longer? An' their Injun niggers—ain't we seen their clothes in the comic op'ras an' them without their clothes in the monkey cage at Central Park? An' their Hong-Kong China Regiment an' all the other Chinos is jus' the same as yer meet in the pipe joints in Mott Street. Then,' says he, 'come all the *dagos*. These leather necks of Macaroni *dagos* we've seen a swarmin' all over Mulberry Bend an' Five Points; the Sauerkraut *dagos* looks fer all the woild like they was goin' ter a Schützenfest up by High Bridge; the Froggie *dagos* you'll find packed in them Frenchy restaraws in the Thirties—where yer git blue wine— and them Vodki *dagos* only needs a pushcart ter make yer think yer in Baxter Street.'

"Buck, he could sure talk, but Ranch, he wasn't much on chin-chin. Little an' dark an' quiet he was, an' jus' crazy fer dogs. Any old mutt'd do fer him—jus' so's it was in the shape of a pup. He was fair wild fer 'em. He picked up a yeller cur out there the day after the Yangtsin fight, an' that there no-account, mangy, flea-bitten mutt had ter stay with us the whole time. If the pup didn't stand in me an' Buck an' Ranch, he swore he'd quit too, so we had to let him come, an' he messed an' bunked with our outfit right along. Ranch named him Daggett, after the Colonel, which was right hard on the C. O., but I bet Ranch thought he was complimentin' him. Why, Ranch considered himself honoured if any of the pup's fleas hopped off on him. The pup he kep' along with us right through everything; Ranch watchin' him like the apple of his eye, an' he hardly ever was out of our sight, till one night about a week after we quartered in the temple he didn't turn up fer supper. He was always so reg'lar at his chow that Ranch he begin ter git the squirms an' when come taps an' Daggett hadn't reported, Ranch had the razzle-dazzles.

"Nex' mornin' the foist thing he must go hunt that pup, an' went a scoutin' all day, me an' Buck helpin' him—but nary pup; an' come another supper without that miser'ble mutt, an' Ranch was up an alley all right, all right. He was all wore out, an' I made him hit the bunk early an' try ter sleep; but, Lord! No sooner he'd drop off 'n he git ter twitchin' an' hitchin' an' wake up a-yelpin' fer Daggett. Long about taps, Buck, who's been out on a private reconnaissance, comes back an' whispers ter me: 'Ssst, Bill! The cur's found! Don't tell Ranch; the bloke'd die of heart failure. I struck his trail an' follered it—an' say, Bill, what'n thunder do yer think? Them heathen Chinos has *et him*!' Lord, now, wouldn't that jolt youse? Them Chinos a-eatin' Daggett! It give me an awful jar, an' Buck he felt it, too. That there mutt had acted right decent, an' we knew Ranch would have bats in the belfry fer fair if he hoid tell o' the pup's finish; so says Buck; 'Let's not tell him, 'cause he's takin' on now like he'd lost mother an' father an' best goil an' all, an' if he knew Daggett was providin' chow fer Chinos he'd go clean bug house an' we'd have ter ship him home ter St. Elizabeth.'

"I says O. K. ter that, an' we made it up not ter let on ter Ranch; an' now here comes the spook part yer been a-waitin' fer.

"Four or five nights later I was on guard, an' my post was the farthest out we had on the north. There was an ol' road out over that way, an' I'd hoid tell it led ter a ol' graveyard, but I hadn't never been there myself an' hadn't thought much about it till 'long between two an' three o'clock, as I was a-hikin' up an down, when somepin' comes a-zizzin' down the road hell-fer-leather on to me, a-yellin' somepin' fierce. Gee, but I was skeered! I made sure it was a spook, an' there wasn't a bit o' breath left in me. I was all to the bad that time fer sure.

Before I had time ter think even, that screamin', streakin' thing was on me an a-grabbin' roun' my knees; an' then I see it was one o' them near-Christian Chinos, an' he's skeered more'n me even. His eyes had popped clean out'n their slits, an' his tongue was hangin' out by the roots, he was that locoed. I raised the long yell fer corporal of the guard, which happened, by good luck, ter be Buck, an' when he come a-runnin', thinkin' from the whoops I give we was bein' rushed by the hole push of Boxers, the two of us began proddin' at the Chink ter find out what was doin'. Took us some time, too, with him bein' in such a flutter an' hardly able ter even hand out his darn ol' pigeon English, that sounds like language comin' out of a sausage machine. When we did savvy his line of chop-suey talk, we found out he'd seen a ghost in the graveyard, an' not only seen it but he knew who the spook was an' all about him. We was gittin' some serious ourselves an' made him tell us.

"Seems it was a mandarin—that's a sort o' Chink police-court judge (till I got ter Tientsin I always thought they was little oranges), an' this tangerine's—I mean mandarin's—name was Wu Ti Ming, an' he'd been a high mucky-muckraker in his day, which was two or three hundred years back. But the Emprer caught him deep in some sort o' graft an' *took away his button* an' all o' his dough.

"'Lord!' says Buck when we come ter this, 'don't that prove what heathens Chinks is? Only one button ter keep on their clothes with, an' the Emprer he kin take it away! What did this here Judge Ming do then, John? Use string or pins?' This here John didn't seem ter savvy, but he said that the mandarin took on so fer his button an' his loss of pull in the ward that it was sure sad ter see, an' by an' by the Emprer got busy again with him an' had him finished up fer keeps; had him die the 'death of a thousand cuts,' says John. It sounded fierce ter me, but Buck he says:

"'Pshaw! Anybody who's been shaved reg'lar by them lady barbers on Fourth Avenyer would 'a' give the Emprer the merry ha-ha—'

"After Ming was cut up they took the remains of his corpse an' planted him in this here graveyard up the road; but he wouldn't stay planted an' began doin' stunts at night, 'topside walkee-walkee' an' a-huntin' fer his lost button. He'd used ter have the whole country scared up, but fer the last twenty years he'd kep' right quiet an' had hardly ever come out; but now sence the foreign devils come (ain't that a sweet name fer us?) he's up an' at it again worse than ever, an' the heathens is on their ear. Fer four nights now they'd seen him, wrapped in a blue robe, waitin' an' a-huntin' behind tombstones an'

166

walkin' round an' round the graveyard lie a six days' race fer the belt at Madison Square. John had jus' seen him on the wall, an' that was why he come chargin' down the road like forty cats.

"'Will Mr. Ming's sperrit walk till he gits that button back?' Buck asts. John says: 'Sure.'

"'Well,' says Buck, 'why don't yer give him one?'

"'No can give. Only Emplor, only Son of Heaven give.'

"'Well, look here,' says Buck, 'we sand rabbits ain't no sons of Heaven, but I'll be darned if we couldn't spare a button ter lay the ghost of a pore busted police-court judge, who's lost his job an' his tin, if *that's* all he wants back. What time does he come out at, John? Could we see him termorrer night?' 'Sure could we,' says John; 'he'll show us the way, but he won't wait with us; he's bad enough fer his.'

"So Buck takes John an' goes back ter the guard shack, as it's most time fer relief, an' after I got back we told John ter git the hook, an' we talked things over, an' Buck he was just wild ter see if he couldn't lay that Chino ghost. His talents was achin' ter git action on him; anythin' like that got up his spunk. Says I:

"'Maybe Ranch kin help. We'll tell him termorrer after guard mount. It'll take his mind off Daggett.'

"'No, yer don't,' says Buck. 'Don't yer dare tell him. He's nervous as a cat over the pup as it is, an' this spook business is awful skeery; I'm feelin' woozy over it meself. I'm all off when it comes ter ghosts—that is, if it's a real ghost. And things here in Pekin' is so funny the odds is all in favour of its bein' the sure thing. I ain't afeard o' no kinds o' people, but I sure git cold feet when I'm up against a ghost. Wouldn't that jar youse? An' me a soldier; when it's a soldier's whole business not ter *git* cold feet. But I'm bound I'll have a show at that ol' spook even if it *does* skeer me out o' my growth. Only don't yer dare tell Ranch.'

"Nex' night, right after eleven o'clock rounds, me an' Buck slipped outer our blankets, sneaked out past the guard, an' met John, who was waitin' fer us in the road jus' beyond where the last sentry woulder seen him. It was cold as git out. Jus' the same kind o' early cold as tonight, an' John's teeth was chatterin' like peas in a box—he was some loco with skeer, too, you bet.

"'Which way?' says Buck, an' John spouts a lot o' dope-joint lingo an' takes us up a side alley, where there's a whole bunch o' Chinos waitin' fer us, an' they begun a kowtowin' an' goin' on like we was the whole cheese. Turned out that John had jollied 'em that the Melican soldier mans was big medicine an' would make Judge Ming quit the midnight hike an' cut out scarin' 'em blue. That jus' suited Buck; he was all there when it come ter play commander in chief. He swelled up an' give 'em a bundle o' talk that John put in Chino fer 'em, an' then finished up by showin' 'em a button—a ol' United States Army brass button he'd cut off his blue blouse—an' tol' 'em he was goin' ter bury it in Ming's grave so as ter keep him bedded down.

"An' them simple idiots was pleased ter death, an' the whole outfit escorted us over ter the graveyard, but they shied at the gate (Lord, I hated ter see 'em go—even if they *was* heathens!), an' let John take us in an' show us where ter wait. He put us in behind a pile o' little rocks in about the middle o' the place near where Judge Ming hung out, an' then retired on the main body at the double, leavin' us two in outpost alone there together. I hadn't never been ter a Chino buryin' ground before, an' night time wasn't extree pleasant fer a foist introduce. There was a new moon that night—a little shavin' of a thing that hardly gave no light, an' from where we was there was a twisty pine tree branch that struck out right acrost it like a picture card—two fer five. The graveyard was all dark an' quiet, with little piles o' rocks an' stone tables ter mark the graves, an' a four or five-foot wall runnin' all round it; an' somehow, without nothin' stirrin' at all, the whole blame place seemed chock full o' movin' shadders. There wasn't a sound neither; not the least little thing; jus' them shadders; an' the harder yous'd look at 'em the more they seemed ter move. It was cold, too, like I told yer—bitin' cold—an' me an' Buck squatted there tight together an' mos' friz. We waited, an' we waited, an' *we waited*, an' we got skeerder, an' skeerder, an' *skeerder*, an', gee! how we shivered! Every minute we thought we'd see Judge Ming, but a long time went by an' he didn't come an' he *didn't* come. There we set, strung up tight an' ready ter snap like a banjo string, but nothin' ter see but the shakin' shadders an' nothin' ter hear—nothin' but jus' dead, dead silence.

"All of a suddent Buck (he kin hear a pin drop a mile away) nearly nips a piece out'n my arm as he grips me. 'Listen!' says he.

"I listened an' listened, but I didn't hear nothin', an' I told him so.

"'Yes, yer do, yer bloke yer,' he whispers, 'Listen. Strain your years.'

"Then way off I did begin ter hear somepin'. It was a long, funny, waily cry, sort o' like the way cats holler at each other at night. 'Oh-oo-oo, oh-oo-oo!' like that, an' it come nearer an' nearer. Then all of a suddent somepin' popped up on the graveyard wall about a hundred yards away—somepin' all blue-gray against the hook o' the moon—an' began walkin' up an' down an' hollerin'. I knew it was sayin' words, but I was so far to the bad I didn't know nothin' an' couldn't make it out. I never thought a feller's heart could bang so hard against his ribs without bustin' out, an' me hair riz so high me campaign hat was three inches off'n me head. I hope ter the Lord I'll never be so frightened again in all my livin' days. I set there in a transom from fear an' friz ter the spot. I don't know nothin' o' what Buck was doin', as my lamps was glued ter the spook. It jumped down from the wall, callin' an' whistlin' an' begin runnin' round the little stone heaps. I seen it was comin' our way, but I couldn't move or make a sound; I jus' set. All of a suddent Buck he jumps up an' makes a dash an' a leap at the spook, an' there's a terrible yellin' an' they both comes down crash at the foot of a rock pile, rollin' on the little pebbles; but Buck is on top an' the spook underneath an' lettin' off the most awful screeches. Gosh, they jus' ripped the air, them spooks' yells did, an' they turned my spell loose an' I howled fer all I was worth. Then Buck, he commenced a-yawpin' too, but me an' the spook we was both raisin' so much noise I didn't savvy what he said fer some time. Then I found he was cussin' me out.

"'Come here, you forsaken — —,' he howls. 'Quit yellin'! I say *quit yellin*'! Don't yer see who this is? Come here an' help me.'

"'You think I'm goin' ter tech that Ming spook?' I shrieks.

"'You miser'ble loony,' he yells back, 'can't yer see it ain't no Ming? It's Ranch!'

"Well, so it was. It was Ranch skeered stiff an' hollerin' fer dear life at bein' jumped on an' waked up in the middle of a graveyard that-away. Pore ol' feller had had Daggett on his mind, an' went sleepwalkin' an' huntin' wrapped in his blanket.

"'An',' says Buck ter me, 'if youse hadn't been in such a dope dream with skeer, you'd 'a' sensed what he was a-yellin'. He was callin' "Oh-oo-oo, oh-oo-oo, here Daggett! Here, boy!" an' then he'd whistle an' call again: "Here, Daggett! Here, Daggett!" That's how I knew it was Ranch; an', besides, he told me onct that he sleepwalked when he got worried. But you, you white livered—' an' then he cussed me out some more.

"'Smarty,' I says, 'if yer knew so blame well it was Ranch, why did yer give him the flyin' tackle like yer done an' git him all woiked up like this?'

"'Well,' says Buck sort o' sheepy, 'I was some woiked up meself, an' time he come along I give him the spook's tackle without thinkin'; I was too skeered ter think. Hush, Ranch. Hush, old boy. It's jus' me'n Bill. Nobody shan't hoit yer.'

"We comforted pore ol' Ranch an' fixed him up, an' then when he felt better told him about things—all but how Daggett was et—an' I

169

wrapped his blanket around him an' took him back ter quarters while Buck went a-lookin' fer John an' his gang.

"He found 'em about half a mile off, in front of a Mott Street joss house, all prayin' an' burnin' punk an' huddled together, skeered green from the yellin's they'd heard. Buck, he give 'em a long chin-chin about layin' the ghost, an' how Judge Ming wouldn't never come back no more; an' then he dragged 'em all back (they pullin' at the halter shanks with years laid back an' eyes rollin'), ter him bury his United States button on Ming's rock pile. He dropped it in solemn, an' said what the Chinks took ter be a prayer; but it was really the oath he said. Buck havin' onct been a recruitin' sergeant, knew it by heart all the way from 'I do solemnly swear' ter 'so help me, Gawd.' Buck says I oughter seen them grateful Chinos then: they'd 'a' give him the whole Chino Umpire if they could. They got down an' squirmed an' kissed his hands an' his feet an' his sleeve. They wanted ter escort him back ter camp, but he bucked at that, an' said no, as he was out without pass an' not itchin' fer his arrival ter be noticed none.

"After that we took toins watchin' Ranch at night, an' got him another mutt ter love, an' he didn't wander any more, so Judge Ming seemed satisfied with his United States button, an' kep' quiet. But them Chinks was the gratefullest gang yer ever seen. They brought us presents; things ter eat—fruit, poultry, eggs, an' all sorts of chow, some of it mighty funny lookin', but it tasted all right; we lived high, we three. The other fellers was wild ter know how we woiked it. An' I tell yer I ain't never been skeered o' ghosts sence—that is, not ter speak of—*much!*"

Bill, paused, drew a long breath, and looked at the clock. "Gee!" said he, "most nine o'clock. I got ter go over ter K troop ter see Sergeant Keefe a minute—I promised him. Adios, fellers. Thanks fer the smokin'."

"Keep the change, hombre. Thanks for yo' tale," shouted Whitney after him as he disappeared down the hall.

"Well!!" said Stone, and looked at Hansen.

"Well!!" responded Hansen. The big Swede shook with laughter. "Iss he not the finest liar! Yess? I wass in the Fourteenth myselluf. That wass my company—Chay. He wass not even the army in then—in nineteen hund'erd."

"Yes," said Stone, "I knew, but I wasn't goin' to spoil his bloomin' yarn. I happened to see his enlistment card only this mornin', and the only thing he was ever in before was the Twenty-third Infantry after they came back from the Islands. He's never even been out of the States."

"But where did he get it from?" asked Whitney. "His imagination is equal to most anything but gettin' so many facts straight. Of co'se I noticed things yere an' there—but the most of it was O. K."

"I tell you," said Hansen, grinning, "he got it from an old Fourteenth man—Dan Powerss—at practice camp last Chuly. He an' I wass often talking of China. He wuss in my old company an' wass then telling me how he an' the other fellerss all that extra chow got. I tank Bill he hass a goot memory."

"But the nerve of him!" cried Whitehall, "tryin' ter pass that off on us with Hansen sittin' right there."

"It iss one thing he may have forgot," smiled Hansen.

"Well, who cares anyway?" said Stone. "It was a blame good story. An' now clear out, all of you. I want to hit the bunk. Reveille does seem to come so early these cold mornin's. Gee! I wish I knew of some kind of button that would keep *me* lyin' down when Shorty wants me to get up an' call the roll."

The Spectre Bridegroom

Washington Irving

He that supper for is dight,
He lyes full cold,
I trow, this night!
Yestreen to chamber I him led,
This night Gray-Steel has made his bed.

Sir Eger, Sir Grahame and Sir Gray-Steel

On the summit of one of the heights of the Odenwald, a wild and romantic tract of Upper Germany, that lies not far from the confluence of the Main and the Rhine, there stood, many, many years since, the Castle of the Baron Von Landshort. It is now quite fallen to decay, and almost buried among beech trees and dark firs; above which, however, its old watch tower may still be seen, struggling, like the former possessor I have mentioned, to carry a high head, and look down upon the neighbouring country.

The baron was a dry branch of the great family of Katzenellenbogen, and inherited the relics of the property, and all the pride of his ancestors. Though the warlike disposition of his predecessors had much impaired the family possessions, yet the baron still endeavoured to keep up some show of former state. The times were peaceable, and the German nobles, in general, had abandoned their inconvenient old castles, perched like eagles' nests among the mountains, and had built more convenient residences in the valleys; still the baron remained proudly drawn up in his little fortress, cherishing with hereditary inveteracy, all the old family feuds; so that he was on ill terms with some of his nearest neighbours, on account of disputes that had happened between their great-great-grandfathers.

The baron had but one child, a daughter; but nature, when she

172

grants but one child, always compensates by making it a prodigy; and so it was with the daughter of the baron. All the nurses, gossips, and country cousins assured her father that she had not her equal for beauty in all Germany; and who should know better than they? She had, moreover, been brought up with great care under the superintendence of two maiden aunts, who had spent some years of their early life at one of the little German courts, and were skilled in all branches of knowledge necessary to the education of a fine lady. Under their instructions she became a miracle of accomplishments. By the time she was eighteen, she could embroider to admiration, and had worked whole histories of the saints in tapestry, with such strength of expression in their countenances, that they looked like so many souls in purgatory. She could read without great difficulty, and had spelled her way through several church legends, and almost all the chivalric wonders of the Heldenbuch. She had even made considerable proficiency in writing; could sign her own name without missing a letter, and so legibly, that her aunts could read it without spectacles. She excelled in making little elegant good-for-nothing lady-like knickknacks of all kinds; was versed in the most abstruse dancing of the day; played a number of airs on the harp and guitar; and knew all the tender ballads of the Minnelieders by heart.

Her aunts, too, having been great flirts and coquettes in their younger days, were admirably calculated to be vigilant guardians and strict censors of the conduct of their niece; for there is no duenna so rigidly prudent, and inexorably decorous, as a superannuated coquette. She was rarely suffered out of their sight; never went beyond the domains of the castle, unless well attended, or rather well watched; had continual lectures read to her about strict decorum and implicit obedience; and, as to the men—pah!—she was taught to hold them at such a distance, and in such absolute distrust, that, unless properly authorized, she would not have cast a glance upon the handsomest cavalier in the world—no, not if he were even dying at her feet.

The good effects of this system were wonderfully apparent. The young lady was a pattern of docility and correctness. While others were wasting their sweetness in the glare of the world, and liable to be plucked and thrown aside by every hand, she was coyly blooming into fresh and lovely womanhood under the protection of those immaculate spinsters, like a rosebud blushing forth among guardian thorns. Her aunts looked upon her with pride and exultation, and vaunted that though all the other young ladies in the world might go astray, yet, thank Heaven, nothing of the kind could happen to the heiress of Katzenellenbogen.

But, however scantily the Baron Von Landshort might be provided with children, his household was by no means a small one; for Providence had enriched him with abundance of poor relations. They, one and all, possessed the affectionate disposition common to humble relatives; were wonderfully attached to the baron, and took every possible occasion to come in swarms and enliven the castle. All family festivals were commemorated by these good people at the baron's expense; and when they were filled with good cheer, they would declare that there was nothing on earth so delightful as these family meetings, these jubilees of the heart.

The baron, though a small man, had a large soul, and it swelled with satisfaction at the consciousness of being the greatest man in the little world about him. He loved to tell long stories about the dark old warriors whose portraits looked grimly down from the walls around, and he found no listeners equal to those that fed at his expense. He was much given to the marvellous, and a firm believer in all those supernatural tales with which every mountain and valley in Germany abounds. The faith of his guests exceeded even his own: they listened to every tale of wonder with open eyes and mouth, and never failed to be astonished, even though repeated for the hundredth time. Thus lived the Baron Von Landshort, the oracle of his table, the absolute monarch of his little territory, and happy, above all things, in the persuasion that he was the wisest man of the age.

At the time of which my story treats, there was a great family gathering at the castle, on an affair of the utmost importance: it was to receive the destined bridegroom of the baron's daughter. A negotiation had been carried on between the father and an old nobleman of Bavaria, to unite the dignity of their houses by the marriage of their children. The preliminaries had been conducted with proper punctilio. The young people were betrothed without seeing each other, and the time was appointed for the marriage ceremony. The young Count Von Altenburg had been recalled from the army for the purpose, and was actually on his way to the baron's to receive his bride. Missives had even been received from him from Wurtzburg, where he was accidentally detained, mentioning the day and hour when he might be expected to arrive.

The castle was in a tumult of preparation to give him a suitable welcome. The fair bride had been decked out with uncommon care. The two aunts had superintended her toilet, and quarrelled the whole morning about every article of her dress. The young lady had taken advantage of their contest to follow the bent of her own taste; and fortunately it was a good one. She looked as lovely as youthful bridegroom could desire; and the flutter of expectation heightened the lustre of her charms.

The suffusions that mantled her face and neck, the gentle heaving of the bosom, the eye now and then lost in reverie, all betrayed the soft tumult that was going on in her little heart. The aunts were continually hovering around her; for maiden aunts are apt to take great interest in affairs of this nature. They were giving her a world of staid counsel how to deport herself, what to say, and in what manner to receive the expected lover.

The baron was no less busied in preparations. He had, in truth, nothing exactly to do; but he was naturally a fuming bustling little man, and could not remain passive when all the world was in a hurry. He worried from top to bottom of the castle with an air of infinite anxiety; he continually called the servants from their work to exhort them to be diligent; and buzzed about every hall and chamber, as idly restless and importunate as a blue-bottle fly on a warm summer's day.

In the meantime the fatted calf had been killed; the forests had rung with the clamour of the huntsmen; the kitchen was crowded with good cheer; the cellars had yielded up whole oceans of *Rheinwein* and *Fernewein*; and even the great Heidelberg tun had been laid under contribution. Everything was ready to receive the distinguished guest with *Saus und Braus* in the true spirit of German hospitality— but the guest delayed to make his appearance. Hour rolled after hour. The sun, that had poured his downward rays upon the rich forest of the Odenwald, now just gleamed along the summits of the mountains. The baron mounted the highest tower, and strained his eyes in hope of catching a distant sight of the count and his attendants. Once he thought he beheld them; the sounds of horns came floating from the valley, prolonged by the mountain echoes. A number of horsemen were seen far below, slowly advancing along the road; but when they had nearly reached the foot of the mountain, they suddenly struck off in a different direction. The last ray of sunshine departed—the bats began to flit by in the twilight—the road grew dimmer and dimmer to the view; and nothing appeared stirring in it but now and then a peasant lagging homeward from his labour.

While the old castle at Landshort was in this state of perplexity, a very interesting scene was transacting in a different part of the Odenwald.

The young Count Von Altenburg was tranquilly pursuing his route in that sober jog-trot way in which a man travels toward matrimony when his friends have taken all the trouble and uncertainty of courtship off his hands, and a bride is waiting for him, as certainly as a dinner at the end of his journey. He had encountered at Wurtzburg a youthful companion in arms with whom he had seen some service on the frontiers: Herman Von Starkenfaust, one of the stoutest hands and worthiest hearts of German chivalry, who was now returning from the army. His father's castle was not far distant from the old fortress of Landshort, although an hereditary feud rendered the families hostile, and strangers to each other.

In the warm-hearted moment of recognition, the young friends related all their past adventures and fortunes, and the count gave the whole history of his intended nuptials with a young lady whom he had never seen, but of whose charms he had received the most enrapturing descriptions.

As the route of the friends lay in the same direction, they agreed to perform the rest of their journey together; and, that they might do it the more leisurely, set off from Wurtzburg at an early hour, the count having given directions for his retinue to follow and overtake him.

They beguiled their wayfaring with recollections of their military scenes and adventures; but the count was apt to be a little tedious, now and then, about the reputed charms of his bride and the felicity that awaited him.

In this way they had entered among the mountains of the Odenwald, and were traversing one of its most lonely and thickly wooded passes. It is well known that the forests of Germany have always been as much infested by robbers as its castles by spectres; and at this time the former were particularly numerous, from the hordes of disbanded soldiers wandering about the country. It will not appear extraordinary, therefore, that the cavaliers were attacked by a gang of these stragglers, in the midst of the forest. They defended themselves with bravery, but were nearly overpowered, when the count's retinue arrived to their assistance. At sight of them the robbers fled, but not until the count had received a mortal wound. He was slowly and carefully conveyed back to the city of Wurtzburg, and a friar summoned from a neighbouring convent who was famous for his skill in administering to both soul and body; but half of his skill was superfluous; the moments of the unfortunate count were numbered.

With his dying breath he entreated his friend to repair instantly to the castle of Landshort, and explain the fatal cause of his not keeping his appointment with his bride. Though not the most ardent of lovers, he was one of the most punctilious of men, and appeared earnestly solicitous that his mission should be speedily and courteously executed.

"Unless this is done," said he, "I shall not sleep quietly in my grave!" He repeated these last words with peculiar solemnity. A request, at a moment so impressive, admitted no hesitation. Starkenfaust endeavoured to soothe him to calmness; promised faithfully to execute his wish, and gave him his hand in solemn pledge. The dying man pressed it in acknowledgment, but soon lapsed into delirium—raved about his bride—his engagements—his plighted word; ordered his horse, that he might ride to the castle of Landshort; and expired in the fancied act of vaulting into the saddle.

Starkenfaust bestowed a sigh and a soldier's tear on the untimely fate of his comrade, and then pondered on the awkward mission he had undertaken. His heart was heavy, and his head perplexed; for he was to present himself an unbidden guest among hostile people, and to damp their festivity with tidings fatal to their hopes. Still, there were certain whisperings of curiosity in his bosom to see this far-famed beauty of Katzenellenbogen, so cautiously shut up from the world; for he was a passionate admirer of the sex, and there was a dash of eccentricity and enterprise in his character that made him fond of all singular adventure.

Previous to his departure he made all due arrangements with the holy fraternity of the convent for the funeral solemnities of his friend, who was to be buried in the cathedral of Wurtzburg near some of his illustrious relatives; and the mourning retinue of the count took charge of his remains.

It is now high time that we should return to the ancient family of Katzenellenbogen, who were impatient for their guest, and still more for their dinner; and to the worthy little baron, whom we left airing himself on the watch-tower.

Night closed in, but still no guest arrived. The baron descended from the tower in despair. The banquet, which had been delayed from hour to hour, could no longer be postponed. The meats were already overdone; the cook in an agony; and the whole household had the look of a garrison that had been reduced by famine. The baron was obliged reluctantly to give orders for the feast without the presence of the guest. All were seated at table, and just on the point of commencing, when the sound of a horn from without the gate gave notice of the approach of a stranger. Another long blast filled the old courts of the castle with its echoes, and was answered by the warder from the walls. The baron hastened to receive his future son-in-law.

The drawbridge had been let down, and the stranger was before the gate. He was a tall, gallant cavalier mounted on a black steed. His

177

countenance was pale, but he had a beaming, romantic eye, and an air of stately melancholy.

The baron was a little mortified that he should have come in this simple, solitary style. His dignity for a moment was ruffled, and he felt disposed to consider it a want of proper respect for the important occasion, and the important family with which he was to be connected. He pacified himself, however, with the conclusion, that it must have been youthful impatience which had induced him thus to spur on sooner than his attendants.

"I am sorry," said the stranger, "to break in upon you thus unseasonably—"

Here the baron interrupted with a world of compliments and greetings; for, to tell the truth, he prided himself upon his courtesy and eloquence.

The stranger attempted, once or twice, to stem the torrent of words, but in vain, so he bowed his head and suffered it to flow on. By the time the baron had come to a pause, they had reached the inner court of the castle; and the stranger was again about to speak, when he was once more interrupted by the appearance of the female part of the family leading forth the shrinking and blushing bride. He gazed on her for a moment as one entranced; it seemed as if his whole soul beamed forth in the gaze, and rested upon that lovely form. One of the maiden aunts whispered something in her ear; she made an effort to speak; her moist blue eye was timidly raised; gave a shy glance of inquiry on the stranger; and was cast again to the ground. The words died away; but there was a sweet smile playing about her lips, and a soft dimpling of the cheek that showed her glance had not been unsatisfactory. It was impossible for a girl of the fond age of eighteen, highly predisposed for love and matrimony, not to be pleased with so gallant a cavalier.

The late hour at which the guest had arrived left no time for parley. The baron was peremptory, and deferred all particular conversation until the morning, and led the way to the untasted banquet.

It was served up in the great hall of the castle. Around the walls hung the hard-favoured portraits of the heroes of the house of Katzenellenbogen, and the trophies which they had gained in the field and in the chase. Hacked corselets, splintered jousting spears, and tattered banners were mingled with the spoils of sylvan warfare; the jaws of the wolf and the tusks of the boar grinned horribly among cross-bows and battle-axes, and a huge pair of antlers branched immediately over the head of the youthful bridegroom.

The cavalier took but little notice of the company or the entertainment. He scarcely tasted the banquet, but seemed absorbed in admiration of his bride. He conversed in a low tone that could not be overheard—for the language of love is never loud; but where is the female ear so dull that it cannot catch the softest whisper of the lover? There was a mingled tenderness and gravity in his manner, that appeared to have a powerful effect upon the young lady. Her colour came and went as she listened with deep attention. Now and then she made some blushing reply, and when his eye was turned away, she would steal a sidelong glance at his romantic countenance and heave a gentle sigh of tender happiness. It was evident that the young couple were completely enamoured. The aunts, who were deeply versed in the mysteries of the heart, declared that they had fallen in love with each other at first sight.

The feast went on merrily, or at least noisily, for the guests were all blessed with those keen appetites that attend upon light purses and mountain air. The baron told his best and longest stories, and never had he told them so well, or with such great effect. If there was anything marvellous, his auditors were lost in astonishment; and if anything facetious, they were sure to laugh exactly in the right place. The baron, it is true, like most great men, was too dignified to utter any joke but a dull one; it was always enforced, however, by a bumper of excellent Hockheimer; and even a dull joke, at one's own table, served up with jolly old wine, is irresistible. Many good things were said by poorer and keener wits that would not bear repeating, except on similar occasions; many sly speeches whispered in ladies' ears, that almost convulsed them with suppressed laughter; and a song or two roared out by a poor, but merry and broad-faced cousin of the baron that absolutely made the maiden aunts hold up their fans.

Amidst all this revelry, the stranger guest maintained a most singular and unseasonable gravity. His countenance assumed a deeper cast of dejection as the evening advanced; and, strange as it may appear, even the baron's jokes seemed only to render him the more melancholy. At times he was lost in thought, and at times there was a perturbed and restless wandering of the eye that bespoke a mind but ill at ease. His conversations with the bride became more and more earnest and mysterious. Lowering clouds began to steal over the fair serenity of her brow, and tremors to run through her tender frame.

All this could not escape the notice of the company. Their gayety was chilled by the unaccountable gloom of the bridegroom; their spirits were infected; whispers and glances were interchanged, accompanied by shrugs and dubious shakes of the head. The song and the laugh grew less and less frequent; there were dreary pauses in the conversation, which were at length succeeded by wild tales and supernatural legends. One dismal story produced another still more dismal, and the baron nearly frightened some of the ladies into hysterics with the history of the goblin horseman that carried away the fair Leonora; a dreadful story which has since been put into excellent verse, and is read and believed by all the world.

The bridegroom listened to this tale with profound attention. He kept his eyes steadily fixed on the baron, and, as the story drew to a close, began gradually to rise from his seat, growing taller and taller, until, in the baron's entranced eye, he seemed almost to tower into a giant. The moment the tale was finished, he heaved a deep sigh and took a solemn farewell of the company. They were all amazement. The baron was perfectly thunder-struck.

"What! going to leave the castle at midnight? Why, everything was prepared for his reception; a chamber was ready for him if he wished to retire."

The stranger shook his head mournfully and mysteriously; "I must lay my head in a different chamber to-night!"

There was something in this reply, and the tone in which it was uttered, that made the baron's heart misgive him; but he rallied his forces and repeated his hospitable entreaties.

The stranger shook his head silently, but positively, at every offer; and, waving his farewell to the company, stalked slowly out of the hall. The maiden aunts were absolutely petrified—the bride hung her head, and a tear stole to her eye.

The baron followed the stranger to the great court of the castle, where the black charger stood pawing the earth and snorting with impatience. When they had reached the portal, whose deep archway was dimly lighted by a cresset, the stranger paused, and addressed the baron in a hollow tone of voice which the vaulted roof rendered still more sepulchral.

"Now that we are alone," said he, "I will impart to you the reason of my going. I have a solemn, an indispensable engagement—"

"Why," said the baron, "cannot you send someone in your place?"

"It admits of no substitute—I must attend it in person—I must away to Wurtzburg cathedral—"

"Ay," said the baron, plucking up spirit, "but not until to-morrow—to-morrow you shall take your bride there."

"No! no!" replied the stranger, with tenfold solemnity, "my engagement is with no bride—the worms! the worms expect me! I am a dead man—I have been slain by robbers—my body lies at Wurtzburg—at midnight I am to be buried—the grave is waiting for me—I must keep my appointment!"

He sprang on his black charger, dashed over the drawbridge, and the clattering of his horses' hoofs was lost in the whistling of the night blast.

The baron returned to the hall in the utmost consternation, and related what had passed. Two ladies fainted outright, others sickened at the idea of having banqueted with a spectre. It was the opinion of some, that this might be the wild huntsman, famous in German legend. Some talked of mountain sprites, of wood-demons, and of other supernatural beings, with which the good people of Germany have been so grievously harassed since time immemorial. One of the poor relations ventured to suggest that it might be some sportive evasion of the young cavalier, and that the very gloominess of the caprice seemed to accord with so melancholy a personage. This, however, drew on him the indignation of the whole company, and especially of the baron, who looked upon him as little better than an infidel; so that he was fain to abjure his heresy as speedily as possible, and come into the faith of the true believers.

But whatever may have been the doubts entertained, they were completely put to an end by the arrival, next day, of regular missives confirming the intelligence of the young count's murder, and his interment in Wurtzburg cathedral.

The dismay at the castle may well be imagined. The baron shut himself up in his chamber. The guests, who had come to rejoice with him, could not think of abandoning him in his distress. They wandered about the courts, or collected in groups in the hall, shaking their heads and shrugging their shoulders at the troubles of so good a man; and sat longer than ever at table, and ate and drank more stoutly than ever, by way of keeping up their spirits. But the situation of the widowed bride was the most pitiable. To have lost a husband before she had even embraced him—and such a husband! if the very spectre could be so gracious and noble, what must have been the living man! She filled the house with lamentations.

On the night of the second day of her widowhood, she had retired to her chamber, accompanied by one of her aunts who insisted on sleeping with her. The aunt, who was one of the best tellers of ghost stories in all Germany, had just been recounting one of her longest, and had fallen asleep in the very midst of it. The chamber was remote, and overlooked a small garden. The niece lay pensively gazing at the beams of the rising moon, as they trembled on the leaves of an aspen-tree before the lattice. The castle-clock had just tolled midnight, when a soft strain of music stole up from the garden. She rose hastily from her bed, and stepped lightly to the window. A tall figure stood among the shadows of the trees. As it raised its head, a beam of moonlight fell upon the countenance. Heaven and earth! she beheld the Spectre Bridegroom! A loud shriek at that moment burst upon her ear, and her aunt, who had been awakened by the music, and had followed her silently to the window, fell into her arms. When she looked again, the spectre had disappeared.

Of the two females, the aunt now required the most soothing, for she was perfectly beside herself with terror. As to the young lady, there was something, even in the spectre of her lover, that seemed endearing. There was still the semblance of manly beauty; and though the shadow of a man is but little calculated to satisfy the affections of a love-sick girl, yet, where the substance is not to be had, even that is consoling. The aunt declared she would never sleep in that chamber again; the niece, for once, was refractory, and declared as strongly that she would sleep in no other in the castle: the consequence was, that she had to sleep in it alone: but she drew a promise from her aunt not to relate the story of the spectre, lest she should be denied the only melancholy pleasure left her on earth—that of inhabiting the chamber over which the guardian shade of her lover kept its nightly vigils.

How long the good old lady would have observed this promise is uncertain, for she dearly loved to talk of the marvellous, and there is a triumph in being the first to tell a frightful story; it is, however, still quoted in the neighbourhood, as a memorable instance of female secrecy, that she kept it to herself for a whole week; when she was suddenly absolved from all further restraint, by intelligence, brought to the breakfast table one morning, that the young lady was not to be found. Her room was empty—the bed had not been slept in—the window was open, and the bird had flown!

The astonishment and concern with which the intelligence was received, can only be imagined by those who have witnessed the agitation which the mishaps of a great man cause among his friends. Even the poor relations paused for a moment from the indefatigable labours of the trencher, when the aunt, who had at first been struck speechless, wrung her hands, and shrieked out, "The goblin! the goblin! She's carried away by the goblin!"

In a few words she related the fearful scene of the garden, and concluded that the spectre must have carried off his bride. Two of the domestics corroborated the opinion, for they had heard the clattering of a horse's hoofs down the mountain about midnight, and had no doubt that it was the spectre on his black charger, bearing her away to the tomb. All present were struck with the direful probability; for events of the kind are extremely common in Germany, as many well-authenticated histories bear witness.

What a lamentable situation was that of the poor baron! What a heart-rending dilemma for a fond father, and a member of the great family of Katzenellenbogen! His only daughter had either been rapt away to the grave, or he was to have some wood-demon for a son-in-law, and, perchance, a troop of goblin grandchildren. As usual, he was completely bewildered and all the castle in an uproar. The men were ordered to take horse, and scour every road and path and glen of the Odenwald. The baron himself had just drawn on his jack-boots, girded on his sword, and was about to mount his steed to sally forth on the doubtful quest, when he was brought to a pause by a new apparition. A lady was seen approaching the castle, mounted on a palfrey, attended by a cavalier on horseback. She galloped up to the gate, sprang from her horse, and falling at the baron's feet, embraced his knees. It was his lost daughter, and her companion—the Spectre Bridegroom! The baron was astounded. He looked at his daughter, then at the spectre, and almost doubted the evidence of his senses. The latter, too, was wonderfully improved in his appearance since his visit to the world of spirits. His dress was splendid, and set off a noble figure of manly symmetry. He was no longer pale and melancholy. His fine countenance was flushed with the glow of youth, and joy rioted in his large dark eye.

The mystery was soon cleared up. The cavalier (for in truth, as you must have known all the while, he was no goblin) announced himself as Sir Herman Von Starkenfaust. He related his adventure with the young count. He told how he had hastened to the castle to deliver the un-welcome tidings, but that the eloquence of the baron had interrupted him in every attempt to tell his tale. How the sight of the bride had completely captivated him, and that to pass a few hours near her, he had tacitly suffered the mistake to continue. How he had been sorely perplexed in what way to make a decent retreat, until the baron's goblin stories had suggested his eccentric exit. How, fearing the feudal hostility of the family, he had repeated his visits by stealth—had haunted the garden beneath the young lady's window—had wooed—had won—had borne away in triumph—and, in a word, had wedded the fair.

Under any other circumstances the baron would have been inflexible, for he was tenacious of paternal authority, and devoutly obstinate in all family feuds; but he loved his daughter; he had lamented her as lost; he rejoiced to find her still alive; and, though her husband was of a hostile house, yet, thank Heaven, he was not a goblin. There was something, it must be acknowledged, that did not exactly accord with his notions of strict veracity, in the joke the knight had passed upon him of his being a dead man; but several old friends present, who had served in the wars, assured him that every stratagem was excusable in love, and that the cavalier was entitled to especial privilege, having lately served as a trooper.

Matters, therefore, were happily arranged. The baron pardoned the young couple on the spot. The revels at the castle were resumed. The poor relations overwhelmed this new member of the family with loving kindness; he was so gallant, so generous—and so rich. The aunts, it is true, were somewhat scandalized that their system of strict seclusion and passive obedience should be so badly exemplified, but attributed it all to their negligence in not having the windows grated. One of them was particularly mortified at having her marvellous story marred, and that the only spectre she had ever seen should turn out a counterfeit; but the niece seemed perfectly happy at having found him substantial flesh and blood—and so the story ends.

The Spectre of Tappington
From *The Ingoldsby Legends*

Richard Barham

"It is very odd, though; what can have become of them?" said Charles Seaforth, as he peeped under the valance of an old-fashioned bedstead, in an old-fashioned apartment of a still more old-fashioned manor-house; "'tis confoundedly odd, and I can't make it out at all. Why, Barney, where are they?—and where the d—d are you?"

No answer was returned to this appeal; and the lieutenant, who was, in the main, a reasonable person—at least as reasonable a person as any young gentleman of twenty-two in "the service" can fairly be expected to be—cooled when he reflected that his servant could scarcely reply extempore to a summons which it was impossible he should hear.

An application to the bell was the considerate result; and the footsteps of as tight a lad as ever put pipe-clay to belt sounded along the gallery.

"Come in!" said his master. An ineffectual attempt upon the door reminded Mr. Seaforth that he had locked himself in. "By Heaven! this is the oddest thing of all," said he, as he turned the key and admitted Mr. Maguire into his dormitory.

"Barney, where are my pantaloons?"

"Is it the breeches?" asked the valet, casting an inquiring eye round the apartment;—"is it the breeches, sir?"

"Yes, what have you done with them?"

"Sure then your honour had them on when you went to bed, and it's hereabouts they'll be, I'll be bail"; and Barney lifted a fashionable tunic from a cane-backed arm-chair, proceeding in his examination. But the search was vain; there was the tunic aforesaid, there was a smart-looking kerseymere waistcoat; but the most important article of all in a gentleman's wardrobe was still wanting.

"Where *can* they be?" asked the master, with a strong accent on the auxiliary verb.

"Sorrow a know I knows," said the man.

"It *must* have been the devil, then, after all, who has been here and carried them off!" cried Seaforth, staring full into Barney's face.

Mr. Maguire was not devoid of the superstition of his countrymen, still he looked as if he did not quite subscribe to the *sequitur*.

His master read incredulity in his countenance. "Why, I tell you, Barney, I put them there, on that arm-chair, when I got into bed; and, by Heaven! I distinctly saw the ghost of the old fellow they told me of, come in at midnight, put on my pantaloons, and walk away with them."

"May be so," was the cautious reply.

"I thought, of course, it was a dream; but then—where the d—l are the breeches?"

The question was more easily asked than answered. Barney renewed his search, while the lieutenant folded his arms, and, leaning against the toilet, sunk into a reverie.

"After all, it must be some trick of my laughter-loving cousins," said Seaforth.

"Ah! then, the ladies!" chimed in Mr. Maguire, though the observation was not addressed to him; "and will it be Miss Caroline or Miss Fanny, that's stole your honour's things?"

"I hardly know what to think of it," pursued the bereaved lieutenant, still speaking in soliloquy, with his eye resting dubiously on the chamber-door. "I locked myself in, that's certain; and—but there must be some other entrance to the room—pooh! I remember—the private staircase; how could I be such a fool?" and he crossed the chamber to where a low oaken door case was dimly visible in a distant corner. He paused before it. Nothing now interfered to screen it from observation; but it bore tokens of having been at some earlier period concealed by tapestry, remains of which yet clothed the walls on either side the portal.

"This way they must have come," said Seaforth; "I wish with all my heart I had caught them!"

"Och! the kittens!" sighed Mr. Barney Maguire.

But the mystery was yet as far from being solved as before. True, there *was* the "other door"; but then that, too, on examination, was even more firmly secured than the one which opened on the gallery—two heavy bolts on the inside effectually prevented any *coup de main* on the lieutenant's *bivouac* from that quarter. He was more puzzled than ever; nor did the minutest inspection of the walls and floor throw any light upon the subject: one thing only was clear—the breeches were gone! "It is *very* singular," said the lieutenant.

* * * * * * * *

Tappington (generally called Tapton) Everard is an antiquated but commodious manor-house in the eastern division of the county of Kent. A former proprietor had been high-sheriff in the days of Elizabeth, and many a dark and dismal tradition was yet extant of the licentiousness of his life, and the enormity of his offenses. The Glen, which the keeper's daughter was seen to enter, but never known to quit, still frowns darkly as of yore; while an ineradicable blood-stain on the oaken stair yet bids defiance to the united energies of soap and sand. But it is with one particular apartment that a deed of more especial atrocity is said to be connected. A stranger guest—so runs the legend—arrived unexpectedly at the mansion of the "Bad Sir Giles." They met in apparent friendship; but the ill-concealed scowl on their master's brow told the domestics that the visit was not a welcome one; the banquet, however, was not spared; the wine-cup circulated freely—too freely, perhaps—for sounds of discord at length reached the ears of even the excluded serving-men, as they were doing their best to imitate their betters in the lower hall. Alarmed, some of them ventured to approach the parlour, one, an old and favoured retainer of the house, went so far as to break in upon his master's privacy. Sir Giles, already high in oath, fiercely enjoined his absence, and he retired; not, however, before he had distinctly heard from the stranger's lips a menace that "there was that within his pocket which could disprove the knight's right to issue that or any other command within the walls of Tapton."

The intrusion, though momentary, seemed to have produced a beneficial effect; the voices of the disputants fell, and the conversation was carried on thenceforth in a more subdued tone, till, as evening closed in, the domestics, when summoned to attend with lights, found not only cordiality restored, but that a still deeper carouse was meditated. Fresh stoups, and from the choicest bins, were produced; nor was it till at a late, or rather early hour, that the revellers sought their chambers.

The one allotted to the stranger occupied the first floor of the eastern angle of the building, and had once been the favourite apartment of Sir Giles himself. Scandal ascribed this preference to the facility which a private staircase, communicating with the grounds, had afforded him, in the old knight's time, of following his wicked courses unchecked by parental observation; a consideration which ceased to be of weight when the death of his father left him uncontrolled master of his estate and actions. From that period Sir Giles had established himself in what were called the "state apartments," and the "oaken chamber" was rarely tenanted, save on occasions of extraordinary festivity, or when the Yule log drew an unusually large accession of guests around the Christmas hearth.

On this eventful night it was prepared for the unknown visitor, who sought his couch heated and inflamed from his midnight orgies, and in the morning was found in his bed a swollen and blackened corpse. No marks of violence appeared upon the body; but the livid hue of the lips, and certain dark-coloured spots visible on the skin, aroused suspicions which those who entertained them were too timid to express. Apoplexy, induced by the excesses of the preceding night, Sir Giles's confidential leech pronounced to be the cause of his sudden dissolution. The body was buried in peace; and though some shook their heads as they witnessed the haste with which the funeral rites were hurried on, none ventured to murmur. Other events arose to distract the attention of the retainers; men's minds became occupied by the stirring politics of the day; while the near approach of that formidable armada, so vainly arrogating itself a title which the very elements joined with human valour to disprove, soon interfered to weaken, if not obliterate, all remembrance of the nameless stranger who had died within the walls of Tapton Everard.

Years rolled on: the "Bad Sir Giles" had himself long since gone to his account, the last, as it was believed, of his immediate line; though a few of the older tenants were sometimes heard to speak of an elder brother, who had disappeared in early life, and never inherited the estate. Rumours, too, of his having left a son in foreign lands, were at one time rife; but they died away, nothing occurring to support them: the property passed unchallenged to a collateral branch of the family, and the secret, if secret there were, was buried in Denton churchyard, in the lonely grave of the mysterious stranger. One circumstance alone occurred, after a long-intervening period, to revive the memory of these transactions. Some workmen employed in grubbing an old plantation, for the purpose of raising on its site a modern shrubbery, dug up, in the execution of their task, the mildewed remnants of what seemed to have been once a garment. On more minute inspection, enough remained of silken slashes and a coarse embroidery, to identify the relics as having once formed part of a pair of trunk hose; while a few papers which fell from them, altogether illegible from damp and age, were by the unlearned rustics conveyed to the then owner of the estate.

Whether the squire was more successful in deciphering them was never known; he certainly never alluded to their contents; and little would have been thought of the matter but for the inconvenient memory of one old woman, who declared she heard her grandfather say, that when the "strange guest" was poisoned, though all the rest of his clothes were there, his breeches, the supposed repository of the supposed documents, could never be found. The master of Tapton Everard smiled when he heard Dame Jones's hint of deeds which might impeach the validity of his own title in favour of some unknown descendant of some unknown heir; and the story was rarely alluded to, save by one or two miracle-mongers, who had heard that others had seen the ghost of old Sir Giles, in his night-cap, issue from the postern, enter the adjoining copse, and wring his shadowy hands in agony, as he seemed to search vainly for something hidden among the evergreens. The stranger's death-room had, of course, been occasionally haunted from the time of his decease; but the periods of visitation had latterly become very rare—even Mrs. Botherby, the housekeeper, being forced to admit that, during her long sojourn at the manor, she had never "met with anything worse than herself"; though, as the old lady afterwards added upon more mature reflection, "I must say I think I saw the devil *once.*"

Such was the legend attached to Tapton Everard, and such the story which the lively Caroline Ingoldsby detailed to her equally mercurial cousin, Charles Seaforth, lieutenant in the Hon. East India Company's second regiment of Bombay Fencibles, as arm-in-arm they promenaded a gallery decked with some dozen grim-looking ancestral portraits, and, among others, with that of the redoubted Sir Giles himself. The gallant commander had that very morning paid his first visit to the house of his maternal uncle, after an absence of several years passed with his regiment on the arid plains of Hindustan, whence he was now returned on a three years' furlough. He had gone out a boy—he returned a man; but the impression made upon his youthful fancy by his favourite cousin remained unimpaired, and to Tapton he directed his steps, even before he sought the home of his widowed mother—comforting himself in this breach of filial decorum by the reflection that, as the manor was so little out of his way, it would be unkind to pass, as it were, the door of his relatives, without just looking in for a few hours.

But he found his uncle as hospitable, and his cousin more charming than ever; and the looks of one, and the requests of the other, soon precluded the possibility of refusing to lengthen the "few hours" into a few days, though the house was at the moment full of visitors.

The Peterses were from Ramsgate; and Mr., Mrs., and the two Miss Simpkinsons, from Bath, had come to pass a month with the family; and Tom Ingoldsby had brought down his college friend the Honourable Augustus Sucklethumbkin, with his groom and pointers, to take a fortnight's shooting. And then there was Mrs. Ogleton, the rich young widow, with her large black eyes, who, people did say, was setting her cap at the young squire, though Mrs. Botherby did not believe it; and, above all, there was Mademoiselle Pauline, her *femme de chambre*, who "*mon-Dieu'd*" everything and everybody, and cried "*Quel horreur!*" at Mrs. Botherby's cap. In short, to use the last-named and much-respected lady's own expression, the house was "choke-full" to the very attics—all save the "oaken chamber," which, as the lieutenant expressed a most magnanimous disregard of ghosts, was forthwith appropriated to his particular accommodation. Mr. Maguire meanwhile was fain to share the apartment of Oliver Dobbs, the squire's own man; a jocular proposal of joint occupancy having been first indignantly rejected by "Mademoiselle," though preferred with the "laste taste in life" of Mr. Barney's most insinuating brogue.

* * * * * * * *

"Come, Charles, the urn is absolutely getting cold; your breakfast will be quite spoiled: what can have made you so idle?" Such was the morning salutation of Miss Ingoldsby to the *militaire* as he entered the breakfast-room half an hour after the latest of the party.

"A pretty gentleman, truly, to make an appointment with," chimed in Miss Frances. "What is become of our ramble to the rocks before breakfast?"

"Oh! the young men never think of keeping a promise now," said Mrs. Peters, a little ferret-faced woman with underdone eyes.

"When I was a young man," said Mr. Peters, "I remember I always made a point of—"

"Pray, how long ago was that?" asked Mr. Simpkinson from Bath.

"Why, sir, when I married Mrs. Peters, I was—let me see—I was—"

"Do pray hold your tongue, P., and eat your breakfast!" interrupted his better half, who had a mortal horror of chronological references; "it's very rude to tease people with your family affairs."

The lieutenant had by this time taken his seat in silence—a good-humoured nod, and a glance, half-smiling, half-inquisitive, being the extent of his salutation. Smitten as he was, and in the immediate presence of her who had made so large a hole in his heart, his manner was evidently *distrait*, which the fair Caroline in her secret soul attributed to his being solely occupied by her *agrèmens*: how would she have bridled had she known that they only shared his meditations with a pair of breeches!

Charles drank his coffee and spiked some half-dozen eggs, darting occasionally a penetrating glance at the ladies, in hope of detecting the supposed waggery by the evidence of some furtive smile or conscious look. But in vain; not a dimple moved indicative of roguery, nor did the slightest elevation of eyebrow rise confirmative of his suspicions. Hints and insinuations passed unheeded—more particular inquiries were out of the question—the subject was unapproachable.

In the meantime, "patent cords" were just the thing for a morning's ride; and, breakfast ended, away cantered the party over the downs, till, every faculty absorbed by the beauties, animate and inanimate, which surrounded him. Lieutenant Seaforth of the Bombay Fencibles bestowed no more thought upon his breeches than if he had been born on the top of Ben Lomond.

****

Another night had passed away; the sun rose brilliantly, forming with his level beams a splendid rainbow in the far-off west, whither the heavy cloud, which for the last two hours had been pouring its waters on the earth, was now flying before him.

"Ah! then, and it's little good it'll be the claning of ye," apostrophized Mr. Barney Maguire, as he deposited, in front of his master's toilet, a pair of "bran new" jockey boots, one of Hoby's primest fits, which the lieutenant had purchased in his way through town. On that very morning had they come for the first time under the valet's depurating hand, so little soiled, indeed, from the turfy ride of the preceding day, that a less scrupulous domestic might, perhaps, have considered the application of "Warren's Matchless," or oxalic acid, altogether superfluous. Not so Barney: with the nicest care had he removed the slightest impurity from each polished surface, and there they stood, rejoicing in their sable radiance. No wonder a pang shot across Mr. Maguire's breast as he thought on the work now cut out for them, so different from the light labours of the day before; no wonder he murmured with a sigh, as the scarce dried window-panes disclosed a road now inch deep in mud! "Ah! then, it's little good claning of ye!"—for well had he learned in the hall below that eight miles of a stiff clay soil lay between the manor and Bolsover Abbey, whose picturesque ruins,

"Like ancient Rome, majestic in decay,"

the party had determined to explore. The master had already commenced dressing, and the man was fitting straps upon a light pair of crane-necked spurs, when his hand was arrested by the old question—
"Barney, where are the breeches?"

They were nowhere to be found!

* * * * * * * *

Mr. Seaforth descended that morning, whip in hand, and equipped in a handsome green riding-frock, but no "breeches and boots to match" were there: loose jean trousers, surmounting a pair of diminutive Wellingtons, embraced, somewhat incongruously, his nether man, *vice* the "patent cords," returned, like yesterday's pantaloons, absent without leave. The "top-boots" had a holiday.

"A fine morning after the rain," said Mr. Simpkinson from Bath.

"Just the thing for the 'ops," said Mr. Peters. "I remember when I was a boy—"

"Do hold your tongue, P.," said Mrs. Peters—advice which that exemplary matron was in the constant habit of administering to "her P." as she called him, whenever he prepared to vent his reminiscences. Her precise reason for this it would be difficult to determine, unless, indeed, the story be true which a little bird had whispered into Mrs. Botherby's ear—Mr. Peters, though now a wealthy man had received a liberal education at a charity school, and was apt to recur to the days of his muffin-cap and leathers. As usual, he took his wife's hint in good part, and "paused in his reply."

"A glorious day for the ruins!" said young Ingoldsby. "But Charles, what the deuce are you about? you don't mean to ride through our lanes in such toggery as that?"

"Lassy me!" said Miss Julia Simpkinson, "won't yo' be very wet?"

"You had better take Tom's cab," quoth the squire.

But this proposition was at once over-ruled; Mrs. Ogleton had already nailed the cab, a vehicle of all others the best adapted for a snug flirtation.

"Or drive Miss Julia in the phaeton?" No; that was the post of Mr. Peters, who, indifferent as an equestrian, had acquired some fame as a whip while travelling through the midland counties for the firm of Bagshaw, Snivelby, and Ghrimes.

"Thank you, I shall ride with my cousins," said Charles, with as much nonchalance as he could assume—and he did so; Mr. Ingoldsby, Mrs. Peters, Mr. Simpkinson from Bath, and his eldest daughter with her album, following in the family coach. The gentleman-commoner "voted the affair d—d slow," and declined the party altogether in favour of the gamekeeper and a cigar. "There was 'no fun' in looking at old houses!" Mrs. Simpkinson preferred a short *séjour* in the still-room with Mrs. Botherby, who had promised to initiate her in that grand *arcanum*, the transmutation of gooseberry jam into Guava jelly.

****

"Did you ever see an old abbey before, Mrs. Peters?"

"Yes, miss, a French one; we have got one at Ramsgate; he teaches the Miss Joneses to parley-voo and is turned of sixty."

Miss Simpkinson closed her album with an air of ineffable disdain.

Mr. Simpkinson from Bath was a professed antiquary, and one of the first water; he was master of Gwillim's Heraldry, and Mill's History of the Crusades; knew every plate in the Monasticon; had written an essay on the origin and dignity of the office of overseer, and settled the date on a Queen Anne's farthing. An influential member of the Antiquarian Society, to whose "Beauties of Bagnigge Wells" he had been a liberal subscriber, procured him a seat at the board of that learned body, since which happy epoch Sylvanus Urban had not a more indefatigable correspondent. His inaugural essay on the President's cocked hat was considered a miracle of erudition; and his account of the earliest application of gilding to gingerbread, a masterpiece of antiquarian research. His eldest daughter was of a kindred spirit: if her father's mantle had not fallen upon her, it was only because he had not thrown it off himself; she had caught hold of its tail, however, while it yet hung upon his honoured shoulders. To souls so congenial, what a sight was the magnificent ruin of Bolsover! its broken arches, its mouldering pinnacles, and the airy tracery of its half-demolished windows. The party were in raptures; Mr. Simpkinson began to meditate an essay, and his daughter an ode: even Seaforth, as he gazed on these lonely relics of the olden time, was betrayed into a momentary forgetfulness of his love and losses; the widow's eye-glass turned from her *cicisbeo's* whiskers to the mantling ivy; Mrs. Peters wiped her spectacles; and "her P." supposed the central tower "had once been the county jail." The squire was a philosopher, and had been there often before, so he ordered out the cold tongue and chickens.

"Bolsover Priory," said Mr. Simpkinson, with the air of a connoisseur—"Bolsover Priory was founded in the reign of Henry the Sixth, about the beginning of the eleventh century. Hugh de Bolsover had accompanied that monarch to the Holy Land, in the expedition undertaken by way of penance for the murder of his young nephews in the Tower. Upon the dissolution of the monasteries, the veteran was *enfeoffed* in the lands and manor, to which he gave his own name of Bowlsover, or Bee-owls-over (by corruption Bolsover)—a Bee in chief, over three Owls, all proper, being the armorial ensigns borne by this distinguished crusader at the siege of Acre."

"Ah! that was Sir Sidney Smith," said Mr. Peters; "I've heard tell of him, and all about Mrs. Partington, and—"

"P. be quiet, and don't expose yourself!" sharply interrupted his lady. P. was silenced, and betook himself to the bottled stout.

"These lands," continued the antiquary, "were held in grand serjeantry by the presentation of three white owls and pot of honey—"

"Lassy me! how nice!" said Miss Julia. Mr. Peters licked his lips.

"Pray give me leave, my dear—owls and honey, whenever the king should come a rat-catching into this part of the country."

"Rat-catching!" ejaculated the squire, pausing abruptly in the mastication of a drumstick.

"To be sure, my dear sir; don't you remember the rats came under the forest laws—a minor species of venison? 'Rats and mice, and such small deer,' eh?—Shakespeare, you know. Our ancestors ate rats ('The nasty fellows!' shuddered Miss Julia, in a parenthesis); and owls, you know, are capital mousers—"

"I've seen a howl," said Mr. Peters; "there's one in the Sohological Gardens—a little hook-nosed chap in a wig—only its feathers and—"

Poor P. was destined never to finish a speech.

"*Do* be quiet!" cried the authoritative voice; and the would-be naturalist shrank into his shell, like a snail in the "Sohological Gardens."

"You should read Blount's *Jocular Tenures*, Mr. Ingoldsby," pursued Simpkinson. "A learned man was Blount! Why, sir, His Royal Highness the Duke of York once paid a silver horse-shoe to Lord Ferrers—"

"I've heard of him," broke in the incorrigible Peters; "he was hanged at the Old Bailey in a silk rope for shooting Dr. Johnson."

The antiquary vouchsafed no notice of the interruption; but, taking a pinch of snuff, continued his harangue.

"A silver horse-shoe, sir, which is due from every scion of royalty who rides across one of his manors; and if you look into the penny county histories, now publishing by an eminent friend of mine, you will find that Langhale in Co. Norf. was held by one Baldwin *per saltum, sufflatum, et pettum*; that is, he was to come every Christmas into Westminster Hall, there to take a leap, cry hem! and—"

"Mr. Simpkinson, a glass of sherry?" cried Tom Ingoldsby, hastily.

"Not any, thank you, sir. This Baldwin, surnamed *Le*—"

"Mrs. Ogleton challenges you, sir; she insists upon it," said Tom still more rapidly, at the same time filling a glass, and forcing it on the *sçavant*, who, thus arrested in the very crisis of his narrative, received and swallowed the potation as if it had been physic.

"What on earth has Miss Simpkinson discovered there?" continued Tom; "something of interest. See how fast she is writing."

The diversion was effectual; every one looked towards Miss Simpkinson, who, far too ethereal for "creature comforts," was seated apart on the dilapidated remains of an altar-tomb, committing eagerly to paper something that had strongly impressed her; the air—the eye in a "fine frenzy rolling"—all betokened that the divine *afflatus* was come. Her father rose, and stole silently towards her.

"What an old boar!" muttered young Ingoldsby; alluding, perhaps, to a slice of brawn which he had just begun to operate upon, but which, from the celerity with which it disappeared, did not seem so very difficult of mastication.

But what had become of Seaforth and his fair Caroline all this while? Why, it so happened that they had been simultaneously stricken with the picturesque appearance of one of those high and pointed arches, which that eminent antiquary, Mr. Horseley Curties, has described in his *Ancient Records*, as "a *Gothic* window of the *Saxon* order"; and then the ivy clustered so thickly and so beautifully on the other side, that they went round to look at that; and then their proximity deprived it of half its effect, and so they walked across to a little knoll, a hundred yards off, and in crossing a small ravine, they came to what in Ireland they call "a bad step," and Charles had to carry his cousin over it; and then when they had to come back, she would not give him the trouble again for the world, so they followed a better but more circuitous route, and there were hedges and ditches in the way, and stiles to get over and gates to get through, so that an hour or more had elapsed before they were able to rejoin the party.

"Lassy me!" said Miss Julia Simpkinson, "how long you have been gone!"

And so they had. The remark was a very just as well as a very natural one. They were gone a long while, and a nice cosy chat they had; and what do you think it was all about, my dear miss?

"O lassy me! love, no doubt, and the moon, and eyes, and nightingales, and—"

Stay, stay, my sweet young lady; do not let the fervour of your feelings run away with you! I do not pretend to say, indeed, that one or more of these pretty subjects might not have been introduced;

but the most important and leading topic of the conference was—Lieutenant Seaforth's breeches.

"Caroline," said Charles, "I have had some very odd dreams since I have been at Tappington."

"Dreams, have you?" smiled the young lady, arching her taper neck like a swan in pluming. "Dreams, have you?"

"Ah, dreams—or dream, perhaps, I should say; for, though repeated, it was still the same. And what do you imagine was its subject?"

"It is impossible for me to divine," said the tongue; "I have not the least difficulty in guessing," said the eye, as plainly as ever eye spoke.

"I dreamt—of your great-grandfather!"

There was a change in the glance—"My great-grandfather?"

"Yes, the old Sir Giles, or Sir John, you told me about the other day: he walked into my bedroom in his short cloak of murrey-coloured velvet, his long rapier, and his Raleigh-looking hat and feather, just as the picture represents him; but with one exception."

"And what was that?"

"Why, his lower extremities, which were visible, were those of a skeleton."

"Well?"

"Well, after taking a turn or two about the room, and looking round him with a wistful air, he came to the bed's foot, stared at me in a manner impossible to describe—and then he—he laid hold of my pantaloons; whipped his long bony legs into them in a twinkling; and strutting up to the glass, seemed to view himself in it with great complacency. I tried to speak, but in vain. The effort, however, seemed to excite his attention; for, wheeling about, he showed me the grimmest-looking death's head you can well imagine, and with an indescribable grin strutted out of the room."

"Absurd! Charles. How can you talk such nonsense?"

"But, Caroline—the breeches are really gone."

****

On the following morning, contrary to his usual custom, Seaforth was the first person in the breakfast parlour. As no one else was present, he did precisely what nine young men out of ten so situated would have done; he walked up to the mantelpiece, established himself upon the rug, and subducting his coat-tails one under each arm, turned towards the fire that portion of the human frame which it is considered equally indecorous to present to a friend or an enemy. A serious, not to say anxious, expression was visible upon his good-humoured countenance, and his mouth was fast buttoning itself up for an incipient whistle, when little Flo, a tiny spaniel of the Blenheim breed—the pet object of Miss Julia Simpkinson's affections—bounced out from beneath a sofa, and began to bark at—his pantaloons.

They were cleverly "built," of a light-grey mixture, a broad stripe of the most vivid scarlet traversing each seam in a perpendicular direction from hip to ankle—in short, the regimental costume of the Royal Bombay Fencibles. The animal, educated in the country, had never seen such a pair of breeches in her life—*Omne ignotum pro magnifico!* The scarlet streak, inflamed as it was by the reflection of the fire, seemed to act on Flora's nerves as the same colour does on those of bulls and turkeys; she advanced at the *pas de charge*, and her vociferation, like her amazement, was unbounded. A sound kick from the disgusted officer changed its character, and induced a retreat at the very moment when the mistress of the pugnacious quadruped entered to the rescue.

"Lassy me! Flo, what *is* the matter?" cried the sympathizing lady, with a scrutinizing glance levelled at the gentleman.

It might as well have lighted on a feather bed. His air of imperturbable unconsciousness defied examination; and as he would not, and Flora could not, expound, that injured individual was compelled to pocket up her wrongs. Others of the household soon dropped in, and clustered round the board dedicated to the most sociable of meals; the urn was paraded "hissing hot," and the cups which "cheer, but not inebriate," steamed redolent of hyson and pekoe; muffins and marmalade, newspapers, and Finnan haddies, left little room for observation on the character of Charles's warlike "turn-out." At length a look from Caroline, followed by a smile that nearly ripened to a titter, caused him to turn abruptly and address his neighbour. It was Miss Simpkinson, who, deeply engaged in sipping her tea and turning over her album, seemed, like a female Chrononotonthologos, "immersed in cogibundity of cogitation." An interrogatory on the subject of her studies drew from her the confession that she was at that moment employed in putting the finishing touches to a poem inspired by the romantic shades of Bolsover. The entreaties of the company were of course urgent. Mr. Peters, "who liked verses," was especially persevering, and Sappho at length compliant. After a preparatory *hem!* and a glance at the mirror to ascertain that her look was sufficiently sentimental, the poetess began:—

"There is a calm, a holy feeling,
"Vulgar minds, can never know,

"O'er the bosom softly stealing,—
"Chasten'd grief, delicious woe!
"Oh! how sweet at eve regaining
"Yon lone tower's sequester'd shade—
"Sadly mute and uncomplaining—"

"—*Yow!*—*yeough!*—*yeough!*—*yow!*—*yow!*" yelled a hapless sufferer from beneath the table. It was an unlucky hour for quadrupeds; and if "every dog will have his day," he could not have selected a more unpropitious one than this. Mrs. Ogleton, too, had a pet—a favourite pug—whose squab figure, black muzzle, and tortuosity of tail, that curled like a head of celery in a salad-bowl, bespoke his Dutch extraction. Yow! yow! yow! continued the brute—a chorus in which Flo instantly joined. Sooth to say, pug had more reason to express his dissatisfaction than was given him by the muse of Simpkinson; the other only barked for company. Scarcely had the poetess got through her first stanza, when Tom Ingoldsby, in the enthusiasm of the moment, became so lost in the material world, that, in his abstraction, he unwarily laid his hand on the cock of the urn. Quivering with emotion, he gave it such an unlucky twist, that the full stream of its scalding contents descended on the gingerbread hide of the unlucky Cupid. The confusion was complete; the whole economy of the table disarranged—the company broke up in most admired disorder—and "vulgar minds will never know" anything more of Miss Simpkinson's ode till they peruse it in some forthcoming Annual.

Seaforth profited by the confusion to take the delinquent who had caused this "stramash" by the arm, and to lead him to the lawn, where he had a word or two for his private ear. The conference between the young gentlemen was neither brief in its duration nor unimportant in its result. The subject was what the lawyers call tripartite, embracing the information that Charles Seaforth was over head and ears in love with Tom Ingoldsby's sister; secondly, that the lady had referred him to "papa" for his sanction; thirdly, and lastly, his nightly visitations and consequent bereavement. At the two first times Tom smiled suspiciously—at the last he burst out into an absolute "guffaw."

"Steal your breeches! Miss Bailey over again, by Jove," shouted Ingoldsby. "But a gentleman, you say—and Sir Giles, too. I am not sure, Charles, whether I ought not to call you out for aspersing the honour of the family."

"Laugh as you will, Tom—be as incredulous as you please. One fact is incontestable—the breeches are gone! Look here—I am reduced to my regimentals; and if these go, to-morrow I must borrow of you!"

Rochefoucault says, there is something in the misfortunes of our very best friends that does not displease us; assuredly we can, most of us, laugh at their petty inconveniences, till called upon to supply them. Tom composed his features on the instant, and replied with more gravity, as well as with an expletive, which, if my Lord Mayor had been within hearing might have cost him five shillings.

"There is something very queer in this, after all. The clothes, you say, have positively disappeared. Somebody is playing you a trick; and, ten to one, your servant had a hand in it. By the way, I heard something yesterday of his kicking up a bobbery in the kitchen, and seeing a ghost, or something of that kind, himself. Depend upon it, Barney is in the plot."

It now struck the lieutenant at once, that the usually buoyant spirits of his attendant had of late been materially sobered down, his loquacity obviously circumscribed, and that he, the said lieutenant, had actually rung his bell three several times that very morning before he could procure his attendance. Mr. Maguire was forthwith summoned, and underwent a close examination. The "bobbery" was easily explained. Mr. Oliver Dobbs had hinted his disapprobation of a flirtation carrying on between the gentleman from Munster and the lady from the Rue St. Honoré. *Mademoiselle* had boxed Mr. Maguire's ears, and Mr. Maguire had pulled *Mademoiselle* upon his knee, and the lady had *not* cried *Mon Dieu!* And Mr. Oliver Dobbs said it was very wrong; and Mrs. Botherby said it was "scandalous," and what ought not to be done in any moral kitchen; and Mr. Maguire had got hold of the Honourable Augustus Sucklethumbkin's powder-flask, and had put large pinches of the best Double Dartford into Mr. Dobbs's tobacco-box; and Mr. Dobbs's pipe had exploded, and set fire to Mrs. Botherby's Sunday cap; and Mr. Maguire had put it out with the slopbasin, "barring the wig"; and then they were all so "cantankerous," that Barney had gone to take a walk in the garden; and then—then Mr. Barney had seen a ghost.

"A what? you blockhead!" asked Tom Ingoldsby.

"Sure then, and it's meself will tell your honour the rights of it," said the ghost-seer. "Meself and Miss Pauline, sir—or Miss Pauline and meself, for the ladies comes first anyhow—we got tired of the hobstroppylous scrimmaging among the ould servants, that didn't know a joke when they seen one: and we went out to look at the comet—that's the rorybory-alehouse, they calls him in this country—and we walked upon the lawn—and divil of any alehouse there was there at all; and Miss Pauline said it was bekase of the shrubbery maybe, and why wouldn't we see it better beyonst the tree? and so we went to the trees, but sorrow a comet did meself see there, barring a big ghost instead of it."

"A ghost? And what sort of a ghost, Barney?"

"Och, then, divil a lie I'll tell your honour. A tall ould gentleman he was, all in white, with a shovel on the shoulder of him, and a big torch in his fist—though what he wanted with that it's meself can't tell, for his eyes were like gig-lamps, let alone the moon and the comet, which wasn't there at all—and 'Barney,' says he to me—'cause why he knew me—'Barney,' says he, 'what is it you're doing with the *colleen* there, Barney?'—Divil a word did I say. Miss Pauline screeched, and cried murther in French, and ran off with herself; and of course meself was in a mighty hurry after the lady, and had no time to stop palavering with him any way: so I dispersed at once, and the ghost vanished in a flame of fire!"

Mr. Maguire's account was received with avowed incredulity by both gentlemen; but Barney stuck to his text with unflinching pertinacity. A reference to *Mademoiselle* was suggested, but abandoned, as neither party had a taste for delicate investigations.

"I'll tell you what, Seaforth," said Ingoldsby, after Barney had received his dismissal, "that there is a trick here, is evident; and Barney's vision may possibly be a part of it. Whether he is most knave or fool, you best know. At all events, I will sit up with you to-night, and see if I can convert my ancestor into a visiting acquaintance. Meanwhile your finger on your lip!"

****

'Twas now the very witching time of night, When churchyards yawn, and graves give up their dead.

Gladly would I grace my tale with decent horror, and therefore I do beseech the "gentle reader" to believe, that if all the *succedanea* to this mysterious narrative are not in strict keeping, he will ascribe it only to the disgraceful innovations of modern degeneracy upon the sober and dignified habits of our ancestors. I can introduce him, it is true, into an old and high-roofed chamber, its walls covered in three sides with black oak wainscoting, adorned with carvings of fruit and flowers long anterior to those of Grinling Gibbons; the fourth side is clothed with a curious remnant of dingy tapestry, once elucidatory of some Scriptural history, but of *which* not even Mrs. Botherby could determine. Mr. Simpkinson, who had examined it carefully, inclined to believe the principal figure to be either Bathsheba, or Daniel in

200

the lions' den; while Tom Ingoldsby decided in favour of the king of Bashan. All, however, was conjecture, tradition being silent on the subject. A lofty arched portal led into, and a little arched portal led out of, this apartment; they were opposite each other, and each possessed the security of massy bolts on its interior. The bedstead, too, was not one of yesterday, but manifestly coeval with days ere Seddons was, and when a good four-post "article" was deemed worthy of being a royal bequest. The bed itself, with all the appurtenances of *palliasse*, mattresses, etc., was of far later date, and looked most incongruously comfortable; the casements, too, with their little diamond-shaped panes and iron binding, had given way to the modern heterodoxy of the sash-window. Nor was this all that conspired to ruin the costume, and render the room a meet haunt for such "mixed spirits" only as could condescend to don at the same time an Elizabethan doublet and Bond Street inexpressibles.

With their green morocco slippers on a modern fender, in front of a disgracefully modern grate, sat two young gentlemen, clad in "shawl pattern" dressing-gowns and black silk stocks, much at variance with the high cane-backed chairs which supported them. A bunch of abomination, called a cigar, reeked in the left-hand corner of the mouth of one, and in the right-hand corner of the mouth of the other—an arrangement happily adapted for the escape of the noxious fumes up the chimney, without that unmerciful "funking" each other, which a less scientific disposition of the weed would have induced. A small Pembroke table filled up the intervening space between them, sustaining, at each extremity, an elbow and a glass of toddy—thus in "lonely pensive contemplation" were the two worthies occupied, when the "iron tongue of midnight had tolled twelve."

"Ghost-time's come!" said Ingoldsby, taking from his waistcoat pocket a watch like a gold half-crown, and consulting it as though he suspected the turret-clock over the stables of mendacity.

"Hush!" said Charles; "did I not hear a footstep?"

There was a pause—there *was* a footstep—it sounded distinctly—it reached the door it hesitated, stopped, and—passed on.

Tom darted across the room, threw open the door, and became aware of Mrs. Botherby toddling to her chamber, at the other end of the gallery, after dosing one of the housemaids with an approved julep from the Countess of Kent's "Choice Manual."

"Good-night, sir!" said Mrs. Botherby.

"Go to the d—l!" said the disappointed ghost-hunter.

An hour—two—rolled on, and still no spectral visitation; nor did aught intervene to make night hideous; and when the turret-clock sounded at length the hour of three, Ingoldsby, whose patience and grog were alike exhausted, sprang from his chair, saying:

"This is all infernal nonsense, my good fellow. Deuce of any ghost shall we see to-night; it's long past the canonical hour. I'm off to bed; and as to your breeches, I'll insure them for the next twenty-four hours at least, at the price of the buckram."

"Certainly.—Oh! thank'ee—to be sure!" stammered Charles, rousing himself from a reverie, which had degenerated into an absolute snooze.

"Good-night, my boy! Bolt the door behind me; and defy the Pope, the Devil, and the Pretender!"

Seaforth followed his friend's advice, and the next morning came down to breakfast dressed in the habiliments of the preceding day. The charm was broken, the demon defeated; the light greys with the red stripe down the seams were yet *in rerum naturâ*, and adorned the person of their lawful proprietor.

Tom felicitated himself and his partner of the watch on the result of their vigilance; but there is a rustic adage, which warns us against self-gratulation before we are quite "out of the wood."—Seaforth was yet within its verge.

* * * * * * * *

A rap at Tom Ingoldsby's door the following morning startled him as he was shaving—he cut his chin.

"Come in, and be d—d to you!" said the martyr, pressing his thumb on the scarified epidermis. The door opened, and exhibited Mr. Barney Maguire.

"Well, Barney, what is it?" quoth the sufferer, adopting the vernacular of his visitant.

"The master, sir—"

"Well, what does he want?"

"The loanst of a breeches, plase your honor."

"Why, you don't mean to tell me—By Heaven, this is too good!" shouted Tom, bursting into a fit of uncontrollable laughter. "Why, Barney, you don't mean to say the ghost has got them again?"

Mr. Maguire did not respond to the young squire's risibility; the cast of his countenance was decidedly serious.

"Faith, then, it's gone they are sure enough! Hasn't meself been looking over the bed, and under the bed, and *in* the bed, for the matter of that, and divil a ha'p'orth of breeches is there to the fore at all:— I'm bothered entirely!"

"Hark'ee! Mr. Barney," said Tom, incautiously removing his thumb, and letting a crimson stream "incarnadine the multitudinous" lather that plastered his throat—"this may be all very well with your master, but you don't humbug *me*, sir:—Tell me instantly what have you done with the clothes?"

This abrupt transition from "lively to severe" certainly took Maguire by surprise, and he seemed for an instant as much disconcerted as it is possible to disconcert an Irish gentleman's gentleman.

"Me? is it meself, then, that's the ghost to your honour's thinking?" said he after a moment's pause, and with a slight shade of indignation in his tones; "is it I would stale the master's things—and what would I do with them?"

"That you best know: what your purpose is I can't guess, for I don't think you mean to 'stale' them, as you call it; but that you are concerned in their disappearance, I am satisfied. Confound this blood!—give me a towel, Barney."

Maguire acquitted himself of the commission. "As I've a sowl, your honour," said he, solemnly, "little it is meself knows of the matter: and after what I seen—"

"What you've seen! Why, what *have* you seen?—Barney, I don't want to inquire into your flirtations; but don't suppose you can palm off your saucer eyes and gig-lamps upon me!"

"Then, as sure as your honour's standing there, I saw him: and why wouldn't I, when Miss *Pauline* was to the fore as well as meself, and—"

"Get along with your nonsense—leave the room, sir!"

"But the master?" said Barney, imploringly; "and without a breeches?—sure he'll be catching cowld—!"

"Take that, rascal!" replied Ingoldsby, throwing a pair of pantaloons at, rather than to, him: "but don't suppose, sir, you shall carry on your tricks here with impunity; recollect there is such a thing as a treadmill, and that my father is a county magistrate."

Barney's eye flashed fire—he stood erect, and was about to speak; but, mastering himself, not without an effort, he took up the garment, and left the room as perpendicular as a Quaker.

* * * * * * * *

"Ingoldsby," said Charles Seaforth, after breakfast, "this is now past a joke; to-day is the last of my stay; for, notwithstanding the ties which detain me, common decency obliges me to visit home after so long an absence. I shall come to an immediate explanation with your father on the subject nearest my heart, and depart while I have a change of dress left. On his answer will my return depend! In the meantime tell me candidly—I ask it in all seriousness, and as a friend—am I not a dupe to your well-known propensity to hoaxing? have you not a hand in—"

"No, by heaven, Seaforth; I see what you mean: on my honour, I am as much mystified as yourself; and if your servant—"

"Not he:—If there be a trick, he at least is not privy to it."

"If there *be* a trick? why, Charles, do you, think—"

"I know not *what* to think, Tom. As surely as you are a living man, so surely did that spectral anatomy visit my room again last night, grin in my face, and walk away with my trousers; nor was I able to spring from my bed, or break the chain which seemed to bind me to my pillow."

"Seaforth!" said Ingoldsby, after a short pause, "I will—But hush! here are the girls and my father. I will carry off the females, and leave you a clear field with the governor: carry your point with him, and we will talk about your breeches afterwards."

Tom's diversion was successful; he carried off the ladies *en masse* to look at a remarkable specimen of the class *Dodecandria Monogynia*— which they could not find—while Seaforth marched boldly up to the encounter, and carried "the governor's" outworks by a *coup de main*. I shall not stop to describe the progress of the attack; suffice it that it was as successful as could have been wished, and that Seaforth was re-ferred back again to the lady. The happy lover was off at a tangent; the botanical party was soon overtaken; and the arm of Caroline, whom a vain endeavour to spell out the Linnaean name of a daffy-down-dilly had detained a little in the rear of the others, was soon firmly locked in his own.

What was the world to them, Its noise, its nonsense and its "breeches" all?

Seaforth was in the seventh heaven; he retired to his room that night as happy as if no such thing as a goblin had ever been heard of, and personal chattels were as well fenced in by law as real prop-erty. Not so Tom Ingoldsby: the mystery—for mystery there evidently was—had not only piqued his curiosity, but ruffled his temper. The watch of the previous night had been unsuccessful, probably because it was undisguised. To-night he would "ensconce himself"—not in-deed "behind the arras"—for the little that remained was, as we have seen, nailed to the wall—but in a small closet which opened from one corner of the room, and by leaving the door ajar, would give to its occupant a view of all that might pass in the apartment. Here did the young ghost-hunter take up a position, with a good stout sapling under his arm, a full half-hour before Seaforth retired for the night. Not even his friend did he let into his confidence, fully determined that if his plan did not succeed, the failure should be attributed to himself alone.

At the usual hour of separation for the night, Tom saw, from his concealment, the lieutenant enter his room, and after taking a few turns in it, with an expression so joyous as to betoken that his thoughts were mainly occupied by his approaching happiness, proceed slowly to disrobe himself. The coat, the waistcoat, the black silk stock, were gradually discarded; the green morocco slippers were kicked off, and then—ay, and then—his countenance grew grave; it seemed to occur to him all at once that this was his last stake—nay, that the very breeches he had on were not his own—that to-morrow morning was his last, and that if he lost *them*—A glance showed that his mind was made up; he replaced the single button he had just subducted, and threw himself upon the bed in a state of transition—half chrysalis, half grub.

Wearily did Tom Ingoldsby watch the sleeper by the flickering light of the night-lamp, till the clock striking one, induced him to increase the narrow opening which he had left for the purpose of observation. The motion, slight as it was, seemed to attract Charles's attention; for he raised himself suddenly to a sitting posture, listened for a moment, and then stood upright upon the floor. Ingoldsby was on the point of discovering himself, when, the light flashing full upon his friend's countenance, he perceived that, though his eyes were open, "their sense was shut"—that he was yet under the influence of sleep. Seaforth advanced slowly to the toilet, lit his candle at the lamp that stood on it, then, going back to the bed's foot, appeared to search eagerly for something which he could not find. For a few moments he seemed restless and uneasy, walking round the apartment and examining the chairs, till, coming fully in front of a large swing-glass that flanked the dressing-table, he paused as if contemplating his figure in it. He now returned towards the bed; put on his slippers, and, with cautious and stealthy steps, proceeded towards the little arched doorway that opened on the private staircase.

As he drew the bolt, Tom Ingoldsby emerged from his hiding-place; but the sleep-walker heard him not; he proceeded softly downstairs, followed at a due distance by his friend; opened the door which led out upon the gardens; and stood at once among the thickest of the shrubs, which there clustered round the base of a corner turret, and screened the postern from common observation. At this moment Ingoldsby had nearly spoiled all by making a false step: the sound attracted Seaforth's attention—he paused and turned; and, as the full moon shed her light directly upon his pale and troubled features, Tom marked, almost with dismay, the fixed and rayless appearance of his eyes:

There was no speculation in those orbs That he did glare withal.

The perfect stillness preserved by his follower seemed to reassure him; he turned aside, and from the midst of a thickest laurustinus drew forth a gardener's spade, shouldering which he proceeded with great rapidity into the midst of the shrubbery. Arrived at a certain point where the earth seemed to have been recently disturbed, he set himself heartily to the task of digging, till, having thrown up several shovelfuls of mould, he stopped, flung down his tool, and very composedly began to disencumber himself of his pantaloons.

Up to this moment Tom had watched him with a wary eye; he now advanced cautiously, and, as his friend was busily engaged in disentangling himself from his garment, made himself master of the spade. Seaforth, meanwhile, had accomplished his purpose: he stood for a moment with his streamers waving in the wind,

occupied in carefully rolling up the small-clothes into as compact a form as possible, and all heedless of the breath of heaven, which might certainly be supposed at such a moment, and in such a plight, to "visit his frame too roughly."

He was in the act of stooping low to deposit the pantaloons in the grave which he had been digging for them, when Tom Ingoldsby came close behind him, and with the flat side of the spade—

****

The shock was effectual; never again was Lieutenant Seaforth known to act the part of a somnambulist. One by one, his breeches—his trousers—his pantaloons—his silk-net tights—his patent cords—his showy greys with the broad red stripe of the Bombay Fencibles were brought to light—rescued from the grave in which they had been buried, like the strata of a Christmas pie; and after having been well aired by Mrs. Botherby, became once again effective.

The family, the ladies especially, laughed; the Peterses laughed; the Simpkinsons laughed;—Barney Maguire cried "Botheration!" and Ma'mselle Pauline, "Mon Dieu!"

Charles Seaforth, unable to face the quizzing which awaited him on all sides, started off two hours earlier than he had proposed:—he soon returned, however; and having, at his father-in-law's request, given up the occupation of Rajah-hunting and shooting Nabobs, led his blushing bride to the altar.

Mr. Simpkinson from Bath did not attend the ceremony, being engaged at the Grand Junction meeting of *Sçavans*, then, congregating from all parts of the known world in the city of Dublin. His essay, demonstrating that the globe is a great custard, whipped into coagulation by whirlwinds and cooked by electricity—a little too much baked in the Isle of Portland, and a thought underdone about the Bog of Allen—was highly spoken of, and narrowly escaped obtaining a Bridgewater prize.

Miss Simpkinson and her sister acted as brides-maids on the occasion; the former wrote an *epithalamium*, and the latter cried "Lassy me!" at the clergyman's wig. Some years have since rolled on; the union has been crowned with two or three tidy little off-shoots from the family tree, of whom Master Neddy is "grandpapa's darling," and Mary Anne mamma's particular "Sock." I shall only add, that Mr. and Mrs. Seaforth are living together quite as happily as two good-hearted, good-tempered bodies, very fond of each other, can possibly do; and that, since the day of his marriage, Charles has shown no disposition to jump out of bed, or ramble out of doors o' nights—though from his entire devotion to every wish and whim of his young wife, Tom insinuates that the fair Caroline does still occasionally take advantage of it so far as to "slip on the breeches."

In the Barn

Burges Johnson

The moment we had entered the barn, I regretted the rash good nature which prompted me to consent to the plans of those vivacious young students. Miss Anstell and Miss Royce and one or two others, often leaders in student mischief, I suspect, were the first to enter, and they amused themselves by hiding in the darkness and greeting the rest of our party as we entered with sundry shrieks and moans such as are commonly attributed to ghosts. My wife and I brought up the rear, carrying the two farm lanterns. She had selected the place after an amused consideration of the question, and I confess I hardly approved her judgment. But she is native to this part of the country, and she had assured us that there were some vague traditions hanging about the building that made it most suitable for our purposes.

It was a musty old place, without even as much tidiness as is usually found in barns, and there was a dank smell about it, as though generations of haymows had decayed there. There were holes in the floor, and in the dusk of early evening it was necessary for us to pick our way with the greatest care. It occurred to me then, in a premonitory sort of way, that if some young woman student sprained her ankle in this absurd environment, I should be most embarrassed to explain it. Apparently it was a hay barn, whose vague dimensions were lost in shadow. Rafters crossed its width about twenty feet above our heads, and here and there a few boards lay across the rafters, furnishing foothold for anyone who might wish to operate the ancient pulley that was doubtless once used for lifting bales. The northern half of the floor was covered with hay to a depth of two or three feet. How long it had actually been there I cannot imagine. It was extremely dusty, and I feared a recurrence of my old enemy, hay fever; but it was too late to offer objection on such grounds, and my wife and I followed

208

our chattering guides, who disposed themselves here and there on this ancient bed of hay, and insisted that we should find places in the centre of their circle.

At my suggestion, the two farm lanterns had been left at a suitable distance, in fact, quite at the other side of the barn, and our only light came from the rapidly falling twilight of outdoors, which found its way through a little window and sundry cracks high in the eaves above the rafters.

There was something about the place, now that we were settled and no longer occupied with adjustments of comfort, that subdued our spirits, and it was with much less hilarity that the young people united in demanding a story. I looked across at my wife, whose face was faintly visible within the circle. I thought that even in the half-light I glimpsed the same expression of amused incredulity which she had worn earlier in the day when I had yielded to the importunities of a deputation of my students for this ghost-story party on the eve of a holiday.

"There is no reason," I thought to myself, repeating the phrases I had used then—"there is no reason why I should not tell a ghost story. True, I had never done so before, but the literary attainments which have enabled me to perfect my recent treatise upon the 'Disuse of the Comma' are quite equal to impromptu experimentation in the field of psychic phenomena." I was aware that the young people themselves hardly expected serious acquiescence, and that, too, stimulated me. I cleared my throat in a prefatory manner, and silence fell upon the group. A light breeze had risen outside, and the timbers of the barn creaked persistently. From the shadows almost directly overhead there came a faint clanking. It was evidently caused by the rusty pulley-wheel which I had observed there as we entered. An iron hook at the end of an ancient rope still depended from it, and swung in the lightly stirring air several feet above our heads, directly over the centre of our circle.

Some curious combination of influences—perhaps the atmosphere of the place, added to the stimulation of the faintly discernible faces around me, and my impulse to prove my own ability in this untried field of narration—gave me a sudden sense of being inspired. I found myself voicing fancies as though they were facts, and readily including imaginary names and data which certainly were not in any way premeditated.

"This barn stands on the old Creed place," I began. "Peter Creed was its last owner, but I suppose that it has always been and always will be known as the Turner barn. A few yards away to the south you will find the crumbling brick-work and gaping hollows of an old foundation, now overgrown with weeds that almost conceal a few charred timbers. That is all that is left of the old Ashley Turner house."

I cleared my throat again, not through any effort to gain time for my thoughts, but to feel for a moment the satisfaction arising from the intent attitude of my audience, particularly my wife, who had leaned forward and was looking at me with an expression of startled surprise.

"Ashley Turner must have had a pretty fine-looking farm here thirty years or so ago," I continued, "when he brought his wife to it. This barn was new then. But he was a ne'er-do-well, with nothing to be said in his favour, unless you admit his fame as a practical joker. Strange how the ne'er-do-well is often equipped with an extravagant sense of humour! Turner had a considerable retinue among the riffraff boys of the neighbourhood, who made this barn a noisy rendezvous and followed his hints in much whimsical mischief. But he committed most of his practical jokes when drunk, and in his sober moments he abused his family and let his wife struggle to keep up the acres, assisted only by a half-competent man of all work. Finally he took to roving. No one knew how he got pocket-money; his wife could not have given him any. Then someone discovered that he was going over to Creed's now and then, and everything was explained."

This concise data of mine was evidently not holding the close attention of my youthful audience. They annoyed me by frequent pranks and whisperings. No one could have been more surprised at my glibness than I myself, except perhaps my wife, whose attitude of strained attention had not relaxed. I resumed my story.

"Peter Creed was a good old-fashioned usurer of the worst type. He went to church regularly one day in the week and gouged his neighbours—any that he could get into his clutches—on the other six. He must have been lending Turner drinking money, and everyone knew what the security must be.

"At last there came a day when the long-suffering wife revolted. Turner had come home extra drunk and in his most maudlin humour. Probably he attempted some drunken prank upon his over-taxed helpmate. Old Ike, the hired man, said that he thought Turner had rigged up some scare for her in the barn and that he had never heard anything so much like straight talking from his mistress, either before or since, and he was working in the woodshed at the time, with the door shut. Shortly after that tirade Ashley Turner disappeared, and no one saw or heard of him or thought about him for a couple of years except when the sight of his tired-looking wife and scrawny children revived the recollection.

"At last, on a certain autumn day, old Peter Creed turned up here at the Turner place. I imagine Mrs. Turner knew what was in store for her when his rusty buggy came in sight around the corner of the barn. At any rate, she made no protest, and listened meekly to his curt statement that he held an overdue mortgage, with plenty of back interest owing, and it was time for her to go. She went. Neither she nor anyone else doubted Creed's rights in the matter, and, after all, I believe it got a better home for her somewhere in the long run."

I paused here in my narration to draw breath and readjust my leg, which had become cramped. There was a general readjustment and shifting of position, with some levity. It was darker now. The rafters above us were invisible, and the faces about me looked oddly white against the shadowy background. After a moment or two of delay I cleared my throat sharply and continued.

"Old Creed came thus into possession of this place, just as he had come to own a dozen others in the county. He usually lived on one until he was able to sell it at a good profit over his investment; so he settled down in the Turner house, and kept old Ike because he worked for little or nothing. But he seemed to have a hard time finding a purchaser.

"It must have been about a year later when an unexpected thing happened. Creed had come out here to the barn to lock up—he always did that himself—when he noticed something unusual about the haymow—this haymow—which stood then about six feet above the barn floor. He looked closer through the dusk, and saw a pair of boots; went nearer, and found that they were fitted to a pair of human legs whose owner was sound asleep in his hay. Creed picked up a short stick and beat on one boot.

"'Get out of here,' he said, 'or I'll have you locked up.' The sleeper woke in slow fashion, sat up, grinned, and said:

"'Hello, Peter Creed.' It was Ashley Turner, beyond question. Creed stepped back a pace or two and seemed at a loss for words. An object slipped from Turner's pocket as he moved, slid along the hay, and fell to the barn floor. It was a half-filled whisky-flask.

"No one knows full details of the conversation that ensued, of course. Such little as I am able to tell you of what was said and done comes through old Ike, who watched from a safe distance outside the barn, ready to act at a moment's notice as best suited his own safety and welfare. Of one thing Ike was certain—Creed lacked his usual browbeating manner. He was apparently struggling to assume an unwonted friendliness. Turner was very drunk, but triumphant, and his satisfaction over what he must have felt was the practical joke of his life seemed to make him friendly.

"'I kept 'em all right,' he said again and again. 'I've got the proof. I wasn't working for nothing all these months. I ain't fool enough yet to throw away papers even when I'm drunk.'

"To the watchful Ike's astonishment, Creed evidently tried to persuade him to come into the house for something to eat. Turner slid off the haymow, found his steps too unsteady, laughed foolishly, and suggested that Creed bring some food to him there. 'Guess I've got a right to sleep in the barn or house, whichever I want,' he said, leering into Creed's face. The old usurer stood there for a few minutes eying Turner thoughtfully. Then he actually gave him a shoulder back onto the hay, said something about finding a snack of supper, and started out of the barn. In the doorway he turned, looked back, then walked over to the edge of the mow and groped on the floor until he found the whisky-flask, picked it up, tossed it into Turner's lap, and stumbled out of the barn again."

I was becoming interested in my own story and somewhat pleased with the fluency of it, but my audience annoyed me. There was intermittent whispering, with some laughter, and I inferred that one or another would occasionally stimulate this inattention by tickling a companion with a straw. Miss Anstell, who is so frivolous by nature that I sometimes question her right to a place in my classroom, I even suspected of irritating the back of my own neck in the same fashion. Naturally, I ignored it.

"Peter Creed," I repeated, "went into the house. Ike hung around the barn, waiting. He was frankly curious. In a few minutes his employer reappeared, carrying a plate heaped with an assortment of scraps. Ike peered and listened then without compunction.

"'It's the best I've got,' he heard Creed say grudgingly. Turner's tones were now more drunkenly belligerent.

"'It had better be,' he said loudly. 'And I'll take the best bed after to-night.' Evidently he was eating and muttering between mouthfuls. 'You might have brought me another bottle.'

"'I did,' said Creed, to the listening Ike's great astonishment. Turner laughed immoderately.

"A long silence followed. Turner was either eating or drinking. Then he spoke again, more thickly and drowsily.

"'Damn unpleasant that rope. Why don't you haul it up out of my way?'

"'It don't hurt you any,' said Creed.

"'Don't you wish it would?' said Turner, with drunken shrewdness. 'But I don't like it. Haul it away.'

"'I will,' said Creed.

"There was a longer silence, and then there came an intermittent rasping sound. A moment later Creed came suddenly from the barn. Ike fumbled with a large rake, and made as though to hang it on its accustomed peg near the barn door. Creed eyed him sharply. 'Get along to bed,' he ordered, and Ike obeyed.

"That was a Saturday night. On Sunday morning Ike went to the barn later than usual and hesitatingly. Even then he was first to enter. He found the drunkard's body hanging here over the mow, just about where we are sitting, stark and cold. It was a gruesome end to a miserable home-coming."

My audience was quiet enough now. Miss Anstell and one or two others giggled loudly, but it was obviously forced, and found no further echo. The breeze which had sprung up some time before was producing strange creakings and raspings in the old timbers, and the pulley-wheel far above us clanked with a dismal repetitious sound, like the tolling of a cracked bell. I waited a moment, well satisfied with the effect, and then continued.

"The coroner's jury found it suicide, though some shook their heads meaningly. Turner had apparently sobered up enough to stand, and, making a simple loop around his neck by catching the rope through its own hook, had then slid off the mow. The rope which went over the pulley-wheel up there in the roof ran out through a window under the eaves, and was made fast near the barn door outside, where anyone could haul on it. Creed testified the knot was one he had tied many days before. Ike was a timorous old man, with a wholesome fear of his employer, and he supported the testimony and made no reference to his eavesdropping of the previous evening, though he heard Creed swear before the jury that he did not recognize the tramp he had fed and lodged. There were no papers in Turner's pockets; only a few coins, and a marked pocket-knife that gave the first clue to his identity.

"A few of the neighbours said that it was a fitting end, and that the verdict was a just one. Nevertheless, whisperings began and increased. People avoided Creed and the neighbourhood. Rumours grew that the barn was haunted. Passers-by on the road after dark said they heard the old pulley-wheel clanking when no breeze stirred, much as you hear it now. Some claim to have heard maudlin laughter. Possible purchasers were frightened away, and Creed grew more and more solitary and misanthropic. Old Ike hung on, Heaven knows why, though I suppose Creed paid him some sort of wage.

"Rumours grew. Folks said that neither Ike nor Creed entered this barn after a time, and no hay was put in, though Creed would not have been Creed if he had not sold off the bulk of what he had, ghost or no ghost. I can imagine him slowly forking it out alone, daytimes, and the amount of hay still here proves that even he finally lost courage."

I paused a moment, but though there was much uneasy stirring about, and the dismal clanking directly above us was incessant, no one of my audience spoke. It was wholly dark now, and I think all had drawn closer together.

"About ten years ago people began calling Creed crazy." Here I was forced to interrupt my own story. "I shall have to ask you, Miss Anstell, to stop annoying me. I have been aware for some moments that you are brushing my head with a straw, but I have ignored it for the sake of the others." Out of the darkness came Miss Anstell's voice, protesting earnestly, and I realized from the direction of the sound that in the general readjustment she must have settled down in the very centre of our circle, and could not be the one at fault. One of the others was childish enough to simulate a mocking burst of raucous laughter, but I chose to ignore it.

"Very well," said I, graciously; "shall I go on?"

"Go on," echoed a subdued chorus.

"It was the night of the twenty-eighth of May, ten years ago—"

"Not the twenty-eighth," broke in my wife's voice, sharply; "that is to-day's date." There was a note in her voice that I hardly recognized, but it indicated that she was in some way affected by my narration, and I felt a distinct sense of triumph.

"It was the night of May twenty-eighth," I repeated firmly.

"Are you making up this story?" my wife's voice continued, still with the same odd tone.

"I am, my dear, and you are interrupting it."

"But an Ashley Turner and later a Peter Creed owned this place," she persisted almost in a whisper, "and I am sure you never heard of them."

I confess that I might wisely have broken off my story then and called for a light. There had been an hysterical note in my wife's voice, and I was startled at her words, for I had no conscious recollection of either name; yet I felt a resultant exhilaration. Our lanterns had grown strangely dim, though I was certain both had been recently trimmed and filled; and from their far corner of the barn they threw no light whatever into our circle. I faced an utter blackness.

"On that night," said I, "old Ike was wakened by sounds as of someone fumbling to unbar and open the house door. It was an unwonted hour, and he peered from the window of his little room. By the dim starlight—it was just before dawn—he could see all of the open yard and roadway before the house, with the great barn looming like a black and sinister shadow as its farther barrier. Crossing this space, he saw the figure of Peter Creed, grotesquely stooped and old in the obscuring gloom, moving slowly, almost gropingly, and yet directly, as though impelled, toward the barn's overwhelming shadow. Slowly he unbarred the great door, swung it open, and entered the blacker shadows it concealed. The door closed after him.

"Ike in his secure post of observation did not stir. He could not. Even to his crude imagining there was something utterly horrible in the thought of Creed alone at that hour in just such black darkness as this, with the great timbered chamber haunted at least by its dread memories. He could only wait, tense and fearful of he knew not what.

"A shriek that pierced the silence relaxed his tension, bringing almost a sense of relief, so definite had been his expectancy. But it was a burst of shrill laughter, ribald, uncanny, undeniable, accompanying the shriek that gave him power of motion. He ran half naked a quarter of a mile to the nearest neighbour's and told his story."

* * * * * * * *

"They found Creed hanging, the rope hooked simply around his neck. It was a silent jury that filed from the barn that morning after viewing the body. 'Suicide,' said they, after Ike, shivering and stammering, had testified, harking back to the untold evidence of that other morning years before. Yes, Creed was dead, with a terrible look on his wizen face, and the dusty old rope ran through its pulley-wheel and was fast to a beam high above.

"'He must of climbed to the beam, made the rope fast, and jumped,' said the foreman, solemnly. 'He must of, he must of,' repeated the man, parrot-like, while the sweat stood out on his forehead, 'because there wasn't no other way; but as God is my judge, the knot in the rope and the dust on the beam ain't been disturbed for years.'"

At this dramatic climax there was an audible sigh from my audience. I sat quietly for a time, content to allow the silence and the atmosphere of the place, which actually seemed surcharged with influences not of my creation, to add to the effect my story had caused. There was scarcely a movement in our circle; of that I felt sure. And yet once more, out of the almost tangible darkness above me, something seemed to reach down and brush against my head. A slight motion of air, sufficient to disturb my rather scanty locks, was additional proof that I was the butt of some prank that had just missed its objective. Then, with a fearful suddenness, close to my ear burst a shrill discord of laughter, so uncanny and so unlike the usual sound of student merriment that I started up, half wondering if I had heard it. Almost immediately after it the heavy darkness was torn again by a shriek so terrible in its intensity as completely to differentiate it from the other cries which followed.

"Bring a light!" cried a voice that I recognized as that of my wife, though strangely distorted by emotion. There was a great confusion. Young women struggled from their places and impeded one another in the darkness; but finally, and it seemed an unbearable delay, someone brought a single lantern.

Its frail light revealed Miss Anstell half upright from her place in the centre of our circle, my wife's arms sustaining her weight. Her face, as well as I could see it, seemed darkened and distorted, and when we forced her clutching hands away from her bared throat we could see, even in that light, the marks of an angry, throttling scar entirely encircling it. Just above her head the old pulley-rope swayed menacingly in the faint breeze.

My recollection is even now confused as to the following moments and our stumbling escape from that gruesome spot. Miss Anstell is now at her home, recovering from what her physician calls mental shock. My wife will not speak of it. The questions I would ask her are checked on my lips by the look of utter terror in her eyes. As I have confessed to you, my own philosophy is hard put to it to withstand not so much the community attitude toward what they are pleased to call my taste in practical joking, but to assemble and adjust the facts of my experience.

A Shady Plot

Elsie Brown

So I sat down to write a ghost story.

Jenkins was responsible.

"Hallock," he had said to me, "give us another on the supernatural this time. Something to give 'em the horrors; that's what the public wants, and your ghosts are live propositions."

Well, I was in no position to contradict Jenkins, for, as yet, his magazine had been the only one to print my stuff. So I had said, "Precisely!" in the deepest voice I was capable of, and had gone out.

I hadn't the shade of an idea, but at the time that didn't worry me in the least. You see, I had often been like that before and in the end things had always come my way—I didn't in the least know how or why. It had all been rather mysterious. You understand I didn't specialize in ghost stories, but more or less they seemed to specialize in me. A ghost story had been the first fiction I had written. Curious how that idea for a plot had come to me out of nowhere after I had chased inspiration in vain for months! Even now whenever Jenkins wanted a ghost, he called on me. And I had never found it healthy to contradict Jenkins. Jenkins always seemed to have an uncanny knowledge as to when the landlord or the grocer were pestering me, and he dunned me for a ghost. And somehow I'd always been able to dig one up for him, so I'd begun to get a bit cocky as to my ability.

So I went home and sat down before my desk and sucked at the end of my pencil and waited, but nothing happened. Pretty soon my mind began to wander off on other things, decidedly unghostly and material things, such as my wife's shopping and how on earth I was going to cure her of her alarming tendency to take every new fad that came along and work it to death. But I realized *that* would never get me any place, so I went back to staring at the ceiling.

217

"This writing business *is* delightful, isn't it?" I said sarcastically at last, out loud, too. You see, I had reached the stage of imbecility when I was talking to myself.

"Yes," said a voice at the other end of the room, "I should say it is!" I admit I jumped. Then I looked around.

It was twilight by this time and I had forgotten to turn on the lamp. The other end of the room was full of shadows and furniture. I sat staring at it and presently noticed something just taking shape. It was exactly like watching one of these moving picture cartoons being put together. First an arm came out, then a bit of sleeve of a stiff white shirtwaist, then a leg and a plaid skirt, until at last there she was complete,—whoever she was.

She was long and angular, with enormous fishy eyes behind big bone-rimmed spectacles, and her hair in a tight wad at the back of her head (yes, I seemed able to see right through her head) and a jaw— well, it looked so solid that for the moment I began to doubt my very own senses and believe she was real after all.

She came over and stood in front of me and glared—yes, positively glared down at me, although (to my knowledge) I had never laid eyes on the woman before, to say nothing of giving her cause to look at me like that.

I sat still, feeling pretty helpless I can tell you, and at last she barked: "What are you gaping at?"

I swallowed, though I hadn't been chewing anything.

"Nothing," I said. "Absolutely nothing. My dear lady, I was merely waiting for you to tell me why you had come. And excuse me, but do you always come in sections like this? I should think your parts might get mixed up sometimes."

"Didn't you send for me?" she crisped.

Imagine how I felt at that!

"Why, no. I—I don't seem to remember—"

"Look here. Haven't you been calling on heaven and earth all afternoon to help you write a story?"

I nodded, and then a possible explanation occurred to me and my spine got cold. Suppose this was the ghost of a stenographer applying for a job! I had had an advertisement in the paper recently. I opened my mouth to explain that the position was filled, and permanently so, but she stopped me.

"And when I got back to the office from my last case and was ready for you, didn't you switch off to something else and sit there drivelling so I couldn't attract your attention until just now?"

"I—I'm very sorry, really."

"Well, you needn't be, because I just came to tell you to stop bothering us for assistance; you ain't going to get it. We're going on Strike!"

"What!"

"You don't have to yell at me."

"I—I didn't mean to yell," I said humbly. "But I'm afraid I didn't quite understand you. You said you were—"

"Going on strike. Don't you know what a strike is? Not another plot do you get from us!"

I stared at her and wet my lips.

"Is—is that where they've been coming from?"

"Of course. Where else?"

"But my ghosts aren't a bit like you—"

"If they were people wouldn't believe in them." She draped herself on the top of my desk among the pens and ink bottles and leaned towards me. "In the other life *I* used to write."

"You did!"

She nodded.

"But that has nothing to do with my present form. It might have, but I gave it up at last for that very reason, and went to work as a reader on a magazine." She sighed, and rubbed the end of her long eagle nose with a reminiscent finger. "Those were terrible days; the memory of them made me mistake purgatory for paradise, and at last when I attained my present state of being, I made up my mind that something should be done. I found others who had suffered similarly, and between us we organized 'The Writer's Inspiration Bureau.' We scout around until we find a writer without ideas and with a mind soft enough to accept impression. The case is brought to the attention of the main office, and one of us assigned to it. When that case is finished we bring in a report."

"But I never saw you before—"

"And you wouldn't have this time if I hadn't come to announce the strike. Many a time I've leaned on your shoulder when you've thought *you* were thinking hard—" I groaned, and clutched my hair. The very idea of that horrible scarecrow so much as touching me! and wouldn't my wife be shocked! I shivered. "But," she continued, "that's at an end. We've been called out of our beds a little too often in recent years, and now we're through."

"But my dear madam, I assure you I have had nothing to do with that. I hope I'm properly grateful and all that, you see."

"Oh, it isn't you," she explained patronizingly. "It's those Ouija board fanatics. There was a time when we had nothing much to occupy us and used to haunt a little on the side, purely for amusement, but not any more. We've had to give up haunting almost entirely. We sit at a desk and answer questions now. And such questions!"

She shook her head hopelessly, and taking off her glasses wiped them, and put them back on her nose again.

"But what have I got to do with this?"

She gave me a pitying look and rose.

"You're to exert your influence. Get all your friends and acquaintances to stop using the Ouija board, and then we'll start helping you to write."

"But—"

There was a footstep outside my door.

"John! Oh, John!" called the voice of my wife.

I waved my arms at the ghost with something of the motion of a beginner when learning to swim.

"Madam, I must ask you to leave, and at once. Consider the impression if you were seen here—"

The ghost nodded, and began, very sensibly, I thought, to demobilize and evaporate. First the brogans on her feet grew misty until I could see the floor through them, then the affection spread to her knees and gradually extended upward. By this time my wife was opening the door.

"Don't forget the strike," she repeated, while her lower jaw began to disintegrate, and as my Lavinia crossed the room to me the last vestige of her ear faded into space.

"John, why in the world are you sitting in the dark?"

"Just—thinking, my dear."

"Thinking, rubbish! You were talking out loud."

I remained silent while she lit the lamps, thankful that her back was turned to me. When I am nervous or excited there is a muscle in my face that starts to twitch, and this pulls up one corner of my mouth and gives the appearance of an idiotic grin. So far I had managed to conceal this affliction from Lavinia.

"You know I bought the loveliest thing this afternoon. Everybody's wild over them!"

I remembered her craze for taking up new fads and a premonitory chill crept up the back of my neck.

"It—it isn't—" I began and stopped. I simply couldn't ask; the possibility was too horrible.

"You'd never guess in the world. It's the duckiest, darlingest Ouija board, and so cheap! I got it at a bargain sale. Why, what's the matter, John?"

I felt things slipping.

"Nothing," I said, and looked around for the ghost. Suppose she had lingered, and upon hearing what my wife had said should suddenly appear—Like all sensitive women, Lavinia was subject to hysterics.

"But you looked so funny—"

"I—I always do when I'm interested," I gulped. "But don't you think that was a foolish thing to buy?"

"Foolish! Oh, John! Foolish! And after me getting it for you!"

"For me! What do you mean?"

"To help you write your stories. Why, for instance, suppose you wanted to write an historical novel. You wouldn't have to wear your eyes out over those musty old books in the public library. All you'd have to do would be to get out your Ouija and talk to Napoleon, or William the Conqueror, or Helen of Troy—well, maybe not Helen—anyhow you'd have all the local colour you'd need, and without a speck of trouble. And think how easy writing your short stories will be now."

"But Lavinia, you surely don't believe in Ouija boards."

"I don't know, John—they are awfully thrilling."

She had seated herself on the arm of my chair and was looking dreamily across the room. I started and turned around. There was nothing there, and I sank back with relief. So far so good.

"Oh, certainly, they're thrilling all right. That's just it, they're a darn sight too thrilling. They're positively devilish. Now, Lavinia, you have plenty of sense, and I want you to get rid of that thing just as soon as you can. Take it back and get something else."

My wife crossed her knees and stared at me through narrowed lids.

"John Hallock," she said distinctly. "I don't propose to do anything of the kind. In the first place they won't exchange things bought at a bargain sale, and in the second, if you aren't interested in the other world *I* am. So there!" and she slid down and walked from the room before I could think of a single thing to say. She walked very huffily.

Well, it was like that all the rest of the evening. Just as soon as I mentioned Ouija boards I felt things begin to cloud up; so I decided to let it go for the present, in the hope that she might be more reasonable later.

After supper I had another try at the writing, but as my mind continued a perfect blank I gave it up and went off to bed.

The next day was Saturday, and it being near the end of the month and a particularly busy day, I left home early without seeing Lavinia.

Understand, I haven't quite reached the point where I can give my whole time to writing, and being bookkeeper for a lumber company does help with the grocery bills and pay for Lavinia's fancy shopping. Friday had been a half holiday, and of course when I got back the work was piled up pretty high; so high, in fact, that ghosts and stories and everything else vanished in a perfect tangle of figures.

When I got off the street car that evening my mind was still churning. I remember now that I noticed, even from the corner, how brightly the house was illuminated, but at the time that didn't mean anything to me. I recall as I went up the steps and opened the door I murmured:

"Nine times nine is eighty-one!"

And then Gladolia met me in the hall.

"Misto Hallock, de Missus sho t'inks you's lost! She say she done 'phone you dis mawnin' to be home early, but fo' de lawd's sake not to stop to argify now, but get ready fo' de company an' come on down."

Some memory of a message given me by one of the clerks filtered back through my brain, but I had been hunting three lost receipts at the time, and had completely forgotten it.

"Company?" I said stupidly. "What company?"

"De Missus's Ouija boahrd pahrty," said Gladolia, and rolling her eyes she disappeared in the direction of the kitchen.

I must have gone upstairs and dressed and come down again, for I presently found myself standing in the dimly lighted lower hall wearing my second best suit and a fresh shirt and collar. But I have no recollections of the process. There was a great chattering coming from our little parlour and I went over to the half-opened door and peered through.

The room was full of women—most of them elderly—whom I recognized as belonging to my wife's Book Club.

They were sitting in couples, and between each couple was a Ouija board! The mournful squeak of the legs of the moving triangular things on which they rested their fingers filled the air and mixed in with the conversation. I looked around for the ghost with my heart sunk down to zero. What if Lavinia should see her and go mad before my eyes! And then my wife came and tapped me on the shoulder.

"John," she said in her sweetest voice, and I noticed that her cheeks were very pink and her eyes very bright. My wife is never so pretty as when she's doing something she knows I disapprove of, "John, dear I know you'll help us out. Mrs. William Augustus Wainright 'phoned at the last moment to say that she couldn't possibly come, and that leaves poor Laura Hinkle without a partner. Now,

John, I know *some* people can work a Ouija by themselves, but Laura can't, and she'll just have a horrible time unless you—"

"Me!" I gasped. "Me! I won't—" but even as I spoke she had taken my arm, and the next thing I knew I was sitting with the thing on my knees and Miss Laura Hinkle opposite, grinning in my face like a flirtatious crocodile.

"I—I won't—" I began.

"Now, Mr. Hallock, don't you be shy." Miss Laura Hinkle leaned forward and shook a bony finger almost under my chin.

"I—I'm not! Only I say I won't—!"

"No, it's very easy, really. You just put the tips of your fingers right here beside the tips of my fingers—"

And the first thing I knew she had taken my hands and was coyly holding them in the position desired. She released them presently, and the little board began to slide around in an aimless sort of way. There seemed to be some force tugging it about. I looked at my partner, first with suspicion, and then with a vast relief. If she was doing it, then all that talk about spirits—Oh, I did hope Miss Laura Hinkle was cheating with that board!

"Ouija, dear, won't you tell us something?" she cooed, and on the instant the thing seemed to take life.

It rushed to the upper left hand corner of the board and hovered with its front leg on the word "Yes." Then it began to fly around so fast that I gave up any attempt to follow it. My companion was bending forward and had started to spell out loud:

"'T-r-a-i-t-o-r.' Traitor! Why, what does she mean?"

"I don't know," I said desperately. My collar felt very tight.

"But she must mean something. Ouija, dear, won't you explain yourself more fully?"

"'A-s-k-h-i-m!' Ask him. Ask who, Ouija?"

"I—I'm going." I choked and tried to get up but my fingers seemed stuck to that dreadful board and I dropped back again.

Apparently Miss Hinkle had not heard my protest. The thing was going around faster than ever and she was reading the message silently, with her brow corrugated, and the light of the huntress in her pale blue eyes.

"Why, she says it's you, Mr. Hallock. What *does* she mean? Ouija, won't you tell us who is talking?"

I groaned, but that inexorable board continued to spell. I always did hate a spelling match! Miss Hinkle was again following it aloud:

"'H-e-l-e-n.' Helen!" She raised her voice until it could be heard at the other end of the room. "Lavinia, dear, do you know anyone by the name of Helen?"

"By the name of—? I can't hear you." And my wife made her way over to us between the Book Club's chairs.

"You know the funniest thing has happened," she whispered excitedly. "Someone had been trying to communicate with John through Mrs. Hunt's and Mrs. Sprinkle's Ouija! Someone by the name of Helen—"

"Why, *isn't* that curious!"

"What is?"

Miss Hinkle simpered.

"Someone giving the name of Helen has just been calling for your husband here."

"But we don't know anyone by the name of Helen—"

Lavinia stopped and began to look at me through narrowed lids much as she had done in the library the evening before.

And then from different parts of the room other manipulators began to report. Every plagued one of those five Ouija boards was calling me by name! I felt my ears grow crimson, purple, maroon. My wife was looking at me as though I were some peculiar insect. The squeak of Ouija boards and the murmur of conversation rose louder and louder, and then I felt my face twitch in the spasm of that idiotic grin. I tried to straighten my wretched features into their usual semblance of humanity, I tried and—

"Doesn't he look sly!" said Miss Hinkle. And then I got up and fled from the room.

I do not know how that party ended. I do not want to know. I went straight upstairs, and undressed and crawled into bed, and lay there in the burning dark while the last guest gurgled in the hall below about the wonderful evening she had spent. I lay there while the front door shut after her, and Lavinia's steps came up the stairs and—passed the door to the guest room beyond. And then after a couple of centuries elapsed the clock struck three and I dozed off to sleep.

At the breakfast table the next morning there was no sign of my wife. I concluded she was sleeping late, but Gladolia, upon being questioned, only shook her head, muttered something, and turned the whites of her eyes up to the ceiling. I was glad when the meal was over and hurried to the library for another try at that story.

I had hardly seated myself at the desk when there came a tap at the door and a white slip of paper slid under it. I unfolded it and read:

Dear John,
I am going back to my grandmother. My lawyer will communicate with you later.

"Oh," I cried. "Oh, I wish I was dead!"

And:

"That's exactly what you ought to be!" said that horrible voice from the other end of the room.

I sat up abruptly—I had sunk into a chair under the blow of the letter—then I dropped back again and my hair rose in a thick prickle on the top of my head. Coming majestically across the floor towards me was a highly polished pair of thick laced shoes. I stared at them in a sort of dreadful fascination, and then something about their gait attracted my attention and I recognized them.

"See here," I said sternly. "What do you mean by appearing here like this?"

"*I* can't help it," said the voice, which seemed to come from a point about five and a half feet above the shoes. I raised my eyes and presently distinguished her round protruding mouth.

"Why can't you? A nice way to act, to walk in sections—"

"If you'll give me time," said the mouth in an exasperated voice, "I assure you the rest of me will presently arrive."

"But what's the matter with you? You never acted this way before."

She seemed stung to make a violent effort, for a portion of a fishy eye and the end of her nose popped into view with a suddenness that made me jump.

"It's all your fault." She glared at me, while part of her hair and her plaid skirt began slowly to take form.

"My fault!"

"Of course. How can you keep a lady up working all night and then expect her to retain all her faculties the next day? I'm just too tired to materialize."

"Then why did you bother?"

"Because I was sent to ask when your wife is going to get rid of that Ouija board."

"How should I know! I wish to heaven I'd never seen you!" I cried. "Look what you've done! You've lost me my wife, you've lost me my home and happiness, you've—you've—"

"Misto Hallock," came from the hall outside, "Misto Hallock, I's gwine t' quit. I don't like no hoodoos." And the steps retreated.

"You've—you've lost me my cook—"

225

"I didn't come here to be abused," said the ghost coldly. "I—I—"
And then the door opened and Lavinia entered. She wore the brown hat and coat she usually travels in and carried a suitcase which she set down on the floor.

That suitcase had an air of solid finality about it, and its lock leered at me brassily.

I leaped from my chair with unaccustomed agility and sprang in front of my wife. I must conceal that awful phantom from her, at any risk!

She did not look at me, or—thank heaven!—behind me, but fixed her injured gaze upon the waste-basket, as if to wrest dark secrets from it.

"I have come to tell you that I am leaving," she staccatoed.

"Oh, yes, yes!" I agreed, flapping my arms about to attract attention from the corner. "That's fine—great!"

"So you want me to go, do you?" she demanded.

"Sure, yes—right away! Change of air will do you good. I'll join you presently!" If only she would go till Helen could *de*-part! I'd have the devil of a time explaining afterward, of course, but anything would be better than to have Lavinia see a ghost. Why, that sensitive little woman couldn't bear to have a mouse say boo at her—and what would she say to a ghost in her own living-room?

Lavinia cast a cold eye upon me. "You are acting very queerly," she sniffed. "You are concealing something from me."

Just then the door opened and Gladolia called, "Mis' Hallock! Mis' Hallock! I've come to tell you I'se done lef' dis place."

My wife turned her head a moment. "But why, Gladolia?"

"I ain't stayin' round no place 'long wid dem Ouija board contraptions. I'se skeered of hoodoos. I's done gone, I is."

"Is that all you've got to complain about?" Lavinia inquired.

"Yes, ma'am."

"All right, then. Go back to the kitchen. You can use the board for kindling wood."

"Who? Me touch dat t'ing? No, ma'am, not dis nigger!"

"I'll be the coon to burn it," I shouted. "I'll be glad to burn it."

Gladolia's heavy steps moved off kitchenward.

Then my Lavinia turned waspishly to me again. "John, there's not a bit of use trying to deceive me. What is it you are trying to conceal from me?"

"Who? Me? Oh, no," I lied elaborately, looking around to see if that dratted ghost was concealed enough. She was so big, and I'm rather a smallish man. But that was a bad move on my part.

"John," Lavinia demanded like a ward boss, "you are hiding some-*body* in here! Who is it?"

I only waved denial and gurgled in my throat. She went on, "It's bad enough to have you flirt over the Ouija board with that hussy—"

"Oh, the affair was quite above-board, I assure you, my love!" I cried, leaping lithely about to keep her from focusing her gaze behind me.

She thrust me back with sudden muscle. "*I will* see who's behind you! Where is that Helen?"

"Me? I'm Helen," came from the ghost.

Lavinia looked at that apparition, that owl-eyed phantom, in plaid skirt and stiff shirtwaist, with hair skewed back and no powder on her nose. I threw a protecting husbandly arm about her to catch her when she should faint. But she didn't swoon. A broad, satisfied smile spread over her face.

"I thought you were Helen of Troy," she murmured.

"I used to be Helen of Troy, New York," said the ghost. "And now I'll be moving along, if you'll excuse me. See you later."

With that she telescoped briskly, till we saw only a hand waving farewell.

My Lavinia fell forgivingly into my arms. I kissed her once or twice fervently, and then I shoved her aside, for I felt a sudden strong desire to write. The sheets of paper on my desk spread invitingly before me.

"I've got the bulliest plot for a ghost story!" I cried.

The Lady and the Ghost

Rose Cecil O'Neill

It was some moments before the Lady became rationally convinced that there was something occurring in the corner of the room, and then the actual nature of the thing was still far from clear.

"To put it as mildly as possible," she murmured, "the thing verges upon the uncanny"; and, leaning forward upon her silken knees, she attended upon the phenomenon.

At first it had seemed like some faint and unexplained atmospheric derangement, occasioned, apparently, neither by an opened window nor by a door. Some papers fluttered to the floor, the fringes of the hangings softly waved, and, indeed, it would still have been easy to dismiss the matter as the effect of a vagrant draft had not the state of things suddenly grown unmistakably unusual. All the air of the room, it then appeared, rushed even with violence to the point and there underwent what impressed her as an aerial convulsion, in the very midst and well-spring of which, so great was the confusion, there seemed to appear at intervals almost the semblance of a shape.

The silence of the room was disturbed by a book that flew open with fluttering leaves, the noise of a vase of violets blown over, from which the perfumed water dripped to the floor, and soft touchings all around as of a breeze passing through a chamber full of trifles.

The ringlets of the Lady's hair were swept forward toward the corner upon which her gaze was fixed, and in which the conditions had now grown so tense with imminent occurrence and so rent with some inconceivable throe that she involuntarily rose, and, stepping forward against the pressure of her petticoats which were blown about her ankles, she impatiently thrust her hand into the—

She was immediately aware that another hand had received it, though with a far from substantial envelopment, and for another mo-

228

ment what she saw before her trembled between something and nothing. Then from the precarious situation there slowly emerged into dubious view the shape of a young man dressed in evening clothes over which was flung a mantle of voluminous folds such as is worn by ghosts of fashion.

"The very deuce was in it!" he complained; "I thought I should never materialize."

She flung herself into her chair, confounded; yet, even in the shock of the emergency, true to herself, she did not fail to smooth her ruffled locks.

Her visitor had been scanning his person in a dissatisfied way, and with some vexation he now ejaculated: "Beg your pardon, my dear, but are my feet on the floor, or where in thunder are they?"

It was with a tone of reassurance that she confessed that his patent-leathers were the trivial matter of two or three inches from the rug. Whereupon, with still another effort, he brought himself down until his feet rested decently upon the floor. It was only when he walked about to examine the *bric-à-brac* that a suspicious lightness was discernible in his tread.

When he had composed himself by the survey, effecting it with an air of great insouciance, which, however, failed to conceal the fact that his heart was beating somewhat wildly, he approached the Lady.

"Well, here we are again, my love!" he cried, and devoured her hands with ghostly kisses. "It seems an eternity that I've been struggling back to you through the outer void and what-not. Sometimes, I confess I all but despaired. Life is not, I assure you, all beer and skittles for the disembodied."

He drew a long breath, and his gaze upon her and the entire chamber seemed to envelop all and cherish it.

"Little room, little room! And so you are thus! Do you know," he continued, with vivacity, "I have wondered about it in the grave, and I could hardly sleep for this place unpenetrated. Heigho! What a lot of things we leave undone! I dashed this off at the time, the literary passion strong in me, thus:

"Now, when all is done, and I lie so low, I cannot sleep for this, my only care; For though of that dim place I could not know; That where my heart was fain I did not go, Nor saw you musing there!

"Well, well, these things irk a ghost so. Naturally, as soon as possible I made my way back—to be satisfied—to be satisfied that you were still mine." He bent a piercing look upon her.

"I observe by the calendar on your writing-table that some years

229

have elapsed since my—um—since I expired," he added, with a faint blush. It appears that the matter of their dissolution is, in conversation, rather kept in the background by well-bred ghosts.

"Heigho! How time does fly! You'll be joining me soon, my dear."

She drew herself splendidly up, and he was aware of her beauty in the full of its tenacious excellence—of the delicate insolence of Life looking upon Death—of the fact *that she had forgotten him.*

He rose, and confronted this, his trembling hands thrust into his pockets, then turned away to hide the dismay of his countenance. He was, however, a spook of considerable spirit, and in a jiffy he met the occasion. To her blank, indignant gaze he drew a card from his case, and, taking a pencil from the secretary, wrote, beneath the name:

Quiet to the breast Wheresoe'er it be, That gave an hour's rest To the heart of me. Quiet to the breast Till it lieth dead, And the heart be clay Where I visited. Quiet to the breast, Though forgetting quite The guest it sheltered once; To the heart, good night!

Handing her the card he bowed, and, through force of habit, turned to the door, forgetting that his ghostly pressure would not turn the knob.

As the door did not open, with a sigh of recollection for his spiritual condition, he prepared to disappear, casting one last look at the faithless Lady. She was still looking at the card in her hand, and the tears ran down her face.

"She has remembered," he reflected; "how courteous!" For a moment it seemed he could contain his disappointment, discreetly removing himself now at what he felt was the vanishing-point, with the customary reticence of the dead, but feeling overcame him. In an instant he had her in his arms, and was pouring out his love, his reproaches, the story of his longing, his doubts, his discontent, and his desperate journey back to earth for a sight of her. "And, ah!" cried he, "picture my agony at finding that you had forgotten. And yet I surmised it in the gloom. I divined it by my restlessness and my despair. Perhaps some lines that occurred to me will suggest the thing to you—you recall my old knack for versification?

"Where the grasses weep O'er his darkling bed, And the glow-worms creep, Lies the weary head Of one laid deep, who cannot sleep: The unremembered dead."

He took a chair beside her, and spoke of their old love for each other, of his fealty through all transmutations; incidentally of her beauty, of her cruelty, of the light of her face which had illumined his darksome way to her—and of a lot of other things—and the Lady bowed her head, and wept.

The hours of the night passed thus: the moon waned, and a pallor began to tinge the dusky cheek of the east, but the eloquence of the visitor still flowed on, and the Lady had his misty hands clasped to her reawakened bosom. At last a suspicion of rosiness touched the curtain. He abruptly rose.

"I cannot hold out against the morning," he said; "it is time all good ghosts were in bed."

But she threw herself on her knees before him, clasping his ethereal waist with a despairing embrace.

"Oh, do not leave me," she cried, "or my love will kill me!"

He bent eagerly above her. "Say it again—convince me!"

"I love you," she cried, again and again and again, with such an anguish of sincerity as would convince the most sceptical spook that ever revisited the glimpses of the moon.

"You will forget again," he said.

"I shall never forget!" she cried. "My life will henceforth be one continual remembrance of you, one long act of devotion to your memory, one oblation, one unceasing penitence, one agony of waiting!"

He lifted her face, and saw that it was true.

"Well," said he, gracefully wrapping his cloak about him, "well, now I shall have a little peace."

He kissed her, with a certain jaunty grace, upon her hair, and prepared to dissolve, while he lightly tapped a tattoo upon his leg with the dove-coloured gloves he carried.

"Good-by, my dear!" he said; "henceforth I shall sleep o' nights; my heart is quite at rest."

"But mine is breaking," she wailed, madly trying once more to clasp his vanishing form.

He threw her a kiss from his misty finger-tips, and all that remained with her, besides her broken heart, was a faint disturbance of the air.

LEONAUR

ALSO FROM LEONAUR

AVAILABLE IN SOFTCOVER OR HARDCOVER WITH DUST JACKET

TROS OF SAMOTHRACE 1: WOLVES OF THE TIBER *by Talbot Mundy*—
When his ship is taken and his crew slaughtered Tros of Samothrace is captured by
Imperial Rome.

TROS OF SAMOTHRACE 2: DRAGONS OF THE NORTH *by Talbot Mundy*—Tros of Samothrace burns for vengeance and has declared himself the implacable
enemy of Rome.

TROS OF SAMOTHRACE 3: SERPENT OF THE WAVES *by Talbot Mundy*—Tros, his allies and the forces of Rome have drawn apart to prepare for the
conflict to come.

TROS OF SAMOTHRACE 4: CITY OF THE EAGLES *by Talbot Mundy*—As
Tros of Samothrace continues in his attempts to confound Caesar's plans for the invasion of Britain, he journeys to the Eternal City to seek the aid of its great leaders—
and Caesar's opponents—Cato, Pompey and the Vestal Virgins themselves!

TROS OF SAMOTHRACE 5: CLEOPATRA *by Talbot Mundy*—Cleopatra—
Queen of Egypt—is a formidable character ever ready to play the game of intrigue,
betrayal and shifting loyalties to suit her own objectives. Blood will surely be spilt
and once again Tros finds himself inexorably caught up in monumental events that
threaten his life and those he loves.

TROS OF SAMOTHRACE 6: THE PURPLE PIRATE *by Talbot Mundy*—The
epic saga of the ancient world—Tros of Samothrace—draws to a conclusion in this
sixth—and final—volume. Julius Caesar has been assassinated and Queen Cleopatra of
Egypt finds herself in a perilous position and desperate for allies to secure her power.

THE ILLUSTRATED & COMPLETE BRIGADIER GERARD *by Sir Arthur
Conan Doyle*—These are the adventures of Conan Doyle's incomparable French
hero-the finest swordsman in the Light Cavalry-Etienne Gerard. Arranged for the
first time in historical chronological order, his many enthusiasts can now properly
appreciate his colourful career as he fights, loves and blunders his way through the
Napoleonic epoch-from his earliest adventure as a young blade determined to reach
his lady love despite the unwelcome attention of her fathers bull-through many campaigns and special missions-to the bloody field of Waterloo, the downfall of his beloved Emperor and beyond. This is the complete collection of these classic stories. What
makes this edition exceptional is the inclusion of nearly 140 illustrations-mostly by
the famed military artist William Barnes Wollen-which accurately portray the spirit of
the stories and the uniforms and scenes of the events they portray.

LEONAUR

ALSO FROM LEONAUR